FAMILY
BLESSINGS

FAMILY
BLESSINGS

LaVyrle Spencer

G. P. PUTNAM'S SONS

NEW YORK

G. P. Putnam's Sons
Publishers Since 1838
200 Madison Avenue
New York, NY 10016

ISBN 0-399-13906-0

Printed in the United States of America

*To the memory of
our beloved daughters
Sarah and Beth*

Do not stand at my grave and weep
I am not there, I do not sleep.
I am a thousand winds that blow,
I am the diamond glints on snow,
I am the sunlight on ripened grain,
I am the gentle autumn rain.
When you awaken in the morning's hush,
I am the swift uplifting rush
   of quiet birds in circled flight,
I am the soft stars that shine at night.
Do not stand at my grave and cry,
I am not there, I did not die.

Many thanks to my nephew,
Officer Jason Huebner
of the Anoka Police Department,
Anoka, Minnesota, for his help
during the research and writing
of this book. Love you, Peanut.

Thanks also to Dawn and Bob Estelle
of Stillwater Floral for
their help with information
about the florists' trade.

Chapter 1

FOR Christopher Lallek life couldn't have been better. It was payday, his day off, all the junk was scraped out of his old beat-up Chevy Nova, and his brand-new Ford Explorer had come into Fahrendorff Ford. It was an Eddie Bauer model, top of the line, with a four-liter V-6 engine, four-wheel drive, air-conditioning, tilt wheel, compact digital disc player and leather seats. The paint color was called wild strawberry, and it was wild, all right, wilder than anything he'd ever owned. Within an hour the papers would all be signed and he'd be slipping behind the wheel of his first new vehicle ever. All he needed was his paycheck.

He swung into the parking lot of the Anoka Police Station, cranked his old beater in a U-turn and, out of long practice, backed the car against the curb beside two black-and-white squads parked the same way near the door.

He sprang out whistling "I've Got Friends in Low Places" and took a happy leap onto the sidewalk, scanning the sky from behind a pair of mirrored sunglasses strung with hot-pink Croakies. Perfect day. Sunny. Couple of big white fluffy clouds in the east. Eighty degrees now shortly before noon, and by the time all the guys met at the lake it would be pushing ninety and the water would feel great. Greg was going to stop and price oversized inner tubes; Tom was bringing his jet-ski; and Jason had the use of his folks' speedboat for the day. Some of the guys would bring beer. Chris would pick up a couple of six-packs of soda and some salami and cheese, maybe a pint of that herring in cream sauce that he and Greg loved so much, and drive out there in his shiny new truck playing his new Garth Brooks CD—hey, hell of a deal.

He unlocked the plate-glass door and walked into the squad room, still whistling. Nokes and Ostrinski, both in uniform, were standing beside the computer table, looking sober, talking.

"Hey, what's new, guys?"

They looked up and fell silent, watching him poke a hand into his mail cubicle, come up with an envelope and rip it open. "Payday at last—hot damn!" He swung around, scanning the check, then slapped it against his palm. "Eat your heart out, boys, my new Explorer came in at last and it's all dealer-prepped and ready for pickup! If you want to go outside and administer last rites to my old Nova—" It struck him suddenly that neither Nokes nor Ostrinski had moved. Or smiled. Nor had they said a word since he'd come in. From the patrol room two more uniformed officers came silently through the doorway, looking equally as solemn as the two already there.

"Murph, Anderson . . ." Christopher greeted, wary now. He'd been a police officer for nine years: He recognized this silence, this somberness, this stillness too well.

"What's wrong?" His eyes darted from man to man.

His captain, Toby Anderson, spoke in a grave tone. "It's bad news, Chris."

Christopher's stomach seemed to drop two inches. "An officer went down."

"Afraid so."

"Who?"

Nobody spoke for ten seconds.

"Who!" Chris shouted, his dread mounting.

Anderson replied in a low, hoarse voice. "Greg."

"Greg!" Christopher's features registered bald-faced surprise, followed by disbelief. "Wait a minute. Somebody's got their wires crossed here."

Anderson only shook his head sadly. His gaze remained steady on Christopher while the others studied their shoes.

"But you're wrong. He's not on duty today. He left the apartment no more than an hour ago to come over here and get his check, then he was going to the bank, then he had to stop by his mother's house, and as soon as I picked up my Explorer we were going to buy a water tube and go out to Lake George."

"He wasn't on duty, Chris. It happened on his way here."

Christopher felt the truth shoot through his nerves to his extremities and turn them prickly. He felt his head go light.

"Oh, shit," he whispered.

Anderson spoke again. "A pickup ran a red light and hit him broadside."

Shock created havoc inside Christopher and hammered his features into hard, unaccepting lines. He dealt with tragedies daily, but never before with the death of one of the force. Certainly not with the death of a best friend. He stood in the grip of conflicting reactions, his human side sending heat and weakness streaming through his insides, while the trained lawman maintained an analytical exterior. When he spoke his voice came out patchy and gruff. "He was on his motorcycle."

"Yes . . . he was."

Anderson's pause, his throaty voice precluded the need for details. Christopher's throat closed, his chest constricted and his knees began trembling, but he stood his ground and asked the questions he'd ask if Greg were some stranger, little realizing that shock had him operating as if by remote control.

"Who responded to the call?"

"Ostrinski."

Christopher's eyes found the young police officer, who appeared pale and shaken. "Ostrinski?"

Ostrinski said nothing. He looked as though he'd been crying. His lips were puffy and his face pink.

"Well, go on . . . tell me," Christopher insisted.

"I'm sorry, Chris, he was dead by the time I got there."

Out of nowhere came a hot smack of anger. It sent Christopher whirling in a half circle, flinging a chair out of his way. "God*damn* it!" he shouted. "Why Greg?" Beset by passion, he lashed out with the most simplistic blame. "Why didn't he ride with me! I *told* him I didn't mind taking him by his mother's house! Why did he have to take his motorcycle?"

Anderson and Ostrinski reached out as if to comfort Christopher, but he recoiled. "Don't! Just . . . just let me . . . I need . . . give me a minute here . . ." He spun away from them, marched two steps to an abrupt halt and exclaimed again, "Shit!" Fear roiled within him, spawned by a shot of adrenaline that turned him hot, cold, trembly, made him feel as if his entire body could no longer fit inside his skin. Working as a cop, he'd seen reactions like this dozens of times and had never understood them. He'd often thought people hard when their response to the news of death took the form of anger. Suddenly it was happening to him, the quick flare of absolute rage that made him storm about like a warrior rather than cry like a bereaved friend.

As swiftly as the anger struck, it fled, leaving him shaken and nauseated. Tears came—hot, stinging tears—and a hurt in his throat.

"Aw, Greg," he uttered in a strange, cracked voice. "Greg . . ."

His fellow officers came up behind him and offered support. This time he accepted the touch of their arms and hands on his shoulders. They murmured condolences, their voices, too, strangled by emotions. He turned, and suddenly Captain Anderson's arms were around him, big burly arms trained in the martial arts, clasping him hard while both men strained to withhold sobs.

"Why Greg?" Chris managed. "It's just so damned unfair. Why not some . . . some dealer selling coke to school kids or some parent who's beating on his k . . . kids twice a week? Hell, we got a hundred of 'em in our files."

"I know, I know . . . it's not fair."

Christopher's tears streamed. He stood in his captain's grip, his chin pressed to Anderson's crisp collar with its fifteen-year chevrons, listening to the bigger man swallow repeatedly against his ear, feeling the captain's handcuff case pressing his belly while the other officers stood nearby feeling useless and vulnerable.

Anderson said, "He was a good man . . . a good officer."

"Twenty-five years old. Hell, he'd hardly even lived."

Anderson gave him a bluff thump on the shoulder and released him. Christopher lowered himself to a chair and doubled forward, covering his face with both hands. Visions of Greg flashed through his mind:

earlier this morning in the apartment they shared, shuffling out of his bedroom with his brown hair standing on end, scratching his chest and offering the usual bachelor good morning: "I gotta pee like a race-horse. Outa my way!" Then plodding from the bathroom to the kitchen, where he stood holding the refrigerator door open for a good minute and a half, staring inside, asking, "So what time're you going to get the new Explorer?" Reaching inside for a quart of orange juice and drinking half of it from the carton, belching and finally letting the door close.

He couldn't be dead! It wasn't possible!

Only one hour ago he was standing by the kitchen cupboard eating a piece of toast, dressed in bathing trunks and a wrinkled T-shirt that said MOUSTACHE RIDES FREE! "I gotta stop by my Mom's," he'd said. "The end busted off one of her garden hoses and she asked me to put a new one on."

Greg was always so good to his mother.

Greg's mother . . . aw, Jesus, Greg's poor mother. The thought of her brought a fresh shot of dread and grief. The woman had been through enough without this. She didn't need some strange police chaplain coming to her door to break the news.

Christopher drew a shaky breath and straightened, swiping a hand under his nose. Somebody handed him some hard napkins from the coffee room. He blew his nose and asked in a husky voice, "Has the chaplain informed his family yet?"

"No," Captain Anderson answered.

"I'd like to do it, sir, if that's all right."

"You sure you're up to it?"

"I know his family. It might be easier coming from me than from a stranger."

"All right, if you're sure you want to do it."

Chris drew himself to his feet, surprised at how weak he felt. His body was trembling everywhere—knees, stomach, hands—and his teeth were juddering together as if he'd just stepped into subzero cold.

Anderson said, "You okay, Lallek? You look a little unsteady. Maybe you'd better sit back down for a minute."

Chris did. He hit the chair as if he'd been bulldozed, closed his eyes and drew several deep breaths only to feel tears building once more.

"It's just so hard to believe," he mumbled, clutching his head and shaking it. "An hour ago he was standing in the kitchen eating toast."

Ostrinski said, "And yesterday when he went off duty he was talking about you guys going out to the lake."

Chris opened his eyes and saw Pete Ostrinski through a wavery pool of tears, a six-foot-four giant, only twenty-five years old, wearing a stricken expression. "Hey, Pete, I'm sorry, man. You're the one who responded to the call and here I sit blubbering when you took the biggest shock."

Ostrinski said, "Yeah," choked on the word and turned away to dry his eyes.

Chris took a turn at comforting, rising to drape an arm across Pete Ostrinski's shoulders and give his thick neck a squeeze.

"Is he at the morgue already?"

Ostrinski could scarcely get the words out. "Yeah, but don't go over there, Chris. And whatever you do, don't let his mother go. He was broken up pretty badly."

Chris squeezed Ostrinski's shoulder once more and let his hand drop disconsolately.

"This is going to kill his mother."

"Yeah . . . mothers are tough."

Their records technician, a woman named Ruth Randall, had been standing silently in the doorway leaning against the door frame as if uncertain what to say or do, just as they all were. The door from the parking lot opened and closed and another on-duty uniformed officer arrived. "I just heard," Roy Marchek said, and the crowded room fell utterly silent. Every person in it dealt with tragedies on a daily basis and had, of necessity, become somewhat inured to them. This death, however—one of their own—hit them in a way that made the impersonal dealings of past police calls feel like cakewalks.

The outside door opened again and the police chaplain, Vernon Wender, arrived. He was a man in his forties, with erect stature, thinning brown hair and silver-rimmed glasses. Captain Anderson nodded a silent hello as Wender stepped past Ruth Randall and moved into the squad room among the men.

"We've lost a good one," he said in a respectfully subdued voice. "A terrible tragedy." A stultifying silence passed while everyone struggled with their emotions. "The last time I talked to Greg he said to me, 'Vernon, you ever think about how many people hate their jobs? Well, not me,' he said. 'I love being a cop. It feels good to be out there helping people.' Maybe you'll all feel better if you dwell on that. Greg Reston was a happy man." Wender let some seconds tick away before adding, "I'll be here all day long if any of you need to talk . . . or pray . . . or reminisce. I think we'd all feel a little better if we said a prayer right now."

Throughout the prayer Christopher lost touch with the chaplain's words. He was thinking of Greg's family, especially his mother, and the shock that lay ahead for her. She was a widow with two other children—Janice, twenty-three, and Joey, fourteen—but Greg had been the oldest, the one she'd relied on most since the death of her husband nine years ago. "A strong woman," Greg had called her countless times, "the strongest woman I know . . . and the best." In all his life Christopher Lallek had never heard anyone praise a mother the way Greg Reston had praised his. The relationship between them had been one of mutual respect, admiration and love, the kind that brought a hollow lump of envy to Christopher's stomach as he'd heard about it over the past couple of years since Greg had joined the force. Greg and his mother could talk about anything—sports, money, sex, philosophy, even the occasional hurt feelings that crop up in the best-balanced families. Whatever it was, those two had discussed it, and afterward Chris would hear about it from Greg. He knew more about Mrs. Reston than many people knew about their own mothers, and because of it he had acquired a vicarious admiration and respect for her such as he'd never had for his own parents.

The prayer ended. Feet shuffled. Somebody blew his nose. Chris drew a deep, shaky sigh and said to Wender, "Greg and I are . . . were roommates. I'd like to tell his family."

The chaplain squeezed his arm and said, "All right, but are you sure you're okay yourself?"

"I'll make it."

Wender dropped his hand and nodded solemnly.

Outside, the sun was still radiant. It hurt his burning eyes. He covered them with his dark glasses and got into his car, scarcely noticing the hot upholstery beneath his bare legs. He started the engine then forgot to put the car in gear. *He's not really dead. He's going to pull in beside me and come over here and lean his hands against the car door and say, "See you out at the lake."*

Only he wouldn't.

Never again.

Christopher had no awareness of passing time, only of a lump of sorrow so overwhelming it controlled every atom of his being. Sluggishly he put the car in gear and pulled out onto the street, functioning within a haze of emotions that removed him from the mundane process of operating an automobile. He searched for Greg's face as he'd last seen it, struggling to recall the absolute final glimpse he'd had of his friend. Greg had been going out the apartment door—that was it—dressed for the beach with a red bill cap on his head, an apple in one hand and his keys in the other. He'd anchored the apple between his teeth while opening the door, then had taken a bite and said with his mouth full, "See you in an hour or so."

A bill cap instead of a helmet.

Swimming trunks instead of jeans.

A T-shirt instead of a leather jacket.

Not even any socks inside his dirty white Nikes.

Chris knew only too well what happened to the victims of motorcycle accidents who failed to wear proper gear.

Skulls crushed . . .

Bones laid bare by the hot blacktop . . .

Skin burned . . .

Sometimes their shoes were never found.

A car horn shook Christopher back to the present. The world swam beyond his tears. He'd been driving at ten miles an hour in a thirty-mile zone and had just gone through a stop sign without slowing. Hell, he was in no condition to be operating a vehicle. He'd be the next one to kill somebody if he didn't look out.

He dried his eyes on his shirt shoulders and speeded up to thirty, trying to push the horrifying images from his mind. He had to get his emotions pulled together before he reached Mrs. Reston's house.

The thought of her brought a billow of dread. A mother—God almighty, how do you tell a mother a thing like this? Especially a mother who's lost a child before?

She had lost her secondborn to SIDS—Sudden Infant Death Syndrome—when Greg had been so young he'd scarcely remembered it. But she'd talked about that time with Greg, after he'd gotten older. It had been her philosophy that Greg had admired so and set out to duplicate. She'd held that nothing was as important as the happiness of her marriage and her family, and to let either be undermined by extended grief would have been unpardonable. She'd had a responsibility to be a happy mother and wife for her husband and surviving son, and she'd done so by immediately trying to get pregnant again. The result had been Greg's younger sister, Janice, two years his junior. Nine years later Joey had been born.

Then at age thirty-six, Greg's mother had been widowed, losing a husband she'd loved immensely. He had died of a brain aneurysm after lingering for three days in a hospital bed. But Mrs. Reston had shown the same grit as before. Left with three children who needed her, no career, and a measly $25,000 in life insurance, she had refused to curl up with grief and self-pity. Instead, she'd consulted a vocational counselor, taken some business courses, spent a year in a trade school, bought herself a florist shop and established a firm foundation for supporting her children for as long as need be.

Strong? The woman was the Rock of Gibraltar. But even rocks can crack under intense pressure.

Driving to her house through the noon heat on this tragic late June day, Christopher Lallek wondered how to break the news that she'd lost another child. There simply was no good way.

Her house wasn't far from the station, just two miles or so. After spending most of the drive oblivious to his surroundings, Christopher became startlingly alert as he turned onto Benton Street. It was a shaded avenue that followed a bend of the Mississippi River, with older, well-maintained houses on both sides. Hers was several blocks off Ferry Street, facing southwest, across the street from the river. It was a nice old rambler, white with black shutters and a beige brick planter full of red geraniums flanking the front step. The maples in the yard were mature and as perfectly round as lollipops, as if they'd had professional pruning their entire lives. Around their trunks pink and white petunias bloomed inside circles of brick. The grass was neatly mowed but drying near the curb where an oscillating sprinkler fanned desultorily back and forth. It threw water across Christopher's windshield and his left elbow as he pulled into the driveway and stopped before an oversized detached garage. The garage door was up. One stall was empty; the other held her car, a five-year-old blue Pontiac sedan with some rust surrounding a bumper sticker that said FLOWERS MAKE LIFE LOVELIER.

Chris turned off his engine and sat awhile, staring into the garage at the testimony of her life: rakes and hoes, a garden cart, a bag of charcoal, her dead husband's workbench with tools still hanging above it, an old yellow bicycle hanging from the rafters, probably Greg's.

A new swell of grief struck and he pinched the bridge of his nose while an invisible winch seemed to tighten around his chest. He felt as if he'd swallowed a tennis ball.

Damn you, Greg, why didn't you wear a helmet?

He sat awhile, crying, dimly registering the thought that Mrs. Reston shouldn't leave her garage door open this way; anybody could walk right in and steal anything in sight. Greg used to scold her for it but she'd laughingly reply, "I've known every person on this block for twenty years and nobody locks their garages. Besides, who'd steal anything from me? Who'd want that junk out there? If they need it that badly, let them come in and take it."

But Christopher was a police officer who knew the dangers of leaving doors unlocked, just as Greg had.

Who would warn her to lock up from now on? Who would remind her to have the oil changed in her car? To replace her furnace filter? Who would fix her hoses?

Christopher dried his eyes, put his sunglasses back on, drew a fortifying breath and opened his car door.

Outside, the heat from the blacktop driveway beat up through the soles of his blue rubber thongs. It struck him suddenly what he was wearing—a man shouldn't bring news like this dressed in beach clothes. He closed up three shirt buttons and was rounding the hood of his car when he encountered the garden hose lying coiled on the driveway waiting for Greg to replace its end.

Everything inside him mounded up volcanically again.

Oh hell, would every reminder of Greg bring this awful affliction? Sometimes the force of it seemed as if it would send his ribs flying in two directions like a pair of gates bursting open. His life would be a series of reminders from now on; would every one bring this terrible desolation and urge to cry?

He stepped around the coiled hose and continued toward the front door.

It was open.

He stood awhile, looking through the screen, summoning courage. Inside, from some distant room, a radio softly played an old Neil Diamond song. The front hall led straight to the rear of the house, where a kitchen table stood before an open sliding glass door. A sheer drapery was being sucked and blown against the screen. Beyond it he could see a deck and a big backyard, shaded by trees, where he was supposed to come with Greg for a Fourth of July picnic. He made out the silhouettes of other things: a bouquet on the table, a sweater hanging on the back of a chair, a soda can and purse atop a stack of books, as if she was getting ready to go someplace.

Deeper in the house a faucet ran, then stopped. A female voice sang a line along with Neil Diamond, then disappeared as if around a bedroom doorway off to his right.

He stood in the shade of a small entry roof with a wall jutting to his right and the strong-smelling geraniums poking up out of the planter at his left.

The button for the doorbell was black, mounted in a pitted brass casing.

In his entire life Christopher Lallek had never dreaded doing anything as much as ringing that doorbell.

He knocked instead—somehow a knock seemed gentler—knocked and waited with the tennis ball still filling his throat.

Lee Reston shut off the water, polished the faucet, hung up the towel and gave her head a little shake, watching in the bathroom mirror as her plain brown hair fell into its customary place. Sometimes she thought about letting it grow, doing something different with it, but she'd never felt comfortable with fuss. Her hair parted where it would and hung in a short, simple Julie Andrews cut, a blow-and-go hairdo that suited her just fine and seemed to go well with the childish freckles that plagued her whenever summer came. She gave a yank on the knot holding her wraparound denim skirt at the waist, glanced at her plain white blouse and twirled both of her tiny gold stud earrings in her ears the way she'd been instructed when she'd had them pierced many years ago.

Singing a line from "Cracklin' Rosie," she shut off the bathroom light and zipped around the corner into her bedroom, took a shot of hand lotion from a dispenser on her dresser and was rubbing it in when she heard a knock on the front door.

"Coming!" she yelled, glancing at her wristwatch. Five to twelve already and she was due at the shop at noon. Ah, well, her sister Sylvia was there handling things. She and Sylvia didn't watch clocks on one another.

She cut through the living room on her way to the front door wondering if she'd have to buy a new rubber hose. That darned Greg had promised three times already that he'd come over and fix it, but no luck yet.

Rounding the living room archway into the front hall she was surprised to find her son's apartment mate on the step.

"Christopher!" she greeted, smiling, opening the screen door. "What are you doing here? I thought you and Greg were going to the lake. Come on in."

"Hello, Mrs. Reston."

"He's not here, if you're looking for him. He promised he'd come over today to put a new end on my hose, but he never showed up. He still might though. You can wait for him if you want."

He stepped inside, wearing bathing trunks and a wild orange-and-green Hawaiian-print shirt, his hairy legs bare, his feet in rubber thongs. As she looked up she saw her distorted reflection in his mirrored sunglasses, which were looped from ear to ear by a hot-pink string.

She stood before him, still working the flowery-smelling lotion into her hands, impatient to be off to work.

"I understand you can join us for the Fourth. That's great. We're going to try injecting a turkey with garlic juice and doing it on the grill. Then if we can stand one another's breath for the rest of the day we'll play some volleyball and bocce. How does that sound?"

He didn't answer. In very slow motion he removed his sunglasses and lowered them gently to the limits of the hot-pink string. She could see immediately he'd been crying.

"Christopher, what is it?" She took a step toward him.

He swallowed once and his Adam's apple drifted down like an ice cube dropped into a drink.

"Mrs. Reston . . ."

She knew things about this young man that he didn't know she knew, about his pitiable childhood and the parents who'd treated him as if he were a mistake they never should have made.

"Christopher . . ." She touched his arm, prepared to let Sylvia work alone a little longer. "You need to talk?"

He cleared his throat, caught both her hands and gripped them hard. They were still sleek from lotion and smelled like honeysuckle.

"Mrs. Reston, I have some terrible news." He'd decided the best way to say it was straight out, avoiding any prolonged limbo. "There's been a very bad accident. Greg is dead."

Her face changed neither shape nor line. Her eyes either. "Greg?" she repeated in a perfectly normal voice, as if the message he'd delivered was too bizarre to be believable.

"I'm so sorry," he whispered.

For the longest time she didn't move, only stood before him while the shock waves rippled in and changed her life. Finally she covered her mouth with both hands and stared at Christopher while tears made her rust-colored eyes gleam like polished copper. "Greg," she uttered in a squeaky, distorted voice.

"He was on his way over here. A car ran a red light and hit him broadside. He was dead by the time our squad car reached the scene."

"Oh my God," she whispered, her hands dropping slowly. "Not Greg . . . oh no, not Greg."

Involuntary spasms replaced her indrawn breaths, each one accompanied by a tick in her throat. Her mouth opened and stayed open in a wide, silent call. It erupted at last in a dolorous, elongated syllable as Christopher caught her in his arms and felt his sunglasses bruise his chest. He pulled them free and held her as hard as human arms can hold. Her keening took on a pitiful tone like a child playing a high, uncertain violin note—"No . . . no . . . noooooo . . ."—squeaky, sliding off-tune near Christopher's ear with her face pointed toward heaven. Finally, when it seemed her lungs would burst from lack of air, she broke into wretched, full-scale weeping that racked her body. He held her firmly, feeling her weight deliver itself into his safekeeping until her knees finally buckled and she hung on him.

"Not another one . . ." she mourned. "No . . . not another one."

His heart broke. Surely it did, for he felt the splintering deep within, putting pressure on his bones, his belly, his lungs.

"H . . . he . . . w . . . was . . . c . . . coming . . . ov . . . er . . . to . . . fix . . . my . . . ho . . . ho . . . h . . ." She could not complete the word.

"Yes . . ." he whispered in a strangled voice. "He was coming to fix your hose." She began quaking terribly, and he lowered her to the floor. It was hardwood, cool against his bare knees as he held her from tipping sideways. She drooped with her forehead against his throat, against the bare triangle of hair and skin above his ridiculous Hawaiian shirt, to which she clung, sobbing and sobbing, rocking and rocking, pushing so hard against him that he swayed backward with each lunge.

"He tr . . . tried to f . . . fix it o . . . o . . . once but he b . . . bought the wr . . . wrong-sized end."

"I know . . ." he said, "I know . . . ," rubbing her back, aching from pity, wishing he could spare her this, bring Greg back, bring her other dead baby back, or her husband to help her through this ordeal. Instead, here he knelt and did his best at comforting, not quite a stranger but certainly not a friend, merely a young man she'd met a few times in passing to whom she'd been kind because he worked and lived with her son.

They knelt together so long his shirtfront grew soaked. His knees began aching. She was still weeping and rocking and keening. He gripped her arms and set her on the floor, leaned her back against the hall wall and sat with an arm around her while she wept against his chest.

Wept and rocked. Rocked and wept. Until the blue denim of her skirt was dotted with dark spots.

"I'll be right back." He propped her against the wall, then hurried off to hunt for Kleenex, which he found in the kitchen and took back to her. He sat down again, put the blue flowered box on her lap, pulled out three tissues for himself and three that he stuffed into her hand. It lay limp on her lap while she sat like a muscleless lump, propped against the wall. He put an arm around her and gave her all the time she needed, resting a cheek on her hair and stroking her arm, wiping her face now and then, and his own, dropping the used blue Kleenexes on the floor beside them.

Out on the street a car passed. The sprinkler splattered across the end of the driveway ten times . . . fifteen . . . twenty . . . . Her head felt hot in the hollow of his shoulder. Her bare arm stuck to his.

Finally she let out a ragged sigh and rolled her head upright, running the heel of her hand up her forehead. He removed his arm from around her and wondered what to do next. She blew her nose hard and discarded the Kleenex.

"Oh God," she whispered, as if unsure she had strength for more than remaining slump-shouldered against the wall. Her eyes closed and residual sobs jerked her body.

"Where's Janice?" he asked.

Tears seeped from between her eyelashes and she bit her lip to hold in some squeaking sobs. She drew her knees up, crossed her arms on them and buried her head, her shoulders shaking.

He put a hand on her shoulder blade. "Where is she?" he whispered.

"In S . . . San Fr . . . Francisco."

"San Francisco?"

"With her fr . . . friend K . . . Kim."

That's right. Greg had said his sister was going out west for a week's vacation.

"How about Joey?"

"Joey's up at G . . . Gull Lake with the Wh . . . Whitmans."

"Someone will have to call them."

Her shoulders shook as she remained bowed over. He didn't know what to do: forget the details or begin handling them, let her cry or encourage her to stop, get help or leave her alone.

"Your sister—is she at the store?" he asked.

She nodded into her arms.

He went onto one knee beside her, looking down on her short disheveled hair, which was brown with copper highlights. "Would you like me to call her to come and be with you?"

"N . . . no." She lifted her head at last and swiped below her eyes with her open hands. "No, I'll call her." She sniffed once, hooked the Kleenex box and began rising unsteadily. When she rocked on her heels he reached out to help her, rising with her, waiting with a grip on her arm while she hung her head, drying her eyes once more.

At last she gave him a forced, quavery smile. Without returning it, he draped his arm around her shoulders and walked her slowly toward the kitchen. There was a phone on the counter but the table seemed safer. He pulled out a chair and guided her onto it, then sat down himself, on the chair with her sweater slung over the back. Her purse, Coca-Cola and books were still stacked on the table, a reminder of the happy, normal routine he had interrupted.

"We don't have to call anybody yet. Just take your time."

She propped her head with one hand and turned her face to the sliding door, where the curtain still luffed in the warm summer air.

He waited in silence, so wrapped up in her grief he had momentarily set his own aside.

"Do I have to go and identify him?" she asked, turning her puffy face to him.

"No. His driver's license did that."

She closed her eyes and sighed in relief, opened them and asked, "Did you see him?"

"No."

"Do you want to?"

"I don't know."

"Do you know if he was smashed up badly?"

"I didn't ask." Literally speaking, it was the truth. He hadn't asked. "Was he in his car?"

He rose and tried three cupboard doors before finding glasses. He filled one with ice from the freezer and returned to the table, popped open the Coke can and filled the glass for her.

"Was he in his car?" she repeated, stoic and insistent, ready to go on to the next step.

Christopher went to stand at the sliding glass door with his back to her, his feet spread wide and his bare toes digging into the spongy blue rubber of his thongs. "No. On his motorcycle."

After a brief silence while she absorbed the news, her high, peculiar violin voice played some short, muffled, staccato notes. He turned to find her with the drink untouched, both elbows propped on the table, both hands covering her face. He moved behind her and bracketed her neck with both hands, just to let her know he was there, just the touch of someone who cared.

"You don't have to see him at all. What purpose will it serve?"

"I don't know ... I have to ... I'm his m ... mother ... oh God oh God oh God ..."

"You need your family here. Should I call your sister . . . or your mother?"

"I'll c . . . call." She mopped her face and gained enough control to rise wearily, pushing off the tabletop with both hands.

He watched her walk into the U-shaped work area of the kitchen and pick up a white phone. The dial tone hummed for fifteen seconds before she dropped the receiver into the cradle without dialing and doubled over the counter.

He went to her immediately and said, "I'll call. Who?"

She seemed incapable of making the decision. "I don't know," she squeaked, beginning to cry again. "I d . . . don't kn . . . know. I don't want to p . . . put them through this."

"Here." He took her back to the table. "Just sit down and I'll take care of it. Where's your phone book?"

"In the d . . . drawer . . . over th . . . there."

He found her personal phone book in the second drawer he tried, and looked up the number of her flower shop. When he'd dialed she looked back over her shoulder at him, holding a blue Kleenex plastered over her mouth with one hand, her eyes red and running.

"Absolutely Floral," a woman answered.

"Is this Mrs. Eid?" he asked.

"Yes, it is."

"Mrs. Eid, are you there all alone or is there someone there with you?"

Her voice became suspicious. "Who is this?"

"I'm sorry, this is Christopher Lallek. I'm a friend of your nephew Greg Reston. I'm at your sister's house and I'm afraid I have some very bad news. Greg has been killed in a motorcycle accident."

He pictured Mrs. Eid with her mouth wide open during the silence, then dropping into a chair when she whispered, "Oh my God."

"I'm sorry to give you the news so abruptly. Is someone there with you?"

She had begun to cry and was muffling the sound with her hand. Throughout the conversation his eyes had not left Mrs. Reston. She rose from her chair and came around the cabinet to take the receiver.

"Sylvia? . . . Oh, Sylvia . . . I know . . . oh God . . . yes . . . no, no . . . neither one of them . . . yes . . . oh, yes, please . . . thank you."

She needed his arms again and turned into them after hanging up.

"She's coming," she whispered, and clung. The smell of her hand lotion became fixed in his memory while they stood in the kitchen waiting for her sister. Other impressions were stored away, too. The exact angle of the afternoon light falling through the trees in the backyard. The way the curtain kept flapping. The distant burping of a lawn mower being started. The smell of freshly cut grass. The sight of a bouquet of flowers blurring, then clearing, then blurring again as his eyes filled and refilled, familiar garden flowers whose names he did not know. A photograph of Greg stuck into the corner of a framed print on a blue-papered wall. The beads of condensed moisture running down the side of an iced glass of Coke the way Greg's mother's tears rolled down her face. The feel of her denim skirt against his bare legs. Her hot face stuck to the side of his neck and his own shirt plastered to his skin by their combined tears. A note on her refrigerator door that said *Give Greg the leftover lasagna.* Another that said *Janice, NW Flight 75, 1:35.* The ceaseless drone of that mower. The radio playing Vince Gill's mournful "When I Call Your Name."

Greg's mother whispering brokenly, "Oh, he loved this song."

Chris replying, "Yes, I know. He played it all the time." They both had loved the song; they'd both owned the CD.

Sorrow spilling upward in Christopher and Lee Reston as they realized how many such sad reminders lay in the days, months and years ahead.

They heard the car pull in and separated. Her forehead was marked with an oval red spot where it had stuck to his neck, crossed by a deeper red crease from his hot-pink Croakies.

Footsteps pounded up the sidewalk. The front door opened and Lee ran toward it, trailed by Christopher, who stood back and watched the first of many sorrowful embraces he would witness in the coming days. He saw her tears begin again and swallowed down his own.

"Oh, Lee . . ." As her name was spoken in sympathy he thought, *It's too much for one woman—a baby, a husband, now a full-grown son.*

"Why, Sylvia, why?" she wailed.

Sylvia could only answer, "I don't know, honey, I don't know."

The two sisters clung and wept together.

"Oh, Greg . . . Greg . . ." The name escaped Lee Reston as a lament, a long woeful call to her beloved boy who would never hear his name spoken again.

Christopher Lallek, standing by listening, watching, felt his desolation deepen with every passing minute. He was thirty years old, but was experiencing the cruel impact of true grief for the first time in his life. He was stunned by how lost and uncertain he felt. All the past concerns of his life seemed paltry and inconsequential when weighed against the awful finality of death. How consuming and powerful it was, robbing one of the will to think, to move, to force one's limbs to bend toward the next eventuality.

If he felt so, how must she feel, the mother?

She withdrew from her sister's embrace and Sylvia Eid drew back to find Christopher hovering nearby. Through her tears she managed to speak the words "You're Christopher." He found himself clinging to the strange woman with an intensity he would not have imagined yesterday. He, who held people at bay, who radiated toward no one—least of all strangers—was locked breast to breast with a woman he'd scarcely spoken to before.

They gave each other momentary solace, then turned back to the one who needed it more. Each with an arm around Lee, they urged her toward the living room and sat her on the sofa between them—an odd spot at noon on a weekday, but the place that seemed fitting for mourning. Lee Reston clung to her sister's hand, repeating the chant that Christopher would hear over and over again in the next three days.

"He was . . . he was coming over here to . . . to put a new end on a hose for me."

Why did it start his tears again? Because it was a reminder of how blithely he had taken life for granted until an hour ago? Because it was a reminder of how Greg had cared for his mother? Because it was one of those simple everyday things that speaks of love and devotion so much more loudly than words?

The women made it over another emotional hurdle, then Sylvia asked, "How did you find out?"

"From Christopher. He came over as soon as he heard."

Sylvia looked over at him with reddened eyes. "How did you find out?"

"I . . ." He had to clear his throat and start again. "I went into the station to pick up my paycheck and they told me."

Lee Reston looked up through her tears. She squeezed the back of his hand. "What a horrible shock that must have been for you. And then you

29

had to ... to come over here and tell me." He looked down at her hand covering his and relived the shock, but found some control deep down within that kept his hand steady and his eyes dry. He turned his hand over, linked his fingers with hers and whispered hoarsely, "He loved you so damned much."

She let her eyes close, battling for control; opened them to reveal large, rust-colored irises brimming with tears. "Thank you," she whispered, squeezing his hand tenaciously.

In that moment while they sat connected by grief and sympathy for each other some ineffable bond was forged.

He had given her what she needed to make it through the next hour.

She had recognized that he'd had the toughest job of all, coming here to break the news to her.

"I'll be here for you ... whatever you need," he promised, and the promise went as deep as his love and grief for her son.

"Thank you, Christopher," she said, squeezing his hand even harder, appreciating him fully for the first time, admitting how comforting a man's presence was and that she'd undoubtedly call on him again and again throughout the terrible days ahead.

Chapter 2

*L*EE Reston felt as if she were moving through a phantasm, at moments so steeped in grief it rendered her incapable of anything more than weeping. At other times she'd operate almost as if outside herself, facing the next dread and unavoidable duty.

Janice must be called.

"Janice . . ." Merely speaking her name brought tears welling, along with a great unwillingness to shatter her daughter's world a moment sooner than necessary.

"I'll call Janice," Sylvia offered.

"Thank you, Sylvia, but Janice should hear it from me."

"Oh, Lee, why put yourself through it?"

"I'm her mother. I'll do it."

There was within Lee Reston a vein of implacability so strong it sometimes amazed even her. To escape in a faint, to collapse uselessly would have been totally out of character. What needed facing, she faced. Always had, always would. Sylvia was here, and the young man, Christopher. She would rely on their support and do what must be done.

She did, however, allow Sylvia to dial the phone. Lee's hand shook as she took the receiver, and her legs felt rubbery. A chair was nudged behind her knees—a sudden blessing—and she withered down to it.

Janice sounded agonizingly happy. "Mom, hi! What a surprise! Five more minutes and we'd have been out the door. We're going to Fisherman's Wharf today!"

Oh, Janice, my beloved daughter, how I wish I didn't have to do this to you.

"Honey, I'm afraid I'm going to have to ask you to come home. I have some very sad news. Janice, dear, I'm so sorry . . . there's been a very bad motorcycle accident." Saying it for the first time was like hearing it for the first time: shock and horror coupled with a sense of unreality, as if it were someone else speaking the words about her son. "Our sweet Greg is dead."

"Oh no . . . no . . . nooooo. Oh, Mom . . . Oh God . . . no . . ."

She gripped the receiver in both hands, wanting to be there with Janice, to hold her, cradle her, help her through this. Instead they were separated by 2,000 miles and she could only listen to her daughter weep. "No, no, it can't be true!"

"Oh, Janice, darling, I wish I were there with you." Through those terrible minutes on the phone, Lee was vaguely aware of Sylvia's arm surrounding her shoulders and Christopher standing nearby.

"Janice, you'll have to . . . to get the first . . . first fl . . . fl . . ." She broke into tears and tried to stifle them so Janice wouldn't hear. Sylvia turned her into a hug and Chris took the receiver.

"Janice, this is Christopher Lallek. I'm here with your mother and so is your aunt Sylvia. I'm so sorry . . . yes, we're all in shock."

Her voice was broken and distorted by weeping. She asked questions and he answered—the difficult ones a mother should not have to repeat. Afterward he said, "Janice, put Kim on the phone." Realizing Janice was too overwrought with shock to function well, he spoke to the other young woman about changing plane reservations, told her to call back and that he'd be out at the airport himself to pick up Janice whenever she came in. With these details handled, he returned the phone to Mrs. Reston and listened to a painful goodbye.

"J . . . Janice? . . . Yes . . . me too . . . Please hurry."

Hanging up, Lee felt depleted. Still, she said, "I may as well call Joey too and get it over with."

"Let me," Sylvia pleaded in a whisper. "Please, let me."

"No, Sylvia. This one I have to do, too. And the mortuary. Then I'll let you and Christopher do the rest."

As it turned out, the Whitman family couldn't be reached. It was a hot summer afternoon: They were probably out on the lake.

Lee said, "We'll keep trying them." She stared at the telephone, which seemed both friend and enemy. She'd been through this before; she knew what must be done but resisted making the move to pick up that instrument once more and order a caretaker of dead bodies to take care of her son's. *Dear God . . . on his motorcycle.* The image struck with horrendous force but she buried it behind a memory of Greg hale and smiling as he drove his cycle out of her driveway, lifting a hand in farewell, shouting, "Thanks for the good grub, Ma. You're a helluva cook!"

Other memories came, of the day Bill died, and their three-month-old baby, Grant. She shuddered and summoned a picture of her two remaining children, thinking, *I'm lucky, I'm lucky, I've still got them. I'll be strong for them.*

Keeping their images clearly before her, she dialed the mortuary. She did fine until the question "Where is he?"

Suddenly reality dropped and crushed her. "Why . . . where?" she repeated, casting her eyes around as if searching for the answer in the paint on the walls. "I . . . I don't . . . oh, goodness . . ."

Immediately Christopher came and took the phone. He spoke in a clear, authoritative voice. "This is police officer Christopher Lallek of the Anoka Police Department, a friend of the deceased. May I answer any questions?"

He listened and said, "Mercy Hospital morgue."

"At ten-thirty today."

"A motorcycle accident."

"Yes."

"Yes, I think so."

"910-8510."

"Faith Lutheran."

"Yes, if she doesn't have one we have one at the police department."

"If it would be all right I think she'll need a little time to make that decision. Some of the family members haven't even been informed yet."

"Yes, tomorrow would be better."

"I think nine would be fine. Thank you, Mr. Dewey."

When he'd hung up he wrote Walter Dewey's name and number on a pad beside the phone and told Lee, "You'll need to meet with him, of course, but tomorrow is time enough. He suggested nine o'clock and I said I thought that would be fine. Meanwhile you don't have to worry about making any other arrangements. He'll take care of everything."

"Greg is at the morgue already?"

"Yes. At Mercy Hospital. When the department responds to a fatality that's where they're taken. Mr. Dewey will handle everything."

It struck Lee again how glad she was to have Christopher Lallek here. He, too, must still be in the throes of shock, but he was hiding it well, taking over some of the unpleasant tasks as a husband would if she still had one . . . or as a grown son would. Whenever she was near crumbling, he stepped in and relieved her without being asked to. She recognized that having him here—not only a masculine presence but also Greg's best friend—moving around her kitchen, lifting her burdens in whatever way possible, was much like having Greg himself here.

She left Sylvia and went to him. "Christopher," she said, putting her hands on the short sleeves of his wild Hawaiian shirt. "Thank you. I'm sorry I broke down and left that to you."

"You've got a right to break down, Mrs. Reston. This is one of the worst days of your life."

"Of yours too," she said understandingly.

"Yes . . . it is. But . . ." He looked at the notes on her refrigerator door. "I think he'd want me to help you any way I could, so if you don't mind, I'll stick around."

She hugged him hard and they listened to each other gulp down wads of grief. She rubbed the center of his back with both hands as if he were her own son, and for the briefest flash it felt like holding Greg again.

The telephone rang.

Sylvia answered while the other two watched and listened.

"Yes, Kim. Northwest flight three fifty-six . . . Seven fifty-nine. I've got it." She wrote it down and listened for a while. "I'm sorry your vacation has been ruined, but it's so kind of you to come back home with her. She'll need your support, I'm sure." After another pause, she said, "Seven fifty-nine, yes. I'm not sure which one of us will be there to pick you up, but somebody will. Please tell her her mother is doing all right. We're still here with her and she'll have someone with her every minute. Yes. Yes. All right, see you then."

When she'd hung up, Sylvia said, "Kim is coming home with Janice, so try not to worry about her, Lee."

That was only the first call of many. The afternoon wore on, bringing the reality of the staggering number of telephone calls necessitated by an unexpected death. Sylvia and Christopher took turns making them— to Sylvia's husband, Barry, who showed up at the house within fifteen minutes after receiving the news; to Lee's mother and father, who broke into noisy weeping and needed much calming before the conversation could be continued; to the next-door neighbor and dear friend Tina Sanders, who came immediately, too. To the flower shop. To the Whitmans' again and again and again with no response.

The house began filling with people. Neighbors arrived asking what they could do. Sylvia began organizing them with calling lists. While they were writing down names and telephone numbers the oddest impulse came over Lee. She turned, lifted her head and actually opened her mouth to ask the question *Did anyone call Greg yet?* Just like on any normal day. Startled, she caught herself before phrasing it, and the reality of his death struck her afresh. She stood in midst of a circle of women who were poring over her phone book, wondering how it could be possible she'd never call Greg again, never hear him laugh, never see him walk into this kitchen and open the refrigerator door looking for leftovers, never see him marry, have children. Could it really be true that his death had prompted all the hubbub around her?

Someone brought in a thirty-six-cup percolator and soon the house was filled with the smell of coffee. Someone else brought in a platter of sliced fruit, then a coffee cake appeared. Lee's parents arrived needing more consolation than they were able to give, and she found herself giving the support despite the fact she still needed it so badly herself. But for them the news was fresh. There was a fleeting moment when she was holding her mother, feeling the older woman's sobs quaking them both, that Lee thought, *I've got to get out of here! I can't stand this a minute more!* But the door opened and someone else came in. Someone else who needed to shed first tears on Lee's shoulder, and grip her in a desperate embrace. In the midst of the growing gaggle of mourners Christopher found Lee and quietly told her, "Mrs. Reston, I've got Joey on the phone."

Her heart began pounding and her limbs felt suddenly leaden. She went dutifully to the phone and he followed, then stood with his back to her as if shielding her from the others in the room while she faced this next heartrending duty.

"Joey?"

"Hi, Mom, is something wrong? How come Chris called me?"

"Joey, honey, this is the hardest thing I've ever had to tell you. It's . . ."

While she paused to steady herself he said in a panicky voice, "Is somebody hurt, Mom? Is Janice okay?"

"It's not Janice, Joey . . . it's Greg."

"Greg?" His voice cracked into a high falsetto. "What happened?"

"Greg had a motorcycle accident, honey."

He said really softly, "Ohhh."

"Greg is dead, honey."

He said nothing for the longest time. When he spoke, his voice sounded the way it had a year ago when it was first changing. "Dead? But . . . but how can he be?"

"I know it's hard to believe but it's really true. It happened this morning."

"But . . . but he was gonna take me and the guys to Valley Fair next week."

"I know, dear, I know."

"Aw Jeez, Mom . . ." He was trying not to cry, but the falsetto and the broken phrasing gave him away. "It's not fair."

She whispered, "I know, Joey."

"How we gonna get along without him?"

"We will . . . you'll see. It'll be hard, but we've still got each other. And lots of people who love us. Aunt Sylvia is here with me now, and Grandpa and Grandma and a lot of the neighbors, and Christopher, and Janice is coming home tonight. But I need you here too, okay?"

He barely got out, "Okay."

"I love you. And we're going to be okay. You'll see. We're going to make it through this."

"Okay. Mrs. Whitman wants to talk to you now."

Mrs. Whitman sounded terrified. "Dear God," she said. "We'll leave immediately. We'll have Joey home as soon as we can get him there. Oh, Lee, I'm so sorry."

Lee hung up the phone and dried her eyes to find Chris still shielding her from the rest of the room. He turned and said quietly, "That was a tough one."

"Yes."

"Does someone need to drive up there and get him?"

"No, they're bringing him back."

"You're sure? Because I'll go. I'd be happy to."

Gratitude flooded her. She laid a hand on his arm. "I know you would, but no. They're leaving immediately. But, Chris, if you meant it when you said you'd go to the airport to get Janice and Kim, I'd really appreciate it."

He covered her hand and squeezed it. "Of course I meant it."

"Because if I went out to get Janice, I might not be here when Joey gets home, and I—" She could feel her emotions cracking again but he forestalled another breakdown.

"Don't say another word. I'll be there when her plane touches down. Now how about you? You making it okay? Do you want some coffee or something?"

"No thank you, Christopher, but have some yourself."

"No, I couldn't eat a thing. Feel like it'd come back up."

It was late afternoon. The neighbors had begun returning with hot foods, sandwiches, salads. The front screen door seemed to open and close incessantly and the murmur of voices filled the place.

Sylvia came into the kitchen and said, "Lloyd is here, Lee."

"Lloyd. Oh, Lloyd." She immediately moved toward the front hall, where her father-in-law had just come in. His hair was as silver as the rims of his glasses. A trim man of medium height, he had the gentlest face of any human being she'd ever known, with features that even in sorrow looked accepting and kind.

"Lee," he said. Nothing more. Only folded her in his arms and held her for the longest time while they both relived the day they'd grieved this way for Bill, his son. Odd how she loved this man. More than her own father, for she felt more at ease with him, could talk to him more honestly, could bare her soul with him. He wasn't Bill—she had never mistakenly substituted him for Bill—but in Lloyd Reston's arms she felt closer to her husband than anywhere else. It felt as if Bill were here with her now, fortifying her, as Lloyd said quietly, "Life is so full of sorrow, and we've had our share, haven't we, little one? But we'll weather this one, too. We know we can because we've done it before."

When he pulled back there were tears in his eyes and on his cheeks, but he demonstrated none of the histrionics of her own mother and father, and she found this calming.

"Do the children know?"

"Yes. They're on their way."

"Good." He squeezed her shoulders. "You'll feel better once they're with you. Are there too many others? Are we overwhelming you?"

"No. They all mean well, and they need to gather because it's scary for them, too. It might not be their son, but they all realize it could be someday. Let them stay."

Her pastor arrived, Reverend Ahldecker, and as she was being consoled by him she looked out through the screen door to see Christopher, alone in the front yard, turning off the lawn sprinkler, which had been running in one spot all day. He gathered in the hose, coiling it between the shrubs by the front door. His chin was resting on his chest and his motions were slow and methodical. There were tears running down his face.

His sad solitude touched her deeply. Alone out there, winding up the hose, crying the tears he withheld in the house while offering his support to her. Time and again he had sensed when she needed him, and now it was time to return the favor.

"Excuse me, Reverend Ahldecker, I'll be right back."

She went outside, closing the screen door silently. Approaching him from behind she slipped her arms around his waist, spread her hands on his chest where his sunglasses still hung and laid her cheek between his shoulder blades. His shirt was hot from the late afternoon sun. His heartbeat was steady but his breathing irregular, caught at intervals by swallowed sobs. At her touch, his hands fell lifelessly to his side, the hose still trailing from his fingers. They stood so for long moments, the sprinkler head dripping water onto the sidewalk and splashing their ankles. Neither of them noticed. Neither of them cared.

Their shadows, from behind, stretched along the wet concrete like gray cutouts. Evening was approaching. From a telephone wire nearby a mourning dove called. Some distance away, another answered—like the two of them, calling and answering each other's mourning throughout this bizarre and unspeakably sad day.

At last Christopher drew in a great sigh and expelled his breath with a shudder. "I loved him, you know? And I never told him."

"He knew it. And he loved you, too."

"But I should have told him."

"We tell people those things in countless ways. Last week he said you brought him two cinnamon tornados from Hans's bakery. And I recall times when you washed his car just because you were washing your own, and drove out to give him a jump start when his battery was dead, and returned his video rentals so he wouldn't have to pay an overdue charge. Those are all ways in which we say I love you. He knew it. Don't ever think he didn't."

"But I should have said it."

"Don't be so hard on yourself, Christopher. I'm sure he knew."

"No one ever taught me how to say it. I never had . . ."

He cut the remark short and her mother's heart went out to him for the love he'd never had at home.

"Did he ever say it to you?"

Christopher dropped his gaze to the green rubber hose, scratching it absently with a thumbnail. "No."

"But do you doubt it?"

He shook his head.

"Let me tell you something, Christopher." She stepped back, turned him around and looked up at him. "From the time you two became roommates, he never once took leftovers from here without asking if I had enough for you, too. 'He's never had much home cooking, Mom,' he'd say, 'so put in extra for Chris.' And I did, and he'd take them for you because that was one of his ways of saying he loved you. And there was never a holiday he wasn't worried about you being alone. That's why he invited you here to be with us. And didn't he fix something on that disreputable old car of yours just a couple of weeks ago? Some fuse for the air conditioner or something? I know he did, so don't you waste a minute of your precious life regretting that you never told him. Because he knew it just like you knew it."

Christopher sniffed and wiped his nose with the edge of one hand. Lee found a tissue in her skirt pocket and handed it to him.

"If it'll make you feel better, promise yourself that from now on you'll tell people how they matter to you. If you love someone, tell him."

He blew his nose and nodded at the sidewalk. "I will."

"All right," she said. "Feeling better now?"

He blew out a deep breath. "Yeah. Thanks."

"I've been through this before, you know. I'm an old hand at handling grief, and I know that there's a good year or more of it ahead for both of us. I also know that it doesn't always strike you conveniently when you're off duty, or during daylight hours, or in the privacy of your own home. Grief is an ill-mannered bastard. It strikes you when you least expect it to. When that happens, just remember, Christopher, I'm here and you can come to me anytime, night or day. And somehow we'll muddle through. Okay?"

He nodded again and murmured, "Thanks, Mrs. Reston."

"And now you have to leave for the airport, and I have to speak to Reverend Ahldecker."

She braved a smile. There wasn't a trace of makeup left on her face. Her skin was red and roughened by all the tears and tissues that had worried it that day. Studying her, Christopher saw the resemblance to Greg in the shape of her eyebrows and lips.

"I can see why he loved you so much, and admired you. You're very wise and very strong."

She gave him a gentle shove toward his car and said, "Go on now, before you start me crying again."

At Twin Cities International Airport, Northwest flight 356 taxied to a stop at Gate 6. Janice Reston reached in the overhead compartment for her carry-on bag and waited leadenly for the door to be opened and the passengers to bump their way up the aisle ahead of her.

She wondered if her mom was waiting inside the terminal, or Aunt Sylvia and Uncle Barry. Maybe Grandpa and Grandma Hillier. She had cried throughout most of the flight from San Francisco, staring out the window while the sun moved around behind the plane and reflected off its silver wing. Kim had dried her eyes often, too, then had opened a book that lay unread on her lap while she clasped Janice's hand and Janice had talked through her grief.

Now, walking up the jetway and into the airport she was surprised to see Christopher Lallek waiting at the top of the ramp.

"Chris," she cried, and dropped her canvas bag as he came forward to scoop her into his arms.

"Janice . . ."

"Oh, Chris, how can it be true?"

She clung to him, her arms doubled around his neck while weeping assailed her once more. He held her so firmly only her toes grazed the floor while passengers threaded their way around them and Kim looked on with fresh tears in her eyes. Janice had imagined being in Chris's arms since the first time she'd met him two years ago, when Greg had joined the Anoka police force and the two had begun sharing an apartment. Never had she imagined him holding her for such a reason. He was thirty, she only twenty-three. He'd always treated her like Greg's kid sister, old enough to be in college and out on her own, but far too young to date. Suddenly, in the space of a few hours, death had stepped in and trivialized age differences. Their mutual bereavement brought them together simply as two people who had loved someone they'd lost. Only that loss mattered while they clung and grieved.

They separated and Chris extended his hand. "Hi, Kim. I'm Christopher Lallek. I'm sorry you had to end your vacation so soon after you got there."

Kim's face, too, looked puffy and red. "There was no question of my staying once I heard the news."

He picked up Janice's carryon and they walked three abreast toward the luggage return.

In his car, heading north to Anoka, Kim sat in back, Janice in front. He answered Janice's questions and reached over to rub her shoulder when she was forced to dig in her purse for Kleenex again and again.

"How's Mom holding up?"

"Like the Rock of Gibraltar, cheering up everybody who comes in the door instead of the other way around. Greg always said she was a strong woman and I've seen it today. I know she'll feel better when you get home though. The hardest thing she did was call you and your brother."

"Is he home yet?"

"He wasn't when I left. The Whitmans were heading back from the lake though to bring him."

They rode along thinking awhile, about their own feelings, and Lee's, and those of a fourteen-year-old boy who had been left the only male in the family. The muffler on Chris's old car was nearly shot; its thunder reverberated in their heads while the rush of hot wind from the partially opened windows moved their hair. The fuse had blown on the air conditioner shortly after Greg replaced it, but Christopher had decided it wasn't worth replacing with the new Explorer soon to arrive. The new Explorer—hell, he hadn't given it a thought since noon. The dealer had probably called his apartment all afternoon wondering what had happened to him. Funny how the new vehicle had lost all importance in light of today's tragedy. The sun was dropping toward the horizon. The outline of downtown Minneapolis appeared veiled in a shimmery pearlescent haze then fell behind them as I-94 curved around it and continued north.

Christopher fixed his eyes on the tar and drove without conscious awareness of changing lanes, working a signal light, maintaining speed. The two women stared out their side windows and Janice thought about how everything had changed since yesterday. How her life would never be quite the same again. All those memories she and Greg had shared of growing up together; there was nobody to reminisce with now, especially about the time before Daddy had died. Joey was so much younger his memories were separate from Janice's. It was Greg she'd played with, had gone to high school with, had cheered for when he ran the 440 and talked with about dating and the boys she'd liked, the girls he'd liked.

His kids would have been her kids' cousins. They'd have played together as they grew up, and would have shared holidays. She'd have baby-sat them sometimes when he and his wife wanted to get away alone. All their kids would have been at each others' birthday parties, graduation parties, weddings. Staring out the car window she felt suddenly cheated and angry. All that time and love invested in someone else's life and now he was gone, and with him so much of her future!

Abruptly she felt guilty for the thought. *How can I be angry? And with whom? Greg? Mom? Dad? The baby that died and didn't have to go through all this heartache and isn't here for me now? Myself for going off to San Francisco instead of spending the last couple of days with him?*

42

She dropped her head back against the seat and said, "Do you feel angry, Chris?"

He glanced over at her. "Yes."

"With whom?"

"With Greg, for not wearing a helmet. With fate. Hell, I don't know."

She felt better then, knowing he'd experienced the same feeling as she—selfish as it seemed.

"I keep thinking about how he never got a chance to get married . . . to have kids."

"Yeah, I know."

"And Mom and all of us. I mean—damn it!—think about birthdays! Think about Christmas!" She had begun to cry again. "They're gonna b . . . be awful!"

She was right. He could only reach over and take her hand.

He thought he had never witnessed anything more pathetic than the reunion of Lee Reston and her children. He stood by, watching the three of them form a knot of sorrow, and would truly have given a good portion of his own life in exchange for the restoration of Greg to them. He heard their weeping, witnessed their ungainly three-way hug, watched the mother's hands stroke her children's heads while their faces were buried against her. He moved away to give them privacy, went into the backyard and sat down on the deck steps leading to the lawn. It was a pretty lawn, deep, reaching 200 feet back toward a row of arbor vitae that divided it from the neighbor's house beyond. At the near end shade trees spread. At the far end flower borders with serpentine edges meandered around three edges of the property surrounding an open stretch of grass that served as a volleyball court during family picnics. He'd been at a couple of these. They lingered in his memory as lucky days, some of the luckiest of his life. Hot dogs and laughter and family and friends— all the things he'd missed in his own life. And Greg had brought him into it all. They'd welcomed him as they'd welcome one of their own— "Beer's over there. Pop's over there and anybody who doesn't help himself to the food goes hungry without sympathy!"

Fourth of July was probably off. He supposed there'd be no picnic here this year. He'd asked his captain for the day off clear back in April. He'd probably go in and volunteer for duty that day so one of the married guys could be with his family. Hell, he had nothing better to do. He was used to volunteering for holidays. Better than sitting around feeling sorry for himself.

He remembered one Fourth of July when he was twelve, thirteen maybe. Junior high and he'd joined the band, asked to play the tuba because there was no money for instruments at his house, and the school provided tubas and drums. He'd chosen tuba and could remember its weight on his shoulder, the feeling of that big cup-sized mouthpiece against his lips, and the surge of excitement when he'd marched down the street with that big brass bell above his head for the first time. There'd been a favorite march: the Klaxon, that was it, and—damn!— how it had stirred his blood when they'd played it. *Pum, pum, pum, pum:* He and the bass drum setting the rhythm as the band strutted down the street. The band director, Mr. Zatner, said the junior band had been invited to march at a parade in the small town of Princeton and they'd all been issued satin capes, maroon on one side, black on the other, and were told to wear black trousers and white shirts.

He went home with a knot in his gut because he knew he'd have to ask his parents to buy him a pair of black pants. They lived in a sleazy apartment above an appliance store a half block off Main. A warped, weathered open stairway led up to it from the alley where the smell of rotting vegetables hung heavy in the warm months from the garbage dollies of the Red Owl store next door. A few times, when there was nothing in the apartment to eat, he'd hung around the back door of the grocery store when the produce people were weeding out the bad stuff.

"Hey, need some help?" he'd asked, and the man in the soiled white apron had said, "Hey, this is one for the record! A kid offering help? Sure, why not?"

They'd tossed away some discolored cauliflower, some fancy kinds of lettuce that looked black and slimy, and bunches of broccoli that looked fine to Chris. Trouble was, he hated broccoli. They came to oranges— soft in spots but far from moldy.

"Hey, these look good yet," Chris had said.

"Not good enough to sell."

"Mind if I eat one?"

"Don't mind at all. Here, have two. Have three." Chris caught the three oranges as the man tossed them his way.

That day he took home oranges, wilted carrots and something called spaghetti squash, which tasted like fodder when he peeled and cooked it. His little sister, Jeannie, complained, "But I don't like it!"

"Eat it!" he'd ordered. "It's good for you and it's another nine days before the old man gets his welfare check."

But they both knew the old man and old lady had to buy their booze first. They bought most of it in a dive the kids referred to as "The Hole," a block from the apartment, down one level from the street, a dank, smoky basement bar where the old man went as soon as he got up in the morning, and where the old lady joined him straight from work. She was a fry cook in a truck stop out on Highway 10, gone from the apartment before the kids woke up in the morning, most nights stumbling home after they'd gone to bed.

Both the old man and old lady were at The Hole the day Christopher came home with the knot in his gut about the black slacks. He boiled Jeannie some macaroni and mixed it with Campbell's tomato soup and after she went to bed, he waited up for his parents.

They came in around midnight, arguing as usual. When they stumbled in, stinking like a barroom floor, the old man wavered in his tracks and spoke with slack lips anchoring a smoking cigarette.

"What the hell you still doing up?"

"I gotta talk to you."

"At midnight, for Chrissake! Punk like you oughta be in bed."

"I would be if you'd have gotten home at a decent hour!"

"You're some smart-ass kid, you know that! Don't tell me when to come home and when not to! I still wear the pants in this family!"

He sure did. They were filthy and smelled bad, like all the rest of him, and hung like a hammock below his protruding beer belly.

"I need some money for a pair of slacks."

"You got jeans."

"Black ones."

"Black ones!" he exploded. "What the hell you need black ones for!"

"For a band uniform. We're marching in a parade and everyone needs to wear white shirts and black slacks."

"A parade! Jesus Christ, they think I got money to fork over every time a parade comes to town! Tell your band director to come over here and tell me to my face that I got to foot the bill for any goddamn band uniform! I'll tell him a thing or two!"

His mother spoke up. "Shh, Ed, shut up for God's sakes! You're gonna wake up Jeannie!"

"Don't tell me to shut up, Mavis! This is my goddamn house! *I can yell as loud as I want to in it!*"

"Dad, I need the money."

"Well, I haven't got it!"

"You had enough to get drunk tonight. Both you and Ma."

"You just watch your mouth, sonny!"

"It's the truth."

"There's nothin' wrong with a man having a little drink or two, and I don't need any smart-ass kid like you tellin' me when I've had enough!"

"Ed, don't start in on him."

"You always stick up for him, goddamn it! Smart-ass kid's got no respect for his elders, that's what. Anytime a smart-ass kid tells his own father—" He belched unexpectedly, his slack lips flapping, the bags under his eyes nearly doing the same.

"I'll be the only one without black slacks."

"Well, that's just too bad, ain't it! Goddamn government bleeds a man for taxes to build schools, then they come beggin' for more! You can wear the jeans you got on, and if that ain't good enough for 'em, screw 'em."

"Dad, please . . . everyone's wearing maroon-and-black capes and my blue jeans will look—"

"Capes!" Ed's head jutted forward. "Capes! Jesus Christ, what're they turning out over there, a bunch of sissies! Capes!" He bellowed with laughter, the buttons over his belly straining as he bent back. With a jeering stare at his son, he straightened, pulled the cigarette from his mouth and squashed it out in an ashtray. "I got no money for sissy uniforms and you can tell your band director I said so."

Christopher and Jeannie shared a dinky bedroom with space for little more than their narrow twin beds and one beat-up chest of drawers. Though he got under his covers without turning on the light, he knew she was over there wide awake. Sometimes she pretended to be asleep when their parents were fighting, but not tonight.

"I hate them," she said matter-of-factly.

"You shouldn't say that."

46

"Why? Don't you?"

He did, but he didn't want his feelings to infect her. Girls were different. Girls needed their moms, especially—a lot longer than boys did.

Jeannie startled him by declaring, "I'm getting out of here as soon as I'm old enough."

Hell, she was only nine. She should be living a carefree life instead of plotting her escape from her family.

"Jeannie, don't say that."

"But it's true. I'm going to run away."

"Aw, Jeannie, come on . . ."

"And when I do, I'm never coming back, except maybe once or twice to see you. You're the only good thing around here."

He lay with a lump in his throat, unable to rebuke her with any amount of conviction, for he'd had the same thoughts himself.

The following week, Mavis slipped him twenty-five dollars. "Here's for those black slacks," she said.

"Thanks," he said without any warmth. He deserved decent clothes, and food on the table, and parents at home and sober now and then. Every kid deserved that much. If it weren't for him Jeannie'd have gone to school even tackier than she did. He made her comb her hair and eat some toast and put on her jacket every morning while the old man snored in his alcoholic stupor and his mother fried eggs at the truck stop to earn enough money for their endless boozing.

Twenty-five dollars slipped into his hand now and then couldn't make up for two drunken parents who didn't have time to raise their kids.

"Your dad didn't mean anything by it. He's had it hard, you know—falling off that loading dock and busting up his back. He was a different man before that happened."

He'd heard this so often, but he didn't buy any of it. Other people had strokes of bad luck in their lives and overcame them. Other moms realized that nine-year-old girls needed somebody to wash and iron their clothes and be home to cook them supper and wish them good-night at bedtime. Ed and Mavis were alcoholics, plain and simple, and she was no better than the old man. They didn't beat their kids, but they didn't have to: Neglect did it for them.

Christopher Lallek marched in that Fourth of July parade dressed in new black jeans. But no parents were there watching from the curb, and the joy of playing the Klaxon had somehow dimmed after his father's disparaging remarks about sissies. The following year he dropped band from his schedule and took Home Ec instead. He figured if he had to cook for himself and Jeannie for the next five years he'd at least learn how. And in Home Ec class he got a free meal now and then.

Christopher sat on the steps of a redwood deck, remembering. Dark had fallen and the first stars were gleaming in the southeast sky. Crickets were singing in Mrs. Reston's garden. Behind him, light glowed through her kitchen door while on her refrigerator hung a note about leftover lasagna. His stomach growled, reminding him he hadn't eaten all day, but he had no urge to do so. He should get up and go home, leave this family to themselves, but he didn't know how he could handle walking into his apartment with all its reminders of Greg. Greg's clothing in the closet, his CDs in the living room, his mail on the kitchen cabinet, his shampoo in the shower, his favorite juice in the refrigerator.

Sweet Jesus, he'd give anything if he had a mom and dad to go to, someone whose house he could walk into and be hugged and held and loved and cared about the way this family cared about one another. Someone who'd turn down the bed in their spare room and come to him as he lay in it and comb his hair back with their fingers and say, "It's going to be all right, son. You lost a friend but you still have us. We love you."

He'd never heard the words from them. Never. He'd never said them to a living soul, not even to Jeannie before she left or to Greg before he died. It was true what he'd told Mrs. Reston: He'd never been taught how.

They still lived in town, Ed and Mavis, in a trashy subsidized housing project where he was called regularly to handle domestics and disturbances of the peace. Last time he'd seen them was maybe three years ago. The old man had a grizzled beard and smelled as bad as ever, sitting in a rocker and sipping cheap whiskey straight from a pint bottle. The old lady had been drinking beer and watching soap operas, the place so filthy only a torching could improve it. He'd been called there to break up a fight in another apartment, and who knows what had prompted him to knock on their door. He wished he hadn't. Nothing had changed. Nothing was going to change.

Behind him, Lee Reston said, "Christopher? What are you doing out there alone in the dark?"

He sighed and rose from the hard wooden step, flexing his back, looking up at the stars.

"Remembering."

She slid open the screen and stepped out, crossing her arms and facing the sky just as he did.

"Yes," she said, then both of them held silent awhile, thinking about the night ahead, the days and months ahead. The crickets went on scraping away and the stocks in the garden gave off a pungent perfume. The moon had risen and dew was forming on the grass, which was growing at this very moment.

Life went on.

They must, too.

"It's time I go," he said.

"Where?"

"Back to the apartment."

"Oh, Christopher . . . shall I . . . would you like someone to . . ."

"It's okay, Mrs. Reston. I'll have to face it sometime. Your children are here now and you need some time alone with them. The captain has cleared me till after the funeral, for as long as I need, actually, so I'll be there at the apartment tomorrow. You'll need some of his clothes, his mail, his car keys . . . whatever. If you want me there when you come to get them just say the word. If you'd rather have me gone, that's okay, too. Now you'd better get some rest. You've had a rough day."

She crossed the deck, her feet clad in nylons, shoes left behind somewhere, and stood above him with her arms crossed and her hair backlit by the kitchen light. "You don't have to go back there yet. You can sleep on the sofa in the living room and we'll go together tomorrow."

For a moment he was tempted. The scene he envisioned earlier flashed through his imagination, of her combing his hair back as he lay on a pillow, of her calm voice saying, "It's okay, Christopher, I'm here and I love you. You're going to be just fine." But she had her family now, and her own grief to work through; she didn't need him hanging around tonight—someone else to worry about and soothe.

"Thanks, Mrs. Reston, but I'll be just fine. You go on back inside and be with your kids. I'll see you tomorrow."

She watched him head around the side of the house toward his car. Just as he reached the corner she called, "Christopher?"

He stopped and looked back at her. The moon had risen and by its light she made out the rim of his short regulation haircut, the busy Hawaiian print on his shoulders, his bare legs and feet, still in the rubber thongs he'd been wearing this morning when he'd been heading for the beach for a day of fun.

"Thank you for all you did today. I couldn't have made it without you."

"Thank you, too," he said, "for letting me stay. I'd have gone crazy if I couldn't have been here with all of you."

He began to move again but she called "Just a minute!" and disappeared inside the kitchen. Momentarily she returned carrying a tinfoil-wrapped square in her hand. She thumped softly down the steps in her stocking feet, the light following her left side as she crossed the grass to put the packet in his hands. "You haven't eaten all day. Warm this up in your microwave . . . promise?"

"I will. Thanks."

It was cold on his palm, chilled from her refrigerator. He didn't have to open it to know it was lasagna.

Chapter 3

*I*N his car, Christopher set the tin-foil packet on the seat, started the engine and with the greatest reluctance headed home.

Home was an apartment in a complex called Cutter's Grove where he and Greg had lived for two years. What had attracted Chris to the buildings at that time was the fact that they were brand-new and he'd be the first renter in his unit. Ask him and he'd admit he had a colossal hang-up about cleanliness. Not only was the apartment going to start clean, anybody who shared it was going to keep it that way!

When he learned that the new guy on the force was looking for a place to live, he'd approached Greg and told him truthfully, "I grew up in filth. I had two alcoholic parents who didn't give a damn whether there was food on the table, much less whether or not the joint got cleaned. So if you don't intend to do your share of KP duty, say so now. It'll save us a lot of friction later on."

Greg had replied, "I grew up with a mother who was widowed at thirty-six and had to leave the house and work from that time on. There were three of us kids left at home. Every Thursday morning she'd roust us out of bed at six o'clock and make us clean until seven, then that night after supper we had to finish the job so the place was shipshape for the weekend. If we didn't do our share of the work around the house we lost all privileges—and that included pocket money and using the car. How's that, Lallek?"

They had assessed each other, grinned, shaken hands and begun a friendship.

When Christopher unlocked the apartment door and turned on the light all was in order, as usual. To his right the kitchen was neat. Straight ahead, the living room was, too. It was decorated—actually decorated—in off-white and cocoa brown. They had agreed when moving in that there was no reason two bachelors had to sit on beer kegs and prop their feet on wooden reels that had formerly held telephone cables. So the place had taken on a personality—with a great big cream-colored sofa and oversized pillows, a pair of overstuffed club chairs, a snazzy brown leather chair with matching ottoman, a monstrous entertainment center that covered one whole wall and a few odds and ends to make the place homey: a fig tree beside the sliding glass doors (donated by Greg's mother, along with a few smaller green plants), a couple of framed posters on the wall, some brass lamps, Danish teakwood tables and on one wall their collection of bill caps. They both liked bill caps and had decided right away to put up a couple of expandable crisscross racks and hang them up where they were easy to grab.

Christopher had remembered right—the red Minnesota Twins cap was gone from the rack. He wondered where it was now and what it looked like. Greg's favorite green one was still there though, the one his grandpa Reston had given him for his last birthday. It said PEBBLE BEACH on it and Greg had always claimed it was shaped the way a bill cap ought to be shaped. Chris shuffled slowly to the rack, took down the green cap and held it a long time. He went to the leather chair and sat down with the sluggish, labored movements of an old man, and put the tinfoil packet on the ottoman and the Pebble Beach cap on his head. He closed his eyes, tipped back against the chair and let memories of Greg flutter over him like film across a screen: playing ball in the summer police league, waterskiing, eating hot dogs—the man had been crazy about hot dogs—riding in his black-and-white cruiser, sitting in the patrol room with his feet up on a table bullshitting with the guys, working around the apartment, turning up the radio when a song came on that he liked, especially anything by Vince Gill.

Memories, memories . . . hell, but they hurt.

In time Christopher rose, put the lasagna in the refrigerator and headed down the hall to the far end of the apartment. Outside Greg's bedroom doorway he lingered a long time, standing in the murky shadows, working up the courage to turn on the bedroom light and face the emptiness. Finally, he did . . . and stood leaning against the door frame coming to grips with the finality of Greg's absence. That gun and holster on the chest of drawers would never be strapped on Greg again. The department badge would never be pinned on, not the tie clasp or the radio, none of the police paraphernalia he'd worn for the past two years. He'd never sleep in this room, wear the uniforms in the closet, look at the family pictures in frames on the dresser, finish reading the Robert B. Parker book with the bookmark sticking out of it, pay the bills that were propped against a mug on his dresser, turn on that radio, put on those earphones, yell from this room, "I'm starved! Let's go out and get a hot dog someplace!"

He used to do that and Chris would yell back, "You and your hot dogs! Gimme a break, will ya, Reston?"

The hot dog jokes never ceased.

For Christmas last year Greg had given him a gift certificate from Jimbo's Jumbo Dogs, a dumpy hot dog wagon on Main Street that had become a town fixture. When you ate one of those gut-rotters with everything on it you tasted it for two days and everyone around you smelled it for three. Many was the time they were cruising in the black-and-white and as they approached Jimbo's, Greg would say, "Pull over."

"Aw, no," Chris would say. "Jeez, come on, not today!"

"Look at it this way: We'll save on Mace," Greg had replied the last time it had happened.

Chris moved into the room, still wearing the green cap. He felt it coming—the welling up, the thick throat, the hot, tight chest and the burning eyes. And he let it in. Let it slam hard and double him over as he squatted on the floor with his back against Greg's bed, his knees drawn up while he held the sides of the green cap against his skull and bawled as he'd never bawled in his life. Great whooping, heaving, terrible sobs that wailed through the room and probably up through the ceiling into the apartment above. He didn't care. He let it out, let its force control and wilt him, taking him one step closer to accepting Greg's death.

It felt terrible.

It felt brutal.

It felt necessary.

"Goddamn it!" he shouted once, then went on weeping until he was spent.

Afterward, he stayed where he was, on the floor, drooping, blowing his nose, wearing Greg's cap, wondering again why the good ones got taken and the slime kept on beating and raping and robbing and dealing and neglecting their kids.

He sat there with his head throbbing at one o'clock in the morning, turning Greg's cap around and around in his hands, caught periodically by a jerky after-spasm, feeling weariness steal in and turn him defenseless. He sighed twice—deep, shuddering sighs—looked around the room and wondered why it was said that crying like this made you feel better.

He felt like shit.

Felt as if his head were going to explode and his eyeballs burst like popcorn.

And he admitted to himself that maybe a little bit of the reason he'd wept so hard was—at long last—for himself, for the child he'd been, the loneliness he'd lived with and the painful memories that today had put him through.

At Lee's house everyone was gone. The children had dressed for bed, where they were reluctant to go alone. As it had been for all of them when Bill had died, the dread of aloneness had returned.

"Come into my bed," she invited, and they did, gladly.

They lay three abreast, sleepless, with Lee in the middle, an arm under each of them.

It took a long while before Joey hesitantly confessed his greatest guilt.

"Hey, Mom?"

"Yes, dear?"

"When you called . . . I didn't mean what I said. I mean, it was stupid, what I said."

"What did you say?"

"That Greg was gonna take me and my friends out to Valley Fair next week. Like that's all that mattered to me, you know what I mean?"

She flexed her right arm and curled him closer.

"Oh, Joey, have you been worrying about that all this time?"

"Well, it must've sounded pretty selfish."

"No, no, Joey honey—don't you worry about it. It was just a human reaction, that's all. It's hard to believe news like this, and when it comes we simply . . . well, we express our disbelief. You know how it is—we go along day by day taking our routine for granted and all of a sudden something like this happens and we think of the most common things and say, 'Gosh, how can it be true when the person we lost left unfinished business?' I remember when your dad died I kept saying, 'But we were going to go on a trip to Florida together.' And today when Christopher came and told me the news I kept blubbering about Greg not having fixed the end of my garden hose yet. So you see, I did the same thing as you. When we hear that someone we love has just died, we don't *think*, we just *react*, so don't worry about it."

Janice said, "Wanna know what I thought about all the way home on the plane?"

"What?"

"About how much I'd been cheated out of when Greg died, because he'll never get married and have kids and have a wife who'll be my sister-in-law, and how awful Christmas is going to be from now on, and that my birthdays will never be the same without him there."

"I think every one of us had those thoughts today."

They lay awhile, studying the faint night-light that picked out shadowed objects in the room—moonbeams through a curtain, the bulky presence of furniture, the dresser mirror reflecting the blue-black expanse before it.

Lee's arms were growing numb. She took them from beneath her children but kept Janice and Joey close to her sides. "Now I'll tell you what I thought—several times today. And when it happened I felt so terrible . . . so . . . well, let me tell you. In the midst of all the planning and the telephoning and people coming and going I'd catch myself

thinking, 'Did anybody call Greg yet?' And then it would strike me—
Greg's dead. He won't be coming. And I'd feel so strange and terribly
guilty that I could have forgotten he'd died, that he was the reason for
all the commotion."

Janice admitted, "The same thing happened to me."

Joey said, "Me too."

They took comfort from the fact that once again they'd apparently
pinpointed a human reaction, then Janice whispered timorously, "Nothing's ever going to be the same."

Her mother replied, "No, that's for sure. But we owe it to ourselves
to keep our lives full and good and as happy as possible, in spite of
Greg's absence. It's what I had to tell myself a thousand times after
Daddy died, and it got me through. When things start to get you down
I want you to think of that. Your happiness is imperative, and you must
work hard at having it."

In time they grew drowsy. They each slept sporadically, tossing
frequently; ultimately, they made it through the first night without
Greg.

In the morning they forced themselves to do the things they must:
bathe, eat, answer the phone . . . again . . . and again . . . and again.
Between the incoming calls, Lee made one of her own, to Lloyd.

"Hello, dear," she said. "It's Lee."

"Little one. It's good to hear your voice, shaky as it is."

"I need to ask you a favor, Lloyd."

"Sure, anything."

"Will you come with me to the funeral director's this morning?"

"Of course I will."

"I don't want to put the kids through that. Sylvia would have come
and so would my folks, but I'd rather be with you."

"That's the nicest thing you could have said to an old man at this hour
of the morning. What time should I pick you up?"

With Lloyd at her side she felt a sense of calm once again, as if Bill
were there with her. Dear, kind Lloyd, the eye in the middle of the
storm—how grateful she was to have him in her life.

She had dealt with Walter Dewey before and knew what to expect:
a man compassionate yet businesslike, asking the questions his occupa-
tion required him to ask.

Death certificate statistics first—birth date, birthplace, progenitors' names, social security number. Facts were easy. The more difficult questions followed—what day they wished to have the services, the visitation time, did they want an organist, a soloist, did they have a cemetery plot, what about flowers, lunch after the ceremony, printed memorial folders? Did they want an open or closed casket? Did she have a recent picture of Greg? Who would act as pallbearers?

At this point Lee seemed beleaguered so Lloyd stepped in. "Young Lallek spoke to me about it yesterday. It seems there'll be law-enforcement officers from all over the state at Greg's funeral. When one of their ranks dies, that's how it is. Would you want some of his fellow officers to act as pallbearers, Lee? There seems no question they'd be honored if you'd let them."

"Yes . . . oh, yes. And wouldn't Greg like that. He loved being a policeman so."

Lloyd squeezed her hand, smiled his benevolent smile. "And if you'd permit a doting grandpa—I thought about this last night when I couldn't sleep—I'd love to give a eulogy."

If it were possible to love Lloyd Reston more Lee would have done so, but all her married life she had loved him for exactly the qualities he was displaying now—lovingness combined with unflappable calm. She had learned so much from this man.

In answer to his question she smiled and turned her hand over to squeeze his. "I know your grandson would approve. Thank you, dear."

They went into a room full of caskets and tried to be analytical rather than emotional. Lloyd finally pointed at a gunmetal silver one and said, "I think I like that one. It's about the same color as that first car of Greg's that I financed for him when he graduated from high school."

They left the funeral director's with a promise that they would call back with the names of the pallbearers for the obituary and would return later that day with a set of Greg's clothing.

There was no avoiding it any longer. This above all pierced the heart—facing the place where he had lived, made happy plans for the future, stored the artifacts of his day-to-day life.

"Well, Dad," Lee said when they were back in Lloyd's car. "I guess it's time to face Greg's apartment."

He reached across the seat and took her hand. "Nobody ever said being a parent was easy. You have to weigh the responsibilities against the rewards. This is one of them. Maybe it'll help to think about all the joy he brought to your life. Remember that time when he and Janice were little and they decided to make you and Bill an anniversary cake? The cake turned out just fine, but, as I remember, they didn't know what *confectioners'* meant so they used plain sugar in the frosting."

"And we ate it." Lee grimaced at the recollection.

"And that Mother's Day when he built you that little birdhouse."

"I still have it."

"I predicted then that that kid was sure to end up being a carpenter. He was awfully handy with a hammer."

"Remember when he was in high school track? Gosh, how I used to enjoy going to those meets."

They went on reminiscing until they reached Greg's apartment. When the engine was cut, they sat looking at the building, loath to approach it.

Lloyd asked, "Do you want me to come in with you?"

"Yes," she whispered. "Please."

Christopher answered their knock, freshly shaven, his hair neatly combed, dressed in jeans and a polo shirt. Lee took a look at his puffy eyes and knew he'd had one hell of a night.

"Hi," she said simply and took him in her arms. They remained together for as long as they needed, remembering yesterday and how they'd been the first two to know, to console each other, to face the calamity. He smelled like fresh after-shave and felt sturdy yet vulnerable as Lee rocked with him, her eyes closed and her heart heavy.

When they parted Chris said, "Hi, Lloyd, how are you?" The two men patted each other's shoulders.

"Well, I've been better," Lloyd answered. "I imagine you put in a bad night yourself."

"Yessir, the worst."

Lee said, "You should've stayed at the house with the kids and me."

"Maybe," he replied. "Maybe. But all I'd have done was put off facing this place. There'd still be tonight, and tomorrow and the next day."

He had, Lee knew as she studied him, the most difficult task of any of them, since he'd been closest to Greg. Even she—mother though she was—had not lived with Greg for over two years. This place was where his absence would be felt most.

"Did you eat my lasagna?" she asked.

"Yes, this morning." He put a hand on his flat stomach and managed a smile. "It was good."

She glanced around the kitchen, reluctant to move farther into the apartment, coming up with one more item of business to delay it a few minutes.

"May I use your phone, Christopher? I'd like to call the shop."

"Sure."

He and Lloyd moved into the living room while she dialed Absolutely Floral.

Sylvia answered.

"Sylvia, you're there?" They employed four designers who came in at staggered hours.

"I thought I'd better come down and see how things were going."

"Everything okay?"

"Just fine. The girls are handling everything. Don't worry about a thing. Did you sleep at all?"

"Not much. Lloyd and I have already seen the funeral director and we've set the funeral for Monday at two P.M. We decided not to have a reviewal."

"Honey, I would have come with you."

"I know, so would Mom and Dad. Lloyd came. We did just fine ... really. But there is something you can do for me at the shop, Sylvia."

"Anything. Just name it."

"I'd like you to call Koehler & Dramm and order three dozen calla lilies, some freesias, gardenias and sword ferns. Everything white and green. Make sure we've got sprengeri and tall myrtle, too ... ." She paused and added, "For Monday."

"Lee, you're not going to arrange it yourself."

"Yes, I am."

"But, Lee ... ."

"He was my son. I want to do it, Sylvia."

"Lee, this is silly. Why not let one of the girls do it? Or me? I'll be happy to."

"It's something I must do, Sylvia, please understand. Lloyd is going to give the eulogy; I'm going to arrange the casket flowers."

It took a while before Sylvia agreed. "Very well. Full or half?"

"Full. We've decided to leave it closed."

Sylvia sighed. "All right, Lee, I'll do it right away."

"Thanks, Sylvia."

"Oh, Lee? I thought you'd want to know. The orders are flooding in for Greg. I think I'll stay here and help the girls, but if you need me, just call and I'll come over, okay?"

"I'll be just fine. I'm here at Greg's apartment with Lloyd and Christopher, and the kids are at home."

"Okay, but call if you need me . . . promise?"

"I will. Thanks, Sylvia."

When Lee hung up and went into the living room she knew the two men had overheard, though they'd been talking softly all the time. She was grateful that neither one said a word to try to dissuade her. Instead they each put an arm around her and stood looking up at the collection of caps on the wall.

Christopher said, "He was wearing his red Twins cap, but his favorite one is still here. It's the one you gave him last year, Lloyd."

Lloyd nodded, and they all realized it was time to pull themselves out of the maudlin mood. Lee moved away from their arms toward the fig tree. "The ficus looks good." She poked a finger in the soil. "So does the pothos . . . and the grape ivy." They made her want to cry, these dumb plants, simply because he'd never water them again. No, it was more than that: They'd been a symbol of his independence, gifts she'd given him when he went out on his own to start his adult life in his first apartment. Only two years he'd had them . . . only two.

"Oh, this is stupid!" she said, angry with herself for starting to cry again. "They're just plants! Just dumb plants!"

"It's not stupid," Christopher said. "I feel the same way every time I look at them . . . and at his hats, and his CDs . . . everything. It's not stupid."

"I know," she said, mollified. "But I'm so tired of crying."

"Yeah," he replied softly, "we all are."

"I might as well face his closet—is that what you're saying?"

He nodded silently and led the way. At the doorway to Greg's room he stepped back and let her enter first. Lloyd had remained behind in the living room.

She took in the room and said, "Was he always this neat?"

"He said you forced him to be. Something about Thursday-morning cleaning."

"Lord, how he hated it."

"Didn't hurt him a bit though."

Chris moved to the dresser. "He got a couple pieces of mail yesterday." He handed them to her. "And I went through his bills this morning. The ones we share for the apartment are taken care of. These are for other things."

She glanced at them.

"This one's for his motorcycle," she said and broke down again.

He held her while she cried, held her hard and motionless, his own eyes dry, her hands clutching the back of his shirt with the envelopes bent in one. "Oh God," she whispered. "Oh God . . ."

It struck him while he stood strong for her, how often he'd held this woman in the past twenty-four hours, closer and longer than he'd held any woman for years. Being relied on by her felt fitting, and each time she turned to him he found his own sorrow eased. The process of grieving was so new to Christopher. He'd seen strangers grieve in the course of his nine years on the force. He'd had psychology courses on handling traumatized victims and their equally traumatized families, but this was the first time true grief had ever touched him. No grandparents, extended family or dear friends of any kind had ever been part of his life, so there'd been no tearful funerals for him. He doubted that when his own parents died he'd care much at all.

This though—this was tough.

Lloyd came to the door holding the green bill cap. His eyes met Christopher's over Lee's shoulder. He waited patiently, his face a map of sadness.

Finally he shuffled into the room and sat down on the bed.

"I've been thinking," he said, almost as if to himself. "The casket's going to be closed. Greg loved this cap the best. And he hardly ever wore dress suits when he was alive. What do you say we bury him in jeans and one of his favorite T-shirts and this cap? Lee, dear, what do you think about that?"

She drew herself out of Christopher's arms and fished for a tissue in her pocket. Wiping her eyes, she managed a snuffly laugh. "In blue jeans and that cap? Oh, Lloyd, you're priceless."

"Well, what do you think?"

"I think that's a wonderful idea."

"Then let's pick a shirt. Chris, which one did he wear most?"

After that it wasn't so hard, opening the closet door, leafing through Greg's clothes. They had interacted as a team, one supporting the other as emotions demanded, and by the time they left the apartment they recognized they'd done a fine job of conquering another hurdle.

Lee said to Chris, "You're coming with us back to the house. You can't stay here alone."

"Thanks, but actually I have to go to the Ford dealer and pick up a new Explorer I ordered. I was supposed to pick it up yesterday, but ..." He shrugged. "I called the dealer and told him I'd be in to get it today."

"Then you'll come over later?"

He hesitated, afraid of spending too much time over there, getting in the family's way.

"Listen, I don't think—"

"Christopher, I insist. What are you going to do here? And besides, the neighbors have been bringing in so much food. Come on."

"All right. I will."

"Oh, I almost forgot. Will you do something for me?"

"Anything."

"Will you speak to your captain and express my thanks to him for offering to have the members of the police force act as pallbearers? Ask him to pick six of them—whomever he thinks. Greg liked a man named Ostrinski, and someone named Nokes."

"Ostrinski and Nokes, sure."

"And you, Christopher ..." She touched his hand. "If ... if you want to, I'd be pleased to have you act as pallbearer. But only if you want to."

"I'd have been hurt if you hadn't asked. Besides, he'd expect it, and so would I if it were the other way around."

She squeezed his hand and released it. "I need the names of the other men as soon as possible so they can be listed in the obituary."

"I'll take care of it all, Mrs. Reston. I'll speak to the captain and call Walter Dewey myself—how's that?"

"That would be a big help, thank you. It seems ..." She felt a renewed surge of gratitude at having him to rely on. "It seems as if I've been leaning on you very heavily, Christopher. Forgive me. You've really helped—I want you to know that. Whenever you're around, things just seem—well, I feel better."

She smiled and he felt better than he had since awakening that morning.

"Me too."

When she was gone he drove over to the station and spoke to the captain, called Walter Dewey, then took care of an unpleasant detail that he didn't want Lee Reston to have to handle: He drove to the impound lot to pick up Greg's key ring. Toby, who ran the lot, knew him and knew he and Greg had been roommates.

"I'm sure sorry, Chris," he said as he handed over the keys.

"Yeah," Chris said, clearing his throat. "He was a good man and a good friend."

Toby clapped a heavy hand on his shoulder and they commiserated in silence.

"I imagine the motorcycle is a loss."

"Yes, it is."

Chris nodded, studying the oily dirt of the yard. "That's good." He hadn't looked around for the machine, nor would he. "I guess that's good, otherwise his mother would have to have it fixed and sell it. This way she'll never have to deal with it at all."

Toby squeezed his shoulder and dropped his hand.

"Family must be takin' it pretty hard."

Chris nodded. Sometimes it was hard to know what to say.

"Well, take 'er easy, okay?" Toby said.

"Yeah, thanks."

The weather had grown muggy. To the east the sky was blue as an Easter egg. To the west the clouds looked like a dirty old hen who'd rolled in the dust. Thunder rumbled in the distance. Nearer, one could almost smell the first wetted-down dust, that summery scent that came just before the rain.

It was approaching 4 P.M. when Christopher drove his spanking new wild-strawberry Ford Explorer out of the parking lot of Fahrendorff Ford. The dust-rain smell whipped in the open windows and mingled with that of new vinyl and an engine burning away the residual factory oils from its metal housing.

This should have been a rip-roaring happy moment. He and Greg had looked forward to it for two months, ever since he'd ordered the vehicle. They had made plans to take a trip in it this fall, maybe down to Denver, where they'd go up into the mountains and search out some old abandoned ghost towns where gold mines had played out. They'd also talked about going up to Nova Scotia to see its rugged coastline, or even wait until winter and drive down to Florida. Whatever place they chose, they were going to take the Explorer.

Suddenly Chris was sick and tired of all these mawkish thoughts. He was cruising along Coon Rapids Boulevard when he shouted at the thin air, "Hey, Greg—look! I got it!" He smiled and let some gladness seep in, let himself enjoy this milestone he'd anticipated for so long. "You there, Reston? Hey, lookit this. I've really got it at last and damn your 'nads for not being here with me! I'll get you for this, you little pecker-head! I'm gonna go to Denver anyway, just you wait and see! And you're gonna be sorry as hell you didn't stick around to go with me!" The Explorer had a faint tick in the right door panel. He'd have to have the dealer look into that. "So how is it up there, Reston? They got hot dogs with everything on 'em? Well, good! You keep 'em up there, okay?"

He drove along feeling unexpectedly happy, realizing something for the first time: that until now he had not accepted Greg's death. With acceptance came a measure of peace and the ability to get on with life. He had no doubt there'd be more bad days, bad hours, maybe even longer stretches when he'd miss Greg terribly, but he'd just learned one way to handle them. Get on with what needed getting on with, and give yourself the right to enjoy what ought to be enjoyed.

He drove over to the police station to show the boys. Out of long practice, he checked the call reports from the last shift—suspicious person, domestic, disturbing the peace, lockout, animal complaint, same stuff as usual. He had a cup of coffee, answered sympathetic questions about the Restons and the funeral plans, and went back out to enjoy his Explorer.

It was raining as he headed over to Lee Reston's house. His new windshield wipers worked great, made a different sound than the ones on the old beater. He put a Vince Gill compact disc in the player and drove slowly, singing along softly when he knew the words, enjoying the quiet snicker of the rain on the metal roof, the occasional ranting of thunder, healing a little.

Vince came on singing "When I Call Your Name" and took the cheer out of the afternoon.

At Mrs. Reston's, several cars stood in the driveway; he parked behind them and ran through the rain to the front door.

Janice answered his knock and opened the screen door. "Come on in. Hi. How are you today?"

"Better. How about you?"

"Tired, sad, sighing a lot."

"Yeah, it's rough." He glanced toward the kitchen where the lights were on and people were gathered around the table. "It looks like you've got plenty of company. I probably shouldn't have come."

She put her arm around his waist and drew him forward. "Don't be silly. This is no time to be alone. Come on . . . join the rest."

Beneath a hanging light fixture people were leaning on their elbows looking at photo albums containing snapshots of grandparents, aunts, uncles, cousins, friends. The counter was arrayed with hot dishes, bowls of salad, platters of sandwich fixings, muffins, cookies and four different cakes in aluminum cake tins.

"Hi, Christopher," Lee greeted from across the room. "Glad you came back. I guess you know everyone except these three. They all went to high school with Greg. This is Nolan Steeg, Sandy Adolphson and Jane Retting."

He nodded to them all while Janice added, "Jane dated Greg when they were in high school. She spent a lot of time over here." She gave the girl a hug from behind; Jane looked as if she'd been crying.

They continued examining the pictures, exclaiming, "Oh, there he is with that terrible cap he used to wear everywhere! Remember how you couldn't get him to take it off at bedtime, Lee?"

"He always loved caps."

"And hot dogs."

"And raw cookie dough."

"Oh, look, there he is at a track meet."

"For somebody only six feet tall he could really run."

"Nolan, look at this one—where was this taken?"

"Taylors Falls. A bunch of us guys used to go over there and take our shirts off and play Frisbee in our cutoffs and see if we could pick up girls."

"My son . . . picking up girls?" Lee said in mock horror.

"My boyfriend . . . picking up girls?" Jane echoed in mock horror.

"He wasn't perfect, you know."

Lee said, "Well, we thought so, didn't we, Jane?" and the two of them shared a sad smile.

The examination of photos went on while Lee worked her way around the table and asked Christopher, "Are you hungry? There's plenty to eat. Let me get you a plate and you can help yourself."

He ate some goulash, some chicken-and-rice casserole, Italian salad, two turkey sandwiches and three pieces of cake, all the while standing, looking over everyone's shoulders at pictures of Greg he'd never seen before. Four times he refused to accept chairs that were offered. Janice handed him a glass of milk. He peered over heads at the open albums. There was Greg as an infant; a two-year-old blowing out birthday candles; holding his new baby sister on his lap; going off to his first day of kindergarten; around age seven, missing his front teeth; with Janice and Joey; the whole family beside a fishing boat holding up their catches; standing spraddle-legged with a basketball under one arm, beginning to stretch out in height; with four grandparents in front of Faith Lutheran Church, probably on his confirmation day; lying flat on the grass with some other boy's head on his stomach, the two of them laughing, wearing prank sunglasses one foot wide; carrying his mother piggyback, her arm raised as if holding a horsewhip; with a group of four teenage boys, one of them Nolan, leaning against somebody's car; dressed in a tux with Jane at his side in her prom formal; with Lee on his high school graduation day; standing beside a black-and-white cruiser in his new uniform and badge; playing volleyball last Fourth of July, balancing the ball on five fingertips with his other arm slung around Christopher's shoulder while Christopher's arm hooked Joey around the neck.

A wave of envy struck Christopher: What a charmed life Greg Reston had had. It wouldn't be so bad to die, having had so many happy memories. Greg had had so much family love, friends, every occasion of his life marked by photographs that preserved them forever, lovingly stored in a photo album by a mother. Now here she was, sharing them with everyone again, helping them heal, passing out food and refilling glasses, touching shoulders as she moved around the table.

He gazed at her and thought, *What a woman.* She caught his eyes and smiled. He looked away quickly, back down to the picture of himself and Greg just as the page was being turned.

He had exactly four photographs of himself as a child, and he didn't know who'd taken them, but to the best of his recollection there'd never been a camera around his house. Of elementary school pictures he had none. He was one of the kids who never brought money to pay for the photo packet when the teacher passed them out. Instead, they went back to the photographer.

His graduation picture he'd paid for himself, for by then he was working in the produce department of the Red Owl, earning fairly decent money.

He took his plate to the kitchen sink and rinsed it off.

Lee Reston came up behind him and said, "Here, let me do that."

"It's done. Should I put it in the dishwasher?"

"Yes, please."

He did so. When he straightened and turned she was near, the two of them isolated from the others by an arm of the kitchen cabinets that divided the working area from the eating area.

"Thank you for taking care of the pallbearers today."

"No need to thank me. I was glad to do it."

"About Greg's things in the apartment . . ."

He shook his head. "Take all the time you need. There's no hurry."

"But you'll probably want a new roommate."

"I haven't decided that yet. It's too soon."

"All right," she agreed quietly. "But I should probably get his car out of the garage."

"I got his keys for you . . . here." He fished them out of his pocket. "But there is no hurry. Nobody cares if it sits there for a few days. His rent is paid up till the first."

She studied the keys in her palm and a veil of sorrow descended over her face again.

"Really, Mrs. Reston," he repeated, "there's no hurry. Take your time getting everything."

Janice overheard and came up to join them. "Mom . . . are you talking about Greg's car?"

Lee cleared her throat and replied, "Yes. I told Chris we should probably get it out of the garage over there. He got the keys for us."

"I was hoping I could use it for a while. It's a lot more reliable than mine."

"Of course you can."

"Mine's been burning oil, and if the front tires last another month I'll be surprised. It would really be a lifesaver."

"Sure, dear, go ahead and use it. Maybe we can even have the title changed over to you and sell yours instead of his."

"I was thinking the same thing, but I didn't want to . . ." Janice shrugged and grew glum. "Well, you know."

Lee squeezed her arm. "I know. But something will have to be done with all his belongings eventually anyway."

"Thanks, Mom."

Christopher said, "If you want me to take the keys I can run it over here anytime. One of the cops can follow me and give me a ride back. Or I can come and get you, Janice, whenever you say."

"I could ride back home with you tonight and get it."

"Sure. That'd be okay. It's raining though."

"I've driven in the rain before. You sure this is okay with you, Mom?"

"Of course it is. It's one more detail taken care of. Go ahead and get it."

"Do you want to go now?" Janice asked Chris.

"Anytime."

"Just let me get my purse."

While Janice was gone he said to Lee, "Is there anything else you need me to do?"

"Oh, Christopher, you've been so helpful already. No, you just go." She walked him to the door, where Janice joined them. "I hope for all our sakes that we can all get some sleep tonight. Janice, be careful driving home in the rain. And, Chris . . ." She gave him one of the hugs she shared so freely, an affectionate, motherly brushing of cheeks that said goodnight and thanks. "You're so kind . . . so thoughtful. Thank you for being here." He wondered if she knew how much he liked the way her hand lingered on his neck before he turned away to open the screen door for Janice.

"Oh, just a minute!" Lee said, and hurried to the kitchen, where a drawer rolled open and tinfoil tore. Momentarily she returned with a neatly folded silvery packet. "It's chocolate cake. For morning."

"Thanks, Mrs. Reston."

In the Explorer, in damp shirts, he and Janice headed for the apartment with the rain-spotted tinfoil between them.

"Your mother is wonderful," he said.

"Everybody always says that. All my high school friends wished she was theirs."

"Does she ever get down?"

"Not very often. She has this saying: It is out of adversity that strength is born. But I don't think Greg's death has really hit her yet."

"It will when she stops supporting everyone else and has some time alone. That's when it really hit me—when I got back to the apartment last night."

She reached over and placed her hand on his bare arm, and let silence roll down the rainy streets with them.

In time she dropped her hand and seemed to realize something. "Christopher! Is this vehicle brand-new?"

"I just got it this afternoon."

"And you didn't say anything?"

He shrugged.

"I thought it smelled new. And it's still got cardboard liners on the floors."

"You're the first one to ride in it."

She gazed at his profile. In the center of this sadness came a moment when pure life zinged through her like a shock of electricity. She had always loved his face, from the first time she'd seen it, a handsome face with clear, tanned skin that always looked freshly scrubbed. Highlighted by the dash lights, his nose, lips and forehead formed an attractive silhouette. In these days when men shaved designs into their heads, or wore their hair in ugly crew cuts or below the ear, his vigorous short hair with its slight curl gave him an all-American look that only added to the overall appearance of squeaky cleanness.

"There've been times when I imagined riding somewhere in a car with you. Too bad the occasion isn't happier."

He had felt her gaze and let her subtle implication pass. "Greg and I had planned to take it to Denver in the fall, maybe to Nova Scotia."

"Funny how every path leads back to him."

"I guess that's natural. When someone dies suddenly he leaves unfinished business."

"We talked about that last night, Mom, Joey and I. We all slept in Mom's bed together and we talked about a lot of our feelings."

He featured Lee gathering her kids in beside her. The picture fit.

"I'll bet she never in her life yelled at you, or swore at you or smacked you."

"Swore at us, no. But we got yelled at when we deserved it. And I got smacked once when I was about five or six years old. I called my uncle Barry a dumb shit."

Chris burst out laughing.

Janice went on. "I must have heard someone else say it—I don't know. And right now I can't even remember what it was that bugged me so about Uncle Barry, but whatever it was I didn't like it, so I called him a dumb shit and Mom slapped my face and made me apologize. Afterwards she hugged me so hard I thought she'd crack my ribs, and she cried too and said she was sorry but I must never talk that way to anybody again."

Where Chris came from the parents called the kids dumb shits and meant it. And afterward there were no tearful apologies.

"You're a lucky girl. She's one fantastic mother." He made a sharp left turn that took them into the parking lot of Cutter's Grove apartments. "Here we are." He wound between the buildings and activated the door of an underground garage. Pulling to a halt beside Greg's white Toyota, he shut off his engine and asked, "Are you gonna be able to handle it?"

"I told you I've driven plenty of times in the rain."

"I'm not talking about the rain."

"I can handle it," she replied in a whisper. "I'm my mother's child." She gave in to impulse, leaned over and kissed him on the jaw. "Thanks for everything, Christopher. My mother said she didn't know what she'd have done without you, and the same goes for me."

The next moment she was out of his vehicle, unlocking the door of Greg's car.

Chapter 4

THE following morning the rain was gone and the sun promised a torrid day ahead.

Christopher awakened at 6:35 and listened to the silence in the apartment. *What am I going to do today?* The wake this afternoon, but between now and then the hours would stretch like a Dalí painting, empty, dry, distorted.

He rolled over and switched on the radio.

Lorrie Morgan was singing about Monday, which was never good anyway. The deejay came on with news about road repairs that would narrow I-694 down to a single lane for the remainder of the summer. The weather report predicted a high of 89 today, clear skies and extreme humidity. The announcer said, "Watching your grass grow might actually be exciting on a day like today."

He thought of Lee Reston's grass and wondered when it had last been mowed. Everybody running around like chickens with their heads cut off, and the house overrun with people, and who, in their despair, gave a damn about whether or not the grass got mowed? It was Joey's job, he supposed, but Joey was having as tough a time as the rest of them dealing with Greg's death.

Chris got up and hit the shower.

At ten to eight, when Lee Reston shuffled to the front door and opened it, she heard noises coming from the garage. She went outside barefoot, onto the cool concrete sidewalk, tightening the belt of a knee-length kimono, peering around the corner of the house to find Christopher Lallek with the garage door raised, pouring gas into her mower. He was dressed in cutoff shorts, a sleeveless blue T-shirt and a hot-pink bill cap that matched the strings on his sunglasses.

"Christopher?" she said, surprised. "What are you doing here?"

"Mowing your lawn."

"Oh, Christopher, you don't have to do that."

"I know what pride you take in your lawn, Mrs. Reston, and there'll be lots of company coming the next couple days."

"Joey can mow it."

"Joey's got all he can handle right now."

"Well . . . all right, but have you had breakfast?"

He gave her a small smile. "I had a piece of chocolate cake."

"Well, at least come in and let me give you some coffee." She led the way into the house while he watched her bare feet from behind. She had shapely calves for a woman of her age, and very small feet.

"The kids are still sleeping." She held the screen door open and he followed her inside.

"How about you?" he asked. "Did you sleep?"

"Oh, a little. You?"

"I did, yes. Woke up early though, and the radio said it's going to be a scorcher later on, so I thought I'd come over and do the lawn while it's still cool."

She poured coffee into two thick blue mugs and they sat down at the table.

"I'll bet you'll be glad when tomorrow is over," he said.

"Going back to work is beginning to sound good."

"You must be getting a little tired of having people in your house."

"At moments, yes."

"Listen, I wasn't going to come in, I was just going to—" She pressed him back into his chair when he began to rise.

"No. Not you. I like being with you. Whenever I am, the disaster seems less disastrous. This is nice, just the two of us sitting here quietly."

Beneath the table she crossed her ankles and propped her heels on a chair seat.

It was shady in the kitchen at this time of day. She hadn't turned on any lights. The room was rather a mess, the counter still covered with cake pans, Tupperware, loaves of bread and neglected mail. Beside the sink a roaster was filled with water, soaking the remnants of somebody's offering. The photo albums were closed and piled on the table along with a bunch of stacked clean coffee cups that someone hadn't known where to put away. The sliding door was open, bringing in the cool, dewy freshness of morning. Out on the lawn a pair of robins cocked their heads, enjoying a healthy breakfast after the previous night's rain.

"I feel the same way," he said. "When I'm over here, I'm closest to Greg. But I don't want to make a pest of myself."

"Tell you what. If you do, I'll let you know."

He sipped his coffee and let his eyes smile at her over the rim of the cup.

"Everybody at the station asked how you were when I was over there yesterday."

"Everybody I know seems to be wondering how I am. Can I tell you something? Without meaning to sound ungrateful for people's good intentions, there was a moment yesterday when the phone rang again, and I heard that question again, and I thought I'd scream and run out of here. I just wanted to hang up and say, 'Leave me alone! How do you think I am!' "

"Well, you'd better get used to it, because from what I've seen of the people you know, they're going to keep calling for a long, long time."

"I must sound ungrateful. What would I have done without all the wonderful people who came and brought love and hugs and food the last two days?"

"Aw, come on, don't be so hard on yourself. You're not ungrateful, you're just human. It's a tough question to answer on the best of days— how are you." He took another sip of coffee and they listened to the birds singing.

"So, how *are* you?" he asked.

They both laughed.

Afterward they felt themselves grow a notch more relaxed with each other.

"Gosh, that felt good." She roughed up her hair with four fingers, the sleeves of her silky kimono falling to her shoulders. "Haven't done that in a long time."

"Me either. Mostly I have long lapses when my mind hardly works. How about you?"

"Same here. You find yourself staring at nothing."

He scratched at his mug with a thumbnail and said, "I did something yesterday that I was quite proud of, though."

"What?"

"I spoke out loud to Greg."

"Really?" She propped her jaw on an upturned palm. "What did you say?"

"I said, 'Hey, Greg, I finally got my new Explorer!' And then I said, 'Damn your 'nads for not being here with me to ride in it!' "

She laughed softly and got a little teary-eyed at the same time.

"We had talked about taking a trip in it this fall, maybe to Denver, maybe to Nova Scotia."

"I didn't know that. But that's ..." She wagged her mug back and forth across the tabletop, then looked up again. "... That's what I value about being with you right now. Talking with you is like talking with him. Getting tidbits about his life that I wasn't privy to in the last couple months. He was always fascinated by Nova Scotia."

"Yeah, I know," Chris said, studying the contents of his mug. "Then yesterday, after I got mad at him I asked him if there were hot dogs up there. ..." He looked up at Lee. "And afterwards I felt so much better. You ought to try it."

She took her mug in both hands and, resting her elbows on the table, studied the yard while he studied her. Her kimono was flowered and crossed at the breast. Above it hung a tiny pearl surrounded by a gold swirl and two small diamonds, suspended on a fine gold chain around her neck. Her neck was thin and long. Her chest was slightly freckled.

He looked away, finished off his coffee and rose. "Well, I'd better get to work."

"Sorry," she said, rising, too. "I got melancholy on you. I didn't mean to."

"Don't apologize, Mrs. Reston. Not to me."

In silence they studied each other. The coffee machine clicked on and sizzled, rewarming the pot. Outside the birds sang. At the other end of the house a toilet flushed.

"All right," she agreed quietly.

"And one more thing. You should keep your garage locked. Anybody could come in and start your mower."

Her mouth hinted at a smile. "You sound just like him."

"I know. Us damn cops never let up, do we?"

He headed for the door and she trailed after him.

"Thanks for the coffee."

"Thanks for mowing."

"The best thing is to keep busy."

"Yes, I've found that out."

He went out and she caught the screen door as it closed, stood with her fingers caught idly on its handle, watching him go down the steps. At the bottom he did an about-face and stood below her, looking up. Strings dangled from his lopped-off jeans onto his thighs. The hair on his sturdy arms and legs was bleached by the sun. His bare feet, in dirty sneakers, were set wide apart.

"I'll tell you something, Mrs. Reston." He slipped his sunglasses on, the pink Croakies flaring back behind his neck. "I've never lost anyone before. I've never been to a funeral. It's damned scary."

He turned and headed for the garage before she could answer.

Thirty-five minutes later he was mowing the backyard when Janice came out the sliding door with a glass of ice water. He glanced up and remembered it was Sunday: She was wearing a pale peach dress and white high-heeled pumps. He went on maneuvering the machine around the edge of the flower beds until she approached. He killed the motor, pushed his cap back on his head, accepted the glass and said, "Thanks."

She watched him drink the ice water, his head tipped back, a trickle of sweat sliding from his short-trimmed sideburn. "Ahhh," he growled, finishing, backhanding his mouth and returning the glass. "Thanks."

"You're welcome. It's really nice of you to do this."

"Keeps me busy."

"Don't make light of it. Mother really appreciates everything you've done for us."

"Yeah, well it goes both ways. Your family's pretty special."

She smiled.

"Did I wake you with the mower?" he asked.

"No. I had to get up and get ready for church anyway. Do you want more water?"

"No, thanks . . . that was great." He nodded at the flower beds. "She do all this?"

"Yes. In her spare time. We keep saying to her, 'Mom, how can you spend all that time in the garden after working with flowers at the shop all day long?' but she just loves it."

He studied some tall blue spiky flowers while she studied him and wondered if he'd ever notice her. He hadn't for two years. Now that Greg was gone Chris wouldn't be around anymore, and she'd never been comfortable with flirting. Furthermore, this wasn't the time for such thoughts.

"Do you go to church, Chris?" Janice asked.

"No."

"Mom said to tell you you can come with us if you want. We can wait for a later service."

"No thanks, I'll just . . ." He gestured toward the mower. "Finish the mowing."

"All right." She fired the ice cubes off the lip of the glass onto the grass and turned toward the house. Halfway there, she called back over her shoulder, "Anytime though. It's an open invitation."

"Thanks."

He watched her walk away in her peachy summer dress with the sun showing the outline of her slip through the skirt, her legs looking firm and polished, her white high heels adding a pleasing curve to her ankles. He watched her, feeling the uneasy regret of a man who knew full well a woman found him attractive though she failed to stir him in the least.

Disquieted, he turned back to work.

A while later, with the mower still buffeting his ears, he saw Mrs. Reston step onto the deck, dressed in a short-sleeved brown-and-white suit and high heels with a purse slung over her wrist. She waved; he waved and watched her walk the length of the deck toward the garage. A moment later, between the two buildings, he saw them drive away for church.

* * *

When he got home the light was blinking on his telephone answering machine. He pushed the message button and Lee Reston's voice came on.

"Christopher, this is Lee. I just wanted to tell you one thing. Funerals aren't bad, Chris. If you think about it, they're really for the living."

He tried to bear that in mind that afternoon as he showered, shaved and dressed in a suit and tie for the wake of his best friend. But when he was in the Explorer with the air-conditioning turned on high, driving toward Dewey's Funeral Home, the stream of cold air couldn't quite dry the sweat on his palms.

The funeral home was one of the prettiest buildings in town, on a shaded corner, looking like a stately southern mansion with white pillars and Palladian windows. Walking toward it, he felt a knot of dread in his stomach. Inside the shadowed building, it was nappy and gloomy, the windows mostly covered to hold out the summer light. But where one might expect to hear recorded organ music, he heard instead—very softly as a background to murmured voices—the sound of Vince Gill's album "I Still Believe in You."

His mouth twisted into a disbelieving half-smile as he smoothed his tie and stepped toward a lectern holding a memorial book. Lee's mother and father were there signing, then whispering together, scowling as they cast their eyes toward the ceiling as if in search of the speakers.

He caught a snatch of their conversation ". . . what in the world she was thinking of!"

"I can just imagine what Aunt Delores will say."

He signed and followed them toward a cluster of people, watching Lee separate herself from them to come forward and greet her parents.

"Hi, Mom. Hi, Dad. I know what you're going to say, but please . . . let's celebrate his life, not his death."

"Oh, Lee, people are whispering."

"Who?" she said, gazing straight into her mother's eyes, gripping Peg Hillier's hands in both of her own. "I talked it over with the kids and it's our choice. It makes our memories happier."

Peg withdrew her hands. "All right, have it your way. Orrin, let's go say hello to Clarice and Bob."

When they'd moved on, Christopher took their place. He and Lee hugged briefly.

"I walked in and heard that music and all of a sudden I could swallow and breathe again. Thanks."

She smiled and squeezed his fingers. "Did you get my message?"

"Yes."

"Then why are your palms damp and trembling?"

He released her hands, making no reply, still uncertain of protocol.

"There's no reason to be afraid."

"I don't know what to do."

"Go up and say hi to him, just like you did in your Explorer. That's all."

He glanced at the casket and felt his insides seize up. She rubbed his sleeve then gave him a gentle nudge. He approached the coffin with his heart racing, dimly aware of the multitude of flowers surrounding the dais like a forest, so strong-smelling it seemed there wasn't enough pure oxygen left to sustain life. He stood between two huge bouquets, looking down at the framed photographs of Greg that smiled up at him from atop the closed metal box. There were two: one in his police uniform and cap, the other a very informal shot of him in a striped polo shirt and the green Pebble Beach cap.

Christopher put his hand on the smooth metal beside the picture. "Hi," he said quietly. "Miss ya."

How inconsiderate life was. It taught you how to deal with everything but the most important parts—marriage, parenthood, death. These people just stumbled through, making plenty of mistakes along the way. Christopher felt himself stumbling and wished again for family, someone whose hand he could hold, who would understand with no further words at this moment.

He dropped his hand from the casket and discovered he felt better.

Behind his shoulder someone said "Hi."

He turned and there stood Joey, disconsolate, his hands in his suit pockets.

"Hi," Chris said, and slung an arm around Joey's neck.

They stood there listening to Vince Gill. Gazing at Greg's picture. Choking on the smell of flowers.

Finally Joey hung his head, whacked at the tears in his eyes and whispered, "Shit."

Chris tightened his affectionate headlock and dropped his cheek against Joey's hair.

"Yeah, that's for sure."

Janice drifted up on his left, twined an arm around his elbow and rested her cheek on his sleeve.

On the far side of the room, Lee Reston accepted a hug from her aunt Pearl and uncle Melvin. As they left her with pats and murmurs, she turned to watch them move away and caught sight of Christopher with Janice and Joey at his side.

What a fine young man he was. Thoughtful beyond mere good manners; considerate of people's feelings; dependable in tens of ways. He had been a role model for Greg when the two of them met—older, more mature, out on his own already. When Greg joined the force Christopher had taken him under his wing and taught him, in a practical fashion, the best way to deal with suspects and perpetrators as well as the many personalities on the force.

He'd taught Greg how to survive on a day-to-day basis, too: how to balance a checkbook, establish credit, live on a budget, keep income-tax records, maintain a car, buy groceries, run a washing machine. Greg had left home and fallen in with a man who had helped him mature in so many ways.

Christopher Lallek—sensible, reliable, willing.

Even the kids sensed it and leaned on him. He was what Greg had been—a cop, a caretaker of a community, one to turn to in emergencies—and all of them had turned to him perhaps more than they ought since Greg's death. But his willingness made one reach toward him, as Joey and Janice were doing now. They might very well be using him as a substitute for the brother they'd lost, but what harm would it do? If they radiated toward him, let them. It was no different for them than it was for Lee: saying goodbye to Greg came easier over stories of his life, which Christopher had shared most recently.

Nonetheless, his vulnerability touched her deeply. How uncharacteristic his uncertainty had been when he'd stared at her with daunted eyes and admitted, *I don't know what to do.* Her mother's heart had reached out to him. It did so again as he stood with his arms around her children, once again the strong one for their sakes.

"Lee . . ." Someone else had come to pay their condolences and she turned to the business at hand.

Nearly two hours later, as she finished bidding goodbye to the last callers, Christopher spoke behind her.

"Mrs. Reston?"

She turned, feeling drained and anxious to go home.

"Would you mind if I took Joey for a little while?"

"No, of course not. Where are you going?"

"I thought I'd take him for a ride in my new Explorer, maybe let him drive it a little, cheer him up some."

"Oh, Christopher, yes, do."

"You'll be all right? Janice will be with you?"

"I'll be fine. I'm going to go home and collapse."

"You're sure? I realize moms need their kids at a time like this, and I don't want to—"

She touched his hand. "Take him. It's just what he needs today."

"Okay." He smiled and stepped back. "And don't worry, I'll bring him back in good shape."

Joey agreed, without much enthusiasm, but once they were out in the summer air, with the late afternoon sun dappling the boulevard, Christopher sensed Joey growing more interested.

"It's new?"

"Brand-new." Chris removed his tie and got the truck moving. "Greg and I were gonna take it out to the lake day before yesterday."

Joey threw him a dubious glance. "How can you talk about him so easy?"

"What else you gonna do? Pretend he didn't exist?"

"I don't know, but I can't talk about him at all without starting to bawl."

"So what's wrong with that? Bawling's okay. I bawled plenty in the last couple days. So did a lot of other cops."

Joey looked out his far window and said nothing.

They were riding along the shady streets of Anoka, heading toward Main. "You hungry?" Chris asked.

"No."

"I am. Mind if I stop for a burger?"

No response. He went through the drive-in window of the Burger King and ordered two cheeseburgers, two fries and two Cokes. Once the food was smelling up the truck, Joey turned to watch Chris unwrapping his sandwich.

"I guess I am sorta hungry," he admitted.

"Help yourself."

Eating burgers and fries, they cruised down Main Street onto High way 10, then headed north toward Ramsey township. In no time at all they were out in the country between cornfields and stretches of woods, where silos stuck up on the horizon and the hot crackle of summer could be felt expanding things all around. Grains bowed in the breeze and crows flapped across the blue sky. On a barbed-wire fence hung a sign advertising hybrid corn. Along a farm driveway a child rode a bicycle. A woman was putting a letter in her rural mailbox and putting up the red flag. A young boy about Joey's age was sitting on a lawn chair in the shade of a pickup truck with a sign that said FIRST CROP GREEN BEANS. A farmer on a tractor was mowing weeds in the ditch ahead of them, spreading the sweet green scent of grass and clover.

That damned old life again—just rolling on.

"How old are you?" Chris asked.

"Fourteen—why?"

"So you haven't got your driver's permit yet."

"You're a cop—you should know."

"Sure I do. Wanna drive?"

Joey's eyes got wide. His back came away from the seat. "You kidding?"

"No, I'm not kidding."

"Won't you get in trouble?"

"What do you intend to do, wreck the thing?"

"No—heck, no—I'd be careful."

"All right then . . ." Chris pulled onto the shoulder. When the gravel stopped rasping, he got out and circled the truck. Joey slid across the front seat and Chris climbed into the passenger seat.

"Adjust the seat if you need to, and the mirror, too. Have you driven before?"

"A little."

"Ask, if there's anything you don't know."

Joey drove cautiously but well. He gripped the wheel too hard and sat with his shoulder blades six inches away from the backrest, but he stayed on his half of the road and kept the speedometer steady at fifty.

Chris reached over and turned on the radio.

"You like country?"

"Yeah."

Travis Tritt was singing "Trouble."

About seven minutes later Joey asked, "Could I turn onto that road?" It was narrow, gravel.

"You're driving."

Brooks & Dunn started in on "Boot Scootin' Boogie."

About five minutes after that, Joey asked, "Can I turn again?"

"You're driving."

They listened to one by Reba McEntire and one by George Strait before Chris asked, "You know where you're going?"

Joey dared remove his eyes from the road for the first time. "No."

Chris chuckled and hunkered down in the seat with a knee wedged against the dashboard. "Sounds good."

They ended up in a little ghost town called Nowthen, got their bearings and made their way back to State Highway 47, where Chris had to take over the wheel. Back in Anoka, Main Street was all but deserted, except for the hot dog wagon, which never seemed to have any business. Passing it put Greg sharply back into both their minds. Chris drove the length of Main and swung past the police department, glancing at the squads backed up near the door. Joey glanced, too, and again Greg was in their thoughts.

Joey remained silent until Chris pulled up at the curb in front of the Reston house. For once there weren't a half dozen cars in the driveway—just Lee's, Janice's and Greg's. Chris reached over and turned down the radio. Joey sat despondently, staring out the windshield and saying nothing.

Finally he said, "I think he came to every game I ever played in. I just keep thinking all the time, Who'll come to my games now?"

"I will," Chris told him.

Joey turned only his head. He studied Chris glumly but made no reply. His eyes looked sheeny.

Chris dropped a hand on his shoulder. "You're gonna do okay, kid. You've got a hell of a family. Stick close to them and they'll get you through."

He saw movement at the front door as Lee stepped near it and looked out through the screen. She stood with her arms crossed like a worried mother who was trying not to be. Even from this distance one could almost sense her relief at Joey's return.

Joey got out and slammed the truck door. Chris lifted a palm in greeting and she did the same, then opened the screen door to wait for her son.

It's got to be tough, Chris thought, *to give your kids their freedom after you've lost two, trying not to worry every minute they're out of your sight.*

He thought about it a lot as he drove home, the picture she made, waiting in the front door with her arms crossed and no smile on her face.

Lee and Sylvia had decided to close Absolutely Floral on Monday, the day of the funeral. Lee was alone when she went in that morning to make the casket spray, which was how she wanted it. Dressed in a lavender smock and listening to Dvořák on the tape player, she arranged one of the most beautiful sprays she'd ever done. It was pungent yet pure, made of fragrant gardenias and clean-lined callas. As she worked she wiped tears on her shoulder.

She could not have verbalized why she had to put herself through this. She was his mother—that was all—and this was her trade, working with flowers. This was one last favor she could do for her son before putting him in the ground.

When the spray was finished she telephoned Rodney, their delivery man, and said quietly, "Okay, Rodney, you can come and get it now."

When he came she unlocked the back door and said, "Hello, Rodney."

Though he was mentally handicapped, Rodney did a fine job of delivering flowers. His lips were pressed firmly together, zipped up tightly to keep him from breaking into tears: It was the first time he'd seen her since Greg's death.

He took off his bill cap and worried it with both hands. "I'm sure sorry, Miss Lee."

"We all are, Rodney," she said, placing a hand on his shoulder. "Thank you."

When he'd taken the spray and left she turned off the tape player and sat down heavily on a stool in the back room between the walk-in cooler and the metal-topped designing table. So peaceful with no customers or employees about, only the buckets of blooms and greens and the familiar herbal smell of cut stems. Lord, it was good to be alone at last. She rested a forearm on the table, glanced down at her hand and noted that it was

83

stained again; after three days away from flowers it had been rather pleasant to have soft, white hands if only for a single day. Now the stains were back. She rubbed at one with a thumb . . . rubbed and rubbed . . . until her vision suddenly wavered. She reached into her smock pocket for a Kleenex and wiped her eyes. Immediately they filled again, faster than before. And finally, there amid the flowers and quiet, truly alone for the first time since Greg's death, she fell across the metal tabletop and let the storm of emotion happen.

She cried his name, "Greg . . . Greg . . . ," and wept noisily, until her face and the tabletop were messy and the metal had turned warm beneath her skin. She let her body lie limp on the shiny steel and allowed her heart's sorrow to spill forth in a rash of self-pity. *It's not fair . . . not fair! All that time and love I put into raising him and now he's gone. All that planning for his future only to be robbed of it on its very threshold.*

When her crying ceased she lay awhile with her cheek in a puddle, resting between the residual sobs that slowly subsided.

Finally she pushed up, wiped her face, and the table, sighed deep and long and sat awhile, gazing around the flower shop, letting some restorative thoughts in to replace the victimized feelings.

Suddenly Greg seemed very close, as if he'd been nearby waiting for her to calm.

"Well, I had you for twenty-five good years, didn't I, hon?" she said aloud. "And what the heck—better twenty-five good ones than a hundred bad ones. Plus I've still got Janice and Joey . . . and dozens of others who'll be gathering for the funeral in less than three hours."

The funeral. She drew a deep breath and rose from the stool. Well, the truth was she'd just conducted her own private funeral for Greg. The one she'd face at two o'clock would be easy by comparison.

The funeral of Greg Reston was attended by 350 law-enforcement officers from all over the state of Minnesota. Their squad cars filled two entire parking lots and more. They made an impressive sight, filing into the church two by two, dressed in their official uniforms of pale blue, navy, brown, and the pure white that designated captains and chiefs. They had come from Twin Cities suburbs and small, distant communities, from police departments, the State Highway Patrol and sheriff's departments representing every one of the eighty-seven counties. Striding in with stately dignity, their badges crossed by black mourning bands, they filled pew after pew until Grace Lutheran Church took on the blurred hues of an impressionistic landscape.

Lee Reston watched them arrive and felt a riffle of astonishment. So many! So impressive! Then, out of all those faces, all those uniforms, one in navy blue stepped forward to distinguish himself.

"Hello, Mrs. Reston." Christopher removed his visored hat and held it under his left arm. His appearance, in full uniform, gave Lee another start, accustomed as she was to seeing him in civilian clothes. The full regalia—navy blue uniform, tie, name tag, badge, belt, gun—added inches to his stature, years to his age and an uncommon dignity to his bearing. It caught her square in her pride and struck within her a new recognition of his manliness.

"Hello, Christopher." They shook hands very formally, Christopher maintaining a military bearing. Their eyes said an empathetic hello, but between them passed a silent message of support that went deeper than the casual sympathies of most mourners who'd weep today and forget next week. The handclasp lengthened while Lee recognized a strength within him to which she responded in an unprecedented way. It was more than bereaved mother to bereaved friend: It was woman to man.

He released her hand and said, "Hello, Janice . . . Joey." Though he'd greeted all three, he directed his following remark straight at Lee. "When Greg died our chaplain came in and talked to us. He said something that I forgot to tell you about. He said the last time he talked to Greg, Greg told him how much he loved being a cop, and how sorry he felt for guys who hate their jobs so much they detest going to work every day. He told Vernon Wender, 'I love my job because I like helping people.' I thought you'd want to know that today. He was very proud of being a cop."

"Thank you, Christopher."

He cleared his throat and glanced at the assembled men nearby. "Let me introduce you to the other officers who are acting as pallbearers." When he'd done so, and she'd shaken all their hands and accepted their condolences, Christopher spoke to her in the same formal manner as earlier.

"Your son was very well liked on the force, Mrs. Reston."

"I'm . . . well, I'm overwhelmed . . . so many of you here today."

"They came from all over the state."

"But so many."

"That's how it is when a peace officer dies."

"But I thought that was only if he died in the line of duty."

"No, ma'am."

A void fell. In the midst of it their eyes met and recognized that his formal attitude felt peculiar after the past three days of close contact.

"Are you going to make it okay today?" he asked, more like his familiar self.

Lee forced a rigid smile and nod.

"Janice? Anything I can do, just say so. Joey . . . I enjoyed our ride yesterday. Anytime you need to do that again, you call me. Maybe next time we can do it in a squad car while I'm on duty . . . with me driving, of course."

He smiled at Joey, who managed a limp smile in return. Then Christopher went away to greet other family members, with the decorum of a man in uniform.

For Lee, the funeral service passed not as a series of hazy impressions, as she'd expected, but as very distinct ones observed by a clearheaded woman who'd done her deepest mourning and was now mourning more for those around her.

Christopher maintained his stiff demeanor while bearing the coffin along with five of his fellow officers, his eyes straight ahead, his visor level with the floor, his shoulders erect. She watched him and thought of her own son in uniform, proud to wear it, liked by those he served with. In those thoughts she found very little sadness.

The white flowers she had arranged covered two-thirds of the coffin; everyone cried harder to learn Lee herself had arranged them.

Grampa Lloyd gave a eulogy with a smile on his face, and made everyone laugh aloud with recollections of Greg as a boy.

Janice and Joey held her hands all through it.

Reverend Ahldecker had a summer cold and sneezed several times in the middle of his prayers.

Sally Umland played the organ as flawlessly as an organ can be played, but Rena Tomland was away on summer vacation, so the soloist—a stranger—was rather mediocre.

Lee's mother—bless her misguided heart—had bought a new black suit for the occasion and was looking with judgmental if tearful eyes at all the summer colors on the women around her.

There was no denying that the presence of so many law-enforcement officers added a measure of pride that filled Lee and strengthened her throughout the service. Afterward, the procession of cars stretched for a mile and a half, every vehicle gleaming, directed through town by on-duty police officers who halted traffic at intersections, then removed their hats and placed them over their hearts as the cortege passed.

At the cemetery the law-enforcement officers circled Greg's grave and created a corridor to it through which Chris and the other pallbearers carried the casket. Graveside prayers were intoned, a bugler played taps, then six officers drew and discharged their pistols in a final good-bye salute.

Dust to dust: It was done.

The cars drove away, one by one. The family lingered, friends touched them, murmuring, dabbing at eyes. An old aunt plucked a gardenia from the casket spray as a keepsake. People held hands, walking slowly to their cars, appreciating life, the blue sky and beautiful earth, perhaps each other more than they had in recent days.

Lee put her arms around her children. She walked between them toward the car, sensing perhaps inappropriately the feeling of her high-heeled shoes sinking into the grass. It was a sensation peculiar to funerals: What other occasion put a woman in high heels on grass? She wondered how she could dwell on such a ridiculously unimportant thing at the saddest moment of her life. Moments of strife were like that though; they brought with them their own little escapes. While she thought of her high heels her eyes were dry.

There followed two hours in the church hall amid the smell of percolating coffee, a macaroni-tomato hot dish and Jello laced with bananas.

Again Lee was overcome by the number of those who had come to pay last respects today.

High school friends of Greg's, policemen and their wives, customers from her store, former business acquaintances of Bill's, people from whom she bought floral supplies, members of the Faith Lutheran congregation whom she scarcely knew, grade school and high school friends of Janice's and Joey's, some along with their parents. Greg's high school track coach was there, as well as his ninth-grade English teacher, who brought along a poem Greg had written when he'd been her student. Even some people who said he'd been their paper boy when he was twelve years old.

"I can't believe it," she said over and over again, accepting their sympathies, their handclasps and their genuine caring. "I can't believe it. All these people."

"He touched a lot of lives," her mother said.

And he would go on touching them for years to come. There was his old girlfriend, Jane Retting, who'd never stopped calling him. And Nolan Steeg, who approached Lee timidly and asked if he could have some little memento of Greg, any small thing that had belonged to him. And Janice, who would continue to drive his car. Joey, who wanted his tape and CD collection. His grandparents, who kept Greg's picture on their living room wall. And Christopher Lallek, who would return to the apartment the two men had shared.

When the church hall emptied, he was one of the last remaining, collapsing metal folding chairs and carrying a few dirty coffee cups to the pass-through window for the hot, tired cooks.

Lee was standing near the door with a cluster of family members who were discussing details of dividing the work that remained: recording the offerings, addressing thank-you cards, distributing flowers to retirement homes. Peg Hillier handed a book and a small white box to Lee and said, "This is the memorial book and the rest of the memorial folders. What do you want to do with the sympathy cards that haven't been opened? Do you want us to take them or do you want to?"

She glanced at Chris, standing apart, waiting, still dressed in his crisp navy blue uniform with the black-crossed badge. She wanted to rush to him and say, "Take me for a ride in your new truck so I don't have to face one more detail or hear one more sad voice or make one more decision! Just take me out of here!"

Instead, she answered her mother, thanked her relatives, expressed her appreciation to the church circle ladies who were finishing the kitchen cleanup and left the building with a bunch of unopened sympathy cards, plus the gift cards from perhaps twenty floral arrangements.

As she emerged into the late afternoon sun, she breathed a sigh of relief. Joey and Janice were sitting on the grass in the shade with a bunch of their and Greg's friends—Kim, Nolan, Sandy, Jane, Denny Whitman. She looked around for Christopher but he was nowhere in sight. His Explorer was gone, too. An unexpected siege of disappointment swamped her. She had no right to feel let down; what would he want to hang around this gloomy group for? He'd done more than his share and had been on hand practically every minute since Friday afternoon.

"Did Christopher leave?" she called to the young people.

Janice answered, "Yes. He said to tell you he was sorry he didn't get to say goodbye, but you were busy."

"Oh."

"He said he'll call you soon."

Lee turned away to hide her disappointment. She'd been thinking about going home and putting a couple of lounge chairs on the deck and maybe even opening up a couple of beers and sitting beside him without saying one damned word. She had no idea why, but out of all who'd offered, his was the only company she wished for tonight. Not her own kids', not her parents', neighbors', friends'. When they were around she was forced to talk, give hugs, put out food, pick up empty glasses, watch them get falsely cheery and morose by turns, rub shoulders, listen to them. All she wanted was simple quiet and someone to share it with.

But those were her children over there, and she couldn't say to them, *Leave me alone for a while.*

"Are you ready to go home now?" she called.

"Sure, but is it all right if these guys come too for a while?"

Lee withheld a sigh. They needed their own support system, too, and these young people were thoughtful to provide it.

"Fine," she answered.

They picked themselves up from the grass, brushing wrinkles from their clothes, and she realized it would be some time before routine would return to normal and her life would be her own.

Chapter 5

$\mathbf{A}$s Christopher drove home through the hazy golden evening, the tail end of rush hour seemed mistimed: He'd lost sight of the fact that it was Monday and people were going about their regular pursuits, stopping for a loaf of bread, filling their gas tanks, waiting in left-turn lanes. The last four days had effectively removed him from routine, making it seem as if the rest of the world was out of step with the slowed-down pace of his life and the lives of the people about whom he cared. Passersby seemed callous, though he knew full well they had no way of knowing that Greg Reston was dead and he was a man in mourning.

The thought of facing the empty apartment took five miles an hour off his speed. He pictured the Reston kids, surrounded by their friends, visiting on the green grass. He'd considered going over and joining them, but he was too old. He didn't fit in there. The one he'd really wanted to stay with was Lee, but he was too young and didn't fit in there either. Besides, he'd nearly worn out his welcome. He wasn't, after all, one of her family.

With nowhere else to go, he drove home.

Inside, the apartment was quiet and stuffy. He opened the sliding glass doors and stepped out onto the deck, which overlooked the picnic area of Cutter's Grove Park with mere glimpses of the Mississippi River visible beyond a thick stand of verdant woods. The sun was still high, lighting the green treetops and the roof of the park shelter. A couple of mothers were giving a birthday party for a bunch of small kids. Crepe-paper streamers were stretched from the poles supporting the shelter roof. Smoke drifted from the barbecue grills. A bunch of preschoolers were blowing bubbles the size of basketballs and their voices carried up to him. "Look at that one! Look at that one!"

His mother had never given him a birthday party that he could remember.

He went back inside, loosening his tie, unbuttoning his shirt, pulling it out of his trousers, opening the refrigerator and overlooking Greg's orange juice in favor of a Sprite. He popped the top, took a swig from the can and noticed that the red message light was lit on his answering machine.

He pushed the button, listened to it rewind and swigged again as a twelve-year-old voice came on.

"Hey, man, what the hell happened to you! You said we was gonna do something this weekend. You said you'd call and we'd maybe go swimming or something. Shit, man, you're just like all the rest of 'em; never mean what you say. Well, don't bother calling me no more. I got better things to do than sit around waiting for some lyin' no-good pig to call and dish me shit." *Click!*

Judd.

Hell, he'd forgotten about Judd. Chris's hand, holding the Sprite can, dropped tiredly to his side as he stared at the machine.

Judd Quincy, age twelve, male, black, shoplifter, runaway, truant, vandal of school property, bicycle thief, neglected son of two known druggies, a reflection of Christopher Lallek at that age.

The poor little bastard. No question he was one. His mother and "dad" were white. Judd was pale brown. Maybe that was why the old man kicked the shit out of him now and then, and out of the mother, too.

He picked up the receiver and dialed.

"Yeah, say it," the kid answered.

"Judd?"

A pause, then, "Shit, man, whaddyou want?"

"Got your message."

"Yeah, so what."

"So, give me a break, huh?"

"Give you a break! Man, you lied! I sit around this dump all weekend long thinking I'm going out to the lake. Nobody calls. I look like a jerk, man! My friend Noise he says maybe I'm makin' you up! He don't believe no cop would give a fuck about a dipwad like me."

"You back to using that word again?"

"Why the fuck not?"

Chris stared at the floor, rubbing his forehead, picking his way carefully. "Something happen, Judd?"

"Something always happening here. This the most happenin' place you ever seen."

"Something worse than most days?"

"Why don't you just stick it, man! Go on out to the lake with your honky friends!"

"What'd they do, Judd?"

"Didn't do nothin', I told you!"

"So you're okay, then?"

"What do you care?"

Chris decided on a new tack. "Well, I'll tell you what . . . I need a friend right now."

The concept of being needed stopped Judd's attitude. Kids like him knew, from the time they were old enough to think, that they'd never been wanted, much less needed.

"You weirding me out, cop."

On top of everything else, Judd was having an identity crisis. Half the time he talked like a semi-educated white kid, the other half he broke into black rap.

"You got an hour?" Chris asked.

"Do what?"

"Ride. I'll come and pick you up."

"Not here."

"Wherever you say."

Judd thought some. "Seven-Eleven, same like always."

"Seven-Eleven. Give me five to get out of my uniform."

*   *   *

When Chris pulled up in the parking lot of the 7-Eleven, Judd had his shoulder blades against the front window and the sole of one sneaker flattened to the brick wall below it. His hands were buried to the elbows in the pockets of black-and-chartreuse knee-length Zubaz. He had on a faded, stretched-out purple body shirt that would have fit Michael Jordan. His hair was black and curly with a lightning bolt shaved into his skull above his left ear—inexpertly, as if with a home razor.

Judd watched the Explorer roll in, leaving his butt against the wall to show that it didn't mean jack-shit to him if anybody got a new red truck with fancy running boards, a visor and chrome wheels. As the vehicle approached, Judd didn't move, only rolled his eyes to keep up with the truck and its driver.

Chris pulled to a stop and looked at Judd out of the open driver's window.

"Yo," Chris said.

"What you talkin' like a black boy for?"

"What *you* talkin' like a black boy for?"

"I be black."

"You might be, but no sense talking like a dumb one if you ever want to get anywhere in this world. Get in."

Judd pushed himself off the wall and made sure his heels dragged with every step on his way to the truck.

He got in, slammed the door and slouched into his corner, letting his knees sprawl.

"Buckle up. You know the rules."

"Bad-ass cop."

"That's right. Now buckle up."

He did. And started complaining and jabbing a finger with his face all scrunched up. "I could turn you in for dat, you know. Teachers in school can't even make us change how we talk. It's the rules. We got our culture to preserve."

"I'm not your teacher, and if you ask me, you're preserving the wrong side of your culture, and furthermore, who you gonna turn me in to?"

"Somebody."

"Somebody." Chris rolled his eyes and shook his head sardonically.

"Yeah, somebody. Your captain, dat who."

"Dat who? Listen to you, talking like a dummy! I told you, if you want to get out someday and make something of yourself and have a truck like this and a job where you can wear decent clothes and people will respect you, you start by talking like a smart person, which you are. I could hack that oreo talk if it was real, but the first time I picked you up for doing the five-finger discount over at the SA station, you talked like every other kid in your neighborhood."

"Man, you don't know jack-shit about my neighborhood, so what you talkin'!"

"The hell I don't. How many times a month do you think I have to bust asses over there?"

"I'm twelve years old. You not supposed to talk to me like dat."

"Tell you what—I'll make you a deal. I'll talk to you nicer if you'll talk to me nicer. And the first thing you do is stop using that F word. And the second thing you do is start pronouncing words the way your first-grade teacher taught you to. The word is *that,* not *dat.*"

Judd let his mouth get punk-disgusted, rolled his face toward the window and made some breathy sound like "Sheece . . ."

"I know you're doing it to get even with your dad."

"He's not my dad."

"Maybe not, but he pays the rent."

"And buys the cheese and snow."

Cheese and snow meant marijuana and cocaine.

"Is that what went on this weekend?"

Judd grew animated again, his bony knees jutting, his head leading the way as he retorted, "You gonna diss on me the rest of this ride, then you can just let me off!"

"Is that what went on this weekend?" Chris demanded.

Judd crumpled into his corner and looked out the window. "So what you gonna do? Put me in foster care again?" he said disparagingly.

"That what you want?"

Judd's answer was only rebellious silence. There were some who'd been in and out of foster homes so many times they grew cynical about it. Caught in the middle, these poor kids longed for nothing as much as security. It was not to be found, however, in being bounced into a foster home for two or three days while social services came out to their home to do a pep talk and offer a job to the parents, who'd rather live on welfare and get a free ride. The result was always the same. The parents would pledge to reform, straighten up for a day or two, then be back on drugs and alcohol before the week was out.

"All right, I'll tell you," Judd conceded. "They had a party Saturday night. Bunch of their friends come over. They got high and started doing a bone dance in the living room—"

"Bone dance?"

"Yeah. You know." Judd fixed Chris with a look that blended indifference and challenge. "That *word* you won't let me say. Then somebody tried to change partners and this fight breaks out. The old man hits the old lady and one of her teeth goes flyin', and she starts hittin' him back."

"Anybody hit you?"

"No."

"You sure?"

Judd refused to answer.

"What did you do?"

"I went out the window. Went to the Seven 'Leven and called you like you said. But you weren't home. Where the hell were you, man?"

"I was burying my best friend."

If Judd had been any other twelve-year-old his head would have snapped around. But Judd was Judd, and he had little energy to spare on other people's problems. Surviving took all the energy he had. He merely turned his head Chris's way and asked, "Who?"

"Greg. He died in a motorcycle accident on Friday."

Judd contemplated the news. His face remained impassive but there were things going on behind his unblinking eyes. After some time he withdrew even his glance, turning back to the view out the windshield.

"Man, that sucks."

Chris said nothing.

They rode awhile before Judd said, "So you bummed out or what?"

"Yeah. I miss him. It's bad in our apartment without him there."

They rode some more while Chris sensed Judd pondering the idea of the death of a friend, changing subtly, losing some of his defiance. He had no frame of reference, however, for dealing with grief or doling out compassion, so he only repeated, "Man, that sucks."

In a while Chris asked, "You hungry?"

Judd shrugged and looked the other way. Chris pulled through a drive-in window and got a double order of chicken McNuggets, a side salad, four packets of sweet-and-sour sauce and two small cartons of milk. They went to the Round Lake boat landing and sat on a picnic table, watching sunset stain the water.

"Sorry I wasn't there Saturday night," Chris said.

"That's bad, about your friend."

"I've got to get over it though. Nobody said life was fair."

"Nobody I ever knew."

"Still, we've got to keep on keepin' on, you know what I mean?"

Judd ate another nugget and nodded.

"Eat the salad, too. It's good for you. And drink all that milk."

Judd tipped his head and swallowed three times, then swiped his mouth with the back of a hand. "This friend—he got people who treat him good, or he like you and me?"

"He's got a good family. The best."

Judd's head bobbed as he studied his badly worn high-top sneakers planted a foot apart on the picnic bench.

"Want to know something?" Chris said. He let a few beats of silence pass, leaning forward on his knees like a basketball player on the bench. "When I was your age I used to be jealous of the kids who had decent parents. I used to treat them like worms, not talk to them—you know? Problem was, the only one it hurt was me because I didn't have any friends. Life is a bitch without friends. Then I grew up and realized that it was nobody's fault my parents were alcoholics. I could go on carrying a chip on my shoulder or I could shrug it off. I shrugged it off and found out that there are some fine people out there in the world. I decided I was going to be a fine person, too, and not do like my old man and old lady did. And that's why I became a cop."

They sat in the twilight thinking about it while Judd finished his food. In time they walked back to the truck with Chris's hand curled around Judd's skinny neck. Just before they reached the Explorer, Judd said, "This some bitchin' ride, man. Gonna have me one like it someday."

The following day Christopher returned to work. He was scheduled on the dogwatch, 11 P.M. till 7 A.M., and reported with a full half hour to spare, as required. In the locker room the radio speaker crackled from the wall while metal doors clanged and officers exchanged small talk. Nokes came over and hung a hand on Chris's shoulder.

"How you doin', Chris?"

"The locker room seems strange without him."

"Yup, it sure does." Nokes squeezed his neck and shuffled to his own locker to get dressed.

With twenty-nine sworn officers on the Anoka force, Chris wasn't always scheduled on the same shift as Greg, but often enough the two of them had stood back to back in the aisle between the lockers, exchanging small talk and wisecracks that were missed tonight.

Chris got into his bullet-proof vest and shirt, then knotted his tie before the tiny mirror on his locker door where most people kept family pictures. His held only one snapshot of himself and Greg by a black-and-white squad car. He loaded his belt with the paraphernalia of his profession: silent key holder, radio in a leather holder, stream light, Cap-stun, rubber gloves, handcuffs in their leather holder, a 9mm Beretta in its holster and two extra magazines. When he was completely dressed, twenty-six pounds of gear hung on his body, and tonight he felt every one of them.

Fifteen minutes before the shift change, he reported to the patrol room for roll call and sat down with the four others who were coming on duty to watch the updates on LETTN—the Law Enforcement Training Television Network. Today, however, the large-screen TV got sporadic attention. Instead the men, their voices subdued, exchanged remarks about the funeral and Greg's absence, asked Chris questions about the Reston family and whether or not he was going to get a new roommate. Somebody passed him the roll-call book and he took his turn acquainting himself with information on missing persons, stolen vehicles and arrest warrants faxed to the department from the jail since he'd been gone. When roll call ended, Chris wandered into the communications room, greeted the dispatcher and checked the past four days' shift reports, which listed every call answered by the department. Though only twenty miles from Minneapolis, the city of Anoka, population 17,000, had far less crime than the big city, and needed a much smaller police force to fight it.

On Saturday night the department had responded to a total of twenty-three calls; Sunday night only seventeen. Same things as usual: suspicious person, disturbing the peace, simple assault, disorderly conduct. After scanning the clipboard, Chris hung it back on the wall, realizing that apart from the fact that memories of Greg lingered throughout the familiar rooms of the police station, it felt good to be back, occupied once more.

He collected his hat from the patrol room table and said, "I'm outta here, guys."

"Me too," Nokes said, and together they headed out to their squad cars.

He spent the night as he'd spent hundreds of others, guarding the sleeping city. Sometimes he prowled. Sometimes he sat, listening to channel one crackle ceaselessly with the voice of the county dispatcher. He and Nokes both responded to a domestic and found the apartment door open, the TV on and nobody home. He got bad-mouthed by two other apartment tenants when he knocked on their doors to ask questions. Back in his squad car, he cruised until a call from the dispatcher sent him to check out an alert from a motion alarm, which he discovered had been tripped by a falling ceiling panel. He sat in the parking lot of Carpenter's Hall beside a shadowy pine tree and watched cars come over the Mississippi River bridge from Champlin, tracking speeds on his radar. He watched the two red lights on his radar screen and listened to the sound of the signal change as the cars swept abreast and passed him.

He thought about how close he was to Benton Street. Nine blocks away Lee Reston probably lay in bed—asleep or awake? Resting after the past four exhausting days or wide-eyed, in the company of sad memories? He started his engine and rolled out of the Carpenter's Hall parking lot, onto Ferry Street, then left on Benton. A dark, sleeping neighborhood with nothing more than a pair of cat's eyes gleaming at him from beneath a clump of shrubs before it shot across the street. He slowed to a crawl as he approached her house. The lights were off, the garage door was down. Janice's old car was parked in the driveway. Greg's Toyota was nowhere in sight, probably in the garage.

Are you sleeping? he thought. *Or are you lying awake wishing you were? Are you wondering whose headlights are sliding down Benton Street so slowly at this hour of the morning? Well, don't worry. It's just me, keeping watch. Did you work today at your shop or stay home and write thank-you cards? I see you closed your garage door. That's better. Now you keep it closed every night, okay? How are the kids doing? I suppose they're a help to you, reasons for you to make it through another day. I could use a little of that. It was sad in the locker room tonight, Greg's locker closed and locked and no Greg clanging the door open and lipping off. I suppose we'll all get used to it, but it'll take time, won't it?*

At 3 A.M. he ate a full meal at Perkins Restaurant.

At five, when the sky had begun going pinkish in the east, he checked her street again.

At six he cruised it one more time and discovered an oscillating sprinkler fanning back and forth over her front lawn: She was up. Was she having coffee in the kitchen the way the two of them had a couple days ago? It took an effort to roll past without stopping to ask for a cup.

At seven he left his bullet-proof vest in his locker and went home to bed.

The phone rang at 1:30 that afternoon and woke him up.

"Hello, Chris, this is Lee."

"Lee . . ." He twisted around to peer, one-eyed, at the digital clock. "Hi." His voice sounded like somebody scraping paint.

"Oh, no . . . did I wake you?"

"That's okay. No problem."

"I'm sorry. I should have called the station for your schedule before I dialed. Did you work last night?"

"Yeah, dogwatch, but that's okay." He settled on his back and wedged a pillow beneath his head, squinting at the bars of sunlight just beginning to peek through the blinds.

"I really am sorry."

"I usually get up around two anyway. Don't give it another thought." He dredged some sandmen out of his eyes, thinking she could call and wake him every day and he wouldn't mind. "There's stuff I want to do this afternoon anyway. I've got a little rattle in one of the doors on my Explorer and I want to take it in and see if they can get it out of there."

"Everybody got a ride in your Explorer but me. How do you like it?"

"Love it. I'll take you for a ride sometime and you can see for yourself. Joey really liked it, too."

"So I understand. You let him drive."

"I hope you don't mind."

"No, of course not. If it were one of his friends I'd be madder than heck, but with you—one of our men in blue—how can I object?"

"We talked a little . . . about Greg. Got some feelings out in the open."

"He needed that very badly, to talk to a man."

"How's Janice doing?"

"She's very blue and sleeps a lot. I think she'll have more trouble than Joey will, getting over this."

"And you—I won't make the mistake of asking how you're doing. *What* are you doing?"

"Trying to face the idea of going back to work again. It's hard when your thoughts are so scattered. I can't seem to concentrate on anything. But I'll have to go back soon and relieve Sylvia. She's been pulling double duty. Today I'm facing a stack of post-funeral business items that seems endless. That's what I'm calling about. Greg's things."

"I told you there's no rush. You don't have to get them out of here until you're good and ready."

"I know, but it's hanging over me like a storm cloud. I want to get it done with and put it behind me. I thought, if it's okay with you, I'd come over on Sunday. My shop is closed that day and Janice and Joey should both be around to help me."

"I'll still be working the night shift so I'll be here all day. You can come anytime you want."

"You said you usually get up around two?"

"Give me till noon."

"Five hours of sleep? Christopher, that's not enough."

"All right, how about one o'clock?"

"Two is better. I don't want to mess up your sleeping schedule. You cops get little enough of it as it is."

"All right, two. What are you going to use to haul the furniture in?"

"Jim Clements next door said I could use his pickup."

"You okay driving it or do you want me to come over and drive?"

"Jim offered, too, but I'll be just fine. See you Sunday at two."

"Fine."

"And, Christopher?"

"Hm?"

"Please go back to sleep. I feel so bad I woke you."

* * *

She planned to ask the kids at supper that night if they'd help her. Before she could do so, Joey announced that Denny Whitman had asked him to drive up to the lake that day with his family.

"Oh," she said, halting in the midst of setting a bowl of scalloped potatoes on the table. "I sort of made plans for the three of us to go over to Greg's apartment and pack up his things that day. I was counting on both of you to help me." She sat down at her place and Joey began filling his plate.

"On Sunday?" he complained. "Couldn't we do it on Saturday so I could still go up to the lake with the Whitmans? They're only going for that one day."

Lee hid her disappointment and reminded herself he was only fourteen. At that age kids had a lot to learn about their parents' needs, especially in a situation like this. The Whitmans had undoubtedly invited him with the best of intentions, realizing that he needed diversions now more than ever.

"Janice?" she said, glancing at her daughter.

Janice put down her fork and shifted her gaze out the kitchen window while her eyes filled with tears. On her plate, her favorite food in the world was scarcely touched. "Mom . . . I . . . I'm just not ready for that yet. Can't we put it off for a while?"

Lee set her fork down, too.

Janice added, "And anyway, I'm supposed to work on Sunday." She clerked at The Gap store at Northtown Shopping Center. "I'm afraid if I don't go back pretty soon I might lose my job, and I need the money for college. Can't we put it off for a while?"

Lee took Janice's hand and held it on the tabletop. "Of course we can," she said quietly. "Christopher says there's no rush at all."

Janice blinked and her tears fell. She withdrew her hand from Lee's, swiped beneath both eyes, retrieved her fork and filled it with chunks of potato and ham, then stared at it for some time before the fork handle clinked against her plate. "Mom, I'm just not hungry tonight." She lifted her brimming eyes to Lee. "The scalloped potatoes are great—honest. But I think I'll just . . . I don't know . . . go to my room for a while."

"Go ahead. The potatoes will keep till another day."

When Janice was gone Lee and Joey fought the feeling of abandonment, but it won. Joey had eaten only half of his dinner when he, too, said, "Mom, I'm not very hungry either. Could I be excused?"

"Sure," she said. "What are you going to do?"

"I don't know. Maybe go over to the ballpark, watch a couple games."

"All right. Go on," she said understandingly.

He rose and stood by his chair uncertainly. "Want me to help you with the dishes?"

"I can do them. Give me a kiss." He pecked her on the cheek while she patted his waist. "Have a good time and be back by ten."

"I will."

He left the house and she sat at the table, listening to him raise the kickstand of his ten-speed bicycle, then whir away on it until its clickety-sigh disappeared down the driveway. She sat on, lonely beyond words, willing herself to get up and put away the leftovers, rinse the plates, load the dishwasher. These were healthy pursuits that would help lift her spirits. But she was so tired at that moment of falsely trying to lift those spirits. Instead she remained at the table, her chin braced on a palm, staring out the window at the backyard. She could go pull a few weeds in the garden, stake up the delphiniums, which were blooming heavily, pick a bouquet for the kitchen table. She could call her mom or Sylvia, ask Janice if she'd like to go to a movie, go outside and wash the car, get into it and return the various cake pans and Pyrex dishes that people had left here and never come back to collect. She could scribble a few thank-you cards.

She sighed, weary of being the strong one for everyone else's benefit, wishing someone else would take over the duty for just this one evening. She sat on at the table, overcome by a lassitude so enormous it seemed insurmountable.

She turned her head and stared down the front hall at the sunshine bouncing off the white siding and lighting the front entry. Such a sad time of day, suppertime, when you were sitting at a table alone. Jim Clements's truck rolled past; he was a construction worker and just getting home from work. Two young girls in bathing suits rode past on their bicycles. Their ten-year-old chatter filled Lee with sadness. Everybody busy, heading for someplace, to do something with someone.

She was still sitting there morosely when a black-and-white squad car rolled past her line of vision and pulled into her driveway. She was up and out the front door before she realized she felt rescued.

She got outside in time to see Christopher, in full uniform, getting out of the car. His unexpected appearance filled her with sudden happiness.

He slammed the door but left the engine running, and came around the front of the car. She moved toward him eagerly, energized by some new reaction she had not expected. She had always rather clumped him with Greg's friends and thought of him as a boy. But the police officer approaching her was no boy. His navy blue uniform granted him a stature, a respectability, a maturity that caught her unaware. His visored hat was anchored low over his eyes. His uniform shirt, pressed to perfection, was tucked in smoothly, holding chevrons, pins and badges of all sorts. His tie was neatly knotted beneath his tanned chin. The heavy black leather holders on his belt lent him additional authority while his bullet-proof vest added girth to his overall shape.

They met at the front of the car, beside the hot, running engine.

"Hi," he said, removing his sunglasses and smiling.

"Hi." She stuck both hands into the front pockets of her white shorts. "I didn't expect to see you today."

"Some mail came for Greg." He handed it to her.

"Thanks." She glanced down and leafed through four envelopes. "I guess I'd better go to the post office and fill out a change-of-address form. I'll have to add it to the list. I'd forgotten how much paperwork has to be done when someone dies." She looked up again. "I thought you were working the eleven-to-seven shift."

"I'm supposed to be, but one of the guys asked me to exchange shifts with him today." The radio on his belt began crackling out a dispatch, and he reached down without looking to adjust its volume. Greg used to do the same thing. She could never figure out how they could decipher the stuttering radio and carry on a conversation at the same time. "I just passed Joey back there. Said he was heading over to the ballpark."

"Summer leagues," she replied. "Much better than hanging around the dreary house."

"How about you? You just hanging around the dreary house?"

"I'm going back to work pretty soon. I figure I've let Sylvia carry the load long enough. Christopher, about Sunday though . . ."

He waited, standing with his feet planted firmly in thick-soled black regulation shoes.

"The kids can't help me that day. Joey wants to go up to the lake with Denny, and Janice just needs some time yet before she can face the job. So we'll have to do it some other time."

"I'll help you," he said.

"But you've helped so much already."

"I was planning to help anyway. If you want to go ahead, the two of us can probably handle it all ourselves. If you want to wait for the kids to be there with you—well, that's fine too."

"It's not an easy job," she told him. "I've done it before, after Bill died, and it can be devastating."

"Then we could spare the kids, couldn't we?" After a beat he added, watching her very closely, "But I imagine sometimes you get a little tired of sparing the kids and wish they'd spare you."

How intuitive, she thought. For a man so young, he could read her with amazing accuracy. Sometimes when she had such thoughts she felt guilty, but hearing him put voice to them filled her with a sense of relief and excused her of the guilt.

"How did you know?" she asked.

On his radio a voice came through, sputtering like arcing electrical current. "Three Bravo Eighteen."

"Just a minute," he told Lee, plucking the radio from his belt and nearly touching it to his lips. She had never before noticed what beautifully sculpted lips he had. "Three Bravo Eighteen."

The crackly voice said, "Eight two zero west Main Street. Apartment number G-thirty-seven. Report of loud voices. Possible domestic in progress. No one to be seen."

"Copy," he said, then to Lee, "Sorry, I've got to go." He slipped his sunglasses back on. "Let me know about Sunday. In my opinion you should wait for your kids, but if you decide to go ahead we can get it done in three hours. Then you can stop dreading it."

She nodded and found herself following him to the door of the squad car, waiting while he got in and scribbled the address on a legal pad beside him on the front seat. He reached for the dash radio to report his car number and the time. "Three Bravo Eighteen en route. Eighteen-oh-nine." He replaced the radio on the dash, put the car into reverse and said out the open window, "You look tired. Get some sleep." A simple farewell, but with a familiarity that unexpectedly stirred a reaction deep within her. It was the kind of blandishment a husband might toss out, the kind that implied caring that went much deeper than the words.

She crossed her arms and watched him leave. She'd seen Greg do it dozens of times, slinging an arm along the top of the seat and craning around to look through the rear window as he pelted backward at ten miles an hour. The car bounced off the concrete apron at the end of the driveway, and he lifted a hand in farewell as he roared away down the street.

Long after he had disappeared she stood in the driveway looking after him.

She returned to work later that week to the blessed balm of routine. Opening the store at 8 A.M., brewing coffee, watering all the arrangements in the cooler and checking their care cards to see what day each was made—the familiar motions brought ease, though often she found herself staring into space. Sylvia asked often, "How are you doing, sis?" Their hired arrangers, Pat Galsworthy and Nancy McFaddon, also showed concern, but Lee found herself answering by rote, rather than expressing what she really felt: that she was absolutely dreading Sunday, when she had to face Greg's possessions.

By Sunday she had put a full nine days between herself and Greg's death, but it helped little in light of the duty that lay ahead. She awakened early, with four hours to spare before church. At six-thirty she was out in the backyard, kneeling on a green rubber pad, pulling quack grass from between the daylilies and wishing it were tomorrow morning and today was behind her.

By two o'clock the temperature had risen to eighty-five degrees and had five more to go. She put on some faded green shorts and a misshapen cotton shirt, forcing herself to move, step by step, get the truck from next door, drive it across town and face the place where her son had lived. She left the truck in the hot parking lot and struggled up to his apartment with a bunch of nested cardboard boxes bumping against her bare leg. Christopher answered the door wearing cutoff blue jeans and a white T-shirt. Gloria Estefan was singing quietly on the radio. No country music today to remind her of Greg.

"Hi," Christopher said, taking the boxes from her, sobered as she was by what they had to do today.

"Hi," she answered, remaining on the threshold.

"Hell of a thing to have to do on a beautiful day like this, isn't it?"

He saw her battling self-pity, but it won and her face began to crumple. The boxes hit the floor and suddenly she was in his arms, being held hard against his sturdy chest. After a moment he said, "I think you should have waited for your kids."

"No, I'll be all right. I promise I will." She withdrew and took a deep breath.

"You sure?"

She nodded hard, as if convincing herself.

He'd known this moment would be difficult for her and had done all he could to make it easier. "I've got his bed all taken apart and I've sorted through our CDs and got all of his put into one box."

She sniffed once, ran a hand beneath her nose and said, "Good. Let's get to work then."

They went directly into Greg's bedroom, where his mattress and box spring were leaning against the wall.

"I washed his bedding and put it in that bag." He pointed. "And the stuff wrapped in newspaper is everything that was on his wall and on top of his chest of drawers—pictures, certificates from the department. His shoot badge and merit badges and all that stuff are in here." He squatted and touched a shoe box. "I took care of returning his gun to the department, and his cuffs and radio and whatever had to be turned in." He lifted his gaze to her before rising slowly to his full height, his palms to his thighs like an uncertain suitor. "I hope I did the right thing. I thought it would make it easier on you."

She touched his bare arm in gratitude. "It does."

They went to work, she turning to Greg's closet, he carrying the bed frame out into the beating heat and loading it on the pickup.

When the contents of the closet were boxed, they carried them out together, followed by the heavy chest with its drawers still full, the mattress and box spring, lugging them down two flights of stairs and onto the bed of the pickup. By the time they finished they were sweating profusely and wiping their foreheads.

Back inside, the air-conditioned halls felt heavenly. In the apartment the venetian blinds were closed on the west windows. The radio was still playing and Lee turned on the kitchen faucet.

"How about a Sprite?" Christopher asked, opening the refrigerator door.

"Sounds good."

He found two cans, two handfuls of ice, and had the soda glugging into a pair of glasses when he turned around . . . and stopped pouring.

Lee was tilted over the sink, scooping handfuls of water onto her face and neck, stretching the collar of her knit shirt and running her hands into it. The hair on her nape was wet, stuck together into short brown arrows. Her green shorts had sneaked up in the back, revealing a rim of white underwear. She turned off the single-lever faucet and began drying her face with both palms. He snatched a hand towel and touched it to her left arm.

"Thanks," she said, grabbing it blindly, turning to him with her face covered, pat-pat-patting at her skin the way men didn't. By the time her eyes appeared above the towel he was pouring their drinks again.

"Hot out there," she said.

He handed her a glass. "This will cool you down."

She took it and drank. He did the same, keeping an eye on her over the rim of his glass. Her face was red from exertion, the hair around it standing out at angles. Her white shirt was damp to the first button.

He pulled a short black comb out of his rear pocket. "Here," he said, handing it to her.

"Oh . . . thanks." She used it without the slightest self-consciousness, and without the need for a mirror, then handed it back to him.

"You want to go through the kitchen next?" he asked.

"I suppose." She looked up at the cabinets. "What's in here?"

"An electric popcorn popper." He opened a bottom door. "He bought the toaster when the old one went kaflooey, and a set of glasses he said we needed. He brought a few dishes from home, I think—these green ones here, and that pitcher. But most of the dishes and silverware I already had when he moved in. We shared the cost of the groceries, but we had an agreement that we'd each buy our own steaks whenever we wanted them. There are a couple of his in the freezer yet. Rib eyes, I think."

He'd been opening and closing cupboard doors as he spoke. When he finally stopped, she said, "Listen, Christopher, this is silly. I'm not going to take his groceries, and these are all things you can use. The few dishes he took from home were just old junk, no family heirlooms, I can assure you. I have no need for anything."

"Not even the popcorn popper?"

"I have one."

"Or the toaster?"

"Keep it."

"How about the rib eyes?"

"You can bring them over on the Fourth of July. Everyone's bringing their own. I've changed my mind about doing the turkey. That was Greg's favorite."

"You mean you're still going to have the picnic?"

"I suppose we could pretend we died right along with him, but I'm not very good at acting like that, are you?"

"No."

"A picnic will be good for us. Play a little volleyball again, get some barbecue smoke in our eyes, go out to the park and watch the fireworks. You'll be there, won't you?"

"I wouldn't miss it."

They raised their glasses and drank again, filling a void that had inexplicably jumped between them as soon as the room grew silent.

"Well," he said, clacking his empty glass on the counter. "I'm going to go sort through the stuff in the bathroom. Why don't you take a look at the living room?"

She went into the room where the radio still played. On the sunny side of the apartment it felt warmer, in spite of the closed blinds. A box of tapes and CDs sat on the floor before the open glass doors of the entertainment unit. The potted tree she'd sent from the shop as a moving-in gift looked healthy, its branches weeping above one end of the sofa. On the wall the crisscross wooden rack held twenty-odd caps, with two pegs empty.

She stood with her thumbnails poking into her thighs, gazing up at it, daunted by it, feeling the suffocation begin, damning it when she'd thought she'd make it through today with flying colors. She steeled herself and selected a cap—a white one with a large maroon A above the bill: Anoka. From his high school days. She carried it to the bathroom doorway and stood for a moment watching Christopher drop things into a black duffel bag balanced on the small vanity top. Quietly, she said, "I'm not sure which ones are his."

Chris stopped pulling things from the drawers and turned to look at her. Her mouth was trembling and her rusty eyes looked vulnerable. She put the cap on her head, dropped one shoulder against the door frame and stuck her hands into her front shorts pockets. "This is a test," she said. "Get through the afternoon without breaking down and bawling . . . because he's never coming back."

"Yeah, I know." His voice broke a little. He was holding Greg's toothbrush and toothpaste in his hands. "This is a hell of a job, too. His hairbrush, razor, after-shave—" Angrily he threw the handful into the duffel bag and braced both hands against the vanity top like a runner stretching. "God, this room even smells like him."

It struck her how self-centered she'd been, considering only her sorrow, not his. "Oh, Christopher, I'm sorry." She moved into the small room, pulling the cap from her head, holding it in one hand while laying the other on his back. "You miss him, too," she whispered. Abruptly he straightened, spun and embraced her. In that white-tiled room with its nostalgic scents of male cosmetics, they closed their eyes while the mirror reflected the two of them locked together, drawing strength from one another, she with Greg's cap still in one hand.

"No, I'm the one who's sorry," he whispered. "I shouldn't have said that. It's hard enough for you without remarks like that."

"But it's hard for you, too, and if we can't be honest with each other about our feelings . . ." She didn't know how to finish.

"God, what a pair we make, huh? Stumbling along and hugging each other every five minutes like this is the end of the world."

"I did so well all week, I thought I could make it through today without this happening. But the caps in the living room . . . somehow I just couldn't handle them."

She opened her eyes and saw herself in the mirror, in Christopher's arms. His head was bent over her far shoulder, his hands clasped on her spine. Their stomachs and bare legs touched and though she realized most hugs of commiseration would remain more guarded, she stayed where she was.

He broke the contact first, drawing back and ordering, "Here, give me the cap." He squeezed the bill into a nice curve, put it on her head and turned her to the mirror, standing behind her with his hands on her shoulders. "There. Look at that. It's a mother in a bill cap and there's not a damn thing wrong with it, okay? Matter of fact, you look pretty good in it. You ought to wear one more often."

He grinned, coaxing a responsive smile from her. She raised both hands and tipped the cap back a little, then grabbed a big, deep, restorative breath and blew it out fast. "All right, I can get through it now. How about you?"

"Me too. Let's get it done and get the truck over to your house. One thing though." He dropped his hands from her shoulders and his mood changed.

"What?" She turned to look up at him.

"There's this kid I know. He's sort of teetering on the brink—not much hope at home, no family life to speak of, both parents druggies trading in their food stamps for money so they can buy their next fix. If you don't mind, I'd like to give him one of Greg's caps. This kid respects cops. He'd like to think he doesn't but he does. A cap could make a difference."

"Sure. Give him any one you want. Give him two."

They got the caps sorted and the bathroom items divided and sifted through some of Greg's papers that were stored in a kitchen drawer. About the living room furniture, Christopher said, "I had some, and we bought some together, but I'd like to keep it all. I have receipts and I'll pay you a fair price for his half of its value. That is, if it's okay with your kids. If they want anything, it's theirs."

"For now, let's leave it here."

"You should take the fig tree though," Christopher said.

"Oh, come on, I can get a dozen more like it wholesale any day I want to. It belongs in that corner."

"All right," he said, "I accept. If you had taken it I'd just go to your store and buy one exactly like it anyway. Thank you."

They shut off the radio, carried the last load out and worked together lashing down the mattress and box spring so they wouldn't blow off. Christopher had put on his sunglasses. Lee's eyes were shaded by the visor of Greg's cap. Heat waves zigzagged off the blacktop.

Christopher tied the last knot and asked, "You okay driving this truck with all that stuff on it?"

"I'm okay."

"All right. I'll be behind you."

He followed her to her house and they unloaded everything into her garage. Janice would be moving back to the U of M campus when school resumed in the fall, and she'd use Greg's bed and leave her own room intact for weekend visits.

By the time they finished and returned the truck to Jim Clements, they were hot and sweaty.

Christopher asked, "Do you know how to swim?"

"Sure."

They were standing in the shade of the garage roof with the overhead door wide open.

"You want to go? Cool off a little bit? We could drive over to the public beach on Crooked Lake."

"Gosh, that sounds good."

She went in, put on a suit and oversized shirt and came back out wearing thongs and carrying two towels.

"Let's go."

He drove.

She clambered into his Explorer and said, "Wow, I like this."

"So do I."

"Did you get the rattle fixed?"

"Yup."

They talked all the way to the lake. About cars. And her business. And how she'd chosen the name Absolutely Floral because it would appear first in the yellow pages, and how Sylvia said Lee was crazy to want a name like that, but her psychology had worked—most of their first-time business came from the yellow pages.

At the lake the beach was crowded. They stripped off their shirts, ran in among children playing in the shallow water and swam out to a diving board. They dove some, swam some, hung on the side of the float and talked some. About surfing, which he'd been watching on TV, and Hawaii, where neither of them had ever been but always wanted to go. They recounted where they'd each learned to swim when they were kids, who they'd swum with. A volleyball plopped into the water ten feet from Chris. He pushed off the raft to return it and they found themselves involved in a game of waterball with a bunch of fun-loving strangers.

They laughed.

And tired.

And worked up a roaring appetite.

When he pulled the Explorer into her driveway she said, "I have some leftover spaghetti I could nuke."

He said, "You're on," and shut off the engine.

She scooped out two servings and warmed them while he fixed ice water and got forks from the drawer she pointed at. Unceremoniously she handed him a plate and a napkin, remarking as she sat down, "Don't tell my mother how I served this."

"What's wrong with this?"

"No place mats, no table setting, letting you get your own water and fork, me in this disgusting shirt and thongs throwing you your plate. My mother would have a shit fit. She's stuck on propriety. One doesn't do the unexpected or the unconventional. Her favorite phrase is 'What would people say?' "

"Shit fit?" He was wearing a smile. His face was shiny from the water and his hair had fallen neatly into place without apparent help from him. "You actually said 'shit fit'?"

She stopped winding spaghetti to meet his amused eyes. "What? I can't say that?"

"It doesn't bother me, it's just that I never heard you say anything like that before. I always thought of you as Mrs. Perfect. Perfect mother, perfect lady, perfect . . . you know what I mean."

"Me?" Her eyes grew big and her mouth dropped open. "I'm far from perfect. What in the world makes you say a thing like that?"

"The way Greg talked about you. In his eyes you could do no wrong."

"I cuss now and then. Does it bother you?"

"No, it makes you human, makes me more comfortable around you. Now what were you saying about your mother?"

"Oh, just that she lives according to Emily Post. Tables set properly, joining the right clubs, dressing properly for dinner, sending thank-you cards, playing Grieg at funerals, not Vince Gill."

"I overheard her remark about that."

"I'm sure. What did she say?"

His eyes grew mischievous. "If I remember right, she said, 'What will people say?' "

Lee grinned and they dug into their spaghetti.

"So what about your mother?" she asked. "What's she like?"

He stopped chewing, stopped winding spaghetti and took a drink of water before answering, "Nothing like yours, believe me."

"You won't tell me?"

He pondered awhile, his eyes leveled on her, before deciding to confide. "She's an alcoholic. So is my father."

"Were they always?"

"Always. She worked as a fry cook on the early morning shift at a truck stop; he didn't work at all that I remember. Claimed he'd hurt his back somehow and couldn't. Most days, by the time I got home from school they'd be down at this place I always called The Hole, pickling their gizzards. Not only didn't she set tables properly, she never set them at all. Any cooking that was done was pretty much left up to me. And I'll guarantee you she never sent a thank-you note in her life—I don't know what the hell she'd have to thank anybody for. She didn't have any friends except the drunks who hung out at that bar. So don't be too hard on your mother. You could have done a lot worse." He said it amiably and she accepted it.

"What about sisters and brothers?"

"One sister."

"Older or younger?"

"Four years younger."

"Where is she now?"

"Jeannie is somewhere on the west coast. She moves around."

"Do you ever see her?"

"Not very often. She ran away when she was fifteen and has been married and divorced three times since then. Last time I saw her she weighed about two hundred fifty pounds and lived off the welfare system, just like our folks did. Jeannie and I don't have a lot in common."

"And your parents? Where are they?"

"They live over on the other side of town in a squalid apartment complex called Jackson Estates. They haven't changed much except that they do their boozing at home now because it's hard for them to get up and down the stairs."

"I've upset you, asking about them."

"No, not really. I gave up expecting them to change a long time ago."

"They must be very proud of you."

"You don't understand. They're not the kind of parents who get proud. To do that you have to get sober first. They haven't been sober in thirty-five years."

"I'm sorry, Christopher," she said quietly.

They finished eating their spaghetti and meatballs. They had progressed through a day running a range of emotions, from low to high, now low again. What they had shared left them undeniably closer, so close, in fact, that he grew uncomfortable as they sat in her cozy kitchen, relaxed in their chairs and exchanging gazes that lasted longer and longer.

He got up and refilled his water glass.

"You want some more?" he asked.

She nodded. That's how it was getting to be between them, comfortable one moment, uncomfortable the next. A man filling a woman's water glass because she was getting to look a little too good to him, and Emily Post and her mother would undoubtedly have a few choice remarks about that.

He drank his water standing up, then reached for their dirty plates. "Well, let's clean this up so I can get out of your hair."

"I'll clean it up."

"No way. I'll help."

They were both clearing the table when Janice came home from work. She walked into the kitchen and dropped her car keys on the table.

"Christopher, hi! What are you doing here?"

"Your mom fed me supper."

A beat of awareness caught and held Janice, pulling the smile from her face. "You helped her move Greg's things, didn't you?"

"Yes."

"I saw them in the garage." She turned to Lee. "Mom, I'm sorry I didn't help."

"It's okay, sweetie." She gave Janice a kiss on the cheek. "It's all done now."

"No, it's not okay. I should have been there. I'm really sorry."

"Christopher helped, so don't say another word about it."

Lee went on swishing a plate under the hot water while Janice studied her, then Chris, then Lee again.

"You sure?"

"I'm sure. You hungry?"

The question convinced Janice her transgression was minor. "Mmm . . . sorta." She nosed along the cabinet to the bowl of cold spaghetti sauce, still in its Tupperware storage dish. With two long rose-colored fingernails she plucked out a meatball. "Boy, it's sweltering out there." She turned, taking a bite, resting her spine against the cabinet edge. "I was thinking about going somewhere for a swim. You interested in going along, Chris?"

He was dressed in his T-shirt again and his cutoffs were nearly dry.

"Actually, your mom and I already did that."

Janice swallowed the last of her meatball with a slight gulp. "You did?" She glanced inquisitively between the two of them.

After an awkward beat of silence Lee offhandedly opened the dishwasher door and said, "It was hot dragging that furniture around. We just cooled off and then grabbed some supper. Do you want me to warm some for you?"

"Mom," Janice said with an air of gentle chiding, "I'm twenty-three years old. You don't have to warm up my supper anymore."

Lee smiled at her daughter, drying her hands on a towel. "Force of habit."

Christopher pushed his chair under the table and said, "Well, I'd better go. I have to work tonight. Thanks for the supper, Mrs. Reston."

"It was the least I could do. Thank you for everything you did today."

He moved toward the door and Janice said, "I'll walk you out." Lee felt a peculiar spurt of resentment at Janice for blithely usurping her place with Christopher. The feeling struck suddenly, then retreated under duress as she told herself her place was not with him. Still, they'd been together all day, working on a decidedly difficult task, and she felt abandoned, watching the two of them walk outside. They looked so young and perfect together.

By his truck door Janice paused, preventing him from getting in. She was dressed in a simple pullover pink blouse and a short jeans skirt. Her tan, bare legs ended in unadorned white flats. She stood on the sides of her heels with her toes curled up off the blacktop, her head tipped to one side. "Thank you for helping her, Chris. I was really a rat not to do it, but I was bummed."

He looked her straight in the eyes, holding his key ring over his index finger. "Sometimes we've got to do things whether we're bummed or not. I didn't mind doing it, but you're right. You and Joey should have helped her today. She needed you."

Janice stared at the chrome edging around his windshield, her mouth contracting.

"Hey, don't cry," he said, touching her chin.

She struggled not to but there was evidence of tears.

"Just be there for her a little more, okay? This is a rough time for her. She carries the brunt of it, taking care of all the details—funeral, cars, paperwork. You know that she wouldn't criticize you in a million years, but she's got feelings too, yet she always puts your feelings first."

"I know," Janice whispered.

They stood awhile in the slanting sun. "You mad at me for saying what I think?"

She shook her head, still staring at the chrome molding.

"You got any objections to me coming around now and then to take her mind off things?"

She shook her head again.

"Okay then . . . see you on the Fourth of July?"

She nodded at the molding.

She was still standing in the driveway holding onto one elbow with the opposite hand when he waved farewell and drove away.

Chapter 6

SERIOUS crime was the exception rather than the rule in the city of Anoka. There were relatively few times when its police officers felt their lives threatened. Now and then a robber was apprehended, or the SWAT team was called out on a drug bust, but for the most part, Christopher Lallek and his fellow officers took their duties in stride.

At 6:20 A.M. on a hazy, hot morning in the first week of July, Christopher was sitting in his squad car yawning. He checked his watch—forty minutes to go—and shifted his stiff rump on the car seat. Glancing up at the movement of vehicles rolling by on Highway 10, he noticed a '78 Grand Prix weaving in and out of traffic.

Immediately he came alert, switched on his reds and pulled out into the westbound lane. He could tell the moment the driver saw the flashing reds because he increased speed and made a reckless lane switch. The inbound lane held more traffic than this one, but the westbound flow was heavy enough to put starch into Christopher's spine and tighten his grip on the wheel.

He caught up with the Grand Prix and followed close on his tail, watching for the driver to look into his rearview mirror.

The driver ignored him.

He gave the siren a short hit and got ignored some more.

He turned on the siren full blast and felt his ire mount as the driver continued pretending the black-and-white wasn't there. He picked up the radio, reported his position and the Grand Prix's plate number and, finally, after a good half mile saw the smart-aleck respond, pulling to a stop on the right shoulder.

Sizzling with temper, Christopher got out of his squad and approached the rusted red vehicle.

The driver had his window down and was slumped slightly toward the wheel. He was perhaps twenty-eight or thirty years old, needed a shave and a haircut, and looked as if he'd been on an all-night bender.

Chris glanced into the car, looking for open bottles, and asked, "Could I see your license, please?"

"Whaffor?" His breath could have cured leather.

"Just show it to me, please."

"If you wanna see my license, tell me what I done wrong."

"Do you have a license?"

The guy shrugged and turned a baggy-eyed expression of disdain Chris's way.

"The license, sir."

" 'S been revoked," the guy mumbled.

Christopher put a hand on his shoulder and said, "Get out of the car, please."

The driver sneered, "Screw you, prick," and tromped on the gas. The edge of the back window glass struck Christopher's arm and carried him six feet down the highway. Even as the pain shot through him he was spun free and found himself running to his squad.

Door slamming! Heart pumping! Siren squealing! The black-and-white fishtailed and sprayed gravel and weeds twenty feet behind him. He grabbed the radio and forced his voice to remain calm. "Two Bravo Thirty-seven. He took off on me, westbound on ten! I'm in pursuit!"

The dispatcher acknowledged and verified the time. "Two B Thirty-seven. Copy WB on ten: oh-six-two-five."

The speed of his pulse seemed to increase with the speed of the car.

Fifty, sixty, seventy miles an hour. He focused his senses and suppressed all natural alarm.

On the radio, a voice: "Three union thirty-one, I'm eastbound on ten, approaching Ramsey Boulevard. Will intercept there." That was a Ramsey car, coming to assist.

Eighty miles an hour, ninety, adrenaline pumping. Up ahead the Ramsey squad, its cherry light flashing, pulled into the left lane. The Grand Prix roared past it with colossal disdain. Christopher pinned his eyes on the road while the Ramsey squad—off his fender at ten o'clock—rocketed down the highway with him. Sweat popped out on his forehead, trailed down his trunk, sealed his body armor against his skin. His palms turned slick. It was work to control the force on the wheel.

He spoke at intervals into the radio, reporting his progress.

"Crossing westbound ten and Armstrong . . . Westbound ten, passing the weigh scale . . ." Familiar landmarks turned into a blur behind him.

A new radio voice said, "Elk River thirty-six thirteen, in position at Highway 169 turnoff westbound on ten, along with SP Unit 403."

Jesus. That made four units. Five counting the suspect . . . at a hundred and ten miles an hour. He shut down his mind to a single track and drove while the damned idiot in the Grand Prix threatened the lives of all the motorists on the highway pretending he was Mario Andretti. For nine miles Christopher drove, anticipating the sharp left curve at the base of the power plant in Elk River. The river itself was on their left. Ahead lay the underpass with its deadly concrete pilings where 169 crossed above 10.

Up ahead he saw the maroon state patrol car and the navy blue Elk River vehicle with its golden elk emblem on the door. There were more flashing reds. Cars scuttled out of the way, left and right.

He reported his position and hung up the radio to lock both hands on the wheel.

The five vehicles converged. Sirens screamed like jet blasts. Red lights flashed everywhere and speeding cop cars filled Christopher's peripheral vision. And somehow as they approached the big curve the four squads had the Grand Prix in a box!

Under the overpass! Into the curve! River water on the left! Huge green hill on the right! Roaring engines and cars inches apart, halfway into a lazy S-curve at ninety miles an hour. Chris's car got bumped. The world tipped and righted itself. On his far right the Ramsey squad lost ground in some loose gravel on the shoulder and fell behind. They hit the second curve and suddenly the suspect's car shot off to the right, into the ditch, up a rise, lost its back bumper and sideswiped a huge tree. The back bumper—a missile now—sailed straight on and wedged itself into the V of the tree's two huge trunks. Hubcaps rolled and bounced. Grass, dirt, dust flew into the air as if a bomb had exploded. The Grand Prix landed on its wheels. The four squads converged on it, bumping over rough grass. Officers out and running. Doors left gaping. Radios clattering. Red lights everywhere. Observers stopping on the shoulder above to stare at the spectacle in wonder.

Christopher ran to the driver's window, his adrenaline pumping like an uncapped gusher. The suspect was alive and cussing a blue streak, kicking the dash, hammering the steering wheel.

"Are you hurt?"

"Sonofabitch!"

Chris tried his door but it was jammed.

"Can you get out?"

"Goddamn it! Look what you did! Motherf—"

He reached in and grabbed the driver's shirt. "Get out. Do it now!"

The driver fought and slapped, refusing to follow orders. Chris and the Ramsey officer reached in and forcefully pulled him out through the window. The Elk River officer had drawn his gun and had it pointed in a two-hand grip at the suspect's head. The state trooper backed him up.

"On your face!" Chris shouted.

Down went the suspect and out came the cuffs.

"Goddamn sonsabitchin' pigs! Whorin' no-good suck-ass cops!" The driver lay facedown in the dirt, calling them every name in the book. Christopher grabbed a handful of red shirt and yanked the jerk to his feet, then propelled him toward his squad car with plenty of upward pressure on the cuffs.

"In the car, asshole!" he shouted, letting off the first steam.

Anger carried him through the rest of his duties. Locking the suspect in the caged backseat. Thanking the assisting officers. Reporting to the dispatcher. Killing his reds and maneuvering the car out of the ditch. Driving the nine miles back to Anoka and going through the booking procedure once he got there.

Forty-five minutes after it was over, the shakes began.

He was on his way home when everything inside him started quivering like a tuning fork. His hand trembled like an old man's as he reached for the button to activate his garage door. Inside, when he'd parked and shut off the engine, his knees felt rubbery as he got out of the Explorer and went upstairs to his apartment. All the way up he felt as if he were falling apart, muscle by muscle. He had trouble getting the key into the lock. When he'd finally managed it, he had trouble getting it out again.

In his apartment he walked around aimlessly from room to room, stripping off his uniform and leaving it scattered. He washed his face in cold water, dried off, went to the refrigerator and opened the door to find he had no purpose in opening it. The walls seemed to press in on him.

He took a thirty-minute run, showered, drank a glass of tomato juice and fried himself an egg sandwich, which he couldn't eat. He closed the blinds, stretched out on his back in the middle of the bed . . . and stared at the ceiling.

The movies liked to glamorize high-speed chases, but he wondered how many movie directors had ever been involved in one. He could still feel the heat in his neck and face. His heart refused to slow down. A pain had settled between his shoulder blades. He was horizontal, but instead of growing more relaxed, he felt like poured concrete—as if he were "setting up."

He forced his thoughts to something else. Lee Reston working with her flowers in a good-smelling shop on Main Street. Judd Quincy and his plan for the Fourth of July. Lee Reston and the garden hose he'd intended to fix for her. Janice Reston and the overt interest she was showing in him. Lee Reston cooling her face with the running water at his kitchen sink.

He checked the clock after forty minutes.

After an hour.

An hour and a half.

By ten-thirty he knew perfectly well he wasn't going to sleep. He felt as if he were on amphetamines.

He rolled to the edge of the bed and sat up with both hands curled over the edge of the mattress. He roughed up his scalp, leaving the hair in furrows. He stared at the mopboard on his left, the nightstand on his right, rewinding the film that had been reeling through his mind for the past two hours: the chase . . . Lee Reston . . . the chase . . . Judd Quincy . . . Lee Reston . . . Lee Reston . . . Lee Reston . . .

No question, he thought of her too much, and not always within the context of mutual grieving. Well, hell, it didn't take Freud to figure out he'd developed a mother complex over her. It was natural, the way she hugged him, rubbed his back, fed him leftovers and relied on him for a few of the difficult tasks as she would rely on a son.

Which is what brought the broken hose back to mind.

A distraction!

He bounded off the bed, brushed his teeth, put on a pair of jeans, a police department T-shirt, sneakers and a gold cap and went down to the garage to make sure his tool box was in the Explorer before heading over to Benton Street.

She wouldn't be home; that was good. He'd been hanging around there too much, but this was different. He'd just sneak in and sneak out and leave the hose repaired. Anything to work off this excess of energy.

He was right. She wasn't home. Neither was Janice. Both of their cars were gone, but the garage door was wide open again. Damn woman needed a week on the force to find out how many open garages get pilfered. The front door of the house was open, too, and Christopher could see right in through the screen, so he figured maybe Joey was around.

He parked in the driveway, took a jackknife out of his pocket, cut off the end of the hose and went to a hardware store to buy a replacement.

Once again at her house, he sat on the front step in the partial shade to do the repair job. It was pleasant there. The concrete was cool. Some ants were busy doing commerce in the cracks of the sidewalk. About five kinds of birds were singing. The neighborhood always seemed populated by birds because it was older and had so many mature trees. The red geraniums in the planter gave off their peculiar peppery smell.

He sat there whistling, working, failing to realize that the jumping nerves from the chase were finally beginning to calm. He went to his truck to look for a pair of pliers and discovered he'd left them in the apartment when he was taking Greg's bed apart. So he went into the garage to look for a pair.

The workbench there was amply outfitted with tools. It looked as if

Bill Reston had been a tinkerer. Neat, too. There were banks of tiny plastic drawers stocked with fastidiously separated screws, bolts, washers and nails. On the wall above the bench every tool had its spot on a pegboard, though it was obvious that in the years since his death those that were used didn't always get replaced. Some were strewn on the bench itself, along with a ball of string, barbecue tools and a few gardening tools in a bucket. The whole area had grown dusty.

He looked up at the pegboard again, finding himself fascinated by these telltale hints of the man Lee Reston had once been married to. Tin snips, glass cutters, wood clamps . . . ah, and a common pair of pliers.

He was sitting on the step clamping the new end on the hose when a voice behind him said, "Hey, Chris, what're you doing here?"

He swung around and found Joey standing in the screen door in gray sweat shorts with sleep-swollen eyes.

"Fixing your mother's hose. You just get up?"

"Yeah."

"Everybody else gone to work?"

"Yeah."

Chris returned to his task and said, "This yard could use some mowing."

"You just mowed it."

"That was more than a week ago. Think you better do it today. You got gas?"

"I don't know."

"Well, go check, will you?"

"I just got up."

"Doesn't matter. Go check anyway."

Joey came outside, barefoot, and went off to the garage. In a minute he returned and said, "Not much."

"I'll go get you some, give you a little time to wake up. Then when I get back you'll mow for your mother, right?"

Joey mumbled, "Yeah, I guess so."

The hose was all fixed. "Okay. See you in a bit."

He got the gas can from the garage, filled it at the Standard Station on the corner of Main and Ferry, then returned to the house. The front door was still open, but Joey was nowhere in sight.

He leaned on the door frame and called inside, "Hey, Joe?"

Momentarily the boy appeared, looking unenthusiastic about the whole deal. Instead of combing his hair he'd put on a baseball cap. However, he was wearing socks and grungy Adidas and eating the first of six slices of peanut-butter-and-jelly toast he had piled on his hand.

"Got that gas," Chris told him. "And I filled the mower."

"Grmm . . ." Joey stepped outside. His mouth was too full to talk.

"Hey, listen . . ." Christopher scratched his head and tilted the bill of his cap way down. The two stood side by side with their toes hanging off the top step, Chris studying the house across the street and the glimpse of river in its backyard while the smell of peanut butter floated around their heads. "I know your mother always made all you kids do your share around the place, and I know it's hard with Greg gone, but nothing's changed. You've still got to help her . . . maybe even more. Give her a little break sometimes. Don't make her ask." He glanced at Joey from the corner of his eye. "Okay?"

Joey considered a moment, consulting the concrete sidewalk below them where the hose had left a wet spot shaped like a dotted J.

"Yeah, okay," he said, when his mouth was empty.

"Great," Chris said. "And when you're done with the mowing, will you put the sprinklers on?"

"Yeah, sure."

"Thanks, Joey." He clapped him between the shoulder blades and left him to get the work done.

Lee called that afternoon and woke him shortly after five.

"Don't tell me I've done it again," she opened when he'd mumbled hello.

"Mrs. Reston . . . that you?"

"Who else consistently ruins your sleep by ringing your phone?"

He stretched. "Rrrr . . ." After a chesty waking-up growl he asked, "What time is it?"

"Ten after five. You told me you sleep till two when you're on the night shift."

"Couldn't get to sleep this morning. I had a high-speed chase."

"Oh, no. Not one of them." Obviously, Greg had talked to her about how hairy high-speed chases were, and how they affected nearly every cop who'd ever donned a uniform. "Did you catch him?"

"Not before he drove in the ditch and got his back bumper stuck four feet up in the air in a tree."

She chuckled.

"Of course, he blamed us."

"Was he drunk?"

"What else? They're the worst ones."

"Well, I'm sorry you had to start your day like that."

"The adrenaline's worn off now that I've slept. Hey, what can I do for you?"

A beat of silence passed before she said, "Thanks for fixing the hose."

"You're welcome."

"And for getting the gas."

"You're welcome."

"And for lighting a fire under Joey. I've no doubt you're the one who's responsible."

"Well, I might have made a remark or two."

"Subtle."

"Well, I *can* be subtle, you know."

"You must have talked to Janice, too. I've noticed a change in her."

"They're both good kids. They just got a little too wrapped up in themselves and sort of forgot how hard it's been for you."

"What can I do to repay you?"

"You really want to know?"

He sensed her surprise before she answered, "Yes."

"Would you mind if I brought a guest with me to your Fourth of July picnic?"

"Not at all."

"It's Judd Quincy. The kid I told you about?"

"The one from the bad home?"

"Yeah. It struck me this morning when I was lying here wide awake thinking about everything in the world but sleep—Judd's probably never even seen a functional family, much less been among them for a holiday. A kid's got to see how it *can* work before he can believe it's possible. He's going to grow up just like his parents unless somebody shows him there's a better way. I can't think of a family in America that'd be a better role model than yours."

"Why, thank you, Christopher. Of course . . . bring him." Her voice had grown warm with understanding.

"And it's okay if he gets Greg's rib eye?"

"Absolutely."

"But listen—let's get this straight before we get there. Judd's on *my* volleyball team."

"Now, wait a minute. You're getting mighty pushy here."

"Well, the kid's built like a used bar stool. All legs and spokes and about as loose in the joints as they come. You don't think I'm gonna let him play on somebody else's team, do you?"

"Well, I think the hostess should get a handicap. We'll have to discuss it more after I've seen him."

"Okay, it's a deal."

Chris lay on his pillow smiling at the ceiling, his wrist cocked above the receiver.

"Well . . ." she said. Then nothing.

"Yeah, I'd better get up."

"And I'd better throw together some sandwiches. Joey's playing ball tonight and I've got to go watch." After a pause, she asked uncertainly, "Want to come?"

"Can't. Got a game of my own."

"Oh, that's right. The police team."

"Yeah."

"First base, right?"

"Right."

"Who's playing center field now?" That had been Greg's position.

"Lundgren, I think. This is my first time back since . . ."

After a pause, she filled in the blank.

"Since Greg died."

"I'm sorry."

"We've got to learn to say it."

"I know, I know. The thing is I have been saying it. I don't know why I pulled back this time."

She put on a cheerful voice. "Well, listen . . . good luck tonight, huh?"

"Thanks. Same to Joey."

"See you on the Fourth."

"Yes, ma'am."

"Eleven o'clock?"

"We'll be there."

* * *

He called Judd and said, "Hi, what's doing?"

"Nada."

"Wanna go to my game tonight? I'll pick you up at the usual spot. Six-thirty."

"Sure. Why not."

At six-thirty that evening Judd was holding up the front wall of the 7-Eleven as usual. Chris wheeled up and the kid got in.

"Heya," Chris said.

"Heya."

"Got a deal for you."

"I don't do deals."

"You'll do this one. It's a Fourth of July picnic with these friends of mine."

The kid couldn't quite maintain his indifference in the face of the news. His head made an eighth turn left and his eyes did the rest.

"Picnic?"

"Yeah. Steak fry. Backyard volleyball. A few pops. Fireworks afterwards over at Sand Creek Park. What do you say?"

"Shit, man, why not?"

"You're gonna have to can the talk like that though. These are nice people."

Judd shrugged. "It's cool. I can do that."

"All right." From the front seat Chris picked up a white bill cap with the maroon letter A. "This is for you."

"For me?"

"Yeah. It was my friend Greg's. His mother said I could give it to you. It's her house we're going to on the Fourth."

Hesitantly, Judd took the cap.

"I'll tell you something," Chris said, "you wear that, you wear it with respect. He was a good cop. He stood for something. When you've got that cap on your head I don't want you stealing bicycles or selling parts or doing any of that crap. Deal?"

Judd considered the cap for a long moment before agreeing. "Deal."

"And one more thing."

"What's that?"

"We've got to get you a new pair of tennies. If you're going to be on my volleyball team I don't want you stumbling over those tongues. Cost us points, you know?"

Judd looked down at his fried tennis shoes, then over at Chris. Realizing he was in danger of showing some emotion here, he settled his shoulders against the back of the seat with his usual unimpressibility.

"New tennies I can handle."

They were almost at the ballpark before he spoke again. "Air pumps?" he asked, cocking a glance at Christopher.

"Air pumps!" Chris exploded. "Gimme a break, kid! You know how much those things cost?"

The kid gave his shoulders a little shrug-n-shimmy then let them droop as if to say, *Air pumps, hell, who needs Air pumps.*

When they reached the ball field and were leaving the truck, Judd hooked the Anoka cap on his curly head with the bill cantilevered over his left ear.

Fourth of July came on the way a Fourth of July ought to. Fair, dry, hot. By the time Christopher pulled up at the curb in front of Lee Reston's house the driveway was full of cars, and music was blaring from the backyard. There was red, white and blue bunting hung above the open garage door and twisted around all the trees in the front yard, where a croquet field was set up. The American flag was waving from its standard on the front stoop post, while below it smaller flags were stuck into the dirt between the geraniums.

Christopher and Judd slammed the truck doors and headed for the backyard. Christopher was wearing a white T-shirt and a horrendous pair of shorts in blinding neon colors. Judd was wearing cutoff jeans, a saggy body shirt, Greg's white cap with the bill sticking out over his left ear and a pair of one-hundred-dollar Air pumps.

For the first time since Christopher had known the kid, his heels weren't dragging.

They stepped into a backyard stippled by maple shade extending clear across the rear of the house and deck where Lee's dad, Orrin Hillier, was dumping charcoal briquettes into a number of portable barbecue grills. From the speaker that had been propped in an open window of the house, band music blasted—raucous marches that made an ex-tuba player itch to have fifteen pounds of brass coiled over his shoulder. Just below the deck in the scattered shade, Janice, Kim, Sandy Adolphson and Jane Retting were wiping off the lawn chairs while Lloyd Reston and Joey unwound a volleyball net in the sunny rear yard between the U-shaped flower beds. Lee's mother, Peg, was out in the flower bed on the left, snipping flowers with a scissors. Sylvia Eid turned from flipping a plastic cloth over a picnic table and hollered, "Get one of those delphiniums, too, will you, Mom? That'll make it red, white and blue." There were some people Chris had met only briefly at the funeral, neighbors, cousins and in-laws. One woman was filling a vase from the garden hose. A man came along and stepped on it, intentionally stopping the water flow, and she took off chasing him, laughing, calling him names, slinging water from the vase that caught him on his left ankle and got his sock soaked. Lee slid open the screen and stepped from the kitchen with a can of lighter fluid.

"Here it is, Dad. And some matches." She was dressed in white Bermuda shorts and a T-shirt printed with a waving American flag. Handing the matches to Orrin, she caught sight of the new arrivals and her face broke into a smile. "Christopher, you made it!" She came down the deck steps.

Hearing Christopher's name, Janice swung around, dropped her rag in a bucket and abandoned the job to come over and welcome him with obvious enthusiasm.

Lee pecked Christopher on the jaw and said, "Glad you came." She stuck out a hand and said, "Hi, Judd. I'm Lee Reston."

Janice said, "Hi, Chris. Hi, Judd, I'm Janice." After shaking his hand she gave Christopher's clothing the once-over. "Cow-a-bunga! Would you look at those shorts! What circus did you get them from?"

"You covet them, I'm sure." He put his hands on his waist and looked down. "Judd here's been telling me I need a little color in my wardrobe. Bought 'em specially for today."

Lee said, "I'd introduce you around, Judd, but everybody will do that themselves. Pop's over there in the coolers. Doritos and Mexican dip on the table over there to hold you over till steak time. Be careful of the one with the little flag sticking out of the middle. It's extra hot. Christopher, you can put your steaks in the cooler till the coals are hot, then would you two mind giving Lloyd and Joey a hand with the volleyball net?"

"Be happy to."

Across the yard Kim called, "Hi, Chris! Who you got there?"

"This is Judd, and he's going to be on *my* volleyball team!" Everyone offered hellos as they moved toward the volleyball net, which by this time was stretched out to its full length on the grass while Joey shook a bunch of aluminum poles out of a cardboard box.

Lloyd came to meet them. "Well, this must be Judd. Nice to meet you. Joey . . . look here."

Joey quit chiming the poles together and approached the new boy with the diffidence of a fourteen-year-old.

"Hi," he said, hanging back a little. "I'm Joey."

"I'm Judd."

After a second of hesitation the two shook hands. Joey said, "Wanna help with these poles?"

"Sure," Judd said.

And so the picnic began.

Orrin touched a match to the briquettes, sending the smell of hot charcoal across the yard. "The Stars and Stripes Forever" came from the speaker, and Janice's friends started an impromptu parade. Lee found an old baton in Janice's room and everybody took turns trying to twirl it. Peg Hillier did surprisingly well and admitted she'd been a majorette in her youth. While she was twirling, dressed in pedal pushers and a loose shirt that covered her slight potbelly, Orrin's eyes got quite avid and he whispered to Joey, "You know, when your grandma was a senior in high school every boy in the class wanted to date her. I was the lucky one." Judd overheard and took a second look at Peg. She threw the baton into the air and missed it. "Try it again, Peg!" "Go for it, Grandma!" everyone shouted. On the third try she succeeded in catching it and the entire crowd cheered. When the song ended she laughed at herself, pressed a palm to her chest and fanned her face with the other hand. Orrin took her by both shoulders and whispered something into her ear, after which she laughed again and gave the baton back to the younger girls.

Joey lugged a box of bocce balls out of the garage and a game started up, going from front yard to back to front again with nobody paying attention to court rules.

Lee came out of the garage with a baseball bat, shouting, "All right, everybody! Time to choose sides for the volleyball game! Christopher and I will be captains!"

She marched toward Christopher and sent the bat on a vertical ride through the air. He caught it low on the barrel, just beneath the trademark, still surprised by her announcement.

"You count knobs?" she asked, slapping a right-handed grip just above his while firing him a mischievous look of challenge.

"Darn right." He gripped it with a right.

Left.

Right.

Left.

Right.

Clear up the bat till only the knob was left. She put a cat claw on it and said smugly, "Me first. I choose Judd."

"Oh, you are really underhanded," he murmured with mock scorn, then shot back, "Joey!"

"Dad."

"Mrs. Hillier." Everybody did a woo-woo number because there were still lots of guys left. "Well, we can't have a husband and wife on the same team!" Christopher claimed. "Too much scrapping! Besides, she twirls a mean baton. I'll bet she's going to be good."

"For heaven's sake, call me Peg," she said, joining his squad.

"Barry."

"Janice."

"Sylvia."

"Hey, I thought we couldn't have a husband and wife on the same team!"

They had a pleasant time haranguing back and forth during the remainder of the choosing up. They had just finished when Nolan Steeg sauntered into the backyard, tall, lean and muscular.

"Hey, we get Nolan!"

"No, we get Nolan!"

Nolan puffed out his chest and spread his arms wide. "Am I wanted?" he hammed. "Take me . . . take me!"

It turned out his cousin, a redheaded kid named Ruffy, was up for the week, and stepped into the backyard right behind Nolan, so each side took one of the power players.

They played a stupendously bad game, with lots of people letting the ball drop two feet in front of their faces. They got into arguments about the out-of-bounds markers and finally laid out four tennis shoes to represent the corners of the court. Lee yelled "Oh, noooo, not the flowers!" the first time the ball headed that way. Then they all watched the ball snap off a yellow lily. Lloyd retrieved the ball, high-stepping into the flower bed and putting the lily behind his left ear with a "Sorry, honey" as he returned to the game. The next time the ball headed for the gardens about four voices chorused *"Oh, noooo, not the flowers!"* After that it became the battle call that inevitably raised laughter as the gardens took a battering and Lee, shrugging good-naturedly, turned her palms up to the sky.

Judd could leap like a pogo stick and every time he got on the front line Lee's team would score. Joey was pretty good at spiking too, and the game picked up momentum. Peg Hillier made a save on the sideline and garnered high fives from her teammates when the point had been made. And twice while Lee and Christopher were playing on their front lines directly opposite each other, they banged chests while going for the ball at the same time. The second time, he knocked her down and stepped on her left ankle when he landed.

Immediately he came under the net. "Sorry. You okay?" He offered her a hand up.

"Yeah, I'm fine." Hopping on one foot, she added, "You big lug."

"You sure?" He brushed some dry grass off her back.

"I'm gonna get you for this," she threatened in the best of humor. "So get back over to your own side of the net."

The game ended when the redheaded cousin named Ruffy accidentally broke wind—very loudly—while going after a tough return on game point, making everyone laugh.

"It's time we put the steaks on," Lee said, heading for the deck, wiping her brow. Someone turned on the garden hose and it got passed from hand to hand for drinks. Beer and soda cans popped. "Who'll take care of the sweet corn?"

Barry and Sylvia did. From a tub of saltwater they fished ears of corn, still in their husks, and slapped them, sizzling, onto one of the grills. They turned them wearing asbestos mitts, while Orrin and Lloyd took over the grilling of the steaks, raising an aroma that made everyone's mouth water. A parade of helpers carried bowls of food from the kitchen. The sun had shifted and tables needed moving into the shade.

Orrin announced, "I think some of this steak is done."

Sylvia stripped the corn husks off the first perfect yellow ear and swabbed it with a paintbrush from the butter kettle. "Corn's ready!"

The slow procession started around the buffet table, past the corn station and over to the grills where the steaks were raising curls of fragrant smoke.

"Anyone want iced tea?"

"Here, Mom, I'll do that." Janice came to take the cold pitcher out of Lee's hands and distribute paper cups.

Lee was nearly the last one to fill her plastic plate with potato salad, baked beans, pickles and steak. She carried it to one of the two long picnic tables where Chris sat with Joey, Judd and some others. "Hey, skootch over," she said, nudging him with her hip. He pulled his plate over and she slid onto the bench beside him.

"How's the corn?" she inquired.

"Mmm . . ." He was butter from dimple to dimple. He grinned at her and chewed another mouthful with his elbows propped on the tabletop. She took up the same pose and went to work, nibbling along a row of buttery yellow kernels. He reached for a salt shaker, sprinkled his corn, and as he settled back into place, his warm bare arm slid down along hers.

They both pulled apart, concentrated on their corn and tried to pretend it hadn't happened.

Across the table Judd and Joey were comparing notes on the music they liked—rap versus country.

From a table nearby, Janice called, "Mom, these baked beans are terrific."

"So is the potato salad," Christopher added. "Bachelors don't get a treat like this very often."

"Even ones who know how to cook?" she inquired.

"I cook pretty simple things, mostly."

"My mother taught me how to make potato salad. She's got a secret."

"What?"

"A little sweet pickle juice in the dressing." Lee raised her voice. "Isn't that right, Mom?"

"What's that?" At another table, Peg turned in her chair and looked back over her shoulder.

"Pickle juice in the potato salad."

"That's right. But yours is every bit as good as mine, honey."

Lloyd came around refilling iced tea glasses. He patted Lee's shoulder. "Nice picnic, dear."

From another table one of the cousins called, "Hey, Aunt Lee?"

"What, Josh?"

"Is it really true that when you were eleven years old you drove Grandpa's car through the window of the dime store?"

Lee dropped her empty corn cob and covered her head with both arms. "Oh my God."

"Did you, Aunt Lee?"

She came up blushing. "Daddy, did you tell him that?" she scolded.

"Did she really, Grandpa?"

"Well now, Josh, I told you it wasn't exactly *through* the window, just a few feet into it."

Christopher smiled down at Lee's right ear, which was as red as the zinnias in her garden.

"What's this?" he teased quietly.

"Daddy, I could crown you!" she blustered.

Christopher teased, "It's no wonder you didn't get upset about Joey driving. At least he waited till he was fourteen. And he didn't do it on the main street of town."

Somebody said, "Hey, what about the time when my dad peed through the screen. Tell 'em, Dad."

It was Orrin Hillier's turn to be put on the hot seat. He laughed and pretended embarrassment, but everyone convinced him to tell the oft-repeated story. "Well, it was when we were kids, and we lived on the farm and I slept with my brother, Jim. Our room was on the second floor, of course, and one summer we got the idea that when we had to get up and go in the middle of the night we could save ourselves the trouble of walking all that way outside to the outhouse by just whizzing through the screen. We got by with it for quite a while, but don't you know, the next year in the spring when my dad was changing the storm windows, he noticed that one of the screens was all rusting out in a perfect circle, about, oh"—he measured off a distance from the ground with one hand—"about wiener high to a couple of snot-nosed boys. And we sure caught it then."

"What happened?"

"We had to shell corn. He put us out in a corncrib with one of those old hand-crank shellers and said, 'Go to work, boys, and don't stop till the crib is empty.' Well, he took pity on us around suppertime, when I suspect my mom stuck up for us, but let me tell you, I've never had blisters like that before or since."

Christopher had been watching Judd's eyes while the story was being told. He had hiked one foot up beneath him on the picnic bench and stretched his neck to see over the heads around him. Like any child of twelve, he had watched the storyteller and listened with his empty fork forgotten against his teeth. He had laughed when the others laughed. He had experienced firsthand the flow of familial lore from one generation to the next, and the fascination showed on his face.

When the story ended he said to Joey, "I thought grampas were like, you know, soybean people, but yours is definitely primo."

Joey smiled and said, "Yeah, I think so too."

They had watermelon for dessert, followed by a watermelon seed spitting contest, which Sylvia won. She received a box of sparklers as her prize.

They played more volleyball, bocce and croquet, and when evening set in ate leftovers, then began cleaning up the yard and the kitchen. By the time they headed for Sand Creek Park, Lee hadn't one item left to fold up, wash or pack away.

Joey said, "Hey, Chris, can I ride with you and Judd?"

"Sure."

"You got room for me, too?" Lloyd asked.

"You bet. Jump right in."

Lee rode with her parents, Janice with all the girls. The cavalcade left the house when the sun was sitting on the rim of the world and the neighborhood resounded with an occasional volley of firecrackers.

At Sand Creek, a huge multifield baseball complex, the surrounding unpaved parkland had been pressed into use as parking lots. The cars, entering bumper to bumper, raised a fine haze of dust that settled like a lanugo on the vehicles as they pulled in. The sky had lost color, faded like an iris left in water too long. The warmth of the day lifted from the sandy earth, met by a press of coolness beginning above. Crayon-colored lights, subdued by dust, blinked and gyrated in the distance where a carnival beckoned. Its enticing clamor drifted across the field, interspersed with the occasional report of firecrackers. Children ran among the cars. Adults walked. The oldest of them carried webbed lawn chairs.

Joey and Judd jogged ahead, raising puffs of dust, talking animatedly as they headed for the carnival and its promise of excitement.

Ambling after them, Lloyd remarked to Chris, "Those two seem to be hitting it off quite well."

"Better than I expected."

Lee called from behind them, "Hey, you two, wait for us."

And that's how Lee ended up beside Christopher, where she seemed to stay the remainder of the night, while Lloyd faded back and fell in beside Lee's folks.

"Want to walk over to the carnival?" Lee asked the older ones.

Her mother replied, "No, I think I've had enough excitement for one day. I'll just settle down on a blanket and wait for the fireworks." Orrin and Lloyd agreed.

"Mind if we go for a while?" Lee asked.

"Of course not. Have fun," her mother replied.

"We'll find you later."

They ambled through the dusty grass toward the red, blue and yellow bars of moving neon, toward the smell of popcorn and Pronto Pups and the sounds of carnival engines and calliope music. All day long they'd been with others; their footsteps slowed as they shared this first time alone.

"Thanks for today," he said, "and especially for letting Judd come."

"You're welcome. I was glad to have you both."

"I don't think he's ever experienced anything like it before. He doesn't have any grandparents that I know of. I was watching his eyes when your dad was telling his story, and the kid was transfixed."

"The rest of us have heard that old story so often we know it by heart."

"That's exactly the point. I wanted him to see how a real family works, and you all certainly gave him a firsthand look."

"Well, you can bring him anytime."

"He and Joey seemed to warm up to each other eventually. They were talking and laughing together quite a bit by the end of the day."

He glanced down at her as they reached the periphery of the carnival. She had put on fresh lipstick before leaving the house, and walked with a sweater folded over her arm. The lights of the carnival stained her face and danced across her eyes, which suddenly grew sad as the sights and sounds amplified. Instinct told him she was remembering Greg, a childhood Greg, perhaps, a little boy begging for one more ride, for money for another treat. In all his life, how many times had Greg Reston been brought here on the Fourth of July by his parents? Year after year until it became tradition. Now the tradition continued without him.

She stopped walking as they reached the midway, stood staring at it while his heart hurt for her.

"Do you want anything?" he offered—a paltry offering, but what else had he?

She shook her head and walked a few steps away, presumably to hide her tears.

He moved up behind her and put a hand on her shoulder. "You brought him here every Fourth when he was a kid, didn't you?"

She nodded stiffly and spoke only after a long silence. "You can go through a day like today and do pretty well. Then you face something like this and it's as if you . . . you expect to see him running toward you through the crowd."

"Eight years old, I bet."

"Eight, nine, ten . . . asking for more money for the rides. I think it's the smells that do it. It happens more often when there's a familiar smell around than at any other time. Have you noticed that?"

"It's still that way in the bathroom at our apartment. It seems worse in that room than anyplace else. Like his after-shave is imbedded in the walls."

They stood motionless, his hand on her shoulder, while people milled past and a man in a white apron and a white paper hat twisted a white paper cone full of pink cotton candy.

"Let's take a ride," he suggested.

"I don't feel much like it."

"Neither do I, but let's do it anyway."

137

She turned, looked back over her shoulder and his hand fell away. "I don't feel like it, Christopher."

"How about on the Ferris wheel?"

She looked at it and realized he was suggesting the right thing to get them over this emotional stone upon which they'd stumbled. "Oh, all right, but I'm afraid I won't be very good company."

He bought a string of tickets, used four and they boarded the Ferris wheel. Her eyes were dry but she looked as if only determination kept them that way. They sat without touching, their bare legs stretched out and crossed at the ankles while the machine took them backward in lurches and starts as others boarded below.

"I've been reading about grief," Christopher told her. "It says that facing places the first time will be hardest and that you shouldn't try facing them all at once. You're supposed to give yourself time. Don't try to be a hero about it."

"I'm not trying to be a hero," she said.

"Aren't you? You made the flowers for his coffin. You went right into his bedroom and cleaned it out. You went right ahead and planned the Fourth of July, the same as always. Maybe you need to cool it for a while and not be quite so strong. Hell, Lee, I've watched you and you blow my mind. All the while I'm admiring your strength, I'm wondering how you do it. I think tonight it's finally catching up with you."

Her anger flared out of nowhere. Her rust-colored eyes flashed his way. "How dare you criticize me! You haven't been through it! You don't know what it's like!"

"No, I haven't. Not like you. But nobody's asking you to be Superwoman."

The Ferris wheel moved and green lights picked out the tracks of tears on her cheeks. Regret shot through Christopher and made his ribs feel too tight.

"Aw, Lee, come here . . . I didn't mean to make you cry." He took her in his arms and cradled her head against his shoulder. "I didn't mean to hurt you. I was trying to get you to see that you can take on too much too soon, and nobody expects it of you. Just give it time, huh?"

Abruptly she huddled against him, her hand folded over his shoulder, gripping it as she wept. They stayed that way while the wheel carried them up into the darkening sky where they seemed to hang like the only two beings on earth. They lurched to a stop and their seat swung. Below, the light and sound seemed far away. Above, the first stars had made their appearance.

He rested his mouth against her hair. It smelled of her and dust and barbecue smoke.

"Lee, I'm sorry," he whispered.

"You're right," she admitted brokenly. "I *have* been acting like Superwoman. I should have waited till the kids could help me with his room. And I should have let well enough alone when we finished the picnic at the house today. Maybe if I hadn't come here I would have made it without doing this again." She sniffed and pulled back, drying her face with her hands. He kept one hand around her nape, his elbow resting on the back of the seat.

"You feel better now?"

She nodded fiercely, as if to convince herself.

"And you're not mad at me?"

She wagged her head twice. "No."

With a slight pressure on her neck he forced her to turn her face, then bent down and kissed her between the eyes. The Ferris wheel moved to its apex and jerked to a stop again. His hold remained loose upon her neck as their eyes met, and lingered, and they wondered about this curious relationship blossoming between them.

"Okay, then, let's enjoy the ride."

She gave him a feeble smile as the Ferris wheel began its steady circling, returning them to the light and sight of activity below. He released her neck but found her hand and, linking their fingers tightly, turned the back of his hand to his bare knee. They rode that way, staring at their joined hands until they realized faces were looking up at them from below, and anyone they knew could be among the crowd. Prudently, he released her hand and they finished their ride in silence, touching no more, but sharing a physical awareness of each other that could be explained only one way.

After their ride, Joey found them and asked his mom for money. Christopher gave him the string of extra tickets and said, "Give half to Judd."

"Gosh, thanks!"

Judd said, "Yeah, thanks, man."

"And meet us back at the car right after the fireworks!" Lee called at their departing backs.

Full dark had fallen as they headed for the baseball fields where everyone was waiting for the display to begin. The park was huge. They had no idea where the others were, and after ten minutes of looking they gave up.

"Want to sit here?" he asked when they found a reasonably good-sized patch of grass surrounded by strangers.

"Why not?"

She spread her sweater and said, "I'll share it."

They dropped onto the small island of white knit, their hips touching, giving themselves that much forbidden contact. When the fireworks started they stretched out their legs, crossed their ankles and braced on their palms behind them.

Spangles of peridots seemed to burst up above, followed by diamonds, rubies, sapphires. Their arms aligned, like earlier at the picnic table. Tonight, however, under cover of darkness, when they touched, they stayed, skin to skin with their faces turned skyward like the hundreds of others surrounding them.

Up in the sky a boom and a whistle . . . another starburst of glitter, blue and red this time . . . pop, pop, pop! . . . and voices in chorus.

"Ohhhhhhh . . ."

"Christopher?" she said, very quietly.

"Hm?" He swung his face to her profile, just beyond their joined shoulders.

"You're very good for me," she said, keeping her eyes on the sky.

Chapter 7

A couple of weeks after the Fourth of July, Janice came home from work one night at 9:45. It was hot in the house and she looked tired as she came down the hall and dropped one shoulder against the open doorway of Lee's bedroom.

"Hi, Mom."

"Hi, honey." Lee was sitting up in bed reading, wearing a pair of short yellow pajamas. "Busy at the store?"

Janice ran a hand through her hair and gave her head a shake. "Not very. Gosh, it's so hot in here, Mom. I wish you'd get air-conditioning."

"Why don't you take a lukewarm shower? That'll make you feel better."

Janice pulled her blouse out of her skirt and unbuttoned it. She lifted her left foot and took off a white flat, hung it over an index finger and did the same with the right, then propped herself against the door casing once more.

"Mom, could I ask you something?"

"Of course." Lee patted the mattress and rested her magazine on her legs. "Come here."

Janice sat on the bed with one knee crooked up, the other foot on the floor. "Mom, what do you do when you've tried everything within the range of good taste to get a guy to notice you . . . only he doesn't?"

"Some guy in particular?"

"Yes . . . Christopher."

Lee sat absolutely still for five seconds, then closed her magazine and put it on the nightstand, giving herself a brief grace period in which to concoct a response. Leaning against the pillows again, she said quietly, "Oh, I see."

"Mom, he treats me like a kid sister and I just hate it."

"There's quite a bit of difference in your ages."

"Seven years, that's not so much. You and Daddy were five years apart."

Lee considered Janice's reply. "That's true. Two more isn't so terribly lopsided."

"Then why doesn't he pay any attention to me? I've tried dropping hints, but he doesn't pick up on them. I've looked in the mirror and I'm not a troll or anything. I've acted like a lady around him, engaged him in conversation, complimented him, dressed nicely, tried in every way I know how to let him know I'm interested and old enough to take it seriously. So what is it?"

"I don't know what to say."

"You're with him a lot. Does he say anything about me?"

"He asks how you are. He's concerned about you just like he is about all of our family."

"Concerned," Janice repeated with a grimace, staring at her white flats as she held them sole to sole in her lap. "Hooray." She sat there looking dejected. Out in the yard crickets were carping. In the living room Joey was watching TV with the volume turned low. Janice's voice grew quiet with sincerity. "I've had a crush on him since the first time Greg introduced him to us. It was at the police station, and he was dressed in his uniform, just pulling up in a squad car. Honest, Mom, he stepped out of that car and my heart just . . . just *flew* into my throat. I'm sure he knows. Kim says I look at him like he's fresh-buttered popcorn."

She raised her disillusioned eyes to Lee and they laughed. Once. Not too cheerily.

Lee opened her arms. "Come here, honey."

Janice stretched across the bed and nestled in the crook of Lee's arm.

"We women have a rotten deal, don't we?" Lee rubbed Janice's hair with her jaw.

"Not anymore. Lots of women ask men out on dates."

"Then why haven't you?"

Janice shrugged. Lee stroked Janice's hair back from her temple and let it fall again and again. It was beautiful hair, mid-back length, auburn, naturally wavy. She had inherited her hair from Bill's side of the family. "I guess I want him to ask me."

At that moment Joey interrupted. "What are you two doing?" He appeared in the doorway and leaned against it where Janice had been. He was dressed in a gray T-shirt and shorts, and filthy white socks with the toes belled out like light bulbs.

"Talking," Lee replied.

"Yeah, I bet I know about what. Janice has got a crush on Chris, hasn't she?" He started to cackle softly, in falsetto.

Janice rolled her head and told her brother, "You know, Joey, it might not hurt you to get a crush on somebody. Maybe you'd grow up a little and pay some attention to your personal hygiene. You've got half the ball diamond on your shirt and I can smell you clear over here."

Lee said, "Could we have a little privacy here, Joe?"

"Yeah, yeah . . . I'm going to bed."

"After you take a shower."

He made a disgusted face and rolled away from the door frame with his shoulders artificially slumped. A minute later the shower started down the hall.

Janice drew herself up and sat with her back to Lee.

"Kim says I should just call him up and ask him to do something. Go to a movie or something. What do you think, Mom?"

"Honey, it's up to you. When I grew up girls didn't do things like that, but I realize times are different now."

"The thing is, I'm scared he'll say no again, then I'll feel like a jerk."

"Again?"

"That one night I asked him if he wanted to go for a swim, but he'd already gone with you. This time though, I'd ask him earlier in the week for a Friday or Saturday night. Maybe make some dinner plans at some place casual." She looked back over her shoulder wistfully. "What do you think?"

Lee studied her daughter and felt a swell of maternal sympathy.

Janice was such a pretty girl. How could any young man brush her off? "I think mothers should stay out of decisions like this."

Janice remained on the crumpled sheets in her crumpled blouse staring at her bare knees. Finally, she gave a rueful laugh. "Well, hell, Mom, you're no help at all," she said, and pulled herself off the bed.

Half an hour later when the house had finally grown quiet, Lee lay in the dark with the pillows mounded under her ear, considering her reaction to what Janice had said. When Janice had mentioned Christopher's name she'd felt a spurt of panic. Or had it been jealousy? How ridiculous. *Either one* was ridiculous, given Christopher's age. He was fifteen years younger than herself and she had no business considering him anything more than a friend. Yet she did. What set him apart was how she'd come to rely on him. He was wise beyond his years, perhaps made so by virtue of his chosen work or his unhappy youth.

In the month since Greg's death she had seen Christopher perhaps a dozen times. It was obvious she was using him as a substitute for Greg. She understood this clearly and supposed her reaction was typical. Any mother who'd lost a child would seek the company of those closest to that child to get over the hurdle of first loss. When the young people were around—any of them—she could talk about Greg with less pain. The girls came by occasionally, and Nolan had even stopped in the flower shop one day, just to say hello.

Then what was so different about Christopher?

She flopped over on her back. The sheets felt sticky and she wondered why she hadn't taken the trouble to have air-conditioning installed after the shop had proven itself and she'd no longer had to watch every penny. Those damned crickets could drive a person crazy. She switched to her side and stretched one leg onto a cool part of the bedding with the top sheet between her legs.

What was so different about Christopher?

He wore a uniform and drove a black-and-white police car. When she saw it pulling into her driveway she had the momentary illusion it was Greg pulling in, Greg stepping from behind the wheel, Greg in that neat navy blue uniform with badges all over the chest. Mercy, Christopher's coloring was even like Greg's. Brown hair, blue eyes, tan face. He had the same stocky build. The police department had a weight room over behind Perkins restaurant where they worked out all the time, and to

Lee every fellow on the force had the thick-necked, toned, muscular shape that spoke of a man keeping fit because someday his life might depend on it.

So what about holding hands with Christopher on the Ferris wheel?

That was comfort, nothing more.

And the kiss between the eyes?

More comfort.

And the compulsion to touch his bare arm?

She tossed a while longer.

No more iced tea after eight o'clock at night if this is what it did to her! She rolled to her other side and stared at the moonlit window, listening to the rasp of crickets and a faint susurrus of leaves as a night breeze filtered past. Then silence. Utter silence, in which she lifted her head off the pillow and looked around the darkened room.

Silly single woman who'd given up those jitters years ago! What in the world had gotten into her tonight? Then she heard it, faintly . . . in the distance . . . a siren . . . so far away even the crickets started up again.

Was he still working night shift? Had he had any more high-speed chases? There . . . see? She didn't even know the answers to these things because she hadn't seen him for two weeks. Wasn't that proof there was nothing untoward about those few moments they'd held hands on the Ferris wheel?

She spent two more weeks without seeing him. During that time she devoted part of every day to settling Greg's business affairs. She'd been fighting with the bank for weeks and was on the phone at the flower shop yet again with someone named Pacey, finding it difficult to get over the loss of Greg when she had to fight these battles daily to clear up his affairs. "But I told you, Mr. Pacey, it's not going through probate. He didn't own enough property to make it worth the trouble."

"In that case my hands are tied."

"Good lord, it's only a four-hundred-dollar savings account!"

"I understand that, but unless he was a minor you have no jurisdiction over his assets, and of course, he was no minor."

"But do you realize, Mr. Pacey, that even after I sent you a copy of his death certificate your computer still sent me another monthly statement? I just want to close it out so that doesn't happen again."

"I'm sorry about that, Mrs. Reston. It sometimes takes a while for the paperwork to be entered into the computer."

"And what about his motorcycle payment? The same thing happened there. I came into the bank over a month ago to let you know he was dead and that his motorcycle was insured. Today I got a notice claiming his payment was overdue and there's a late charge tacked on!"

After a puzzled pause, he asked, "What day did you say you came in?" When she told him, he said, "Just a minute, please," and put her on hold.

She had developed a headache. It seemed to intensify while she stood listening to Barry Manilow sing in her ear. Handling Greg's business affairs became a constant reminder of him—looking at his handwriting in his checkbook register, finding notes he'd made on papers in his files, unearthing evidence of plans he'd had for the future. When snags like this came up—and it was often—she found it harder to cope. Sometimes, after a conversation with someone like Pacey over some tie-up she couldn't control, she'd have herself a brief cry, fueled largely by exasperation.

She was still on hold when the shop door opened and Christopher walked in, dressed in his police uniform. At the same moment, Mr. Pacey returned.

"Mrs. Reston?"

"Yes." Her eyes followed Christopher as he came inside and smiled at her.

"Your son certainly had paid off his car, but the trouble is he used it as collateral against a loan he took out for a motorcycle."

"I know that, Mr. Pacey! I told *you* that the first time I came in! My trouble is that I can't transfer ownership of the car to my daughter without the registration card, and you won't release that without the motorcycle being paid for, and the insurance company is paying for the motorcycle, not me, but they haven't issued a check yet."

She heard him draw a breath of strained patience. "Then wouldn't it be a lot simpler, Mrs. Reston, just to go through probate?"

Her voice was trembling as she said, "Thank you, Mr. Pacey," and slammed down the receiver with such force the bell tinged in the phone.

Christopher stood watching her across the length of the shop. He looked totally out of place amid a tiered display of potted yellow mums and blue hydrangeas. She stood behind a Formica counter with both hands pressed flat upon it, striving to calm herself.

Frustration won out.

She made a fist and thumped it on the counter as hard as she could. "Damn it!" She squeezed her eyes shut.

"What's wrong?" He picked his way between cut flowers and revolving stands of greeting cards to the opposite side of the counter. He rested his forearms on it, bending at the hip and bringing his face down to the level of hers. "Bad day?"

She swung around, presenting her back, hands caught on the edge of the counter, blinking hard at the ceiling.

"Why is it that every time you see me, I'm crying again? I swear I go through *days* without crying, and you walk in here and I'm at it again."

"I don't know," he replied quietly. "Seems to be a rhythm to it, doesn't there? I've sort of been on a downer again myself, so I just thought I'd stop by and see how you're doing."

She turned back to face him, managing a self-deprecating smile. Looking at him in his visored hat and crisp collar and tie, she felt her frustration begin to dissipate. "Oh, hell, I don't know."

"What was that all about on the phone?"

"The joys of settling an estate."

"Ah, I see." He was still bent over the counter, forearms resting on it. The gold band of a wristwatch peeked from under his left cuff. A single bow of a pair of sunglasses was hooked into a pen hole of his shirt pocket. His pose tightened his collar and stretched taut the skin of his neck, which was cinched by a carefully knotted tie held in place by an APD tiepin. As usual, the sight of him in uniform seemed to add ten years to his age and make him her peer.

"Wanna do something?" he asked quietly. "Go to a movie? Walk? Talk? Forget it for a while?"

"When? Tonight?"

"Yeah. I'm on days."

She had an inspiration. "Could we take Janice?"

"Sure," he said without hesitation, straightening and tugging up his leather belt with all its heavy accessories. "Joey too if you want. What should we do?"

"A walk sounds best. A brisk, hard, long walk."

"How about the paved trail west of the Coon Rapids dam?"

"Perfect."

"Should I pick you up?"

"Sure."

"What time?"

She checked her watch. "I'm through here at five-thirty. How about six? I'll pick up some sandwiches to take along."

"Perfect."

"See you then."

She called home immediately. The phone rang nine times and nobody answered. She called The Gap at Northtown. Someone named Cindy told her Janice wasn't scheduled to work that day, which Lee already knew. She called Kim's house. Kim's mother said the two girls had gone down to the university to do some preregistration for fall quarter. She didn't know what time they'd be back.

"Well, if you talk to her, tell her not to eat supper and to meet me at the house at six."

"Will do."

Sylvia had the day off, so Lee locked up the shop herself, swung by the Subway sandwich shop and picked up four combination sandwiches containing everything but the kitchen sink. At home she charged into the house, calling, "Joey, you here?"

"Yo!" he hollered from the depths of his room.

"Wanna go walking with Chris and me?"

"Where?"

She was passing his bedroom door, unbuttoning her waistband as she answered. "Walking trails over by the dam." He was lying on his bed reading a *Hot Rod* magazine.

"Hey, yeah! Only, would it be okay if I took my Rollerblades instead? That walking stuff is heinous."

She laughed and said louder, closing her bedroom door, "I don't care, but hurry and get ready. He'll be here at six. Did Janice come home yet?"

"Haven't seen her all day."

Well, Lee had tried.

She changed into a pair of faded purple knit shorts with a matching T-shirt, put on tennis socks and a pair of Adidas, ran a brush through her hair, wiped her face with a Kleenex, slapped on some fresh lipstick and was shutting off the bathroom light when Christopher knocked on the front door.

"Ready?" he said when she came around the corner into the front hall.

"Yup."

"Where are the kids?"

"Joey's coming." She raised her voice. "Hey, Joe? You all ready?"

He came barreling down the hall and did a Tom Cruise stocking-slide onto the shiny front hall floor, carrying his Rollerblades.

"Where are your shoes?" Lee said.

"I don't need shoes. I'm gonna skate."

She pointed with an authoritative finger at his bedroom. "Get! Your! Shoes!"

Grumbling, he went back to get them. When she turned around Chris was snickering.

"Gnarly adolescent boys!" she whispered. While Joey was gone she jotted a note for Janice and left it on the kitchen table. *Gone walking with Joey & Chris. Sandwich for you in frig. Home early. Love, Mom.*

"Shut the front door when you come out, Joey!" she called, following Christopher outside, letting the screen door slam behind them. "What kind of sandwiches?" he asked, showing pointed interest in the white sack as they walked toward the Explorer.

She hefted the bag. "Salami, ham, cheese, mayo, black olives, lettuce, tomato, onions, Oil of Olay, sassafras root, watercress, potato dumpling, peanut butter, sauerkraut and pigs' ears. What do you mean, what kind of sandwich? You expect a person to remember what they put in those things over there?"

Laughing, he opened the front door of the Explorer for her. "Sorry I asked."

She clambered in the front, leaving the back for Joey. He came out a minute later and they were off, with the windows down and the evening breezing against their ears.

"Thanks for suggesting this, Christopher, it feels so good." She lifted her elbows and face, shut her eyes and ruffled her hair with both hands. "If I have to talk to one more banker or insurance representative or gravestone salesman, I think I'm going to scream."

Christopher glanced at her askance, caught her in profile with her elbows and breasts outlined against the far window. When she broke her pose, he quickly returned his attention to the road. "None of that tonight. The purpose of this walk is to forget all that. Deal?"

She flashed him a smile. "Deal."

The stultifying heat of July had burned itself out and left a more temperate August. By the time they reached the dam it was 6:30 and pleasantly warm. The sky appeared hazy, as if viewed through a steamy window, its colors opaque melon and lavender, while the sun burned through in orange so muted one could look at it with the naked eye. The air smelled of summer's end—drying crops and crisping weeds and the graininess of dust and harvest.

At the dam the Mississippi thundered over the lowered gates, and cars with bicycle carriers were lined up door to door in the angled parking slots. Serious cyclists, in their helmets and gloves, were resting against the guardrails, still seated on their bikes, watching fishermen working the more placid waters above the boil.

Joey grumbled while he put on his Rollerblades. "See, I told you I didn't need shoes." When he finished, he said, "I'm hungry. Can I have my sandwich, Ma?"

"Sure." She fished it out of the sack and handed it to him over the back of the seat while he hung his feet out the open door. "Just make sure you don't leave the paper somewhere along the trail. Have you got a pocket?"

"Yeah, yeah."

He stood beside the truck, wearing a blue baseball cap, scissoring back and forth on his blades, peeling the paper down and taking a first bite big enough to stuff an entire Thanksgiving turkey, then talking with his cheek bulging. "Hurry up, you guys!" In the last year his nose seemed to have mushroomed and lost its boyishness while the rest of his features hadn't quite caught up. His hands had grown to the size of Maine lobsters.

Standing beside him, Lee observed her son and wondered how to get him from fourteen to nineteen in the shortest time possible. She loved him, but this crude, gangly adolescent stage was really the pits.

She leaned across the truck seat and looked in the sack. "You want your sandwich now, Christopher?"

"I'd rather walk on an empty stomach, if you don't mind." He was busy finding his sunglasses, threading the earpieces into their hot-pink string.

"Me too. We'll eat after."

"Better yet, I've got a fanny pack under the seat. We could take the sandwiches along and eat at a picnic stop."

"Sounds good."

Christopher slipped on his sunglasses, locked the truck and carried the blue nylon bag around to Lee's side. She filled it and he buckled it around his waist with the zippered pouch at the rear.

By then Joey was already thirty yards away, swaying gracefully on his Rollerblades, eating his sandwich, caring about little else.

She watched him and said, "Lord, if only he were that graceful on his own feet."

"The miracle is, they actually outgrow it."

"Meanwhile I'm raising the hormonal hurricane. I never knew noses could grow so fast."

They were laughing as they struck out on their walk, heading west along the North Hennepin Trail. It took them through open grassland dotted by brown-eyed Susans and wild asters, between fields of ripe corn where pheasants foraged, through copses of trees that sliced them with intermittent shade. It curved around small marshes where red-winged blackbirds sent forth their distinctive summer call. It passed the remnants of distant farms and an occasional newer house, which looked misplaced next to all that preserved parkland. Bikers occasionally surprised them from behind, passing them in swift puffs of wind, pedaling hard. Other joggers and walkers met them head-on, nodding or speaking winded hellos. Sometimes Joey was visible, sometimes not. He went and returned at will, zooming back at them along the blacktop trail with his blue cap reversed, adding further insult to his adolescent bad looks.

In time Lee squinted at the empty blacktop path that caught the setting sun and turned it to liquid gold. Joey had gone on ahead; the trail stretched for miles, clear out to Elm Creek Park Reserve in the town of Maple Grove.

"I wonder where the hormonal hurricane is," she said.

"Don't worry. He'll be back."

"Are you ready to turn around yet?" she asked.

"Anytime."

They reversed directions, turning their backs on the glare and checking their watches.

"A little over an hour already," Christopher noted. "You tired?"

"Darn right I'm tired, but it feels good."

"Do you do this regularly?"

"Irregularly. In the summer. How about you?"

"I work out regularly in one way or another. Summers a little more outside. Winters, I work out a little more in the weight room, especially after a bad day at work."

They needed their breath for walking, so talking ceased as their shadows grew long on the trail in front of them. The air cooled and frogs began croaking. At a place where the trail crossed a blacktop road a picnic table sat in a clearing. Beside it were bike stands, a garbage can and a drinking fountain. Lee used the fountain first while Christopher waited, standing behind her, watching the curve of her backside as she bent forward to drink. He was growing—he'd discovered—more and more familiar with her curves. She straightened and turned, backhanding her mouth and smiling behind her hand.

He leaned on the fountain with both hands, elbows jutting, sunglasses hanging free and tapping the side of the fountain. She watched the side of his neck as he swallowed, the rhythmic beat of his pulsating skin just below one ear, the line of his backbone beneath his T-shirt, ending where the fanny pack projected from the small of his back. It had been a long time since she'd studied a man's outline in the particular way she found herself studying Christopher's.

He straightened with the sound men make—"Ahh!"—masculine and throaty, a sound she hadn't heard much around her house for many years. With a forearm, he wiped his brow.

"Sandwiches, sandwiches!" she said, clapping twice like a bedouin calling for dancing girls.

"Get 'em out," he said, presenting his back.

She worked the zipper, keeping her eyes on it and nothing else—silly woman, admiring a man fifteen years her junior!—and fished out their supper. At the picnic table they sat down on opposite sides, unwrapped their sandwiches and ate.

And studied each other with mayonnaise in the corners of their mouths. With their hair imperfect and wet around the edges. And their complexions ruddy and unsmooth from exertion. Wearing some of the oldest clothes they owned. Experiencing a comfort level they found with few others.

"So . . ." she began, wiping her mouth on a hard paper napkin printed with an orange-and-black logo. "Any more high-speed chases?"

"No, thank heavens."

"So what's new at the department?"

"I've been made a firearms instructor."

"Wow . . . congratulations."

"Just one of several."

"Still . . . an instructor. Does this mean you'll have to make room for another badge on your chest?"

"Not a badge, just a little pin."

"What does a firearms instructor do?"

"The correct title is range officer. I have to set up quarterly qualification shoots with our duty weapons at the shooting range."

"Where's that?"

"Little park maintenance building behind Perkins."

"The one where the weight room is?"

"Yes."

"I've been in there. Greg took me in once, showed me how the targets move on the metal tracks and put a pair of ear protectors on me and shot off a few rounds. So you have to give the tests?"

"I can design them, too. Next month we're going to be having a gamma shoot that the whole county will participate in."

"What's a gamma shoot?"

"It's done with a gamma machine—it's sort of a simulator."

"And you design the shoots on the simulator?"

"No, the ones I design are done differently."

"How?"

"Well, I'm working on one now. The officers will have to start in the basement and run up three flights of stairs, down a hall, open a door and shoot out six red balloons from a field of twenty-four multicolored ones in two minutes."

"Two minutes?" It seemed long to her.

"Have you ever tried shooting off six accurate rounds in two minutes? Especially when you're breathing like a steam engine and your adrenaline is pumping? If you're on a SWAT team, maybe you've got a gas mask on. Or maybe it's a low-light situation and your reds are flashing, changing the color of everything around you. It's not easy. Even worse, in the test I've designed, they'll have to do it six times, on six different lanes."

"You dreamed this up yourself?"

He shrugged. "There are films and books to give you ideas, and I've been through a lot of qualifying shoots myself in nine years on the force."

"You must be good."

"As good as some, not as good as others. I tend to get less rattled than some of the guys. At least until it's all over . . . then the shakes begin. Like that day of the chase."

He talked about that awful time after all high-risk situations when the adrenaline stops pumping and the shakes set in. How hard it is to concentrate after that, to sleep, to return to normal routine.

"That's why I came and fixed your hose. Couldn't sleep . . . just had to work off that excess energy." A lull fell. Sometimes when this happened—as now—they found themselves studying each other's eyes a little too enjoyably. "So . . . enough about my life. What's going on in yours?"

"Well . . . let's see." She pulled herself from her absorption with him. "School will be starting soon. Right after Labor Day for Joey, two weeks later for Janice. She's had to pay her own way, so it's taking her longer than usual. She was at the U doing some preregistering today. Next week Joey starts football practice, and I'll have to think about taking him out to do some school shopping. His nose isn't the only thing that's been growing this summer. His ankles are hanging out of every pair of jeans he owns." She folded her waxed paper and put it into the sack, then looked off across the open field to the south where twilight was settling. "I hate to see Janice go back to school. The house will seem so empty."

"Will she live in a dorm?"

"Yes."

"So you'll have to move her back. Do you need help with that?"

"I can borrow Jim Clements's truck again."

"Let me know if you need a strong back."

"Thanks, I will."

They sat in silence awhile. A sparrow came and pecked at some crumbs around the garbage can. A gray-haired man and woman came by and said hello. When they'd moved on, Christopher sat with a question in his mind, afraid to pose it, afraid that if he did he might spook Lee and that would be the end of these pleasant times with her. But they'd become friends, good friends. They'd talked about their personal feelings time and again, so what was wrong with talking about this? *Ask her,* an inner voice urged. *Just ask her.* Instead, he rose and threw their trash into the garbage can, gathering courage. Returning to the picnic table, he straddled a bench and rested one arm on the tabletop, looking off at the grass.

"Could I ask you something?"

"Ask."

He turned to watch her face. "Do you ever go out on dates?"

"Dates?" she repeated, as if the word were new to her.

"Yeah, dates." He rushed to explain. "You know, Greg talked a lot about you, but I never heard him mention any guys in your life." He allowed a stretch of silence, then asked, "So do you?"

"No."

"Why?"

"Because when Bill died my kids were enough for me. I just never felt the urge."

"Nine years?" he questioned. "You never dated anybody in nine years?"

"Boy, you've really got your figures down, don't you?" Before he could react to her observation she went on. "They've been busy years. I went to school and started a business. Joey was only five when Bill died. The others were fourteen and sixteen. I didn't have time for dating. Why do you ask?"

He glanced at the grass again. "Because it seems to me it'd be good for you. The way you were today in the shop when I came in, frustrated to the point of tears, handling all this stuff you've had to contend with since Greg died. Seems to me dating would be a distraction. It'd be good for you. Somebody to talk over your feelings with, you know?"

She said quietly, "I seem to talk my feelings over with you," then rushed on as if catching herself at an indiscretion. "And I have my family, the kids . . . I'm not lonely. What about you?"

155

"Do I date?"

"That's the question here, I believe."

"Now and then."

"Who are you dating now?"

"Nobody special. Girls are sort of put off when they find out you're a cop. I guess they're afraid to get serious because they think you're going to get blown away or something . . . I don't know. It's a stressful lifestyle, especially on wives, they say. Ostrinski keeps trying to get me to go out with his sister-in-law. She's divorced, has a couple of kids, had a bad marriage to a guy who lied to her for four years while he played around with anybody and everybody, including one of her best friends. I finally told Ostrinski, okay, I'll take her out. Saturday's the day, but I'm not looking forward to it."

"Why not?"

"Two kids, an ex-husband, all this past history she's trying to get over . . ." He gave a rueful shake of the head.

"Sounds like me," Lee remarked.

"You aren't saying your husband—"

"Oh, heavens no. We had a great marriage. Maybe that's why I haven't dated. What I had was so perfect it'd be hard to . . ."

"Hey, you guys, here you are!" Joey came swooping off the path, panting, bumping over the grass, dropping both palms flat on the picnic table, smelling execrable. "Gol, you know how far I went?"

"Clear to South Dakota, judging by what time it is," his mother replied.

"You mad, Mom?"

"Actually, Christopher and I were talking so hard I hadn't even noticed it's nearly dark."

"Jeez, am I relieved. Guess what? I ran into this girl I know . . . Sandy Parker? And she's having an end-of-the-summer party at her house the last week of vacation and I'm invited."

"A party? With girls? And you want to go?"

"Well, Sandy's not like the other girls. She likes to Rollerblade and fish and stuff like that." He swung his hat bill around to the front and used it as a handle to scratch his head. "I can go, can't I, Ma?"

Lee and Chris pushed up off the table. "You can go." The three of them headed back toward the blacktop trail where Joey immediately pulled ahead. "Wait by the truck for us, okay?" she called after him.

For the short remainder of their walk, and all the way back to Anoka, Lee and Christopher found little to say. He was going out on a date next Saturday and they both knew it was an antidote for the him-and-her situation they'd been nurturing since June: the two of them with their mismatched ages, beginning to enjoy each other's company a little bit too much.

Joey jabbered all the way back to the house, unaware of the deflated moods of the two with him. Back at home, Christopher walked them to the door then waited while Lee unlocked it and Joey passed them in his stocking feet, carrying both his shoes and his skates, his stockings filthy.

She watched the screen door slam behind him and muttered, "I give up."

Neither she nor Christopher laughed as they would have earlier in the evening. Somehow their mood had dulled.

"Joey, come back here and thank Chris!" she called.

He reappeared in the entry hall and said through the screen door, "Oh yeah . . . hey, thanks, Chris. It was fun."

"Sure thing. 'Night, Joey."

He disappeared and a moment later the bathroom door slammed. Lee stood on the step above Chris, telling herself she had no right to react this way to his dating a young woman his own age.

"Yes, it was fun. Thank you. You rescued me again and I needed it."

"So did I."

Joey came banging out of the bathroom and flashed past on his way into the kitchen where the cupboard and refrigerator doors started opening and closing. Lord, it was hard to sort out these feelings with a teenager banging around.

"Well, listen . . ." Lee said. "Have a good time Saturday night. Give the woman a chance. Who knows . . . she might turn out to be somebody you like a lot."

He dropped his foot off the step and stood in what she'd come to think of as his *cop pose*, weight distributed evenly on widespread feet, shoulders back, chest erect, chin level with the earth. His key ring was looped over his index finger and he gave it a jingle, then snuffed it in a tight fist.

"Yeah, right," he said, deep in his throat. "Who knows."

He'd already turned away before saying, "Goodnight, Mrs. Reston."

Chapter 8

O<small>N</small> Saturday night Christopher, Pete Ostrinski, his wife, Marge, and sister-in-law, Cathy Switzer, had a date to go bowling. Summer leagues were done, winter leagues hadn't started: the lanes would be half empty.

Pete and Marge lived in a nice new house over in the Mineral Pond addition on the east side of town: split entry with two bedrooms up, finished, two down, unfinished. The seams still showed between the rolls of sod in the front yard, and inside, the place smelled like new carpet and paint.

Pete answered Christopher's knock and walked him up into the living room, where toys shared equal space with furniture and the two women were waiting. He kissed Marge on the cheek. When introductions were performed, Cathy Switzer rose from her chair and shook Christopher's hand; her palm was damp. She was blonde, sharp-featured, relatively attractive in a bony way, but when she smiled her gums showed.

"Hi, Chris," she said. "I've heard a lot about you."

He smiled. "That makes two of us."

Pete said, "Marge has got some drinks out on the patio," and they trailed after him, attempting to make conversation. Outside, drinking a Sprite while the others drank margaritas, Christopher covertly assessed Cathy Switzer.

Her hair was fluffed up into a huge arrangement of disheveled corkscrews that must have taken her some time to accomplish. He quite hated it. She had tiny breasts, skinny hips and an unearthly thinness that gave her the frail look of a matchstick. Plainly thought: She didn't look healthy.

He remembered Lee's admonition to give the woman a chance, and remarked, "Pete tells me you work for a plumbing supply."

"Yes, in the office. I'm going to school two nights a week though, to get my realtor's license."

So she had goals and ambition.

"And you bowl on a league, I hear."

The conversation bumped along like all conversation on all blind dates has bumped along for aeons. The baby-sitter came home from the park with the kids, providing a welcome diversion just before the foursome left for the bowling alley in Pete's car.

Cathy Switzer—it turned out—brought her own ball.

The first time she delivered it down alley number five, Christopher expected to see her skinny little arm snap off at the elbow. Instead, she went into a downswing in perfect form, right leg crossed behind left, shoulders canted in a perfect follow-through, and put enough backspin on the ball to throw pins halfway to the scoring table, had the setter not descended to scrape them away, still whirring.

Naturally, she got a strike.

Everybody clapped, and Cathy blushed as she returned to her seat next to Chris.

"Nice," he said, grinning at her askance.

"Thanks," she said with a pleasing balance of pride and humility.

They had a lot of fun, playing three games, all won by Cathy in her size seven blue jeans with her top-heavy hair, matchstick arms and her gums that showed when she smiled. Afterward they drove down to Fridley to T. R. McCoy's for some burgers, fries and malts, and sat in a rainbow of neon with Fats Domino's "Walkin'" on the jukebox and James Dean smiling down off the walls beside a '59 Merc.

"I like this place," Cathy said. "Mark and I used to—oops!" She covered her lips with four fingers. "Sorry," she whispered, dropping her eyes to the black Formica tabletop.

"That's okay," Christopher said. "Mark's your ex?"

She looked up at him like Betty Boop and nodded.

"The divorce has been final for nine months, but I still slip and mention him sometimes when I'm not supposed to."

Across the table Marge said, "The ass."

Pete nudged her arm. "Marge, come on now, not tonight."

"All right, sorry I called the ass an ass."

Things got tense after that and they decided to call it a night. When they got back to Pete and Marge's house it turned out Cathy had no car, so Christopher offered to drive her home. In his truck he turned on the radio and Cathy stayed buckled onto her half of the seat.

"You like country?" he asked when the music came on.

She said, "Sure."

While Willie Nelson tried his darnedest to sound less than pitiable, she said, "Sorry I mentioned my ex."

"Hey, listen . . . it's okay. I imagine you were with him for a few years. You've got two kids, I hear."

"Yeah, Grady and Robin. They're five and three. He never comes to see them. He married my best friend and he's busy with her kids now."

He wondered what to say. "That's tough."

"You're only the second guy I've been out with since my divorce. The first one never called back."

"Probably because you took him on the pro bowling tour."

She laughed and said, "Mark hated it when I bowled. It was okay for him to go running all over the country taking my best friend to bed, but he didn't like it when I went out with the girls from work to our bowling league."

He began to regret telling her it was okay to talk about this guy.

"What hurts worst," she went on, "is that a lot of the stuff he'd never do with me and the kids, he does with her and her kids. I know because I talk to his mother, and sometimes she slips and mentions things." She talked nonstop about her ex-husband, barely pausing to give directions to her townhouse. When they got there, she said, "Oh, are we here already?"

"Wait there," he said, got out, pocketed his keys and went around to open her door.

"It's been a long time since a guy has done that for me," she said. "That kind of stuff stopped long before Mark divorced me. That's sort of how I knew something was going on."

He trailed along after her to a concrete walk that took two turns between buildings and led them to a ground-floor door without an outside light. There she took one step up and turned to him.

"Well, I've enjoyed it," she said. "Thanks a lot for the bowling and the burgers and everything."

"I enjoyed it, too," he said. "Especially the bowling, even though you beat everything in sight. It's fun to watch somebody do something that well."

"You're sweet," she said.

"Sweet?" he repeated with a chuckle. "I'm a lot of things, but sweet I don't think is one of them."

"Well, you put up with me crying on your shoulder all night about Mark. That's sweet, isn't it?"

"Hey, listen," he said, taking a step backward. "Good luck. I know it's hard losing someone that way, but I hope everything works out for you and your kids."

She stood in shadow so deep he couldn't make out her face. He had the impression her hands were stuck into the tight front pockets of her jeans, and her puffy hair created a faint nimbus in the dark around her head.

Suddenly he took pity on her. "You know, Cathy, you ought to get over him. Somebody who treats his wife and family like that doesn't deserve any tears."

"Who says I cry about him?"

He saw himself getting in deeper than he wanted with this deluded woman and backed away another step. "Listen . . . I've got to go. Good luck, Cathy."

When he got a yard down the sidewalk she stopped him. "Hey, Chris?"

He turned.

"Would you . . ." She paused uncertainly. "Come here?"

He knew what was coming and experienced little joy in the presumption. Nevertheless he again took pity on her and moved to the base of the stoop, which put their heads on the same level.

"Listen," she whispered, and he heard her swallow as she put her hands on his collar. "I know you're not coming back again either, and that's all right . . . I mean, really it is!" She spoke anxiously. "I mean, I talk too much about Mark and I know that. But before you go, would you mind very much if I kissed you? I mean, it's been a long, long time since he left, and I know you don't like me or anything, and I don't want you to go away thinking I ask strange guys to kiss me all the time. You're a cop, like Pete, and I trust you . . . I mean, I know you think this is a pretty dumb thing to ask, but it's been . . . I've been . . . I've been so lonely . . . and . . . and it would be the sweetest thing you could do for me if you'd just stand there and . . . well, I don't care . . . pretend I'm somebody else if you want . . . and let me kiss you."

Something in his heart twisted. Lonely he understood. Lonely was Judd Quincy waiting with his foot against the wall of the 7-Eleven store. Lonely was little Chris Lallek waiting for his mom and dad to come home so he could ask them for money for a band uniform. Lonely was this skinny, divorced woman laboring under the delusion that she didn't love her philandering husband anymore.

He didn't wait for her to kiss him. He kissed her—an honest, full-mouthed French kiss, holding nothing back. She felt like a bundle of kindling wood in his arms, and he put from his mind the way her gums showed when she smiled, and how unnatural her hair looked, all tortured up three times bigger than her narrow little face.

He'd kissed enough women that he felt the universal pull of all that went along with it; he gave himself over to that universality, to the pre-mating ritual of running hands over backs, and tongues over tongues, and fitting two bodies together so that the line of one obscures the other.

It stopped when Cathy ran her hands down the rear pockets of his jeans and made a place for him between her thighs. His sympathy didn't extend quite that far.

He pulled her arms from behind his neck, stepped back and gripped both her hands hard.

"Listen," he said throatily. "I gotta go. You take care of yourself now."

"Yeah. You too."

When their hands parted and she stayed on her stoop, he couldn't help but breathe a sigh of relief.

* * *

Odd, for a woman he hadn't particularly liked, she stayed on his mind a lot the next couple of days. Then he realized why: He was comparing her to Lee Reston. She had a Dolly Parton hairdo, not Lee's short, unaffected cap, which took wind and weather as it would. She had a profile like an eleven-year-old girl, not the rounded curves of maturity. She had a bony, emaciated face instead of a full, healthy one. And those gums—ye gods. Had he really French-kissed her? Well, hell, the kiss hadn't been so bad if he really stopped to think about it. Cathy Switzer's greatest shortcoming was simple enough for Christopher to understand: She wasn't Lee Reston.

Damn, but that woman stayed on his mind a lot. Not a day went by that he didn't think of her and manufacture excuses to see her, which he most often decided not to act on.

Several days passed after his date without either seeing or speaking to Lee. Then one day he was standing in his kitchen scooping ice cream into a bowl when someone slipped a piece of paper under his door. He reacted like a policeman: leaped and yanked the door open suddenly, to confront whoever was on the other side.

And there was Lee, leaping back in fright.

"Christopher!" She pressed her heart. "Lord, you scared me! I didn't think you were home. I thought you were working days."

"It's my day off." He looked down the hall both ways, then at the envelope on the floor. "What's this?"

"Something of yours I found stuck between Greg's papers. I think it's an insurance card. I must have picked it up when I was taking some things out of your kitchen drawer."

He opened the envelope and perused the item. "Oh yeah . . . I was looking for this."

"Sorry." She shrugged.

"You could have mailed it."

"I know. I was passing by."

He studied her in her green canvas skirt, white blouse and slip-on shoes, her healthy middle-age robustness so different from Cathy Switzer. He had done the right thing; he'd tried a date, tried meeting someone new, but it had only served to point out how much he enjoyed the woman standing before him in the hall.

"Wanna come in?" He stepped back and motioned toward the kitchen.

"No. I've got to go home and fix supper for Joey."

"Oh. Well, okay then." They stood awhile coming to terms with her correct decision before he dropped one shoulder and said, appealingly, "Well, hell, you can come in for a minute, can't you?"

"What were you doing?" She bent forward from the waist, going up on tiptoe to peek around the open door.

"Having a bowl of ice cream."

"At suppertime?"

"Yeah. You want one?"

She settled back down on her heels. "No, I really have to go."

"All right then," he said, accepting her decision, but wishing if she was going to go, she'd go, because they both knew it wasn't what she wanted to do. "Say hi to Joey. I gotta go," he added with a hint of irritation, "my ice cream is melting."

"Well, you don't have to get mad at me." If someone were to point out how childish they sounded they both would have made loud protestations of denial.

"I'm not mad at you."

"All right then, could I change my mind about the ice cream?"

He waved her in, shut the door and followed her into the kitchen, where he took out a glass dish and scooped out ice cream. "You want topping?" He opened a cupboard door and hung a hand from it while taking a tally of its contents. "There's chocolate, caramel and . . ." He picked up a moldy bottle of something, turned and made a perfect shot into a garbage can next to the stove. "I guess there's just chocolate and caramel."

"Caramel," she said.

He drizzled some straight from the jar, caught the stalactite with a finger and sucked it off. Recapping the bottle, he put it away, found spoons, then brought the two sundaes to the kitchen table.

"Sit down," he ordered.

"Thanks."

They ate in silence until half their ice cream was gone. Then Lee asked, "So how was your blind date on Saturday?"

"Great," he answered. "She owned her own bowling ball."

A stretch of silence passed before Lee asked, "So, are you going to see her again?"

"Why do you ask?" He watched her carefully, but she refused to meet his eyes.

"I was just wondering, that's all."

He got up and took their bowls to the sink, rinsed them both and put them in the dishwasher. When he finished, he stayed clear across the room from her, catching his hips and both palms against the edge of the countertop, studying her back while she remained at the table waiting for his answer. After an uncomfortable stretch of silence he sighed—an enormous effort to relieve the tension in his shoulders—and spoke resignedly.

"No," he told her.

She twisted around in her chair and stared at him but said nothing.

"She was pathetic," he added, pushing off the cabinet and returning to the table, where he took the chair at a right angle to her. A fingernail clipper lay on the table. He picked it up and let it slide between the pads of his thumb and index finger time and time again, turning it end for end each time his fingers touched the table.

"She was a skinny pathetic little thing who got dumped by some jerk who had an affair with her best friend, then married her."

"Could we give her a name, please?" Lee requested.

He looked up at her and the fingernail clipper stopped sliding. "Cathy," he said, "Cathy Switzer."

Lee sat with her arms crossed on the table, motionless, studying him.

He threw down the fingernail clipper and went on. "She talked about him all night long. Couldn't stop. How he never liked her to go bowling. How he never came to see his kids anymore. How the first guy she saw after the divorce never came back after one date. And when I walked her to her door she said over and over how she knew she'd talked about him all night long and that I was never going to come back either. Then she asked me to kiss her." He let his eyes wander to Lee and settle there. His voice lost its rough edge. "She said she was lonely, and that she trusted me because I was a cop, and would I just kiss her once and that she didn't care if I pretended she was someone else."

The silence seemed to run itself out into minutes before Lee asked, "And did you?"

It took some time for him to answer, time during which their glances collided and held.

"Yes," he finally said, so low it sounded like someone else had spoken in a faraway room. Their stillness, both with arms crossed on the table, remained absolute. The ambivalence of her question remained: Did he kiss the woman, or did he pretend she was someone else? He thought it best not to fill in the entire truth. The strain in the room got to him, however, and he realized it was the same for her. They had both been dancing around their feelings for each other, afraid to admit them, afraid of this vast difference in their ages and the unwritten rule of propriety it posed. They could go on pretending friendly indifference forever, but he knew and she knew that feelings had begun stirring between them, and one of them had to get it out in the open, because it was hell holding it inside. But there were things she should know first, things he'd told rarely in his life that were important for her to hear.

"I think it's time I told you a little more about myself, Lee. Bear with me, if you will, because some of this you've heard before, and it's rather a long story, but until you hear it all, you can't understand where I'm coming from."

Christopher shifted in his chair, making the wood snap and creak. He picked up the nail clipper again and squeezed it in his palm, concentrating on it as if it were a scientific experiment. "I've told you some of what it was like when I was growing up. How my mom and dad left me to take care of my little sister. All they cared about was where their next drink was coming from. Groceries didn't matter. If there were any in the house, fine. If not, hell with it.

"There was this grocery store two doors down from the apartment where we lived. The Red Owl. I found out what time of day they cleaned out their produce department and I used to make sure I was back there in the alley when this guy named Sammy Saminski used to bring all the wilted stuff out and put it in the dumpster. Some of it was pretty good yet, edible. Sammy would let me take it home. He was a smart guy, Sammy. Didn't take him long to figure out Jeannie and I were living on the stuff. So eventually he started bringing out better stuff. I knew it was still plenty good yet, but I took it anyway. And that's why I learned to cook, so there'd be something on the table for Jeannie and me.

"Mavis and Ed, they might come stumbling in at ten o'clock, maybe midnight—we never knew. How they survived is a mystery to me because I never saw them eat. Just drink and fight, that's all. She used to call the cops on him every once in a while and that's when I first got the idea I'd like to become one, because when I saw that officer walk in in his clean blue uniform I thought for sure he was going to take Jeannie and me away and put us in someplace better, and it was the only time in my life I ever felt safe. It didn't last long though, because instead of taking us, they took the old man. He'd stay in the clink a day or two, and while he was gone Mavis seemed to be around a little more taking care of us. But then Ed would be back out, and he and Mavis would take up their drinking again as if she'd never called the cops in the first place.

"One time when she called them, he had the DTs. He was standing in front of a medicine chest pulling back his lips and looking in the mirror, and he thought there were worms eating his teeth. I can remember Mavis yelling, 'Ed, Ed, there's nothing there!' And he raved, 'Can't you see 'em, Mavis, the goddamn things are eating my teeth!'

"That was one of the worst times I remember. Jeannie and I were both crying. Hell, we didn't know what was going on. And that policeman came and I wanted so damn bad for him to take us out of there. But he didn't." Christopher stared at the fingernail clipper in his hand, then seemed to pull himself from the past and shift his weight on the chair. He settled his back against it and went on.

"Sammy Saminski got me on the payroll at the Red Owl when I was fourteen. He lied about my age. By the time I graduated from high school I was managing the produce department and I'd saved enough money to put myself through two years of vocational school. When I could, I'd give some to Jeannie. She hoarded it away without telling me, and when she was fifteen years old, she ran away."

Christopher cleared his throat. "I think I told you once before that my parents still live here in Anoka. Still drink. Still fight. I don't have anything to do with them."

He looked at Lee—dear, sweet Lee—and decided he didn't care if she saw love in his eyes. He was damned tired of trying to hide it.

"And then you come into my life. And do you know what you are to me? You're all the things they weren't. You're everything a mother should be. You're kind and loving and caring; you're there for your kids no matter what they need. You earn a living and provide for them. They can talk to you about anything, and you love them—you genuinely love them, and they love you back. And all of a sudden I'm right in there being treated like I'm one of them. Then Greg dies and I feel like I've taken his place. And you know what? I love it."

His volume had lowered to a coarse whisper. "Then this woman Saturday night . . . she asks me to kiss her and she says it's okay if I pretend she's someone else. And you know who I was thinking about, don't you, Lee?"

"Christopher, stop!" She jumped up, crossed the room, faced the kitchen sink with her back to him.

"I'm so damned mixed up, Lee."

"Stop, I said!" He could hear terror in her voice.

"You don't want to hear this."

"I don't want to lose your friendship and that's what'll happen if you go on with this."

"Yes, I know. That's why I'm scared."

"Then drop it. Now. Before any more is said."

He considered awhile, waiting for her to turn and face him. When he realized she would not, he whispered, "All right."

She turned on the water. Took a drink. Turned off the water. Set down her glass. All these motions having nothing to do with thirst. Neither of them had looked at the other since she'd leaped from her chair.

She said quietly, "I've got to go."

An aeon seemed to pass while neither of them moved. Then he asked a question.

"How old are you?"

She made a sound—chortle? grunt? he wasn't sure which—and moved to the door, opened it before she spoke.

"Old enough to be your mother."

She went out and left him sitting on his kitchen chair.

Left behind, he remained right there, brooding, disappointed, angry with himself for reading her wrong and opening his mouth, fearing their friendship would end now. Well, what the hell, she was probably scared, too, and she had a lot more at stake than he did.

After twenty minutes he shot to his feet, found his truck keys, drove to the police station, stalked into the squad room and went directly to the computer in the corner. It was on, its screen a quivering green.

He pushed QMR and waited. Nokes sauntered in eating an apple and said, "What the heck are you doing?"

"Looking something up."

"On your day off?"

He slowly turned his chair seat around and gave Nokes a wincing look of long-suffering. "Nokes, haven't you got anything better to do than stand around here crunching that apple in my ear?"

Nokes shrugged and walked down the hall to the communications room.

Query Motor Vehicle was waiting when Christopher turned back to the screen, asking him to put in his initials before it would give out any information.

He entered his initials and the machine sounded a *beep,* giving him the go-ahead.

He typed in her license plate number, pushed the code button and swung around in his chair to listen for the printer in the communications room. It began clattering and he walked down the hall to the room where tonight's dispatcher and records technician, Toni Mansetti and Ruth Randall, were sitting on their respective chairs doing their jobs. Nokes had hooked his buns against a table edge, crossed his legs and was finishing his apple while lazily watching a couple of split-screen televisions that monitored the city parking ramps across the street.

The printer stopped clattering and Christopher reached over Ruth Randall's shoulder to rip the sheet off.

He left the communications room reading the info from the Minnesota Bureau of Driver's Licenses.

Lee Therese Reston
1225 BENTON STREET   ANOKA 55303
SEX/F. DOB/091848.   HGT/506.   WGT/130.   EYE/BRN
PHOTO #: 8082095102.
NO VIOLATIONS
NO HIT
QDP NAM/RESTON, LEE THERESE. DOB/091848

He read the last item again: Date of birth: 9-18-48.
She was forty-four years old.

* * *

Lee had left Christopher's apartment just as upset as he was.

How dare he! she thought, lying awake in the dark that night. How dare he wreck the fragile balance they'd managed during these past couple of months! She needed him, treasured the times they spent together, because she could talk to him about things nobody else seemed to understand. She could be herself—sorrowful or gay—and he accepted whatever mood she was in.

How dare he ruin that by intimating he had other-than-friendly feelings toward her? Anything else was unthinkable, given their ages and his relationship to this family as a whole. Why, Janice had a crush on him! Joey thought he was the neatest thing since pointed footballs, and every other person in the entire family knew how much time he spent around here.

Good god-afrighty, imagine the gasps if anybody got wind of this.

Especially Mother.

August turned the corner into September and Christopher stayed away. Joey started football practice, then school. Lee arranged her working schedule so that she could go to his junior high games in the late afternoons once each week.

At the shop huge bronze and maroon football mums started coming in. The arrangers began putting miniature cattails and preserved gold maple leaves in their fresh bouquets. A new batch of FTD containers came in, shaped like mallard ducks.

Janice moved into her dorm at the university, and Lee stubbornly withheld Christopher's offer of help, pressing her lazy son (who rammed his body against football dummies every afternoon for two hours but said he was too tired to help move the furniture) into duty instead. The three of them—Joey, Janice and Lee—spent a beautiful Sunday after-noon in mid-September lugging Greg's mattress, box spring and bed onto Jim Clements's pickup truck and hauling it thirty miles into the city, then up two flights of stairs at the dormitory.

Janice bid them goodbye with a hug and a promise. "Don't feel so bad, Mom. I've got my car so I'll come home a lot on weekends."

That was, very possibly, the worst week of Lee's life. She began to understand why a lonely woman would ask a strange man to kiss her even though she knew perfectly well he was never going to ask her on a date again.

Such splendid fall days.

Such beautiful fall nights, and after supper—lo!—Joey would come out of the bathroom smelling like deodorant with his hair freshly combed and wearing clean sweat socks *and* shoes.

"A bunch of us kids are going to walk uptown and get a Coke," he'd say. And a bunch of them—boys and girls together—would come in a group and spirit him away. Later, at a very respectable hour, they'd be back in the yard, hanging around the front steps talking and laughing in the moonlight. One of them, she overheard, was named Sandy Parker.

Lee began to feel like a useless old woman.

Then on September eighteenth (a day she'd been dreading as much as she'd dreaded her first root canal) at precisely 10:32 A.M. (she would forever recall the time because she was so used to tracking delivery times, she actually tracked this one made *to* her) Ivan Small, the delivery man for her biggest competitor, Forrest Floral on Fourth Avenue, entered her shop bearing an arrangement of American Beauty roses so huge it made Ivan look like a walking bouquet.

"Mizz Reston?" he said from behind his burden, then set it down on the counter and stepped to one side so he could see her. "I don't know what's going on, but we got an order to deliver this to you here at your shop."

"Are you kidding?" she replied.

"God's truth. Forty-five of them," he said. He wore an expression like the lion in *The Wizard of Oz.*

"Oh God." She covered the bottom of her face and felt herself begin to blush while Sylvia, Pat and Nancy stood in wonderment.

"They're from Mom and Dad," she said hopefully. "Or Lloyd. I'll bet they're from Lloyd."

"There's a card." Ivan plucked it from the foliage and handed it to her.

So help me God, if it's from Christopher and Sylvia reads his name over my shoulder, I'll drive over him with his own cop car!

171

The card said: *Your secret is out.*

Now she'd have some fancy explaining to do.

"Thank you, Ivan," she said. "Oh, wait!"

She opened the cash register and got out five dollars, and felt ridiculous tipping somebody else's flower delivery man at the door of her own shop.

Ivan accepted, said, "Thank you, Mizz Reston," and left.

The second the door closed, all three women asked, "Who are they from?"

"I don't know," Lee lied.

"Well, have you been . . . *dating* anyone?" Sylvia actually seemed to trip over the word.

"Heavens no."

"Then how do you explain it?"

"Your guess is as good as mine."

She took them home and put them in the middle of the kitchen table where never in all her years as a florist had she brought this many roses at one time. The damn fool! These things ran thirty-six dollars a dozen at retail. He'd paid well over one hundred dollars, not counting tax and delivery, for an item she could have gotten from her supplier for half that.

She couldn't help being charmed. Sitting there on her kitchen chair squeezing her mouth, she held in a laugh, but soon it escaped, lilting through the room and making her heart feel light.

"Lallek, you young fool," she said aloud, "what am I going to do with you?"

Joey came home from football practice and actually paused for a full fifteen seconds on his way to the refrigerator.

"Wow, Mom, did you bring them home?"

"They're not throw-aways from my store, if that's what you mean."

"Where'd they come from then?"

"I don't know." She had put the card in her billfold on her way home. "There are forty-five of them."

"One for every hamburger I'm going to eat as soon as Janice gets home and we take you out to eat."

"Are you serious, Joey? Janice is coming home?" She leaped from the chair, the roses forgotten.

"That's right, so get changed. We're going to take you out to the restaurant of your choice. As long as the bill doesn't run over twenty dollars."

Janice came bounding in with a great big hug. "Happy birthday, Mom! Did Joey keep my secret? . . . Gosh, did you bring those flowers home?"

"I've been wondering if they're from Grampa Lloyd. I don't think Mom and Dad would spend that kind of money."

"Grampa Lloyd, huh?" Janice headed toward the bathroom, looking at the flowers over her shoulder. From behind the closed bathroom door she called, "Wasn't there any card?"

Lee Reston pretended she didn't hear, and by the time they were in the car heading for the Vineyard Café, the card was forgotten.

Chapter 9

*S*HE was afraid to call him. Two weeks passed. Three. Then on an afternoon in early October Lee stood on the bleachers of Fred Moore Middle School with a sparse collection of other parents. Down below a game was in progress. Up above weather was churning. A morose layer of low gray scud clouds tumbled along before a pushy wind. Debris, caught in the chain link fence, flapped against it like a playing card against bicycle spokes. The field was wet; they'd had rain the night before. Even from here Lee could see she'd have fun trying to get the stains out of Joey's uniform.

He was a defensive lineman, a position that garnered little glory in most games, especially from moms of ninth graders without men beside them to explain what was happening. But suddenly the line broke and she saw her clumsy son spurt through like O.J. Simpson through an airport, eluding tackles, sidestepping arms, running an abbreviated U-turn and hauling the opposing quarterback smack off his pins!

She stuck her pinkies between her teeth and whistled. "Hey, way to go, Joey!" She whistled again, this time without the fingers, brandishing one fist in the air. She yelled at the top of her lungs, "You could show those Vikings a thing or two!"

On the street above the field, Officer Christopher Lallek parked his black-and-white squad, turned up the collar of his navy blue winter jacket and slammed the door.

Down below, white and blue jerseys darted around like dots on a video screen. He threaded his way inside the chain link fence and giant-stepped down the bleachers, searching for Joey's number. There it was, number eighteen, blue. He was halfway down the steps when the kid made a damned good sack, and the Fred Moore parents sent up some noise. He glanced along the bleachers to his right and there was Lee. She was dressed in a thick blue denim jacket almost to her knees. Her collar was up. Her cheeks were red. And she had two fingers stuck in her mouth, whistling.

Smiling crookedly, he clumped onto the metal bench and moved toward her. She raised a fist and yelled, clapped some, then jammed her hands into her pockets and hunched her shoulders against the wind.

His footfalls made the metal bench clang.

She turned and saw him approaching. The hunch dropped from her shoulders and her eyes grew bright, though her mouth was hidden behind a generous upturned collar.

"Hi," he said, stopping beside her.

It took her a while to answer while their eyes made up for lost days and their pulses got unruly.

"Hi."

The wind ruffled her hair. It buffeted their backs and pushed them from behind.

"Haven't seen you for a while," he ventured.

"No." She finally looked away, back to the football field.

"So how's the game going?" He, too, turned his attention below.

"Fred Moore is behind but Joey just made a great play."

"I saw it. Saw you whistling, too. Pretty impressive. I don't know many women who can whistle like a cattle drover."

They grinned at each other askance, with their collars still hiding their mouths. Another play broke below and she hollered, "Get him! Get him!"

The teams huddled and Christopher returned to studying Lee.

"So, how've you been?"

"Gettin' older," she replied smugly, keeping her eyes steadfastly on the field.

175

"Yeah, so I heard."

They watched two whole plays before she said, "I got your flowers." She turned, her eyes filled with humor. "I didn't know whether to thank you or ram 'em up your nose holes."

"To the best of my recollection, you didn't do either."

"How'd you find out?"

"Ran your plate number through Motor Vehicle Registrations. Lee Therese Reston, September 18, 1948."

"All right, so now you know and maybe you'll understand why I got upset that day."

"Hey, listen. Can we just forget that day? It won't happen again."

She turned back to the field and began alternating feet to warm them up. She was wearing black leggings that disappeared into black patent-leather boots with fur around the ankles.

He watched for her reactions while he said, "I missed you."

She stopped stamping, going motionless for a moment with her hands in her pockets and her eyes on the field. "I missed you too," she said, then swung her face to him. "And I never got so many roses in one bunch in my entire life. Thank you."

"My pleasure," he said.

They spent some seconds enjoying the fact that they'd reconnected before she let her mouth quirk. "You damn fool. I could have gotten them for you at half the price, wholesale."

He reared back and laughed. "Wouldn't have been half as much fun though, would it?"

The ref's whistle blew and they remembered why they were there. The play stopped, however, and the teams went back to their huddles.

"So," she said as if their past contretemps had not happened, "you want to come over Saturday night and have some pot roast with Joey and me?"

With that simple question his life became happy again. "You don't have to ask me twice."

They grinned at each other in anticipation until his radio crackled and he reached for it.

"One Bravo Seventeen."

The dispatcher came back, giving him a staticky message.

"Copy," he replied, and to Lee, who hadn't comprehended a word the dispatcher had said, "Teenage runaway. Gotta go check it out. What time on Saturday?"

"Six-thirty."

He touched his hat, walked two steps away, then came back. "You gonna make gravy?"

"I take it you like gravy?"

"Never learned how to make it myself."

"What's a pot roast without gravy?"

His lingering smile said the last thing he wanted to do at that minute was check out a teenage runaway. "See you."

She swiveled and watched him respond to duty, his thick-soled black shoes making the metal bleacher tremble beneath her feet, the crease in his navy trousers breaking behind the knees, his jacket puffed out above the waist, the leather holders full of heavy paraphernalia hanging thick from his belt, even in back. He turned left, bounded up the steps, taking them two at a time. She watched him climb to the top, turning her back to the field while he shouldered his way around the opening in the chain link fence and walked briskly to his squad car. Opening the door he glanced down, saw her following his progress and raised a hand in farewell.

She saw his smile and waved back, watching until the black-and-white pulled away, amazed at how his return into her life lent it a buoyancy that had been lacking since she'd spooked and cut him out of it. All right, so she might be making a mistake, but Lord it felt good to be looking forward to a night with him again.

On Saturday evening one of those bleak October rains was falling when Christopher arrived at Lee's house. Joey answered the bell and said, "Hi, Chris."

"What do you say, Joe?"

"Saw you at my game Wednesday."

"Sorry I couldn't stick around. I got a call. But I saw your sack. Man, you really nailed him!"

"I got him again in the last quarter, too! Jeez, you should've seen that guy. Took him the whole time-out to get back on his feet, and then after that his linemen were really on me. This one big bruiser . . ."

Lee stuck her head around the kitchen corner and despaired of getting a word in edgewise. She wagged two fingers at Christopher while Joey went on babbling excitedly, moving toward the kitchen with their guest, walking backward without realizing it.

For Christopher, returning to this place, to these people, to these homey comforts filled his heart with a sense of belonging. The table was set for three. Some bronze-colored flowers decorated the middle of it. The kitchen was bright and cozy with the rain beating against the sliding door and the curtains drawn against the dark. The smell in the place made his mouth water—beef and cooked onions, coffee, fragrant steam rising from kettles on the stove. And, of course, there was Lee wearing carpet slippers and a blue sweat suit, moving about, getting a meal ready while her son rambled on as he would with a father or a big brother.

". . . and the coach said, 'Tear their legs off!' and I think I almost did. Hey, Mom, Chris was there when I made my first sack! He saw it!"

"Yes, I know. Hi, Christopher." She was thickening gravy at the stove, and neither of them gave away their gladness at being together.

"Smells good in here."

"You bet your badge. I didn't eat much today. Hope it's okay if I put it on right away. Joey, will you fill the milk glasses?"

Christopher asked, "Can I do something?"

"Sure. You can put this salt and pepper shaker on the table." She handed him the pair. "Then reach up onto the top shelf behind me and get down two bowls for the potatoes and the carrots."

Such plain family activity, but moving around the room together, Christopher and Lee felt a subtle shift in their relationship. Perhaps, for the moment, they simply indulged in playing house. He got down the bowls, she filled them, then put them in his hands. Women set tables differently than men, he noticed. Not only bronze flowers, but bearded wheat sticking out of them, and place mats and a pair of rust-colored candles. She handed him matches and he lit them. There was a jumble of activity—Joey with the milk, Lee opening the oven door, finding pot holders, running water into empty kettles, handing Chris another bowl of food to set on the table.

Then, at last, the three of them sat down to a tableful of steaming foods that Norman Rockwell surely must have painted dozens of times. Roast beef, mashed potatoes, rich dark gravy, bright orange carrots, sweet peas in a thick white sauce, a tossed green salad and something brown, moist and unidentifiable in a casserole dish so hot it burned Christopher's fingers.

"Ouch!"

"You okay?"

"Yeah." Mesmerized, he reached again . . . for the spoon this time. "What's this?"

"Corn-bread stuffing with pork sausage."

"Oh my Go-o-o-d." He drew out the word as if singing a canticle.

They feasted for the better part of an hour while the raindrops tapped against the window like a thousand impatient fingers, while the warmth from the oven suffused the room, and a fourteen-year-old boy amused them all with tales of football and school pranks. They laughed and had refills and Joey asked Christopher what was the first bust he ever made. Christopher wore a self-deprecating grin as he replied that the very first day of work he was watching the crosswalk by Lincoln Elementary when he'd spied a seven-year-old urinating against the corner of the school building. Scared the kid half to death when a great big police officer in an official blue uniform stood above him and gave him a lecture. Forever after, everybody at the station snickered when they recalled that on his first day on the force Chris Lallek busted a seven-year-old for peeing on the school building.

The three at the table laughed and felt relaxed with each other. Lee said, "There's apple cobbler and ice cream." Christopher expanded his chest and rubbed his stomach. "I couldn't hold one more morsel . . ." He released his breath and added, ". . . But give me an extra scoop."

When his dessert was gone, Christopher said, "That's the best meal I've had since the last time I ate at your house. Thanks, Lee."

"It's nice to cook for a man again." It was true. Joey was merely an eating machine. He'd eat metal bolts if they were sautéed in butter. But cooking for a man was different, and there was no denying she'd put extra effort into tonight's meal.

They worked together cleaning up the kitchen, rinsing dishes, loading the dishwasher. Lee was washing off the top of the stove when she paused and said, "Christopher, I know I shouldn't take advantage of you, but would you do me a favor?"

"Name it."

"I put a couple of rugs in the washer the other day and it walked halfway across the basement floor, then afterwards it was sagging way down on one corner. Would you mind leveling it for me?"

"Don't mind at all."

"Joey, will you go downstairs with Chris and show him where?"

Her laundry room was all finished off and brightly lit. A pair of her panty hose hung from a towel bar on a plastic clothespin. Chris thought about taking them off her sometime. Joey got one of his dad's levels and they jostled the machine onto two legs and screwed the other two this way and that until the machine sat level.

Christopher was dusting off the knees of his jeans when she came to the laundry room doorway rubbing lotion into her hands. "Ah, you fixed it. Thank you so much." She walked past him, plucked the panty hose down and folded them. "Most things I'll tackle on my own, but that's one I won't. Thanks again."

She led the way back upstairs. "Anybody for a game of Parcheesi?"

They began a game of Parcheesi, but midway through it Joey got a phone call—obviously from a girl. His voice cracked from contralto to soprano and back again while he said, "Oh, hi, I thought you were going out with your family to your aunt's house tonight . . . Yeah, but just a minute." He covered the mouthpiece with his hand. "Hey, Mom, would you hang this up when I get in your bedroom?"

She complied, and returned to the kitchen table, crooking a knee onto her chair seat while standing beside it. "He'll be on for two hours. The telephone is his newest toy. You want to keep playing or should we watch TV?"

"What do you want to do?"

"Watch TV. I'm tired. I worked today."

"Me too. I'll help you put this away."

When the Parcheesi game was boxed, they went into the living room and she tucked herself into a corner of the sofa while he stretched out on his back on the floor.

"Hey, there are chairs," she said.

"No, this is fine." He tipped his chin up and looked at her backward, then concentrated on the screen.

"All right, stubborn." She tossed him a sofa pillow that landed on his face. He tucked it beneath his head and said, "Thanks."

A situation comedy flickered through its tired scenes before them.

She flicked channels with the remote control. The rain kept pummeling the windows behind the closed curtains. In the bedroom, Joey laughed, then his voice returned to a distant murmur. Lee lowered the volume on the TV. Occasionally her eyes would wander to the figure stretched out across her living room floor, to his flat stomach and crossed ankles and everything in between. Guiltily, she looked away and returned her attention to the television.

But it swerved back to him of its own accord.

"Hey, Christopher?" she said.

"Hm?"

"I've been thinking a lot about the story you told me . . . about your growing up." He lay very still with his hands behind his head. "I'm glad you told me. It makes me understand your relationship with Judd."

"I didn't tell you so you'd feel sorry for me."

"I know that. But I'm glad you did just the same. Your parents . . . they sound like very sad creatures." She waited but he said nothing. "Do you think it would make any difference if you tried to make peace with them?"

"No, I don't."

"Have you ever tried?"

"Drop it, Lee."

"But they're your parents."

He sat up and swung around to face her. "Hey, listen," he said calmly. "We've got to get one thing straight. Don't crusade with me about them. I know it's hard for you to swallow, but I hate them. And with just cause. In my book, a parent doesn't *inherit* the right to respect from his children, he *earns* it. And mine missed the chance years ago."

"But surely everybody deserves a second chance."

"I said, drop it, Lee." She could hear the tight control in his voice.

"But, Christopher, family is so important and they're your—"

"As far as I'm concerned, they're dead."

"Why, Christopher, that's an awful thing to say!"

He leaped to his feet, threw the pillow onto the sofa and headed for the front coat closet.

She was up and after him instantly. "Christopher, I'm sorry." She caught his arm before he reached the front hall. "I'm sorry," she repeated. "It's just that . . ."

He spun on her. "It's just that you live in a dream world, Lee." She had never seen his mouth like that, curled in upon itself in a hard, flat-cheeked face. "You think that just because your mom twirls a baton at a Fourth of July picnic and your dad grills steaks you can somehow get the whole world to do that? Woman, you are *so* naive! You were born into this ideal family, and you raised an ideal one of your own, but they're not all like that. There are millions of Judds in this country— poor, hungry, neglected, scared to death because they don't know what's going to happen to them the next day. And so they turn to drugs and gangs. They become pushers and rapists. Well, I'm one of the few lucky ones who got out—no thanks to my parents. So don't ask me to forgive them, Lee. Don't ever ask that of me, because I won't."

She took his face in her two hands and whispered, "So much anger. I've never seen it before."

He jerked away, twisting his head up and to one side. "Don't!"

She dropped her hands. "I'm sorry," she whispered.

He got his jacket out of the closet. "No, I'm the one who's sorry. I spoiled this perfectly nice Saturday night after you went to so much trouble cooking for me and everything. And I had a good time talking to Joey and . . ." He'd put his jacket on and zipped it up. At the top of the zipper his hands stalled while he looked at her beseechingly. "I'm sorry I ruined it, that's all."

"I shouldn't have brought up the subject of your parents. I promise I won't again, okay?"

He took some gloves out of his pocket and flapped them toward the bedroom. "Okay if I go say goodbye to Joey?"

She stepped back and said, "Sure."

He went down the hall and leaned into her bedroom, glimpsing it for the first time—perfume bottles on a dresser, open closet doors with dresses hanging inside. Joey was lying on top of a blue-flowered bedspread that was all messed up beneath him. The bottom of one enlarged sock was pointed straight at the doorway, propped on top of a knee. Two pillows were piled beneath his head. They, too, had blue floral cases.

"Hey, Joey . . . see ya. Gotta go."

"Already?" Into the phone Joey said, "Just a minute."

Christopher flourished the pair of gloves. "Thanks. I enjoyed it. I'll try to stop by one of your games again before the season is over."

"Yeah, sure . . . hey . . . glad you came."

At the front door Lee was still waiting. He paused before her. Their eyes met, parted, met again. He became preoccupied with stacking and restacking his leather gloves.

"I'm not mad at you," he said. "It's just that . . . well, I'm a little frustrated." He gave in and looked directly into her autumn-colored eyes. They were much the same hue as the flowers she'd put on their supper table. They were eyes he thought of so much when he was away from her, eyes whose mood he'd learned to read so well. When he spoke, his voice came out in a gritty near-whisper. "What are we doing, Lee?"

"Healing," she said.

"Is that all?"

She looked away. "Please, Christopher."

He sighed and tapped his gloves on his palm, then slowly drew them on. So she wanted to pretend this was a platonic relationship. Hell and high water, the idea of it scared him worse than his feelings for her.

"Can I call you again?" he asked.

"I don't know," she said. "This is getting too complicated for me."

"Well, let me add a new wrinkle," he said, and without planning to, he leaned down and kissed her on the mouth, a kiss short enough to prevent immediate trouble but long enough to portend great long-range trouble ahead: This was no son's friend pecking a mother-figure on the cheek. She was still standing with her lips open in surprise when he said, low, "Sorry," and walked out without giving her a chance to speak.

He expected her to call and she did, though not until after eleven that night. He figured Joey must have been on the line all that time and it was the first chance she had to use it.

He was already in bed, lying awake in the dark thinking of her when the phone rang. He rolled over, felt for the receiver and said, "Hello."

"Hello," she returned, then nothing.

He cleared his throat and said, "Now I suppose *you're* mad at *me.*"

"Don't you ever do that again with my son in the house!"

"Why?"

"Oh, for heaven's sake, Christopher, what's the matter with you?"

"What's the matter with me? I don't know whether to treat you like my mother or my lover—that's what's the matter with me! So what do you want me to do? Do you want me to keep the hell out of there? Because I can do that, you know!"

The line got quiet for the longest time. Then she whispered, "Shit." He could almost see her leaning her forehead on the heel of one hand.

"Are you crying?"

"No, I'm not crying!"

He commenced rubbing his eyes, then sighed so hugely it sounded like a horse whickering.

"God, Lee, I don't know," he said, dropping his hand to the mattress. His answer took on more impact because no one had asked the question.

They stayed silent for so long his ears began to ring.

Finally she said, "You know what you just said . . . I mean about not knowing how to treat me? Well, the same is true for me and how to treat you. It's the creepiest thing I've ever been through in my life. You walk in here, and it's like Greg walking in. Only I can distinguish very clearly between you and Greg. You're . . . well, you're very different. You're Christopher, and when I'm with you the strange thing is, I hardly ever even think of Greg anymore. Then you go away and I'm deluged by guilt feelings, like I'm some . . . some pervert. I mean, I've read my psychology, too, you know! And my Greek mythology! I know about the Oedipus complex!" She had grown more agitated and sounded as if she were arguing with herself.

"Guilt feelings about what?"

"Oh, come on . . . this isn't some situation comedy we're playing in. This is real life, and you're not going to trick me into saying things I don't want to."

He said not a word, listening to the faint hum along the telephone wire and feeling their uncertainties stretch in both directions.

Finally she said, "Listen . . . I don't think we should see each other for a while. I've been reading about grief, too, and I'm smart enough to see the similarities between the way I'm acting and what they warn you against doing."

He took in the words, let them settle like a rock in his heart, then said thickly, "Okay . . . if that's the way you want it."

Her voice sounded sheer miserable. "It's not the way I want it. It's the way it's got to be."

"Yes, I understand."

More trembling silence, then she said, "Well . . . it's late. We've got church in the morning."

"Sure."

"Well . . . goodbye."

"Goodbye." Neither of them hung up. When they did, that would be it—their relationship would be over. So they clung to their receivers and the sound of each other's breathing for a few seconds longer. He pictured her in her blue-flowered bed. She pictured him in his mannishly plain one.

Finally, he said, "Thanks again for the supper. I practically felt like Ozzie Nelson."

She couldn't find the wherewithal to laugh. Nothing seemed funny at that moment. It felt as if nothing ever would again.

" 'Bye, Christopher."

" 'Bye, Lee."

This time he hung up, then lay in the dark wondering if her eyes were stinging like his.

For Lee, facing the future without him seemed a cruelty she didn't deserve. It was the abysmal time of year between the first frost and the holiday season, when the prospect of hibernating away indoors for the next six months only dampened her spirits further.

Janice got so busy at college Lee rarely spoke to her unless Lee was the one to initiate the call. Then the conversations were rushed and most often ended by Janice: "Gosh, sorry to run, Mom, but so-and-so is waiting for me and we're running late, as usual."

Joey was smitten by first love. Many evenings after supper he'd spiff up like the froggie goin' a-courtin', and would walk a mile over to Sandy Parker's house, leaving Lee to find her own diversions. Occasionally Joey and Sandy would spend time at her house, monopolizing the living room where they made goo-goo eyes at one another in between tickling sessions on the sofa that were so embarrassing for Lee she'd finally leave them to themselves and hide away in her bedroom reading her *Flowers &* magazine.

Orrin and Peg Hillier set out on an extended trip to New England that would take them south along the entire Atlantic seaboard. They planned to be back in time for Thanksgiving.

Lee had only to call anyone she knew to have a companion for the evening. She went to Donna and Jim Clements' for supper twice, out to the movies with Sylvia and Barry, even to the Rum River Boutique with Nancy McFaddon one evening. There were parent/teacher conferences for Joey at the junior high, and final fall gardening in the backyard, and baked goods to be made for the annual autumn bake sale at church.

However, most evenings Lee spent alone.

One night shortly after ten o'clock she had turned off the lights and was standing at a front window in her pajamas, rubbing lotion into her hands and admiring a big harvest moon, when a black-and-white squad car cruised by so slowly she thought for a moment the driver had probably been able to see her standing in the dark window. She had no doubt it was Christopher. The white door of the car was picked out clearly by the blue-white moonlight, and his speed was so slow she was certain it could be no one else.

Dear God, she got a rush.

Standing there with her hands going motionless she felt her face heat, felt a reaching within, as if an inner voice beyond her control were calling to him.

He didn't stop, of course, just cruised past so silently she felt shaken by the realization that he'd been watching her house at night.

When she went to bed she lay flat on her back with the covers clamped tightly beneath her armpits, flattening her breasts, as if lying motionless and plank-stiff could negate the yearning she'd felt at the window a moment ago.

You've made the right decision, she told herself. *An affair with him would be disastrous. Scandalous. Imagine what people would say.*

Funny, her admonition did little to get her to sleep or to fill the gaping void in her life or to get Christopher off her mind through the days and nights that followed.

She remained firm in her resolve not to see Christopher again as the rains of mid-October turned into the frosts of late October, that stunning time of year when it was so hard to be alone. The world donned its gilded raiments. It burnished apples, turned pumpkins orange in the fields and dried corn upon its stalks.

The town began preparing for Halloween. Since 1920, when its civic leaders had put on its first Halloween celebration to divert old-time pranks such as putting wagons on roofs and overturning outhouses, Anoka had dubbed itself the Halloween Capital of the World. This year, as every year, events happened one upon another. There was a Fiddler Jamboree; the Pumpkin Bowl in which the Anoka Tornadoes played their archrivals, the Coon Rapids Cardinals; a senior citizens' card party, a round-robin horseshoe tournament and Bingo; a pumpkin pie bake-off; a lip-sync contest; and the Gray Ghost 5K Run and One-Mile Fitness Walk. The Knights of Columbus sponsored a haunted house out at the fairgrounds; merchants participated in a Moonlight Madness sale; and students from the Anoka Senior High painted all the store windows downtown. The events were to be culminated in the Friday afternoon kiddies' parade and the Saturday afternoon Grand Day Parade followed by the crowning of Miss Anoka at the senior high.

The entire celebration was supremely good for retail business.

And made one hell of a lot of extra work for the police force.

Being a downtown merchant, and dealing in the products she did, Lee found herself in the thick of it.

It seemed everybody wanted potted chrysanthemums for their door-steps, wind socks shaped like ghosts or a pile of pumpkins to carve into jack-o'-lanterns. More homeowners decorated their yards than didn't, and the town took on a festive air with ghost effigies hanging from front-yard trees and doorways hung with black skeletons. Beside lamp-posts, hay bales, scarecrows and pumpkins appeared. And at Absolutely Floral, dried autumn wreaths for front doors nearly outsold fresh-cut flower arrangements.

On the day the high school seniors came to paint their front window, Lee and Sylvia were busy taking care of some older flowers at the rear of the store. The place smelled like hot apple cider from an electric pot near the front where a sign said HELP YOURSELF. The teenagers were painting the glass, drinking cider and having a wonderful time. The bookkeeper was upstairs in the office doing his biweekly work, and two customers were browsing through the display area where Pat Galsworthy was answering questions for them. Lee was taking care of the unpalatable task of changing the water in a canister of multicolored stocks, a member of the radish family that gave off such a hot radishy smell it burned her eyes.

"Lord, this stuff is foul," she said, transferring the stocks to fresh water, emptying out the old and filling the used container with chlorine bleach and water.

Sylvia went on washing out a container and said, "Mom called yesterday. They were in Brattleboro, Vermont. Did she call you?"

"Not since Tuesday."

"She said it's beautiful there."

"I know. She said they're having trouble moving on."

"Did she talk to you about Thanksgiving?"

"No."

"She wants to have it at her house this year."

"Fine."

"She said that by the time they get back she'll be anxious to cook again and they'll get here in plenty of time for her to make preparations."

"Great. I'm glad I don't have to do it. I'm really not in the mood this year."

"She's going to want us each to bring something, of course."

"She'll ask me to do pies, I'm sure. She loves my pies."

"I'm taking my broccoli casserole and wild rice. Oh, by the way, she said I should tell you to ask Chris."

Lee was pouring Hi-lex water from one container to another. The stream stopped as she looked up at her sister. Sylvia didn't notice and went on talking. "She and Dad really like him. Did you know that when Greg died he even sent them a sympathy card? Mom just can't get over that. And I *know* he really impressed her when he chose her for his volleyball team on the Fourth of July. Have you talked to him lately?"

As Sylvia looked up, Lee snapped back to washing the containers.

"No, I haven't."

"Well, give him a call and tell him he's invited for Thanksgiving dinner."

"Yeah, sure . . . I will."

"So, how's Joey doing with his little heartthrob?" The talk moved on and the subject of Christopher was dropped. The teenagers finished their window painting and came back to thank the owners for letting them do it. Sylvia went to the cooler and sent them each away with an orange carnation. The bookkeeper came downstairs and said he'd finished all his posting and needed some signatures. Lee dried her hands and signed. Sylvia and Pat Galsworthy began getting the store ready for closing. When Pat had said goodbye and left the two sisters alone, Lee turned off the radio and looked across the room at Sylvia, who was donning her coat. She opened her mouth to speak and knew that if she said she didn't want to invite Christopher for the holiday, Sylvia would look at her in stunned amazement and ask "Why?"

She clapped her mouth closed, got on her coat and the two went out the back door together into a swirl of dried leaves that were dancing and rustling like a whirlpool in the close quarters between the buildings. Sylvia had already reached her car before Lee called from beside her own, "Sylvia . . . about Thanksgiving . . ."

Sylvia turned, holding her car keys, waiting.

But Lee had no logical excuse for eliminating Chris from their holiday plans. Suddenly she found herself extemporizing.

"I have a new vegetable recipe I'd like to try. Would you mind making the pies this year?"

Sylvia looked doubtful. "Mom will be disappointed. I can't make crust nearly as well as you."

"Well, maybe I can make the pies and the casserole, too."

"Let's wait till Mom gets home and talk over the menu then."

Chicken! Lee thought when she'd gotten into her car. She sat without starting the engine, gripping the wheel and going nowhere, frustrated and feeling like a jerk for cutting Christopher out when he so looked forward to being with the family on holidays. She was made more miserable by the fact that she was planning a lie, for when the time came she'd tell everybody that Christopher had to work on Thanksgiving day.

The morning of the Grand Day Parade Anoka got crazy well before noon. Thousands of people flooded in, coming to shop, eat lunch and get a good spot on the curb along the parade route. Cars inched along on every side street, looking for parking spaces. Children in costume, hand-towed by their mothers, passed the store windows in droves. Lee looked out between the tempera-painted corn shocks and saw people setting up lawn chairs on the sidewalk out front. Inside, the place was a madhouse. One or two real customers were honestly doing business, but the rest were only creating chaos. Some woman with a bawling baby was looking at greeting cards and wrinkling them when the baby threw itself backward in her arms. A bunch of little boys had discovered the free apple cider and were running in and out, using up her paper cups and bringing their friends in to empty the hot pot. An older woman with a frantic look on her face limped in and asked, "Could I use your toilet, please?" A representative of the Miss Anoka Pageant came tearing in, demanding, "The corsages for the queen candidates—I need them, quick!" The phone rang incessantly. Customers lined up at the checkout counter. The door opened again and the backdraft blew over a wire stand holding a potted cyclamen plant.

At one o'clock, Lee clasped her head and said, "Enough already! Let's lock this place up!"

With a feeling of relief they locked the door, put on their jackets and went out to join the throng on the curb waiting to see the color guard come marching down Main Street to the drumbeat of the Anoka High School band.

Ah, sweet relief! It was a heavenly day, and so good to be outside. Overhead, the sky was deep blue, mottled here and there with puffy white clouds. The temperature on the bank sign read forty-seven degrees, so the sun felt splendid through Lee's denim jacket. Down at the river crossing, the Rum River was frothing over the dam. Along Main Street all the businesses had put out orange-and-black flags, American flags, flags with the school colors and some whose designation was merely decorative.

A police car came inching by, and Lee's heart lurched. But it was someone else at the wheel, not Christopher.

A few yards up the curb some teenagers had gathered and were laughing and jostling each other. One of them threw a basketball-sized pumpkin as high into the air as he could. It hit the blacktop and splattered ten yards, sending people jumping back, then brushing at the orange strings of pumpkin guts hanging from their clothes. Some laughter went up, along with some cursing and complaining.

At the corner of the block Christopher had pulled up his squad car at an angle, cutting off traffic on a cross street. He'd been standing at the front of the car with the flashing reds on, watching the crowd when the pumpkin hit the pavement.

Immediately he headed that way.

He walked along the concrete gutter in front of the gathered crowd, unhurried but authoritative.

Reaching the three rowdy teenage boys, he asked, "You guys throw that?"

One of them said, "Shit no, man. An old lady did. She went that way, didn't she, Kevin?"

Kevin said, "Oh, yeah, way down that way."

Christopher remained calm. "You're going to have to clean it up."

One of the boys said, "Screw you."

An onlooker yelled, "It flew clear over here!"

A block away, the color guard was approaching, followed by the band—seventy pairs of white shoes stomping through all that pumpkin hash. "Now!" Christopher ordered. "Because if that band gets here first, I'm going to start taking names, and I'm sure a lot of these people would be interested in sending you their dry-cleaning bills."

One of the teenagers relented. "What are we supposed to pick it up with?"

Someone handed over a newspaper. The three boys took the paper, went out into the street, scraped up the pumpkin slime with their hands and piled it into the newspaper while Officer Lallek stood by with his thumbs hooked into his belt, watching.

They came running back to the curb just as the American Legion color guard came by with the flags. Behind them, the band was blaring. Christopher pointed down the block in the direction of his patrol car. "There's a garbage receptacle down there."

Grumbling, the boys went toward it.

From the curb in front of her store, Lee Reston had seen it all. She might have willfully cut Christopher out of her life, but the sight of him—particularly in uniform, performing his duties—still had the power to switch her heart into overdrive. There was so much noise that she hadn't heard his voice, but she'd watched without once pulling her eyes from the scene. He looked as strikingly attractive as ever. The color guard passed and she forgot to stand at attention. The band approached and she forgot to watch their synchronized footsteps. Instead, she watched the visor of Christopher's hat above the heads between them, hoping he would turn her way and find her standing there. He removed his hat and placed it over his heart as Old Glory waved past.

He watched the flag.

She watched him.

He stood erect and respectful, raising such a turmoil within her that it felt as if the drums were beating deep in her breast.

The color guard passed and Christopher replaced his hat, leaned over to say something to a small child in the crowd. He laughed, touched the child's head, then straightened, glancing down the street while the band came on, their brass blaring.

As if he sensed himself being studied, he turned and looked over his left shoulder in Lee's direction. Their gazes collided. Neither of them smiled, but he began coming toward her with the same unruffled pace at which he'd approached the boys who'd thrown the pumpkin.

Flustered, she turned her attention to the band, watched their ranks passing by as even as cornrows. The march ended and the drum section took up a street beat—*throom, thr-thr throom!*—tenors and bass drums answering the snares with such booming vigor it battered the eardrums.

Then Christopher was before her and she could no longer keep herself from looking up at his smooth-shaven face. His mouth moved. He must have said hello, though the drums covered it up. She said the word, too, though it was lost in the reverberations around them. Their attraction for each other and denial of it were in the forefront of their encounter, coloring it with polite distancing while the entire city of Anoka and her sister looked on. Finally he realized how long he'd focused on Lee, and touched his hatbrim in a polite hello to Sylvia and Pat Galsworthy. A boy on a BMX bike was doing wheelies, threatening to wipe out the rear corner of the band. "Gotta go," he said, and escaped under the guise of duty.

Against her will, Lee's eyes followed him as he motioned the boy over closer to the curb, then answered a greeting from someone in the crowd with whom he stood talking, Christopher with one foot on the street, one on the curb.

Further contingents of the parade passed by—the grand marshal, kids in costume, the Shriners on their purring Harleys, more kids in costume.

Lee pretended to watch the movement in the street, but all the while she kept Christopher in her peripheral vision. He visited with people. He touched kids on their heads. He caught some candy thrown by a clown and gave it to one of them. He plucked up his radio and put it to his mouth, scowled westward up the street, then turned purposefully and headed back toward his car. Passing Lee, he gave her only a glance, and then he was gone.

The parade kept coming—endless kids in costume, the Forest Lake band, the Hopkins band, a float holding the school cooks from Coon Rapids Senior High, more floats, more bands, the football team on a flatbed truck and the cheerleaders waving pompons, the royalty from the Miss Anoka Pageant—but long before the big red city fire trucks rolled by with their air horns deafening, signaling the parade's end, it had ended for Lee Reston.

Chapter 10

SHE didn't call him about Thanksgiving.

On November eighteenth her parents got back into town and Peg called right away. She wanted Lee to make the pumpkin pies and was planning on twenty-three for the holiday meal. She said, "Chris is coming, isn't he?"

"I'm not sure. I think he has to work."

Peg said, "Oh, what a shame."

Lee hung up, burdened by an enormous load of guilt.

On the Tuesday before Thanksgiving, Peg and Orrin Hillier were at the Red Owl store shopping for their Thanksgiving turkey when Peg turned into the frozen-food aisle and nearly collided with Christopher, just off duty, still dressed in his blues and shopping for his supper.

"Christopher! Well, for goodness sake, it's you!"

"Hello, Mrs. Hillier."

She gave him a hug, which he returned, holding his frozen chicken divan away from her back. He and Orrin shook hands. They stood and talked awhile, about Orrin and Peg's trip to New England, the stupendous fall colors they'd seen and the covered bridges of Vermont. They praised the architectural splendors of Charleston and the fine golf courses of Myrtle Beach.

Then Peg said, "I was so sorry to hear you couldn't make it to our house for Thanksgiving dinner."

Unsure of what was going on, Christopher covered his surprise well. "I'm sorry to miss it, too. You know how a bachelor loves home cooking."

"I was hoping you'd get the holiday off, but Lee said you have to work."

Out of nowhere he blurted the truth. "Not until three."

"Not until three! Why, then, it's settled. We eat at one and you'll be there."

He smiled. "Thanks, Mrs. Hillier. In that case, I will."

"The mulled cider will be hot at eleven, so come early."

"Your family is so good about including me. I just can't thank you enough."

Peg Hillier looked pleased and patted his shoulder. "Nonsense," she said. "You're like one of the family yourself." As proof, he received a grandmotherly hug of farewell.

On the day before Thanksgiving, Lee arranged an elegant centerpiece for Rodney to deliver to her parents' home. It was a lavish mixture of apricot ranunculus, kalanchoes and an abundance of sprayed pomegranates, all tied together with dark trailing ivy and wired bicolored grosgrain ribbon. She put it in a low, gleaming oval of polished brass and signed the card *Happy Thanksgiving and welcome home. Love, Sylvia and Lee.* All the while Lee worked on it she was recalling last Thanksgiving when the family had gathered at her house and Greg had still been alive. How many months since he'd died? Five, yet on given days she was still assaulted by anguish at the realization that he was gone forever. She supposed it was natural that holidays would be the worst.

Lee put the last twist on the wired ribbon and was standing back assessing the arrangement when Sylvia came over to the arranging table and said reverently, "Wow." They stood for a moment admiring the color, balance and texture of the creation.

"It's a masterpiece." Sylvia draped a wrist over Lee's shoulder. "I wish I could arrange something like that just once in my life."

Lee put her arm around Sylvia's waist. "And I wish I was better at the business side of business. It's why we work together so well, isn't it?"

"Mom's going to love it."

"Mm."

To Sylvia, Lee seemed unusually quiet and subdued. "Something wrong?"

Lee only stared at the flowers.

"You thinking of Greg?" Lee got tears in her eyes and Sylvia gripped her shoulder, pulled her over and put her temple against her sister's.

"It's just that it's Thanksgiving . . . the first one without him. We're supposed to give thanks for all our blessings, but I'm not feeling especially blessed right now."

"I know," Sylvia whispered. "I know."

They stood awhile, staring at the flowers, which had paled in importance. In a quiet, lost voice, Lee admitted, "I've been so lonely, Sylvia."

"Oh, honey," Sylvia said sadly.

Lee blinked, scraped the tears off her cheeks and shook herself. "Oh, shoot, I don't know what's the matter with me! I do have plenty to be thankful for, and lots of it is right here at this minute." She gave Sylvia a hug. "Thanks, sis. I feel better now. Just getting it off my chest makes me feel better."

That night at home, Lee tallied up other blessings for which she should be grateful. It snowed that night, a light, fluffy blanket of white. Janice came home from college, Joey stayed home, and the three of them had a lot of fun making four pumpkin pies and an artichoke casserole together.

They awakened on Thanksgiving morning to a pearl-gray sky and a world garbed in ermine. The snow had stopped falling and no wind blew. Still in her nightclothes, Lee looked out the window and said, "Yesss!"

They dressed in their finery, went to church, and from there straight out to the Hillier home.

Peg and Orrin lived several miles north of Anoka beside the Rum River on four very pricey acres covered with red oaks. The trees looked rich beyond description in their new dressing of white. Contrasted against the snow, the black, knurled branches created a stark, stunning tableau like a pen-and-ink drawing. The driveway was long and curved, wending between the oaks on its way to a sprawling, single-level house of salmon-colored brick that had once been featured in a photo layout in *Better Homes and Gardens*. Both inside and out, the place radiated class and good taste. When the house was being custom-built, Peg Hillier had personally chosen every fixture and feature, working not only with the builder, but also with a Minneapolis decorator whose clientele list included officers of the 3M corporation, doctors from the Mayo Clinic and members of the Minnesota Orchestra.

When Lee and the kids arrived, Peg came to answer the door herself, still an impeccably groomed woman in spite of the faint roundness at her middle. "Darlings. Happy Thanksgiving." They all exchanged kisses and hugs, juggling pies and a casserole dish while Orrin came to take their coats and offer hugs, too.

Peg said, "We're having drinks in the study so go right on in."

Lee said, "I had to stop and pick up the ice cream on the way and the carton was a mess. I've got to wash my sticky hands, then I'll be right with you."

In the bathroom a clover-leaf-shaped whirlpool tub was surrounded by carefully placed pots of leafless corkscrew sticks and immense baskets of black and white towels. While Lee washed and dried her hands she heard Sylvia's laugh and a rustle of voices raised in greeting. She opened a drawer, found her mother's brush and ran it through her hair. The doorbell rang. Someone else arrived and voices blended, then faded off toward the study. Sylvia's little granddaughter, Marnie, came running down the hall and into the bathroom, her patent-leather shoes slapping against the tile.

"Hi, Auntie Lee," she said.

"Hi, Marnie!"

"I got a new dress!" It was frosted with lace and ruffled as a tutu.

"Ooo, is it ever pretty!"

"Mommy said to blow my nose." She went up on tiptoe but couldn't reach the tissue box on the vanity counter. Lee helped her and the child chattered all the while ... about her new white tights and how her mom had brought along her snow pants and boots today so she and her brothers could go out and play in the snow later.

Lee snapped off the light and the two of them left the bathroom together.

"Want to go see the flowers?" Lee asked.

The child nodded and offered her hand.

They cut across one end of the entry hall where a great-aunt and uncle were arriving, and moved on toward the rear of the house where the side-by-side dining room and living room looked out over a view that was the house's greatest asset. Roosting high over the river, the building's entire eastern exposure was made of glass, and the view beyond it was splendid today with the water still tumbling between the white wooded banks where squirrels and blue jays added a touch that no decorator, whatever her credits, could have provided.

The tables—two of them butted—were spread in unabashed resplendence, stretching across the archway and spanning both rooms, which were carpeted in palest taupe and decorated with a lot of white upholstery on straight-lined functional furniture. The tables were spread with white damask and set with Bavarian bone china chosen by the decorator to complement the traditional decor.

If there was one thing Peg prided herself on, it was good taste.

Marnie was dancing around, holding one foot up behind her, touching the backs of chairs, too young to be impressed by the lavish layout of finery that glittered and shone before the long, bright windows.

Lee checked the flowers: They looked truly worthy of a Peg Hillier table setting. She wandered along, passing several place settings, noting that her mother had paid her usual attention to every detail. Who but Peg Hillier used place cards anymore?

"Did you make those flowers?" Marnie asked, still dancing on one foot.

"Yes, I did."

"They're pretty."

"Thank you."

Marnie scampered off. Lee took one last look at the flowers and turned toward the sound of happy chatter coming from the study. It was a large room at the front of the house with a brass-screened fireplace where a festive fire burned. Relatives sat on the brown leather sofas or stood in groups chatting with the usual exuberance of arrival time. Peg stood beside a skirted round table ladling hot cider into a crystal cup, adding a cinnamon stick and handing it to . . .

Christopher Lallek!

Lee felt her face go red and her chest constrict.

He took the cup and napkin, smiled and thanked Peg, then put it to his mouth to sip while turning toward Janice, who was talking and smiling up at him, already holding a cup of her own.

She said something and he laughed, then drank again. Over the rim of his cup he saw Lee for the first time, standing stricken in the doorway. Of the two, he managed far more poise than she. No one would have guessed there was the slightest strain between them as he lowered the cup—smile intact—and said to Janice, "Oh, there's your mother."

Lee moved into the room toward him—what else could she do?

Janice turned and said, excitedly, "Mom, why didn't you tell me Christopher was coming?"

"I thought he had to work."

"Not until three, it turned out," he said, then leaned to kiss her cheek. "Happy Thanksgiving, Mrs. Reston. I'm glad I could make it after all."

"So am I," she responded, finding that deep in her heart it was true. Lord, how she'd missed him. They had parted at her request, but she'd come to believe that request—prompted by forces other than what she felt for him—was one of the most misguided of her life. She had said to him once that she was not a lonely woman, then yesterday to Sylvia she'd said just the opposite. Her loneliness had begun, she realized now, since he had come into her life and then been exiled from it.

He was dressed in gray wool trousers, white shirt, blue floral tie and a finely knit shawl collar sweater of navy blue. He was well proportioned, fit, trim, and wore clothing well. So rarely had she seen him in anything other than his uniform or jeans. Shorts in the summer, of course, but his clothing today lent him a new aspect that brought to Lee feelings she hadn't experienced since Bill was alive.

It was sexual attraction, pure and simple. And for the first time, she admitted it.

She watched him with her family. Every person in the room knew him. Everyone liked him. But what, exactly, would their reaction be if she started dating him? *Really* dating him.

Janice looked radiant. She stood beside him, looking up, adoring, offering small talk that often made him laugh. Once she touched his arm; it was only briefly, but Lee understood what kind of feelings women put into touches like that. It was flirtation of the subtlest kind. Studying the two of them as they stood talking, Lee admitted to herself what a beautiful couple they made. He, at thirty, so healthy and well groomed. She, at twenty-three, with her dark wavy hair and perfect skin; not a wrinkle beside her mouth or eyes; in the full flush of youth. Lord in heaven, Lee didn't understand this. How could such a bizarre attraction have happened? Why herself? Why not Janice, who was so much more suitable?

Peg called from the kitchen that she needed help, and Orrin rounded up a few of the women to fill wineglasses and carry bowls. He himself went along to carve the turkey and dig the stuffing from inside the bird.

As Lee circled the table with the wine decanter, she noted what she'd missed earlier: Christopher's place card at a chair between her own and Janice's.

Without asking, she went to the refrigerator, found some cranberry juice and filled his glass with that.

The placement of guests began amid far less than the usual shuffling and shifting, due to Peg's carefully calligraphic place cards. Christopher found himself between the two Reston women and politely seated them both, pulling out their chairs before taking his own.

Orrin said, "Let's all join hands now for a prayer."

Around the table everyone formed a ring. Lee took Joey's hand, on her left, and Christopher's, on her right. His hand was smooth and warm. She was momentarily conscious of her own being rough and dry from too many prickly flower stems and too many dunkings in chlorine water. She was more conscious of a current flowing between them during the warm, firm contact of flesh that seemed to link more than their hands.

Orrin bowed his head.

"Dear Lord, on this day of thanksgiving we give special thanks for everyone around this table, for their health and prosperity and happiness. We thank you for the bounty you've given us, and ask that you watch over us all in the year to come. We also ask that you look after Greg, who's missing from this table this year, but is there with you ..." Lee felt Christopher's fingers tighten on her own and returned the pressure. "... and that you help each of us accept his absence and not question your reason for taking him. Give special strength to Lee, Janice and Joey in the year ahead. Until we gather again next year at this time ... thank you, Lord, for everything."

Few at the table lifted their heads immediately after the prayer.

Neither did Christopher release Lee's hand but held it under the table-
cloth a moment longer and looked over at the tears in her downturned
eyes.

"I'm glad to be here," he whispered, giving her hand an extra squeeze
before finally releasing it.

Oh, that meal. That beautiful, awful, high-tension meal, with Christopher so close she could smell the wool of his sweater, and touch his
sleeve, and watch his hands moving over the silverware, all the while
pretending none of it meant anything out of the ordinary. The family
probably attributed her unusual quiet to Orrin's prayer, though everyone recovered from it nicely and began chattering.

She forced herself to speak to Christopher lest the others wonder at
her reticence.

"Your glass is filled with cranberry juice," she said.

"Thank you."

"So you're on mid-shift today."

"Yes. Three to eleven."

"Will it be busy?"

"Tonight it will. Lot of college kids home for the weekend, getting
together at bars. You know kids and alcohol."

Askance, she watched him put away a helping of potatoes and gravy
that covered half his plate.

"So how about you?" he asked. "Tomorrow's the biggie, huh?"

"That's right—biggest shopping days of the year, tomorrow and
Saturday. I'm not looking forward to it."

"And after that you're into the Christmas rush."

"That's already started. In my business we have to start preparing
permanent Christmas arrangements so they're ready to sell on Thanksgiving weekend."

They talked about superficialities only, locking away what really
mattered and behaving like Greg's friend and Greg's mother with Janice
and Joey near enough to hear every word they said.

At two o'clock Chris checked his watch and said to Peg, "I'm sorry
to do a hit-and-run, but I have to be at roll call in thirty minutes, dressed
like a cop." He pushed back his chair and rose, holding back his tie.
"That means a stop at home first."

Peg looked disappointed. "So soon? But you haven't even had your pie."

"Someone else can have my piece. I'm so full."

201

"I'll send one with you."

"Oh, no, that's not necessary. Everything was so delicious."

They went on exchanging dialogue while he moved away from the table and Peg rose to disregard his polite refusal of the pie. Orrin stood and those around the table bid Christopher farewell. After a moment of indecision, Lee got up too and went with him to the foyer while Orrin got his gray wool chesterfield coat and plaid scarf, holding them as Christopher slipped them on. Peg emerged from the kitchen with a triangular piece of tinfoil.

"Here's your pie. A Thanksgiving dinner just isn't complete without pumpkin pie. Lee made it."

"Thank you," he said. "I see where Lee gets her compulsion to send leftovers home with everybody. And thank you for another wonderful holiday." He kissed Peg's cheek, shook Orrin's hand and kissed Lee's cheek.

She opened the door and said, " 'Bye."

" 'Bye, and thanks again."

She lined the edge of the door with one hand while watching him walk down the wet driveway to his Explorer, which waited in a turn-around some distance away.

The wind had come up and lifted the end of his scarf as he opened the truck door and waved before getting in. He always did that—waved that way—and Lee was struck with warm familiarity watching him do so again.

As usual, from the moment he drove away the ebullience went out of the day.

Lee and the kids stayed till 6:30 P.M., then Janice said she wanted to get home and change clothes: She, too, was going out with a bunch of friends that night.

At home, Joey and Lee changed into sweat suits and turned on the TV while Janice switched on the radio in the bathroom and spent time redoing her makeup and hair. Jane and Sandy came by for her at 8:30, leaving Lee and Joey watching an old rerun of a Waltons Thanksgiving movie.

At 9:15 the doorbell rang.

Lee glanced over at Joey, sprawled on the sofa, and discovered he was sound asleep.

She got up from her chair and went to answer.

Christopher stood on the front step, dressed in uniform, his squad car parked in the driveway behind him with its engine still running and the parking lights on.

She opened the storm door and he held it that way while she stood on the level above him in her sweat suit and slippers.

"I want to talk to you," he said—no smile, no softness, just a statement of fact. "Could you come out to the car for a minute?"

"Joey is here."

"Tell him where you're going and come outside, please."

"Can't we talk in the house?"

"No, not with Joey there."

Suddenly, things inside her began trembling. How indomitable he was to face this head on, far more than she, who had eluded the confrontation in various temporizing ways.

"All right," she said, "let me get my jacket." She opened a coat-closet door and called into the living room, "Joey, Christopher is here. I'm going out in the car to talk to him a minute."

He shifted onto his left side, facing the back of the sofa, and mumbled something while the TV played behind him.

Outside, she preceded Christopher down the walk to his squad car. He opened the passenger door and waited while she got in. Inside it was warm, the heater blowing. A multitude of gear formed a barricade between his half of the seat and hers. A rifle stood barrel-up beside her left knee. On the dash a large radio, glowing with red lights, was mounted beside a larger speaker pointed at the driver's seat. On the seat itself a wooden cup holder was secured in place with space behind it for a bunch of notebooks that were wedged upright. Behind the driver's seat a glass partition divided the front from the back, while behind her a steel mesh partition did the same.

He got in and slammed the door. On the radio, the county dispatcher's voice crackled intermittently. He reached up and lowered the volume, then took off his hat and wedged it behind the speaker. Resting his left wrist on top of the steering wheel, he turned to look at her.

After an uncertain stretch of silence they both spoke at once.

"These past few weeks—" he said.

"I'm sorry about—" she said.

They both clipped off their remarks.

She picked up first. "I'm sorry about the Thanksgiving invitation."

"This isn't about that. I understand perfectly well why you didn't call and ask me."

"It was selfish of me. I'm sorry."

"Apology accepted. Now let me say what I came here to say." He sat back, looking straight out over the steering wheel at her garage door, which was closed for once. "These past few weeks have been bad. I don't like the way things were left between us. I've been miserable, how about you?"

"Lonely." She, too, looked straight out over the dash.

He turned to study her profile, dimly outlined by the pale lights from the dash. The radio light put a ruby haze on the tips of her eyelashes and rouged her cheeks. Her mouth looked somewhat sullen. "I know all the reasons we shouldn't keep seeing each other, but somehow when I add them up they don't seem to matter much. The plain truth is, I want to see you again, and I want it clear that I'm not coming around looking for leftover lasagna, or for sympathy, or to fill in for your son. I want us to be together without all that baggage between us, but I'm working mid-shift right now so the timing is crummy. My next night off is Sunday. Would you go out to a movie with me?"

"What would I tell Joey?"

"Tell him the truth."

"Oh, Christopher, I can't do that."

"Why not?"

"You know why not."

"You didn't hesitate to tell him we were going walking together last summer, or swimming, or riding on a Ferris wheel."

"But the difference was, he went with us most of the time."

"No, the difference is in how *you* perceive us, not in how *he* will. If you tell him you're going out with me, he'll accept it. Just lay it out there, plain and simple."

"I'm scared," she said.

He let out a mirthless nasal huff, rested his elbow on the window ledge, pinched his bottom lip and looked off to his left.

"Well, I am!" she said defensively.

He rolled his head to face her. "Yeah, this is pretty scary, going out to a movie." His tone became more assertive. "Don't make anything of it. Just tell him, 'Chris and I are going out to a movie. See you later,' and walk out with me."

She thought about it awhile and surprised herself by agreeing. "All right, I will."

She seemed to have surprised him, too. He said, disbelievingly, "Really?"

"Yes, really."

He reached for the radio volume though she hadn't even heard the word "Bravo" signaling a call for the Anoka officers.

". . . reporting a vehicle going north on southbound lane of Main."

He plucked his mike from the dashboard and said, "Forty-one to base. Did you copy if that was West Main or East Main?"

"East Main."

"Ten-four," he said, then to Lee. "I've got to go."

She opened her door and the dome light came on. "I'll see you Sunday."

"I'll call with the time."

"Okay." She got out.

"Hey, Lee?"

She leaned down and looked across the seat at him.

"Good pie. I had it on my break."

She smiled and slammed the door.

On Sunday night she didn't have to worry. Janice went back to her own place in the late afternoon; Joey got listless and called Denny Whitman, then announced, "I'm gonna go over to Denny's house and play video games. Can you give me a ride?"

"Sure," she said, giving herself clear sailing, even as far as getting ready was concerned.

With the house to herself, she experienced a sense of ambivalence about what to wear, how much to fuss, whether or not to wear perfume. Lord in heaven, she was going on a date for the first time in twenty-six years. She was terrified!

She put on a pair of blue jeans (an effort to reduce the significance of this event) and a pullover sweater, the same makeup she wore to work every day and the same amount of perfume. Her hair? Well, her hair came as it was. She tugged at it, calling up a memory of Janice's long, young mane, and wondered again how a man of Christopher's age could prefer her over her daughter.

He arrived at the time they'd arranged, and she hurried to the door with a queer tight feeling in her chest, blushing maybe the tiniest bit, wondering what in the world she was letting herself in for.

He was wearing jeans and a red down-filled jacket and acted much less flustered than she.

"Hi," he said, stepping inside and closing the door with the small of his back. "All ready?"

"If you don't mind, I'd like to call Joey first. He's at Denny Whitman's playing video games. I'm not sure if he needs a ride home or not."

"Okay."

While she dialed on the kitchen phone and spoke to Joey, Christopher ambled in behind her and sauntered around the room, looking at this and that, slapping a pair of leather gloves against his thigh. He glanced at a Pyrex baking dish holding leftover peach cobbler on the stove, and at a note on the refrigerator door that said *Pick up watch at jeweler's*. He bent over the kitchen table and read a school announcement Joey had brought home about upcoming teachers' workshop days.

Plainly, he heard her say, "I'm going to a movie with Christopher, but we should be back by nine-thirty," and after a pause, *"The Firm."*

He was watching her and listening quite pointedly when she answered Joey's question about what they were going to see. She spoke for a minute longer, then hung up and told Chris, "Denny's dad will bring him home."

To his credit, Christopher refrained from saying I told you so.

In the front hall he held her denim jacket while she slipped it on; at his truck, he opened her door . . . just like a real date.

During the movie he sat low on his tailbone with both elbows on the armrests. Sometimes their elbows touched. There was a kiss on-screen, and throughout it Christopher and Lee kept their eyes riveted on the scene and wondered what the other was thinking.

In the truck afterward he asked, "Did you like it?"

"Yes. Did you?"

"Not as well as the book."

"Oh, it was better than the book!"

The discussion lasted all the way home. When they got there the lights were on just as she'd left them. Joey's bedroom was in the rear so they couldn't tell if he was home yet or not.

"Do you want to come in and have a piece of peach cobbler and ice cream?" she asked.

"Sure."

They got out and went inside.

Pulling off her jacket she called, "Joey? Are you here?"

No answer.

She threw the jacket on a living room chair and went back to his room to find it dark. When she returned to the kitchen Christopher had hung his jacket on the back of a chair.

"He's still gone. He knows he's got to be home by ten or he's in trouble." It was 9:45.

She got out two sauce dishes, put peach cobbler in them, set them in the microwave and took ice cream from the freezer. When she tried to scoop it out, her muscles bulged, but nothing else moved.

"Can I help?" he asked.

She gave him the ice-cream scoop and opened a drawer to find spoons.

The buzzer went off on the microwave and she carried the two bowls to him, waited while he added the ice cream, then took the desserts to the table while he put the ice cream away in the freezer.

They did all this without ever so much as brushing against each other.

They sat down. The house was intimately quiet—no radio, no television, no Joey moving around anywhere.

She picked up her spoon and gouged into the cobbler, then glanced up to find Christopher intent on her, sitting motionless, his wrists resting against the edge of the table beside his bowl. His blue eyes were steady, smileless, sure.

He said, "Let's get this over with," and took the spoon from her hand, put it back in the bowl and drew her toward him around the corner of the table. She let herself be pulled sideways onto his lap while his arms came around her and his face lifted to kiss her. There was no subtle foolery, no dissembling, not from the first. The kiss was wholly sexual, wet and filled with motion. He tilted his head back, opened his lips and stroked her teeth and tongue. She looped her arms around his neck and let it happen . . . and happen . . . until her heart seemed to expand against her ribs, leaving little room for her lungs to fill and empty. They tasted and stroked each other in the way each had imagined many times, in a whorl of sleek tongues and moist lips, while a full minute slipped away, and then two. In the middle of that time, he shifted her on his lap, dropping her to one side, bending above her until they were twisted together like a pair of tree trunks from a long-ago storm.

It ended lingeringly, with an easing of his hold and a slow unwinding of their bodies until her face was again above his. Their lips parted but stayed close. Their breathing was strident. His hands rested lightly on her sides.

He spoke first, in a voice half-trapped in his throat. "I wasn't sure I could choke down those peaches without getting this out of the way first."

"Me either," she answered, and slipped from his lap to return to her chair.

They picked up their spoons and each ate a bite of warm cobbler and cold ice cream. The air around them seemed smothering, as if it contained too little oxygen for their needs. She glanced up and saw him watching her, his elbows on the table and his spoon leaving his lips. Suddenly, the nine years' dearth of physical affection seemed to catch her like the crack of a whip. It coiled around her body, knocked the spoon from her hand and hauled her from her chair back to his.

It happened so fast. One moment she was safely seated. The next she was standing above him with her hands on his face, lifting it, bending above it and picking up where they'd left off moments ago. And ten seconds after that—without a break in the kiss—she had thrown one leg over his lap and straddled him, striking the table edge with her hip, then taking a ride with him as he pivoted his chair at a sharper angle away from the table.

His arms slid low, pulling her flush against him. She embraced him from her high vantage point, kissing his warm supple mouth while his hands slid around the backs of her thighs and cupped them gently from behind, near the bend of her knees. They shared the flavor of peaches and cream from within each other's mouths, and that sleek fit of two tongues mating, of lips gliding in an endless quest. They had put this off so long it felt like a reward which they shared. They did so, however, sitting smack in view of the front door, while her mind clamored, *Don't come in yet, Joey, please don't come in!*

When things got too crazy inside her, she drew back, as one drugged, realizing she had to get off his lap. "I have to—"

His open mouth cut off the words. His arms snapped her back where she'd been and his shoulder blades came away from the chair. They'd played the song and dance so long that they explored now with exquisite relief, tasting each other and letting their feelings carry the reckless moment. It fled her mind how young he was, for this close, age had no significance. It fled his mind how old she was, for it had never mattered to him nearly as much as it had to her. Kissing, they were merely man and woman, and very facile ones at that.

They ended the kiss mutually, if reluctantly.

Though their mouths parted, their eyes refused. They sat beguiled, breathing hard, a little stunned, his hands still cupping the backs of her thighs in her tight blue jeans.

"Joey could come," she whispered, and slowly swung her leg off him, his right hand trailing around her kneecap, lingering there until she reluctantly backed off and returned to her chair.

They centered themselves before their peach cobbler, which was now surrounded by a lake of melted ice cream. She picked up her spoon and watched the white liquid drip from its tip. She looked up at him.

"Do you know how long it's been since I've done that?"

"No, but I'd like to."

"Nine years."

"Are you kidding? That's not natural."

She shrugged.

"You never kissed anyone since your husband died?"

"A few times I did, a year or so after he died. But never like this. Always testing myself to see if I could, then afterwards feeling as if I wanted to hurry home and brush my teeth."

"And what do you feel like now?"

"I feel . . . a little scared. A little surprised. But brushing my teeth is the farthest thing from my mind."

He gave a smile that was quickly spirited away by the gravity of what had just happened, the call of their bodies for more, the near certainty that this was only the beginning. They sat as they were, with the house's emptiness beating around them, their food forgotten, studying each other in an elaborate silence.

Finally Christopher pushed his chair back and said, "I think I'd better go." His voice sounded like someone else's, throaty with suppressed emotion. He rose and threaded his arms through the sleeves of his jacket, fitted the zipper together and raised it to pocket level. He took out his gloves but held them without putting them on.

She sat on the edge of her chair, tipped forward from the hip, her hands spread on the tight thighs of her blue jeans, looking up at him.

"Thanks for the cobbler," he said. "Sorry I didn't finish it." He looked down at his gloves, then back over at her. "Well, to be honest, I'm really not that sorry."

She grinned timorously and rose as he turned toward the front hall, navigating its length with dilatory footsteps. At the door, he turned back to her.

"Do you want to do something . . ." His pause might have been a shrug. "Whenever? It's hard right now. Our schedules are pretty conflicting."

"Let's just wait and see," she said. "Things are going to get busy at the shop and we'll be staying open evenings between now and Christmas. I think we're going to put on a couple of temporaries for the season, just to clerk for us, but still, my hours will be uncertain."

"Sure," he said, understanding the need to progress cautiously.

"Well," he said, opening the door. "I'll call."

"Yes, do that."

Their belated caution kept them from considering a goodbye kiss. What had happened on the kitchen chair was enough to send him, if not scuttling, most certainly retreating to give thought to what they had initiated here tonight.

Chapter 11

*S*ECRECY came hard for Lee Reston. What she had done surprised and shocked her. She needed desperately to talk about it with someone she could trust. She ran through the list of possibilities. Sylvia? Sylvia was, for all her dear qualities, a staunch prude. She never talked about anything regarding sex. She and Barry were the kind of couple who rarely touched in public and generally demonstrated so little affection for one another Lee had often wondered what they did in their bedroom.

Mother? Mother was so totally out of the question it was absurd to consider her. Propriety was the ultimate force in Peg Hillier's life, and discussing straddling a man fifteen years your junior on a kitchen chair during a first necking session would have drawn only a metaphoric standing in the corner from the older woman.

Janice? Oh, mea culpa, mea culpa. What Lee had done, when measured against Janice's confessed feelings for Christopher, was reprehensible. Merely thinking of Janice made Lee feel like the town harlot. What kind of mother was she anyway?

What about the women who worked for her? She felt it was inadvisable to blur the line between employer and employee with off-hours friendship. It made leadership difficult in negative times.

If only Joey were older. Unfortunately, Joey was at the age where he thought snapping a girl's bra was foreplay. It would be many years yet before she could talk about the birds and the bees with Joey.

Lloyd? She nearly succumbed to the idea that Lloyd might be a guiding light in this impasse, but she felt awkward broaching the subject with the father of her late husband.

Ironically, the only one she could possibly trust with such intimate stuff was Christopher himself, and right now she felt it wiser to keep her distance from him. She had discovered that something he'd said Sunday night was too true for comfort: going as long as she had without kissing a man was unnatural. Now that she'd broken the fast, she was tempted to gorge.

She became distracted at work. On the day after her date with Christopher she and Sylvia were discussing the price of red carnations, which always shot sky-high at holiday time. Sylvia had said she wished they'd pre-booked more the previous month, when the best discounts had been available.

Lee came out of a fog to realize Sylvia had asked her a question.

"Oh, sorry. What was that?"

Sylvia was studying her with a pucker between her eyebrows. "Lee, what in the world is the matter with you today?"

"Nothing. What did you say?"

"I said, do you think we should hire a couple of high school students to cut up Christmas greens and put them in plastic bags?"

"Of course. Good idea. Why pay designers' wages for work like that? Oh . . . and, Sylvia?" Lee paused, giving her full attention to her sister in an effort to erase the frown from her face. "Order a lot of incense cedar, will you? You know how I love the smell of it."

Sylvia said, "Do you feel all right today?"

"I feel fine."

"Then pay attention to what you're doing. You just put those evergreen boughs in the cooler with the carnations."

Lee looked and, sure enough, she'd done exactly what Sylvia had said. There sat a bucket of boughs which, if left in the same cooler, would put the carnations to sleep.

She took the evergreens out and said, sheepishly, "Sorry."

She had been daydreaming about straddling Christopher's lap and kissing him till her jaws ached.

Two days went by and he didn't call. Her shop was on Main Street. The police department was a block off Main on Jackson, meaning the black-and-white cars drove by constantly, coming and going on calls. She seemed to have developed sensors that lifted her head every time a squad car rolled by. Most times there was a smattering of greenery between her and the window, impossible to see through, but sometimes she caught a glimpse of a squad car through it and imagined him behind the wheel. Other times the cars went out on flashing red with their sirens shrilling, and the sound would quicken her heart.

A week after Thanksgiving she was watering some plants in the window when she caught a flash of black-and-white, looked up, and there he was, cruising past on duty. He waved. She waved ... and stood with the watering pitcher forgotten in her hand, her heart doing a circus act against her ribs while she watched the police car roll down Main Street out of sight.

Only minutes later the phone rang beside the cash register at the rear of the store.

"Lee, it's for you," Sylvia called.

"Thanks." Lee set down her watering pitcher and went to the back counter. "Hello?"

"Hello," Christopher said. "You look pretty good in that front window."

She had no idea what to say, so she said nothing, just stood there like a dummy trying to keep her face pale.

"Oh, somebody's there, right?"

"Yes."

"Do you ever get days off in the middle of the week?"

"Sometimes. Now, during the Christmas season when we're open nights, we stagger our hours a little more. What did you want?"

"Some help with a Christmas tree. I've never had one before but I thought I'd put one up this year. Will you help me pick out some decorations?"

Sylvia asked, "Who is it?"

Without covering the mouthpiece, Lee said, "It's Christopher. He wants me to give him a little advice on buying tree ornaments." Into the phone, she asked, "Isn't there any chance of doing it in the evening?"

Sylvia interrupted. "Lee, just a minute."

"Just a minute, Chris."

Sylvia's expression said she felt guilty for what she was about to ask. "I need a day off, too, to do some Christmas shopping. Go ahead and make your plans. I'll fill in for you if you fill in for me. We'll both go nuts if we don't get away from here a little."

Lee asked Chris, "What day did you have in mind?"

"Any day. I'm off next Tuesday and Wednesday though, if you wanted to make a day of it."

"Tuesday?" she asked Sylvia. When her sister nodded, she said, "Tuesday's good, Chris."

"I'll pick you up at your house at ten."

"Fine."

When Lee had hung up, Sylvia lamented, "I don't know how I'm going to get everything done before Christmas. It's the same thing every year. I've been meaning to talk to you about a day off, but things have been so crazy around here I felt guilty to ask."

"You're right though. We'll both go bonkers if we don't get away now and then."

Lee realized something that afternoon that had not struck her before. People were unsuspicious of her comings and goings with Christopher simply because they saw him as a boy, not a man. Because it was inconceivable that a woman of her age would be engaged in any kind of romantic liaison with a man of thirty, their antennae never went up. Furthermore, he had been her son's friend. They saw him, perhaps, as he'd been at the beginning: a son figure who got along well with the family and had been adopted by them because he had none of his own. The concept was simple: familiarity as camouflage.

She found it difficult to digest the fact that on a workday morning in the middle of the week, she was playing hooky from the shop, dressing in play clothes and waiting to go off on a lark with a man who had filled her thoughts with adolescent musings for the past two weeks. Yet she was. There was her very own reflection in the bathroom mirror looking brighter-eyed than usual, her cheeks with so much color she disdained blusher while putting on her makeup. It had been so many years since she'd felt this exhilaration at the thought of being with someone, since she'd examined her mirrored image with some male's projected opinion guiding her judgment of what she saw: a middle-aged woman, reasonably trim, reasonably pleasant-looking, with plain, plain hair, wearing black stretch pants and an aqua-blue turtleneck beneath an oversized thick-knit cotton shirt done in blocks of black, yellow and aqua. She spent a brief worry over whether or not the outfit was too coedish; nothing looked sillier than a woman her age trying to look as though she were eighteen.

Giving herself approval on all but the color spots in her cheeks, she shut off the light.

He arrived promptly. Because she feared her reaction to meeting him the first time after their tryst on the kitchen chair, she was slamming the front door behind her while his Explorer was still bumping over the end of the driveway. He managed to get one foot on the ground while she was halfway down the sidewalk, and waited there in the lee of the open truck door as she reached the other side and got in.

He got in, too, and smiled her way. *Dear God,* she thought, *don't let him lean over and kiss me right here in broad daylight with my neighbors home up and down the street.*

He didn't.

He put the truck in reverse and said, "Where we going?"

She said, "Lindstrom, Minnesota."

"Lindstrom, Minnesota?" It was an hour away.

"If you want to."

"What's there?"

"Gustaf's World of Christmas. Two charming turn-of-the-century houses, side by side on the main street of town, where it's Christmas all year long. I haven't been there for a long, long time, but as I recall, it incites the child in you, plus they have Christmas decorations from all over the world. I think you'll enjoy it."

He shifted to drive, and she felt his eyes linger on her as the truck began rolling down the street. She flashed him a smile, which seemed to be what he was waiting for before settling into his duty as driver.

The day suited their purpose. It was dove-gray with crystal etchings.

Overnight, hoarfrost had formed and was drifting from the trees in glisteny falls. On the boulevards snow piles stood knee-high; toddlers with scarves over their faces slid down them on sheets of blue plastic. Christmas music was playing on the truck radio, and the heater threw out a steady current of warm air.

They left the city behind and bore east into open country.

Christopher said, "I need to buy a Christmas tree. Do you think I should get a fake one or a real one?"

"A real one. Those fake things are abominable. Besides, they don't have any smell."

"So you like the smell of pine?"

"I love it. This is my favorite time of year in the shop because it smells so intoxicating. Just about every arrangement we make has evergreens in it, and we get in a new batch nearly every day. They come in huge boxes and they have to be snipped into usable lengths, and when you're cutting them—especially the incense cedar—there's nothing else like it in the world. Incense cedar has a real lemony smell mixed with the pine. And it stays fragrant forever."

"I never heard of incense cedar. I wouldn't even know what it is."

"You would once you smelled it. We buy lots of other varieties though, too—white pine, balsam, fir, arborvitae, juniper. Juniper is the worst to work with. It really makes a mess of your hands."

He glanced down at her hands, but they were covered by gloves.

"Sylvia just flat refuses to work with it. But Sylvia doesn't do as much arranging as I do. She's the businesswoman. I'm the arranger."

"Did she say anything about your going with me today?"

Their eyes met briefly before he returned his attention to the highway. "No. All she said was that she needs a day off too, to start on her Christmas shopping."

No more was said on the subject.

Christopher said, "Tell me more about what you do every day."

He was the rare person who asked a question, then listened to the answer. As she talked about her shop, she realized that in her life as a mother of three busy offspring, years had gone by since she'd been around anyone genuinely interested in her day-to-day affairs. With Joey and Janice, she was expected to be interested in theirs, but the truth was they rarely asked about hers.

She described an ordinary day in the florists' business: waiting on customers, designing arrangements, throwing out old stock, scrubbing buckets, getting in new flowers, stripping their lower leaves, the various ways they needed hardening before being used in arrangements. She told him that half their flowers came from South America, where pesticides were used more liberally than in the States, and that she occasionally worried about the amount she was absorbing through her hands. Hands, she said, absorbed them more readily than you'd think. He glanced at her hands, but she still had her gloves on.

She described the boxes that came from Colombia by way of Miami, where agents ran metal rods through them, looking for cocaine, so the cartons arrived looking as though they'd been shot full of bullet holes. She told him how much fun it was going to trade shows, and that her next one was coming up in January at the Minneapolis Gift Mart. She said business was very good this winter: They'd just gotten a standing order from a Methodist church for twenty dollars' worth of loose flowers every Saturday, and orders like that were bread and butter because they didn't cost any arranging time, and the bill always got paid. She and Sylvia would have to hire a new designer soon, she said, because Nancy was pregnant and going to quit. He asked how you know a good designer. She replied that you can always tell a good one by her hands: Good ones never wear gloves and work with a Swiss army knife instead of scissors. Christmas time, she said, was especially hard on the hands because of the sap in the evergreens and all the turpentine it took to get rid of it.

He said, "Let me see your hands."

She said, "No."

"You have a thing about your hands, but I've never noticed anything wrong with them."

"They're always a mess."

He said, "A new side of Lee Reston—self-conscious about her hands."

She said, "That's right."

And he didn't ask again.

The yard at Gustaf's was decorated with life-size wooden reindeer wearing willow wreaths around their necks, trailing red-and-green-plaid ribbons.

Inside, it smelled of mulberry. Lights twinkled everywhere. Christmas carols tinkled forth in myriad tones: Swiss bells, carillons, jingle bells and chimes. Ceilings, walls and floors were Disneyesque with holiday trimmings for sale. Balls and bells, toy soldiers and tinsel, tree lights and yard ornaments and a room with so many miniature painted wooden trinkets it felt like walking into a shop in Oslo. Dolls with porcelain faces sat in miniature rocking chairs. Santas of all descriptions beamed upon the colorful array with rosy cheeks and mischievous eyes. A clerk dressed like one of Santa's helpers smiled and said, "Merry Christmas."

"Merry Christmas," they replied in unison.

"Ask, if I can help with anything."

"We will."

They explored every magical room of the old house.

Christopher found a Santa beard and hooked it on behind his ears. "Ho ho ho," he boomed in his best basso profundo. "Have you been a good little girl?"

"Not exactly," she replied, giving him a saucy glance. The words slipped out before she realized how flirtatious they were.

He took off the beard and put it back on the wall, and she knew he was going to touch her shoulder, say something intimate about what had passed between them the last time they were together. To forestall him, she slipped into another room. He came right behind her, hustling around the corner to find her facing the doorway wearing a white mobcap, holding a stuffed white teddy bear to her cheek, singing, "All I want for Chrith-muth ith my two front teeth."

Moments later she discovered him holding up a personalized stocking at least two feet long, pointing at it with his eyebrows raised. Across the top of it was printed CHRIS.

She found a pair of the ugliest earrings in the world, shaped like red electric Christmas lights, and held them up to her ears. "Would you believe they actually light up?"

They laughed and she put them back where they belonged.

The next time she turned around he'd found some mistletoe and was holding it above his head, wearing a rowdy smile.

"Oh, no," she reprimanded. "Nothin' doing. Not in the middle of a public place."

"Oh—what?" he asked innocently, looking around. "You need a kitchen chair?"

"Christopher!" she scolded in a whisper.

He put the mistletoe back in a wooden sleigh and sauntered over to her, putting himself between her and any further progress through the shop. "Touchy subject?" he inquired.

"Not exactly. Well, yes, sort of. I mean, I don't know. I'm just a little amazed at myself for what I did."

"Any regrets?" he asked.

She shook her head slowly, looking up at him at such close range it would have taken only the smallest movement for them to be kissing again right here in Gustaf's World of Christmas.

They chose his tree decorations after that—multicolored miniature lights, gold tinsel garland, some oversized gilded jingle bells, and glass balls that appeared to have snow falling inside them when the light refracted off their transparent surface. They bought a tree stand and a fat red candle surrounded by holly, and a box of delicate ribbon candy, which he claimed he'd never seen before in his life and which totally fascinated him.

They hauled their booty to the truck and he asked, "Are you hungry?" It was 1:30 in the afternoon.

"Ravenous."

He looked up and down the main street of Lindstrom, Minnesota, and said, "Let's take a walk . . . see what we can find."

They found the Rainbow Café, where coffee was served in thick white mugs, and napkins were stored in metal dispensers on the tables, and the locals were telling jokes over coffee at a long Formica bar.

She ordered a Denver sandwich and he opted for a hot beef, mounded with potatoes and gravy, of course.

Afterward, they found a tree lot next to a bank building and bought two fragrant green Norway pines, which they tied on the top of the Explorer before heading back to Anoka.

They rode without talking until well after the truck got warm and cozy. He turned the radio on softly and she sat low on her tailbone with one knee up on the dash. He looked over at her, relaxed, with her fingers linked over her stomach. Her nails were clipped short and the cuticles looked stained and ragged. It only made her more real to him.

"What time does Joey get home?"

She checked her watch and said, "Right about now."

He asked, "Do you have to go home?"

Her head was resting against the back of the seat. She rolled it to face him and they jiggled along the road in the tightly sprung vehicle for another five seconds. He noted that at some time since they'd finished their lunch she'd put on fresh lipstick. She noted that his hair, much like hers, always seemed to look the same. After a whole day of being on the go, shaking snow off of Christmas trees, tying them onto the roof of the truck in the wind, his hair sprang up and away from his face as perfectly as ever. She absolutely loved his hair.

Did she have to go home?

"No," she answered.

She thought he'd never look back at the highway.

He took her to his apartment complex, pushed an activator for an automatic door and drove into an underground garage. The door rumbled shut behind them, they parked, and he said, "If you'll get the packages, I'll get the tree."

When he'd untied it from the roof of the truck she said, "It'll make a mess unless you put it in the stand down here."

"Oh," he said—a novice. "Right."

It took some tools, but he had them in the truck, and after ten minutes he had the tree in the stand and he carried it while she opened doors in front of him. At his own door he handed her the keys and said, "Both locks."

She opened them both, thinking how different she was from Christopher in this regard. She who left her garage door up night and day and often never locked her house; he—the policeman—who recognized the value of a dead bolt.

Inside, he set the tree down and said, "Be right back. Take off your jacket and make yourself at home."

He went to the bathroom and came back out to find her talking to Joey on the kitchen telephone.

"Hi, hon, it's Mom."

"Oh, hey, Mom, I'm glad you called. Are there any of those meat roll-up things left that we had for supper the other night?"

"They're in the refrigerator in a square plastic container with a yellow cover."

"Oh, great! Jeez, I'm starved. We had tripe for school lunch today. Hey, what time are you coming home?"

She looked up and found Christopher standing in the living room doorway, sucking a piece of ribbon candy, watching and listening. "I should be there by eight." Their eyes met and held.

"Good, then I don't have to wait to eat, right?"

"Right. Go ahead and warm up the beef rolls. Zap a potato with it too, if you want. There's sour cream in the fridge."

"Okay. Yeah, that sounds good."

"Well, I'll see you around eight then, okay?"

"Yeah, sure, unless I go over to Sandy's."

"Home by ten, mister, right?"

She could imagine him rolling his eyes. He'd been creeping over the mark lately. "Yeah, right."

"Okay then, 'bye."

When she'd hung up, Christopher asked, "Everything okay?"

"Fine. He had tripe for lunch, but it seems he survived the ordeal."

Christopher chuckled and said, "Come and help me decide where to put this thing."

They lit lamps against the dusky afternoon, turned on the radio and studied his living room furniture.

"Where do you think?" he asked.

They cleared a spot in front of the sliding glass door and pushed the sofa into the exact center of the room facing it. It looked unorthodox, but the view of the tree was great, and with the stereo components on the wall behind the sofa, the sound came through beautifully, too.

Dumping their purchases from the packages, Christopher asked, "What goes on first?"

"Lights," she said, and while he began pulling the tree lights out of their boxes, she said, "Christopher, didn't you *ever* do this at home?"

"Nope," he said, tending to what he was doing.

She heard the brusque note of defensiveness and decided this was no time for unhappy memories. "Well, plug them in first so you can see what you're doing. I think it works best to start at the top and work your way down. How's the ribbon candy?"

"Spicy. Have a piece."

The tree was six feet tall, so he strung the top ones while she did the bottom, and they both sucked the hard candy. They got out the tinsel garland next, while Kenny Rogers came on the stereo with a sentimental song about a married couple playing Santa on Christmas Eve. Lee gave Christopher the end of the garland and said, "Start up at the top." He draped it from branch to branch while she did the same below, weaving back and forth, and somehow she got in his way. The gold-spangled garland caught on her mouth while she was dipping beneath his arm, and as she tried to swing free, it caught on the turtleneck of her shirt, pulled out of his hands and off the last branch he'd decorated.

"Oops, look what I've done. Sorry."

"Hey, there's more on you than on the tree."

She looked up and he saw a single golden filament caught on her lipstick, glistening there like a fragment of a fallen star.

"Hold still," he said, and reached out to remove it with a fingertip. It stuck to her glossy lipstick and he had to use a fingernail to free it, while she stood as still as an hour hand, holding her lips open, looking up at him.

They'd delayed it all day. They'd been responsible, clear-thinking, non-libidinal adults while they were out in public. They had refrained from ardent gazes, touches, intimate exchanges and all the tens of things in which two healthy, red-blooded, attracted people might well have indulged. But her lips were open . . . and he'd touched them with one finger . . . and the kisses they'd shared two weeks ago had remained in their thoughts ever since . . . and around them a gravelly voice was singing about the greatest gift of all.

He dipped his head and put his mouth on hers so tenderly not a hair on her head moved. The golden garland, still in his hand, draped onto the floor where it pooled and glistened like the dropped belts of angels. They remained just so, lips scarcely joined, each tipping slightly toward the other until she teetered a bit and touched his chest to regain her balance. He opened his eyes, caught her hand with his and carried it to his mouth to kiss its roughened knuckles.

Into her eyes, he said softly, "Let's finish this first."

They finished festooning the tree, never touching, politely handing one another ornaments, realizing full well it was only six o'clock.

When the ornaments were hung and the floor was littered with Christmas scree, she knelt to pick up loose pine needles and cardboard boxes and cellophane. He turned off the lamps and went to stand behind and above her, touching the top of her head. "I'll do that tomorrow. Come here." At her delay in rising, he doubled forward, running a hand down her arm to make her drop the cardboard box full of pine needles. "Come here," he whispered again, and pulled her to her feet, then led her to the sofa.

There, he stretched out on his side and drew her down beside him. The cushion gave and she rolled lightly against him. He put a hand on her waist, tipped his head and gave them both the only Christmas gift they wanted at the moment. He wet her lips and abraded her tongue with his own and wiped out all the pent-up longing of that day, and the days before it, and the nights they'd lain awake in their separate beds wondering when this would happen again. They took the sweetest of time, exchanging a candy-flavored kiss that stretched on . . . and on . . . and on . . .

When they opened their eyes they saw red, green, blue and gold lights pieing the walls, the furniture, their clothing and hair.

"Can we talk about it now?" he asked, still with his hand on her waist.

"Talk about what?" she whispered.

"About what we've been feeling since that night. What we've been feeling all day today. What made you resist getting up from your knees and coming over here a minute ago."

A beat passed before she confessed, "Guilt."

"About what?"

"What I did on that kitchen chair."

"You didn't do anything wrong."

"Didn't I?"

"I shouldn't have teased you about it today. I'm sorry. I didn't know it was bothering you so much."

"I've thought about how others would see it—my mother, my daughter, my sister. I think they'd call it seduction."

"It went both ways."

"But I'm fifteen years older than you."

"So you're not allowed to express your emotions?"

"I shocked myself."

"You shocked me, too, but I loved it."

"It's been a very long time, you see, and kissing you was suddenly so irresistible. This is irresistible . . . lying here this way. You were right, it's unnatural to go without . . . without this kind of physical affection for so long. It's been two weeks since we kissed on that kitchen chair, and I haven't been able to think of anything else since."

"And so you feel guilty?"

"Of course, don't you?"

"No. You're female. I'm male. What's there to feel guilty about?"

"Our ages, for one thing."

"I figured that was coming."

"And my long drought, for another. I imagine women can do some pretty dumb things when a younger man pays them some attention after years of none at all."

"Is that all I am to you . . . a younger man paying you some attention?"

"No, you know you're not."

"So what's your big problem with us? All we're doing is kissing."

"You were Greg's friend."

"And that's the first time his name has been mentioned all day long. Do you realize that?"

She hadn't. Her eyes told him so.

"Hey, don't go guilty on me again. It's a healthy sign, you and me spending an entire day together and all we concentrated on was having fun. I thought we did rather well at it, myself."

"We did. I loved it."

"And you don't think it's significant that we never talked about Greg once?"

"Yes, I do. But it's only been six months since his death, and maybe I'm . . . maybe . . ."

"Go on, say it. Maybe you're still going through some grief process and this is part of it."

"Well, maybe it is."

"Maybe. Then again, maybe it's not. And if it is, so what? We're talking about it, it's out in the open. If that's what this is for either one of us, we'll find out soon enough. The glow will wear off and we won't feel so much like being together anymore. Personally, I don't think that's going to happen though."

"Which will be disastrous, too."

"Why?"

"Because Janice has a crush on you."

"I know that."

She picked her head up off his arm. "You do?"

"I've known that for a long time."

"And you'd still do this with me?"

"I never gave her one iota of encouragement. Ask her."

She laid her head back down and admitted, "I don't have to. She's already confided in me."

"There, you see? Now what other hang-ups do you have here?"

"You make it so simplistic."

"It is. All I set out to do was lie here for a while and kiss you and enjoy my first Christmas tree, and maybe make the two of us feel a little less lonely for a while. That's pretty simplistic." His voice turned soft, seductive. "It's just my mouth . . ." He moved closer. ". . . on your mouth."

And what an incredible mouth he had. He was so good at using it, suckling her lips, setting his head in motion and encouraging her to do the same. He kissed her the way she hadn't been kissed since courting days, in the lingering, juicy, slow, sexy way that says, *If this is what we're settling for, let's make it good.* His sweet blandishments worked. She freed her mind of thought and let sensuality pull her into its lair, following his lead and immersing herself in the texture and taste of him. Long liquid kisses led to a dearer fit of their bodies down below. He lifted a knee and she made space for it between her own, welcoming the high, hard pressure he exerted as he lifted it against her warmth.

He made a pleasured sound, "Mmm . . . ," and moved his hand up her back, pressing circles on it, touching her nape, her shoulders, riding his palm flat and hard down her vertebrae to the bend of her spine.

It had been so long since she'd lain with a man, fit herself against one, felt his arousal against her stomach. So long since she'd run her hands over firm, hard shoulders, into short, springy hair. His hair—ah—the feel of it was so different from her own, and when she sifted her fingers through it his scent lifted, the peculiar and individual essence she would ever after recognize as his.

It was as he'd said—this was so unutterably good, she had no desire to desist. His moist lips left hers and wandered her face, dropping kisses where they would—upon her cheek, eyebrow, hairline, nose—dampening her skin, sometimes letting the tip of his tongue mark its passing. He pressed his mouth to her neck, drew three circles with his tongue, bringing forth the scent of the perfume she'd sprayed there that morning.

At last he pulled back and looked into her face.

She opened her eyes and saw his at close range, with the tree lights reflected in them.

"My, you're good at that," she murmured.

"So are you."

"A little out of practice."

"Wanna practice some more?" He grinned.

"I'd love to . . . but my arm is falling asleep." It had been pinned under him for fifteen minutes.

"I can fix that," he said, and rolled on top of her, putting a hand under her back and plumping her over two inches at a time until he lay flush atop her in the center of the couch.

They studied each other's eyes, searching for consent.

"Lee, I meant it," he whispered. "Just kissing, if that's all you want."

"What I want and what I'll allow myself to do are two different things."

He kissed her mouth, bearing his weight on his elbows, crooking one knee along the side of her hip.

When the kiss ended she twined her arms around his neck and drew him down, his face falling above her shoulder.

She sighed. "Oh, Christopher, you feel so good on me I could stay here all night."

"Good idea," he said, intentionally shattering the spell that was getting too tempting. "Should I call Joey or will you?"

She laughed but her stomach refused to lift beneath his greater weight.

"Laugh some more," he said, muffled, near her ear. "Feels great."

Instead she grew still, closing her eyes and appreciating these minutes of closeness, and the realization that she was still desirable, still sexual, with a man again and enjoying it.

"Lee?" he said near her ear.

"What?" she murmured, lazily finger-combing the back of his hair.

He lifted his head and bore his weight on his elbows. "Promise me you won't pull the same tricks you pulled on me at Thanksgiving."

She said, "I'm so sorry for that."

"I want to be with you on Christmas."

"You will be, I promise. But how are we going to keep from giving ourselves away?"

"Trust me. You didn't know how I felt about you until a few weeks ago, did you?"

"I had my suspicions."

"When?" he exclaimed, as if accusing her of fibbing.

"As long ago as the Fourth of July."

"The Fourth of July!"

"When we were sitting side by side eating corn on the cob. And when we banged into each other playing volleyball. And on the Ferris wheel. A woman senses these things before a man does."

"Why didn't you say something?"

"I never would have if you hadn't said something first."

"Why?"

"Because of all the reasons we talked about earlier—the difference in our ages, what my kids would think, the fact that we're still both in mourning and emotionally vulnerable. There are so many reasons they make me question my sanity now."

With his elbows at her shoulders he put his thumbs in the hollows of her cheeks and pushed gently. He watched her lips press into a false pout and relax as his thumbs retreated. He studied her eyes, locked on his and happy, in spite of her words.

When he spoke, his voice was deep with candor and honesty. "Any mother fixation I ever had on you is gone. Do you believe me?"

She studied his face, wiped clean of smiles and teasing. She felt a thrill and a warning inside, that what they'd begun could lead to hurt for both of them if they let this get out of hand. She hooked his neck and brought his mouth close enough to kiss. Once. Fast.

"Yes. And now I must go."

"Why?"

"Because I like this too much. I like you too much. You feel too good and I've had too much fun today and I'm getting so mixed up." His eyes seemed to be studying her as if putting great thought into what she said. "And because I'm afraid of what we've started here. Aren't you?"

Again he considered before answering, "No, I'm not. Not like you." Then he sat back and worked his way off her, grabbed her by both hands and hauled her up. "Come on. I'll take you home."

Chapter 12

THE following Saturday night Lee closed the store at nine after a grueling day spent mostly on her feet. The demand for fresh-cut flower arrangements had become so great she and Sylvia had decided to hire an additional designer now and have her stay on when Nancy quit after the holidays. The new designer was named Leah. She was Asian, and brought to Absolutely Floral a fresh, new visual aspect in flower arranging. Many of her arrangements were minimalistic, asymmetrical and stunning. Lee had watched her work, caught Sylvia's eye and known within ten minutes she was the one they wanted. They had offered her ten dollars an hour, compromised at eleven when she asked for twelve, and believed they were getting a bargain.

However, even with the additional designer, and with Rodney making extra delivery runs each day, they could scarcely keep up with poinsettias for churches, centerpieces for Christmas parties and gift bouquets, both personal and business. There had been three weddings today as well, plus the foot traffic in the store, which got so bad Lee had called Joey over for a few hours just to help bag green plants and carry them out to the cars, take tailings out to the trash, scrub buckets, polish the showcase doors and keep the floor swept in the designing area. She had kept him there till five o'clock, then had given him fifteen dollars and a kiss as thanks before he walked out the door saying, "A bunch of us are going to do something tonight so I won't be home when you get there."

Now it was 9:15 and Lee arrived home nearly exhausted. Her feet hurt, her legs hurt, she had cut her hand on her Swiss army knife and that hurt. She'd been pricked by so many juniper sprigs her hands had developed a puffy red rash. The constant hammering of woody stems had given her a headache. At this time of the year and at Valentine's Day, the banging went on hour after hour until the place sounded like a carpenter's shop instead of a florist. Sitting in the silent house the absence of sound was so abrupt it seemed felt rather than heard.

She threw her coat across one kitchen chair and plunked down on another to scan the mail, too tired to open the two envelopes mixed in with the junk. She yawned, stared absently at Joey's note lying beside the potted pothos on its red plaid runner. *Mom, a bunch of us are going bowling together, then over to Karen Hanson's for sloppy joes. Home by 10:30.* His curfew time was ten, but she was too tired to quibble over trivialities. It was the Christmas season, and he'd come to the shop to help her without complaining. She'd give the kid a break.

She heated up a can of Campbell's tomato soup, put it in a mug and took it, steaming, to the bathroom where she filled the tub, sank into bubbles to her armpits and leaned back, sipping when she remembered to, mostly letting the mug wobble back and forth on her knee while she dozed.

She awoke with a start when the soup spilled down her leg and stained the water orange. Groaning, she sat up, washed, dried, powdered herself from stem to stern and crawled into some warm, soft pajamas. In the living room, she turned on a single lamp and the television, lay down on the sofa and covered herself with an afghan to wait for Joey.

Some time later she awoke again, startled, disoriented after sleep so sound that the hour, day and all basic reason momentarily eluded her. On the screen Raymond Burr was holding forth in an old Perry Mason rerun. It was Saturday night. She was waiting for Joey. Time was . . . she checked her watch . . .

Ten to twelve!

She threw off the afghan and sat up, heart racing from the discombobulating effects of her startled awakening and the sudden plunge into fear for Joey. He was never late! Never! Ten or fifteen minutes lately, since his hormones had started rampaging and little Sandy Parker had come on the scene.

If he was late, there was something wrong.

Oh God, not another one!

The thought skittered through her brain while it was still short of oxygen from getting vertical too fast. She swayed a bit and sat back down to regain her equilibrium. As surely as she knew he hadn't come in, she knew he was dead. It was Greg all over again, and baby Grant. Oh God, a third one, and she'd have only one left. Panic sluiced through her as she rose and ran to his room to find it empty, the bed rumpled but still made from morning, his work clothes from today lying in a heap on the floor beside a pair of hand weights and a carrying case of CDs.

"Joey!" she shouted, turning frantically into the hall, then hurrying toward the kitchen. "Joey, are you here?"

The light was still on over the stove the way she'd left it. There were no empty dishes in the sink, no evidence of recent snacking.

"Oh God . . . oh God . . ." she despaired under her breath, checking her watch against the kitchen clock. "Where can he be?"

It was midnight when she dialed the number for the Anoka police station—not 911, which was routed through a county dispatcher, but the direct line into the station on Jackson Street.

A woman answered and Lee struggled to keep the panic out of her voice.

"This is Lee Reston. I'm Greg Reston's mother, was Greg Reston's mother, I mean. I know this sounds silly, but my fourteen-year-old son Joey is missing. I mean, he didn't come home when he said he would, and he's *always* on time. *Always.* I'm just wondering if by any chance there's been any . . . well . . . report of anything . . . or word of him . . . anything you know of."

"Hi, Mrs. Reston. This is Toni Mansetti. No, I'm sorry. Nothing at all. But I'll certainly put it on the radio and alert the officers on duty."

"No!" she exclaimed, struck by the nebulous illogic that as long as she kept it unofficial he was okay. Then quieter, "No. It's probably something perfectly explainable and he'll come walking in any minute. He was with a bunch of kids so he's probably just fine."

"His name is Joey and he's fourteen?"

"Yes."

"Can you give me a description?"

"Oh listen, no, no, I don't want . . . he'll be . . . just forget it."

"Are you sure?"

"Yes, I'm . . . thank you, Toni. I'm sure he'll show up any minute."

When Toni Mansetti got off the phone she went into the squad room but none of the on-duty officers were around. Christmas season was a violent time of the year and Saturday nights were the worst. Suicides, burglaries, robberies and lots of drunks. Domestics broke out over ridiculous reasons: whose in-laws couples were going to spend Christmas with, who spent too much money on Christmas presents, who was flirting with whom at the company Christmas party. Money shortages, alcohol and loneliness kept 911 ringing more often than at any other time of year. Of the five officers on duty, none were in the squad room when Toni Mansetti checked.

Back at her radio, she called Ostrinski, who was cruising. He picked up immediately.

"Pete, this is Toni. I just had a call from Greg Reston's mother. She sounded a little panicky and said her fourteen-year-old son isn't home yet from some teenage get-together, but she didn't want me to declare him missing. Keep your eyes open though, will you?"

"Ten-four. Toni, is Lallek around there yet?"

"No, he got off at eleven and left right afterwards."

"Do me a favor, will you? Give him a call at home and apprise him of the situation. He's close to that family and I think he'd want to know. He's just like the rest of us, has a hard time sleeping when he gets off mid-shift. He'll probably still be up."

"Copy, Pete. Will do."

Chris had gone to bed but was lying awake when his phone rang. He rolled over, grabbed it in the dark and said, "Yuh."

"Chris, this is Toni down at the station. We just had a call from Greg Reston's mother saying her fourteen-year-old son Joey is missing. We're going to keep an eye out, but Ostrinski thought you'd want to know."

Chris was already out of bed, stretching the phone cord while reaching for his clothes. "What are the details?"

"All she said was that he was with a bunch of friends and that he didn't come home when he said he would. She hung up before I could get a description out of her. She sounded panicked."

"He's about five feet seven, short brown hair a little wavy, no glasses, probably wearing a red jacket with white sleeves—no letter. He looks a lot like Greg. Home address is 1225 Benton Street. Put it on the radio, okay, Toni? And thanks for calling. I'll get over there right away. She'll be going crazy worrying."

"You want me to send a squad over, too?"

"Not yet. I'll call in if I want one."

"Copy. Good luck, Lallek."

Christopher was not a praying man, but a prayer went through his mind, directed at Lee Reston. *Hang on, Lee, I'm coming, I'm coming. He's going to be okay. He's not going to be dead like your other two, but I know what you're going through, so hang on, babe, till I can get there and help you through this!*

While he drove to her house disregarding every driving law he'd ever learned, he found his heart ramming in fear for her and what he knew was going through her mind.

At 12:15 when Lee saw car lights turning into her driveway, she opened the door and went out onto the icy concrete step barefoot, in her pajamas.

The engine and lights were cut, a door slammed and Christopher came striding up the sidewalk.

The sight of him was a gift of greater value than any she'd ever received in her life. His presence—his sturdy, commonsense, trained presence—lifted a portion of the weight from her heart. He knew, always knew when she needed him. It was uncanny.

"Have you heard from him yet?" he asked well before he reached her.

"No. Oh, Christopher, I'm so scared."

She had come halfway down the sidewalk to meet him. He swept her forward in one arm toward the storm door, which had already grown frosty with the inner door open. "Get inside. My God, you haven't even got any shoes on."

The tears she'd held at bay while alone began stinging her eyes now that he was here to carry some of the burden of worry. "He's never done this before. He's always had a curfew and always obeyed it without complaining."

Inside, he shut the doors and she rocketed into his arms. "I'm so glad you're here. How did you find out?"

"The station called me." He hugged her briefly, then gripped her arms to press her back. "Tell me where he was going, what time he left, who he was with."

"He said he was going bowling with a bunch of kids. He left the shop around five o'clock—he'd helped out there this afternoon because we were so busy. After bowling, he said they were all going over to Karen Hanson's house. She's one of the girls he hangs around with. There's a whole bunch of them who always do things together. Here, he left a note."

She led him to the kitchen table. While he read the brief note she told him, "They're all a bunch of really good kids."

"Do you know these Hansons?"

"Yes. I already called there and Karen's mother said the kids went home about ten-fifteen." The tens of dire possibilities implied by the words brought more unwanted tears, but he remained clearheaded and practical.

"Walking?"

"Yes. Different parents give them rides whenever they ask, but a lot of times they just walk in a big group. I never thought to ask him if he needed a ride tonight. He knows that all he has to do is call though and I'll come and pick him up."

"Have you looked in his room?"

"Yes. Nothing."

He headed back there and she followed, stood in the doorway with her arms tightly crossed while he switched on the light and assessed everything slowly. She wondered what his trained eye might pick out that she'd missed, and felt another rush of gratitude for his understanding how hard it would be for her to go through this alone.

"Are these the clothes he was wearing earlier today?"

"Yes."

"Anything missing that you can see?"

"No. Just his jacket, the one he usually wears."

Christopher continued assessing the room while she felt compelled to explain her parental breach.

"I suppose you're wondering why I didn't call earlier, but I came home from work at nine and I was so tired I took a bath and fell asleep on the couch. When I woke up I couldn't believe it was nearly midnight and he wasn't home."

Christopher switched off the light and they went back to the kitchen. "I don't think there's anything to worry about yet. These things happen a lot—kids are reported missing and they just come home later than usual, that's all." He gave her a hug and rubbed her back.

"But he would have called. He knows how I worry."

"How can he know if you've never had to before?"

"Because he knows me, that's all. He wouldn't . . ."

The front door opened and Joey walked in, dressed in his red wool jacket with white leather sleeves, his cheeks rosy from walking in the winter night.

Anger and relief battled in Lee. She marched toward him, demanding, "Where have you been!"

One-handed, he freed his jacket snaps. "With the gang."

"Do you know what time it is!" she bellowed.

He hung his head some while he opened the front closet and hung up his jacket but gave no other sign he shared her concern over the hour.

"It's almost twelve-thirty at night!"

"It's the first time I've ever been late. I don't see what the big deal is."

Lee scarcely controlled the urge to smack him on the side of his head.

"The big deal is that I was worried half out of my mind, that's what the *big deal* is! While you were nonchalantly *hanging out with the gang* I was wondering if you were alive or dead! Calling parents' houses and asking if you were there, finding out you'd left at ten-fifteen. Where have you been since ten-fifteen?"

"At Sandy's," he answered, so quietly she could barely make out the words.

"At Sandy's," she repeated disparagingly. It was then she saw the hickeys on his neck and everything suddenly became clear. The room got uncomfortably silent. Into that silence, Christopher spoke.

"You're okay then, right, Joey?"

Joey shrugged, looked sheepish and mumbled some wordless reply.

Lee stood by feeling guilty for hearing the question she herself should have thought to ask, but she was so angry with the kid, it took an effort to keep from striking him.

To Lee, Christopher said, "I'd better call the station," and moved toward the kitchen telephone. Nobody else spoke while he dialed and said, "Yeah, Toni, this is Chris Lallek. All clear on Joey Reston. You can radio the squads he's home and he's all right."

When he hung up, Joey's face became a mixture of disbelief and embarrassment.

"You had the *police* looking for me?" he said to his mother, his voice cracking with chagrin.

"You don't seem to realize, young man, that things happen to kids your age when they wander around the streets late at night."

"But, gol, Mom . . . the police."

She was about to tear into him again when Christopher said, "Well, now that he's home okay, I'll be going." He walked past Lee and when he got to Joey, curled a hand over his shoulder in passing. "She's right, you know. And you had her awfully scared."

Joey's lips hung open and he stared at the floor, but said nothing.

When Christopher opened the door, the sound seemed to jar Lee from her absorption with her anger. She went to him and stood very close, saying, "Thank you, Christopher, again and again." She banked the strong urge to hug him, but with Joey nearby she could only put a hand on his jacket sleeve. "I can't tell you what it meant to me to see you walking up that sidewalk."

"Anytime," he answered. "See you." Before he left, he said, " 'Night, Joey."

Joey said, "Yeah, g'night."

In Christopher's absence, the silence in the front hall seemed to reverberate. Joey headed for safety, for once bypassing the refrigerator in favor of his room. He hadn't made it to the head of the hall before his mother spoke in the sternest voice possible.

"Joey, come in the living room."

She led the way and sat down stiffly on the sofa, waiting. He followed, walking in that peculiar fashion adopted by guilty teenagers, with their napes high and their chins low. He perched on the edge of a chair at

Lee's right, leaning forward with his elbows on his knees, studying the carpet between his tennis shoes.

"All right, let's talk about it," Lee said.

"Talk about what?" The glance he gave her skittered away again in a millisecond.

"About what you were doing at Sandy's house."

"Nothing. Just watching TV."

"And that's how you got the hickeys on your neck—watching TV?"

It was obvious he hadn't known they were there. He blushed and his hand went up to his shirt collar.

"Were Sandy's parents home?"

It took a while before he shook his head guiltily, still staring at the floor.

"Where were they?"

"At some Christmas party."

Silence again . . . a long, long silence in which Lee's trembling stomach finally began to calm and her anger to dissipate. She leaned forward and reached across the arm of the sofa to cover both of Joey's hands with one of hers. When she spoke her voice held a low hiss of appeal.

"Don't ever do that to me again."

He blinked hard as if tears had formed in his downcast eyes. "I won't."

"I know you think I'm being ridiculous, but since Greg, if I get a little overprotective and jumpy, you'll just have to bear with me. I've never said it before, but it's very hard to be a mother and lose one of your children and not worry every time the others are out of your sight. I've tried really hard to balance my fears with rationalization, but tonight was horrible. Just horrible."

He kept blinking hard at the carpet.

"And don't think I don't understand about what went on tonight, because I do. I've been fourteen and I know how hard it can be to leave your friends when you're having a good time. But, Joey, you and Sandy are only fourteen . . . that's so young."

"Mom, we weren't doing anything, honest."

"Weren't you?"

He met her eyes defiantly. "Just kissing, that's all."

"Standing up or lying down?"

He rolled his eyes and head in disgust. "Jeez, Mom, come on."

"From ten-thirty till twelve-thirty?"

He looked at a far corner of the room and refused to speak.

"Listen," she said, relaxing into a more confidential pose, "there isn't a parent in the world who doesn't face this conversation with every one of her kids, and there isn't a parent in the world who hasn't had to face it with her own parents. I'm not oblivious, you know. I've seen the signs. My goodness, you've grown up practically overnight, and I understand that with that growth comes curiosity, first love, experimenting . . . am I right?"

Joey lurched to his feet and said, "Mom, can I go to bed now?"

"No, you can't," she replied calmly. "If you're old enough to lay down with a girl and get hickeys, you're old enough to make it through this conversation."

Joey sat back down, elbows to knees, linked his fingers loosely and fit his thumbnails together.

She steeled herself and took the plunge, saying the big word. "You've known about intercourse for a long time already; I know because I told you about it myself. Now you're finding out what leads up to it. But, Joey, it's dangerous. Thinking you can indulge in a little foreplay and only go so far can backfire on you, and the next thing you know you're a father."

He met her eyes directly, at last. "Mom, we didn't do that; why won't you believe me?"

"I do believe you, but listen to me anyway. What I'm saying is that now, at your age, the best thing to do is to stay with the group. Be with Sandy—I'm not saying you don't have the right to have a girlfriend—but keep yourselves out of situations where you're alone. I could give you a sermon on condoms, but you get those at school and on TV and in newspapers and just about everywhere you look these days. Right now, I think you need to be a fourteen-year-old boy, maybe kissing girls on doorsteps, okay?"

He nodded halfheartedly. She reached out and tipped up his chin.

"And from now on, if you're going to be late, you call me."

"I will."

"And you'll give some thought to the other?"

He nodded.

"Okay, then, I think it's time we both got some sleep."

She pushed off the couch while he remained in his chair, still dejected. "Come on," she said, refashioning his hair with her fingers. "It's not the end of the world."

He jerked his head away from her touch, sullenly avoiding her gaze.

"All right," she said, "I'm off to bed. Goodnight."

In her room she turned off her bedside lamp and got under the covers but lay looking at the thin thread of light beside her nearly closed bedroom door. The living room lamp snapped off. The bathroom door closed, the toilet flushed, water ran, and in his bedroom she heard Joey's shoes thump to the floor as he took them off.

She had closed her eyes when his voice opened them again. "Hey, Mom?"

"Yes?"

She could see the line of his body cutting off the light along the edge of her door. He pushed it open and stood slump-shouldered, the hall light outlining the hair she had rearranged earlier. "I'm really sorry I scared you," he said. "I never thought about what you said before, I mean, how you worry about us when we're out of your sight. I didn't mean to do that to you."

Her throat began filling instantly.

"Come here," she said.

He walked around the foot of the bed to *her side*, where she'd never stopped sleeping after Bill died, even though it was farther from the door. She put up her arms and he sat on the edge of the mattress, bending over her.

"I love you," she said as they hugged, "and that's the important message in everything that's happened tonight. If I didn't love you I wouldn't care about where you are or what you're doing."

"I love you too, Mom."

And with those words, the knot of sadness dissolved in her throat.

Christopher called the next day, right after church.

"How's everything with Joey?" he asked.

"We had a talk and things came out all right."

"I could see it coming, that's why I thought it was best if I got out of there."

What a kind and caring man he was. It struck Lee again, as it had over and over when she'd lain in bed last night, that whatever her needs, he was always there for her. Turning to him had become so natural for her that it was hard to imagine her life without him. Not only had he come on the run last night, now he was calling the way a true friend would, concerned once more for both her and Joey.

"Christopher, I can't thank you enough for coming. I'd forgotten how stressful it is to handle a teenager without a partner. When I saw you coming up the walk, I felt..." She found it hard to put into words. Even now the thought of him brought a welcome reprise of the relief and gratitude she'd felt last night.

"What?" he prodded.

"Relieved. So relieved to dump my worries on someone else for once. And so often you seem to know how I need you, and you show up as if by magic. It always feels right when I... I turn to you. I guess I rely on you too much, but just to have you there... it means so much to me, Christopher."

"I like being there for you."

The line grew quiet while their feelings extended beyond those of friends into that winsome world of near-lovers.

After a while he cleared his throat. "I've thought about you a lot since Tuesday. Could I see you today? I thought, if you don't have any other plans, I'd take you and Joey out to brunch somewhere."

Disappointment deluged her. "I'm sorry, Christopher, but Lloyd is here. I was just going to start making some chicken for dinner."

"Bring him along. I'd like to see him again, too."

Lee looked toward the wall dividing her from the living room where Lloyd was reading the Sunday paper and Joey was playing a video game on TV.

"All right. I'll ask him." She raised her voice. "Lloyd? Joey? Either one of you interested in going out to Sunday brunch with Christopher?"

Joey came around the corner in his church clothes. The mention of food once again brought him running. "Yeah, sure... where?"

She covered the mouthpiece. "I'm not going to ask him where," she whispered. "That would be rude."

Lloyd called, "That sounds good to me."

She told Christopher, "They both said yes, and that goes for me, too. I'll put the chicken in the refrigerator and cook it tomorrow night."

"How about over at Edinburgh?"

"I've never been there, but I hear it's fabulous."

"I'll pick you up in thirty minutes."

At Edinburgh Country Club, they were seated by a window that looked out across the snow-covered golf course. In the middle of the room an ice carving of a dolphin formed the centerpiece for the main buffet. Around them, in tables of all sizes, extended families were brunching likewise. Everywhere Lee looked she saw grandparents, parents and children: Three generations out for a family get-together, dressed in Sunday clothes, talking and laughing. The four of them—herself, Christopher, Joey and Lloyd—looked as if they were another of those families. For a while she indulged in the fantasy that they were, that she and Christopher were a pair who'd left their home for a pleasant Sunday meal among others. Last night they had handled a crisis over Joey together, and today here they were, like those around them, putting the incident behind them and going on with life.

She sat across the table from Christopher, listening to him talking with Lloyd about the canine units of the Anoka police force, then listening while Lloyd told about a black labrador he'd had when he was a boy on the farm. Joey got into the conversation, too, with an anecdote about his friend's dog who had once chewed the crotches out of all the family's underwear in the dirty-clothes basket.

Everyone laughed, and the waitress came to replenish their coffee.

Lloyd said, "Well, I think I'm going back for more of that fettuccine."

Joey said, "Me too, Grampa. But first I'm gonna have some bread pudding with caramel sauce."

Left alone, Christopher and Lee watched them go. "I like Lloyd," he said.

"So do I."

Christopher's eyes veered back to the woman across the table, catching her watching him steadily, wearing an unmistakable look of admiration. Maybe even love.

"Was your husband like him?"

"I suppose so, in some ways. But Bill was less patient, maybe even a little more judgmental than Lloyd. I think he got that from his mother."

"I'm surprised to hear you say that about Bill."

"Why?"

"Because you told me once you'd had a perfect marriage."

"A perfect marriage doesn't mean the people in it are perfect. Usually it means that they both overlook each other's imperfections."

He thought about that awhile, then asked, "So, didn't you get along with your mother-in-law?"

"I got along with her just fine. But she was judgmental. When Bill died she said I was crazy not to pay off the house with the insurance money so I'd be secure. She thought I shouldn't go to school, shouldn't start a business—what if it failed and all that. Then when Sylvia decided to quit her job with an accounting firm and come in with me, Ruth said it would never work out. Two sisters working together every day—she said we'd be at each other's throats in no time. But we've managed just fine. We each have our fortes and we stick to them. She takes care of the business and I take care of the arranging."

Joey returned to the table with a mountain of the restaurant's signature dessert, which he dug into, doubled over the plate. "Hey, Christopher, guess what," he said with his mouth full.

"What?"

"My birthday is next month and I'm going to be fifteen. That means I can get my driver's permit."

"Your mom better look out then."

Lloyd returned and the talk moved on to a variety of subjects.

Eventually, Christopher checked his watch. "I hate to break this up, but it's after one-thirty and I've got to report for roll call in an hour."

Joey said, "Do I have time for just one more piece of dessert? I didn't get a chance to try that chocolate fool stuff with all the nuts in it."

Lee said, "Go get one, quick, and take it with you in a napkin." Observing him hurry away, Lee remarked, "The bottomless pit," and they all rose, chuckling.

Chris took them home. They thanked him before he drove away, and Lloyd said he thought he'd go home right away, too; he was tired and his Sunday crossword was waiting for him. He drove off only moments after Chris did.

Lee spent the afternoon wrapping Christmas gifts and making popcorn balls, listening to Christmas music on the stereo and enjoying the arrival of a gray twilight that brought a light snow along with it. In the midst of that dusky time of day someone knocked on the front door and she answered to find Christopher there again, this time in uniform with his trusty radio in its leather sleeve on his belt.

"Hi," she said, opening the storm door and letting him in. "Back so soon?"

He held up a napkin with a square grease stain on the bottom. "Joey forgot his chocolate fool in my truck."

"Oh, thanks," she said, taking it from him and carrying it toward the kitchen.

He followed and stopped beside the table, perusing it and the disorderly room. There was a difference between it and the dirty rooms of his youth. This disorder had a homely warmth to it.

"Wrapping gifts, huh?"

"I have been, but I'm about to put this junk away. I've got a backache from bending over too long. Want a cup of coffee or something?"

"No, but what's that I see over there?"

She looked where he was pointing and couldn't help smiling at his boyish pose, the back of his hand to his nose, the index finger straight out. "Why, I believe those are popcorn balls. Could it be you want one?"

He answered with his eyebrows, Groucho Marx style.

"Help yourself." While she began putting away Christmas wrap, he peeled the plastic covering from a pink popcorn ball and bit into it.

"Mmm . . ." It stuck to his teeth and he had to work his jaw to manage chewing. "Did you make them?"

"Aha. Family tradition."

"Mmm . . ."

He leaned against the cabinet, chewing the sticky treat, watching her clean off the table, wipe it with a dishcloth, find a Christmas centerpiece and put it there, then get a broom and begin sweeping. She was wearing a pair of blue jeans and an oversized sweatshirt emblazoned with the words MAD ABOUT MINNESOTA! On her feet she wore white socks with dirty bottoms, reminiscent of her son's. All the while she moved around the room he was remembering lying on his couch kissing her last Tuesday.

"Where's Joey?"

"Sleeping off last night. He's been lost to the world most of the afternoon."

He put the popcorn ball down on the cabinet, sucked off a thumb and finger, went up behind her, took the broom from her hand and angled it against the edge of the table. "Come here," he said, and led her by the hand into the work area of the kitchen where they couldn't be seen from the bedroom hall. "I didn't get a chance to do this this morning, and it's been driving me crazy." He put his arms around her and kissed her, standing in the middle of the messy kitchen with the popcorn popper and dirty kettles and syrup bottles littering the sink and countertop, and bits of ribbon and wrapping paper littering the floor. She gave him no resistance, doubling her forearms behind his neck and leaning against his chest in its metal-bound bullet-proof vest. The kiss began friendly, as if it might be brief, but they started swaying in unison and opened their mouths, and everything felt so lovely that they kept on swaying and soon they were gyrating their heads. He ran his hands up beneath her sweatshirt and over her bare back just above her waistband. Even when his radio crackled and he reached down to adjust the volume, they continued the kissing and swaying.

"Is that for you?" she asked against his mouth.

"No."

They went on pleasuring each other with their mouths until it seemed absurd to continue without doing more; yet they were doing no more.

At last she freed her mouth, but left her arms where they were. "This is so exciting," she teased with a crooked smile. "It's like hugging a brick wall."

"Gotta wear 'em when we're on duty," he said of his flak vest, "but if you want to hug me without it, just name the date and time and I'll be there."

"Tuesday night, seven o'clock. Joey usually goes to the movies because it's dollar night."

"Can't. Gotta work."

"Wednesday night, seven o'clock. Joey *doesn't* go to the movies but what the hell—let's shock him."

"Can't. Gotta work."

She was sort of hanging on him, her mouth pasted with a saucy smile.

"Fine squeeze you are. Get a woman to proposition you, then you dream up excuses."

"How about Tuesday noon at my apartment? I'll fix you lunch."

The word "nooner" flashed through her mind. "Seriously?"

"Mm-hm. Something light that won't make you logy." He grinned suggestively, still rubbing his hands over her warm, smooth back while her chin drilled his chest and he arched back to look down at her.

"It's a date," she said, and slipped from his arms.

The word came to her again and again. Is that what it was going to be? A nooner? Was he anticipating it the way she was? Fearing its complications? Living with this uncertainty about what would happen once they had uninterrupted privacy?

On Tuesday morning, just before shutting off the bathroom light and heading for work, she gazed at herself in the mirror in wide-eyed wonder. Good God, she was heading for a romantic liaison at high noon! There was no other explanation for her preparations. Why else had she shaved her legs, and put on perfume, and scrubbed her fingernails until the flesh tore beneath them? And shaved under her arms and put on her best underclothes, and made sure her pantyhose had no runs, even though they'd be hidden beneath her slacks?

Could it be she was planning to take them off?

No, she was not! She was merely covering all bets.

The morning seemed to crawl. Of all plants to work with, she ended up arranging dyed heather, and it stained her fingers so badly they looked inked. Before she left the store at noon she went into the bathroom and gave them the scrubbing of their lives, then applied some strong-scented almond-oil lotion, as much of it as her hands would absorb. She also refreshed her lipstick and brushed her hair.

"Hey, Syl?" she called, moving through the store. "I might be gone a little longer than usual. Any problem?"

"No. I'll be here. See you when you get back."

Parking in Christopher's parking lot, heading into the building, knocking on his door, she felt as if she were heading toward some nefarious dealings. She was meeting a man for lunch. So what?

So there were butterflies in her stomach and she was fidgeting with her hair when he opened the door.

"Hi."

"Hi."

Her cheeks might have turned the faintest bit pinker.

"You really came. I wasn't sure you would."

"Why not?"

"I don't know. I just wasn't sure."

He stepped back and she walked in, left her boots by the door, let him take her jacket and hang it.

"Hungry?" he asked.

"Ravenous. What are we having?"

"Egg-salad sandwiches and tomato soup."

"I love tomato soup! And egg salad, too."

"Well . . . everything's ready." He gestured to his kitchen table. "I just have to pour the soup. Sit down."

The dishes were some of her old green ones. The sandwiches were plump with egg salad between thick-sliced nine-grain bread, with curly red lettuce showing around the edges. Each sandwich was cut in half and accompanied by a little pile of tiny dill pickles. The silverware was mismatched. Paper towels substituted for napkins. The centerpiece was the fat red candle and holly ring he'd bought the day they were together at Gustaf's. The candle was lit though it was a bright, sunny day.

He put two bowls of steaming tomato soup on the table and sat down.

"Christopher, this is lovely."

"Nothing fancy, like I promised."

"Curly red lettuce."

"I learned about different kinds of lettuce when I worked at the Red Owl store."

"And a centerpiece."

"Largely because of you. If I remember correctly, you were the one who said it's impossible to be lonely with a candle glowing in the room. That's why I bought it."

"I think I recognize the dishes."

"I'm sure you do."

"I got them when Bill and I were first married. It was back before the price of gas flew sky-high. Gas stations used to offer premiums to get customers to come in. A free dish with every fill—that's where these came from."

"They serve the purpose."

"Yes, they do. They make me feel right at home."

They both smiled, biting into their sandwiches and getting egg salad caught on the corners of their mouths.

She asked how Judd was doing, if he'd seen him lately. Christopher said he made sure he saw him every week. This week he'd taken him to the police weight room and let him work out a little.

She asked about Christmas, if there'd be any sort of holiday for the boy at home. He told her that parents like Judd's usually got guilt pangs at holiday time and did *some*thing for their kids. He also said it was high drug- and alcohol-use time of year, so one never knew what could erupt.

She asked him if he'd ever thought about becoming Judd's foster parent.

"No," he answered. "I'm there for him when he needs me, and he knows that. He understands that life dealt him a tough hand, but that he's got to play it out. I'm only there to help him do that. But I've never wanted to have kids of my own, either adopted or otherwise. I've known that since I was twelve years old, forced into the role of parenting my sister."

They sipped their hot soup, ate their sandwiches. He looked at her hands, holding the bread.

"What's that on your fingers?"

She dropped the sandwich and hid the hand in her paper towel on her lap. "Dye. I was working with heather this morning. It's sprayed with this awful stuff that stains just like ink."

He reached over, found her wrist in her lap and carried it up to the tabletop.

"You don't have to hide your hands from me, okay? They're honest hands. I like them."

They finished their food and he said, "Sorry, no dessert. It's too hard to keep in shape eating desserts, and fat cops can't run fast when they need to . . . so . . . this is it."

"I don't need dessert either. This was just perfect."

She rose with dishes in her hand. He took them from her. "Leave them. That's my job."

She was his guest, she realized, and conceded. "All right."

He picked up the soup bowls to rinse while she wandered into the living room and found herself unable to resist testing the soil in every flowerpot there, then looking into the Christmas tree stand to discover it nearly dry.

"Christopher, shame on you. You'll burn the place down if you don't keep your tree watered." She went to the kitchen and asked, "Do you have a coffeepot I can fill it with?" At the kitchen sink she filled the pot, and returned to the living room. On hands and knees, pouring, she realized there was only one gift beneath his tree and wondered who it was from.

He shut off the water and came into the room just as she finished pouring and sat back on her heels. The coffeepot was taken from her hands and discarded to one side as he sat down beside her on one hip, a hand braced on the carpet.

"The gift is for you," he said. "I want you to open it."

"For me?"

He nodded. "Open it."

"But it isn't even Christmas yet, and I don't have anything for you."

"You're here. That's all the gift I need. Open it."

The box was wrapped in silvery-blue foil with a gauzy silver ribbon. The package was shaped like a necktie box. She opened it as eagerly as a child.

Inside she found a plain white business envelope. From inside that she pulled two plane tickets and a color brochure from Longwood Gardens in Kennett Square, Pennsylvania. She barely gave the tickets a glance, but opened the brochure and avidly ran her eyes over photographs of trailing wisteria, statuary, glass houses and profuse blooms of many kinds. On second glance, she saw the tickets were to Philadelphia.

"A trip?" she said, raising excited eyes. "You're giving me a trip?"

"For two. Next summer, in July, when everything's in bloom. You can take whoever you want. I thought you might like to take Sylvia, or maybe even Lloyd."

"Oh, Christopher . . ." She looked down at the beguiling color brochure again and read aloud, "Longwood Gardens . . . a setting of perfect serenity, with its winding paths, temples, passionate bursts of color . . ."

"I went to a travel agent and she helped me pick which one. She said this is one of the best, and I didn't think you'd ever done anything like that before. I thought it was time you did."

"Oh, Christopher . . ." When she lifted her face there were tears in her eyes. She flung both arms around his neck, the brochure crackling against his shoulder. "All my life I've wanted to do something like this."

He hugged her back, smiling at her response, which was exactly the one he'd hoped for. "I'll bet you'll meet a lot of people there with blue fingers, and not one of them will be apologizing."

She kissed him, kneeling in the crook of his hip, tipping her head sharply to one side while his arms spanned half her circumference. Her heart was hammering from excitement over his gift. When she pulled back, she looked square into his eyes and said, "Nobody's ever given me a gift I liked this much. Nobody reads me like you do, Christopher Lallek. How is it that you read me so well?"

"I don't know."

"It's like you see into my head sometimes! If somebody asked me to name the perfect gift for me, I couldn't even name it myself, yet you knew what it was."

He only smiled.

Hugging him, she looked at the brochure over his shoulder. "This cost you a bundle, and I know I should object, but I'm not going to. I want to go too badly! Longwood Gardens! My God, Christopher, you're too good to be true!"

She kissed him again, both of them so perfectly happy at that moment it could only be celebrated thusly: with open mouths that fit less than passionately because they were both smiling; with appreciative hands that ran over one another's sweaters; with sheer joy in being together, and alive, and having one another to spend this improbable sunny December lunch hour with.

He fell to his back, taking her with him, and she reveled in lying across his chest, down one half of his body, letting herself kiss and kiss and kiss him, unable to get enough of the delightful pastime after so many, many manless years. Oh, the warm, liquid interior of his mouth, how good it felt again. And the sturdiness and texture of a strong male body—it, too, filled her with a sense of coming back to a pleasure long abandoned. The kiss changed tone and the glossy brochure in her hand became extraneous. She put it on the rough plush of the carpet and slid it away till it *tinked* against the coffeepot, freeing her hand to slide into his hair. Her right leg lay between his legs and she knew perfectly well what she felt down there; she raised her knee and pressed against it, against the hard, aroused flesh of a man whose desire for her came as a great joy. He raised his knee, too, between her legs, and his head off the floor, rolling them partially onto their sides. He gripped her from behind, hands spread wide on her woolen slacks, catching the curve of her buttocks, thrusting against her while she gave them both some added leverage by putting the sole of her foot on the backside of his calf. He was wearing denim jeans, stiff and heavy through the nylon covering her foot. There had been times after Bill died when she'd wondered if she'd ever do this again, times she'd lain alone in the dark and longed for someone to touch this way, to make her feel alive and sexual.

"Oh, Christopher," she whispered against his mouth, "you feel so good. Everything about you. Hair, muscle, even whiskers. It's been so long since I've felt a man's face this way." She rubbed hers against it, seeking texture from his freshly shaved skin, kissing him wherever she pleased. His hands slid up inside her sweater and cupped her breasts. She shuddered, arched and grew very still, her eyes closed while she absorbed all the wondrous sexual feelings reeling back after all the years. "It's been so long. Sometimes I'd wonder if I might dry up and lose my ability to do this. Now here you are, making me feel it all again after so many years. It's all rushing back, making me feel like a woman. And, ohhh, it feels good."

"What do you want?" he asked in a husky voice while she kissed his face everywhere. "Do you want to make love?"

"I can't. I want to but I can't. I don't have anything and it's—"

"I do."

"You've been planning this."

"We've both been planning this."

"Maybe I have." Her hands were in his hair, but both their eyes were closed. "I thought about the word 'nooner' ever since Sunday night, but if I went and got a contraceptive and brought it along, I would have been . . . you know. I couldn't make myself do it. Christopher, I'm forty-five years old."

"And hornier than you've been since your husband was alive."

"I've got to get back to the shop."

"Yeah, you feel like you're heading back to the shop." Their eyes were still closed. He was caressing both her breasts, sending rivers of feeling from them clear down her limbs. Their legs were still plaited with the sole of her foot wedged behind his calf. He reached behind her as if to unsnap her bra.

"Don't . . . please. This is far enough. Please, Christopher . . . please . . . I'm too tempted."

He returned to caressing her through her bra. "We're going to end up in bed eventually anyway, and you know it."

"My God, I'm being seduced." She had thrown her head back and he was kissing her throat.

"Yes, you are."

"By a boy of thirty."

"Thirty's no boy."

"No, I can feel that."

"So what do you say . . . Mrs. Robinson?"

She smiled and opened her eyes, drawing her head down to meet his gaze eye-to-eye. He was smiling, too, teasing her. They lay on their sides on the carpet, reading one another's faces at close range . . . her rust eyes, his blue ones.

"I just realized I'm doing exactly what I lectured Joey not to do last Saturday night. How do I think I'm ever going to keep on resisting you if we keep this up? Some mother I am, preaching out of one side of my mouth and flirting out of the other, but, damn it, Christopher, you feel so good, I just can't say it enough. But if we go to bed—what then? Where does it lead? What if someone finds out?"

"You've got a lot of hang-ups, you know that? Maybe all it will lead to is us having a good time together, but what's wrong with that? Enjoying each other *in* bed seems to me a natural extension of how we enjoy each other out of bed. Furthermore, we're both single. We're both beyond the age of consent. We both want it a lot."

"Boy, you can say that again." She rolled from him and sat up, feeling shaky and liquid and sensitized. With their legs still tangled she propped an elbow on her knee and rubbed her messy hair back from her face. "All right, suppose we do go to bed. I live in a modern-day world with modern-day problems. I'd want to know something about your past sex life."

He sat up, too—his legs lolling open—and caught one of her feet, put her smooth sole against his genitals and held it there, lightly, with one hand, caressing her through her nylons.

"If a condom isn't enough for you, just say the word and I'll be at a doctor's office tomorrow morning having an AIDS test."

She might live in a modern-day world, but his remark dropped her chin and left her staring at him. Nothing he'd said today had affected her more than these words: what an act of faith for a man to do such a thing.

"You mean it, don't you?"

"Of course I mean it. We'll start with a clean slate."

She stared at him, struck with a fresh new fear: She thought perhaps— dear God, how could it be?—she was falling in love with him. With a man fifteen years her junior.

He went on calmly, "The last time I went to bed with a woman was about two years ago. We dated for about six months, then she moved to Texas on a job promotion. Before that there were four, I think, going way back to high school. I've never been what you might call a ladies' man. Mostly I've been a loner."

She reclaimed her foot from his genitals and sat on it. She took his hand in both of hers, examining it while spreading the fingers wide, then closing them repeatedly.

After some thought, she looked up into his clean, handsome face.

"I need some time to think about this, Christopher. It still doesn't seem right."

"Because I'm younger?"

"Partly."

He looked down at his hand in hers, its fingers opening and closing. "Well, that I can't change. I'll always be younger, and there'll always be those who might accuse you of robbing the cradle. I know that."

A dejected silence fell. She put her hand on his shoulder. "I love my gift very, very much. Of all the people I've ever known in my life, I've never known one as intuitive as you. Not even Bill, and I mean that."

He looked up and gave her a three-cornered smile. "Well, that's a start anyway, isn't it?"

She, too, smiled. "Now I really do have to go back to work. May I use your bathroom first?"

"Sure."

She took her purse along, brushed her hair and applied fresh lipstick. When she came out he was getting her jacket from the closet. He held it while she slipped it on, then turned her by her shoulders to face him.

Angling his head, he gave her a goodbye kiss, gentle and lingering.

When it ended she touched his mouth with the pad of one forefinger. "Thank you for the lunch."

"You're welcome. Anytime."

"And for the tickets."

He only smiled in reply and kissed her finger.

"Christmas Eve," she said quietly, backing away. "Eleven o'clock. I'll wait up for you." One last word came out in a whisper. " 'Bye."

Chapter 13

*C*HRIS was scheduled to work both Christmas Eve and Christmas Day from three to eleven. That shift, on that particular night, was known to be unusually busy with emergency calls, though most of them were not true emergencies: The calls came from lonely people without friends or family who, rather than face Christmas Eve alone, manufactured ailments and went to emergency rooms. There they found people to talk to, someone to pay attention to them, human hands that touched and cared.

Those on duty at the station had come to expect calls from old Lola Gildress, who smelled so bad they had to leave the squad car doors open for a while after dropping her off. Frank Tinker's gallbladder acted up every year, too. He called every patrolman "sonny" and offered them his snuffbox for a pinch, needed a pop can to spit into while he rode in the squad car and always asked them if they'd mind swinging down along Brisbin Street on their way to the hospital. There, he turned rheumy eyes to a two-story house where he'd lived as a boy in a family of six, all of them gone now but him. Elda Minski called, too, as usual, and flounced out of her front door wearing a flea-bitten fox stole, vintage

1930, and a horrendous sequined turban on her bald head, eager to repeat her story of escaping the Russian Revolution and coming to America to sing opera on the same stages where Caruso and Paderewski had performed. The one they all waited for, though, was Inez Gurney, a sweet old woman curled over like a bass clef, who toddled out of her house taking baby steps—the largest she could manage—carrying a tin of German butter cookies for anyone kind enough to wish her Merry Christmas.

Christopher answered Inez's call this year.

When he knocked on her door she was all ready and waiting, wearing a home-knit cap that tied under her chin and ancient rubber boots with zippers up the front and fur above the ankles. The heels of the boots never left the ground when Inez walked.

He touched his hat visor and said, "Emergency call, Mrs. Gurney?"

"Gracious me, yes, but there's no need to hurry." Her *S*'s whistled through false teeth that had outgrown her shrinking gums. "I'm actually feeling a little better. If you'll give me your arm, young man, and carry this . . ."

He took her red tin with the painting of a holiday wreath on top, and escorted her down the path to the squad car.

"I thought the doctors might enjoy a taste of my German butter cookies." She said the same thing every year. "And, of course, you're welcome to sample them yourself. My-oh-my . . ." She tried to look up at the sky but her osteoporosis wouldn't allow it. "Isn't this some heavenly night though? Do you suppose we can see the Star of Bethlehem?"

"I imagine we can, but I wouldn't know which one it is. Would you?"

He stopped in the path to give her time. Again she tried to look up, bending her knees and angling her stiff old body. "No, I suppose not, but when I was a girl my papa taught me to find Cassiopeia and Orion and all the constellations. We lived on a farm near Ortonville, and my-y-y, those skies were big over the prairie. Have you ever been to Ortonville, young man?"

"No, ma'am, I haven't."

"It's farm country. Goose country, too. Why, in the fall those honkers would fly over in battalions, so many of them they'd fair block out the sun. And when they landed in a cornfield you could hear their voices bellering like blow horns clear over to Montevideo. Papa always shot one for Thanksgiving, and one for Christmas, too." They moved on toward the squad car, her hand on his arm, Christopher adjusting his stride to her baby steps while she told him about their Christmas dinners on the farm near Ortonville, her mother's sauerkraut stuffing and precisely what her mother had put into her beets to make them sweet and sour both, and how she herself had never mastered beets like her mother's.

At the squad car she needed help getting in, then swinging her legs to the front.

"Watch your purse," he said, pushing it up so he could slam the door.

Inside, he reported his whereabouts and destination to the dispatcher, and Mrs. Gurney asked, "Would you like to sample my cookies?"

"I certainly would. I'm a bachelor, so I don't get many homemade treats."

"I use only real butter, and cardamom. Some people think it's nutmeg, but it's not, it's cardamom. That's my secret." She had trouble opening the tin. Her fingers bent sharply from the end knuckle and her skin looked like mouse-spotted rice paper. "There we are," she said, when the lid finally gave.

He ate three cookies on the way to Mercy Hospital and told her he'd never tasted anything so delicious in his life, which put a smile on her wizened old face.

At Mercy, in the glaring white lights of the ER, he watched Mrs. Gurney being rolled away in a wheelchair with the tin on her lap, telling a young nurse about the cardamom and real butter she'd used in the cookies she'd brought for the doctors.

Back in his squad car, Christopher felt unutterably sad. The taste of the spice with the strange name—cardamom—lingered in his mouth. The faint smell of mothballs seemed to linger in the car, too, and he had the thought that maybe Mrs. Gurney kept them in her bed to preserve her very body. Poor old thing. Poor lonely old thing. Yet in spite of her loneliness, she had a need to give on Christmas Eve. What was more pitiful than a person with no one to give to?

It made him think of his own parents, who had been given two children and had squandered them both. What were they doing tonight in their dreary little apartment over there at Lincoln Estates? Was there a tree? A special supper? Gifts? Anything? And where was Jeannie? Still shacked up in LA with her drug-pusher? Still fat and greasy-haired and living the reflection of their parents' lives? He imagined what it might be like if Jeannie had stayed around here, graduated from high school, gotten respectably married and had a couple of kids. What would it be like at her house tonight? Would he go there taking gifts to his nieces and nephews, and maybe help some brother-in-law put together toys for the kids' stockings? He tried to imagine his parents as grandparents, but the image wouldn't gel.

Lord, the city streets were so quiet on Christmas Eve. Cars at churches, but nowhere else. For once the bars were closed. Even the lighted Christmas decorations hanging from the lamp poles on Main Street looked forlorn.

He drove by Lee's house, but saw no activity. They, too, were probably at church.

He turned around in the circle at the end of Benton Street and cruised past her house once more, anxious for his shift to end so he could come back.

All the way back uptown his radio was still. At the west end of Main he kept going, right out onto the highway toward his apartment. Making sure his radio was on his belt, he went inside to his own refrigerator, opened the door and stood a long time contemplating the ham. It was wrapped in a mesh bag, must have weighed eighteen pounds, and one like it had been given in gratitude to every person on the staff who had responded to a call and saved the life of some rich people's son after he'd fallen into a swimming pool last summer.

There sat the ham.

Over at Jackson Estates sat his parents.

Reaching for the piece of meat he realized he wasn't so much different from Inez Gurney.

At Jackson Estates the hall smelled like stale cooked vegetables. Its walls were crosshatched with black marks. The corners of the woodwork were worn white. Some doors had been patched where boots had kicked through them. Three candy wrappers and a rusty tricycle sat halfway along the dingy corridor. He knocked at number six and waited. The Wise Men must have made it to Bethlehem faster than his mother made it to the door.

"Hi, Mavis," he said when she opened it.

"What do you want?"

"Just came to wish you Merry Christmas, that's all."

From inside, a gravelly voice yelled, "Who is it, Mavis? And hurry up and shut that goddamned door, will you? This place is built like a goddamn chicken coop!"

"Yeah, yeah!" she bellowed in a coarse whiskey-voice, "quit your bellyachin', you old sonofabitch." To Chris she said, "Well, come on in then, don't stand there in the hall while the old man chews my ass."

As he walked inside he heard his father coughing. The old man was sitting in a dilapidated chair with a metal TV tray beside him. A whiskey bottle and a shot glass shared the tray with a jar of Vicks, the *T.V. Guide*, a box of corn plasters and an empty metal plate from a TV dinner. Between the old man's throne and a similar arrangement four feet away, an artificial Christmas tree about a foot and a half high leaned like the Tower of Pisa, its permanently affixed lights looking hazy through the smoke from Mavis's cigarette, which still burned in an ashtray. She, too, was armed with a bottle and a shot glass. Her chosen libation, however, was peppermint schnapps. The room smelled of it, and the Vicks and the smoke, and the Salisbury steak gravy that congealed on the bottoms of their foil dishes.

"What do you say, Old Man?" Christopher said as he entered the sickening room and thumped the ham down on the adjacent kitchen table.

"Don't say nothin'. Got me a sonovabitch of a cold. What brings you around here all gussied up in your cop uniform? You wanna impress your ma and pa with how important you are?"

"Now, Ed, leave the boy alone," Mavis said, then burst into a fit of crackly coughing measuring about two packs a day on the nico-Richter scale.

"I brought you a ham," Chris told them.

"A ham . . . well, say, that's nice," said Mavis. "Here, have a drink."

"I'm on duty."

"Oh, that's right. Well, what the hell . . . just a little one. It's Christmas."

"I don't drink."

"Oh, that's right."

"He don't drink, Mavis," the old man sneered. "Our holier-than-thou, gun-totin' upstanding citizen cop don't touch the stuff to his lips, do you, Officer?"

Why had he come here again? Why had he set himself up for the hurt these occasional breakdowns in common sense always brought?

"You ought to think about drying out," he said to Ed. "I'll help you anytime you want."

"Come here to deliver your Christmas sermon, did you? I dry out when I *want* to dry out! I've told you that before! Think you can bring a goddamn ham in here and drop it on the table and start preaching, well, just get your ass out!"

"Now, Ed," Mavis said. "Chris, sit down."

"I can't stay. There are still emergency calls coming in even though it's Christmas Eve. I just thought . . ."

What had he thought? That they'd changed? Magically changed while marinating away here day after day in their self-made alcoholic stew?

Jesus, they were so foul and pathetic.

"Have you heard from Jeannie?" he asked.

"Not a word," replied Mavis. "You'd think she'd have the decency to send a card to her mother and dad at Christmastime, but no, not even that."

She didn't see it, didn't see any of it, not how unlovable they were, how undeserving of any consideration from their children. It took more than starting a child in a womb and spewing it forth to make a person deserving of the title "parent."

He felt himself growing physically sick, looking at them.

"Well, listen . . . enjoy the ham. I've got to go."

Mavis came to show him out; he wished she'd have remained in her chair where he need not smell the stale schnapps and smoke on her breath, or let her filthy garments brush his, or see her nicotine-stained fingers on the doorknob.

Thankfully, she didn't touch him or—worse—kiss his cheek as she sometimes remembered to do.

When the door closed behind him he bolted for fresh air, for the blameless, clear, star-studded night where somewhere people prayed in churches and gave each other gifts and sang carols around pianos.

And he thought, *Lee, please, be up when I get there at eleven.*

* * *

The Hillier Christmas tradition held that Orrin and Peg spend Christmas Eve at Lee's house and Christmas Day at Sylvia's. Lloyd came every year around noon of Christmas Eve day and stayed overnight so he'd be there in the morning for the opening of gifts. Janice, of course, was home from college, and to Lee's amazement, little Sandy Parker dropped in on Christmas Eve afternoon for about an hour, too. Though Lee was genuinely friendly to the girl, she found herself studying the fuzzy-haired, sloe-eyed brunette as the person with whom her son had recently begun practicing the rudiments of necking, and possibly—probably—petting.

The young people—dear, thoughtful hearts that they were—knew that this holiday would have a great, sad hole at its heart where Greg had once been, and they stopped over, too—Nolan, Sandy, Jane and Kim.

Candlelight church service was held at six, and afterward Lee fed everyone oyster stew and cranberry cake with hot brandied sauce, their traditional Christmas Eve fare.

They opened their gifts from Orrin and Peg but kept the rest for Christmas morning. They watched Pavarotti perform from some immense gothic temple with a 120-voice choir behind him. They missed Greg so terribly each of them went away to shed private tears at one time or another.

At ten o'clock, Orrin and Peg said they were going home.

Lee said, "Oh, can't you stay a little longer? Christopher gets off at eleven and he's coming over then."

"I'm sorry, honey, we can't. We'll be up fairly early to go over to Sylvia's and open gifts with them."

Janice said, "I didn't know Chris was coming over tonight. I thought he was coming in the morning."

"Poor guy had to work three to eleven on Christmas Eve, so I told him I'd save some oyster stew and cake for him and he could drop by for a midnight snack."

Peg said, "Wish him Merry Christmas from us. We might stop by tomorrow, or if you feel like it, come over to Sylvia's later on in the day."

"We might, but you know how it is. Everybody always likes to hang around here on Christmas Day. Play with their new toys."

When Orrin and Peg were gone, Lee said, "Time to stuff stockings." They had never given up the tradition. Each of them went to their rooms and found sacks of tiny gifts they'd squirreled away during the past few weeks, even Lloyd. The stocking that last year had said *Greg,* this year said *Chris.*

"I hope none of you mind my including Chris this year," Lee said.

Joey said, "Naw. Chris is neat."

Lloyd said, "Since when have any of us minded including Chris?"

Janice said, "I got something special for Chris's stocking."

"What?" her brother asked.

"None of your business. I got something special for you, too."

"What?"

She poked a tissue-wrapped ingot into his sock.

"Lemme see!"

"Get away, nosy!"

The two of them started tussling on the living room floor, and Lloyd smiled broadly at their antics.

They were all still up at 11:15 when Christopher got there. The tree was lit, the television was rerunning an old James Galway Christmas concert, and the stockings were hung from the arms of a dining room chair that had been set beside the tree and pressed into use as a substitute chimney for as long as it had been in the family.

When Christopher stepped in, still in uniform, he held a stack of gifts. The family surrounded him, exclaiming over the packages, taking his jacket, his hat, and wishing him Merry Christmas. Then Janice took his hand and led him into the living room.

"Come and see what's in here for you."

When he saw the stocking with his name on it, a powerful welling seemed to happen in his heart. He stared, battling the sting in his eyes, wondering how he'd managed to get so lucky as to have this family adopt him as they had. As one mesmerized, he reached . . .

And got his hand playfully slapped.

"No, not yet!" Janice scolded. "You have to wait for morning, the same as the rest of us."

"You don't ask much, do you?" he teased in reply.

Janice was now holding the hand she'd slapped, her fingers threaded possessively between Christopher's. "Come down here and look . . . there's more."

Indeed, there were gifts under the tree with his name on them. Several!

"Grampa and Joey and I talked it over, and we all decided you should stay here overnight, that way you'll be here when we all wake up in the morning. Mom, that's okay, isn't it? If Chris stays overnight?"

Christopher began to object. "Hey, wait a minute, Janice, I don't think—"

"Mom, that's okay, isn't it?" she repeated.

"Of course it's okay."

"Grampa sleeps in Greg's room," Janice explained, "and you can sleep on the sofa."

"Janice, really . . . I'm still in my uniform and . . ."

"Joey's got some baggy old sweats, haven't you, Joe?"

The decision seemed to be taken out of Christopher's hands. In short time, he had shucked off his tie, gun belt and bullet-proof vest, and was sitting on the living room floor with a bowl of oyster stew while the others lounged around with second pieces of cake. They turned the television off and kept only the tree lights on; he finished his stew and a piece of cake, and told them about Lola Gildress, Frank Tinker, Elda Minski and Inez Gurney.

He didn't tell them about taking the ham to his folks.

He told Lee later on, when everyone had gone to their rooms and he'd been given a toothbrush, blankets and a pillow, and Joey's sweats. She went down the hall, calling, "Goodnight, everyone," snapping out the lights and tapping on doors. "Everybody wake everybody else in the morning, okay?"

"Okay," they all replied, settling down in their rooms.

She made her way to the kitchen where one last light burned over the kitchen stove. "Joey-y-y-y," she called, "you forgot the kitchen stove light again." On her way past the living room, she called, " 'Night, Christopher. Don't fall asleep with those tree lights on."

He said, "Lee, come here a minute, will you?"

She entered the room where he was lying stretched out on his back with his hands stacked beneath his head, covered to the chest with an old quilt of her mother's.

She stood behind him and said quietly, "Yes?"

He reached a hand above his head. She put hers in it and he hauled her around to the side of the sofa where she knelt on the floor beside him.

He took her face in both his hands, studying what he could see of it

261

with the tree lights behind her. He held it tenderly, his thumbs resting just beside her mouth, fanning softly over her skin.

"I love you, Lee," he said.

She hadn't expected it, not this soon, not this directly. She'd thought maybe, if they ever became intimate, he might say it someday. But this pure revelation, inspired not by some sexual tryst but by the spirit of Christmas, touched her as no passion-inspired words ever could. All within her strove toward a deeper relationship with him. She could no more withhold the words than she could keep from touching his face as she said them.

"I love you too, Christopher."

He didn't kiss her, merely sighed and pulled her down so her head lay on his chest, her forehead against his chin.

"I want to tell you something. I need to tell you, okay?"

With her ear against his chest, she could hear him swallow.

"Of course," she replied.

He waited several beats, as if gathering emotional equilibrium, before launching into it. "I went to see my parents tonight. I had taken Inez Gurney to the hospital and felt so damned sorry for her, all alone with nobody to be with on Christmas Eve. And after I got back in the squad car I started thinking about Mavis and Ed, and I suppose I identified a lot with old Inez. Hell, it was Christmas . . . and they were living right across town . . . and I hadn't seen them at all." He paused ruminatively then started again as if pulling himself from some unwanted wool gathering. "Anyway . . ." He cleared his throat. "I went to see them. I went over to my apartment and got a ham some grateful citizen had given each one of us in the department—and I took it over there." Again she heard him swallow thickly. "It was awful. The two of them, nothing but a pair of sick old drunks who really don't give a shit about me or about themselves. They just sit there drinking their lives away. It's just so damned pointless."

He stared at the tree lights. His tears had turned them into many-pointed stars.

She raised up so she could see his face. "Christopher, listen to me." She saw his glistening eyes, found a corner of the quilt and dried them. "They gave you birth, and for that you should be grateful. Somehow, out of all those misbegotten genes and chromosomes, a few of the right ones went to you and made you a good person who cares about your fellow man. But beyond that, they shirked every responsibility known to sociology. I will never again encourage you to go to them, because they don't deserve you. Alcoholism, they say, is an illness. But character is not. Their character, or lack of it, is inexcusable. Since I've known you, listened to you, learned what your childhood was like and how it's affected your adulthood, I've come to agree with you that parents *earn* love from their children, and they did nothing to earn yours. Now stop feeling guilty because you can't love them."

He kissed her forehead and said, "You're so damned good for me."

She was leaning on his chest with one arm, a hand in his hair while stroking his forehead repeatedly with her thumb. "Yes, I am," she whispered. "And you're good for me too."

He looked at her with some amazement. "Did you really say you love me?"

"Yes, I did. We both did . . . and not in the middle of a thrusting match on the floor either. There's some significance in that, isn't there?"

They both considered it awhile, then he said, "Thanks for the stocking."

"You don't know what's in it yet. Could be a stick and a lump of coal."

He'd been battling some wrenching inner emotions all evening, and they won at last. He gripped her hard, drawing her down against his chest, putting his face in her hair and squeezing his eyes shut against the sting within, the mixture of heavyheartedness and lightheartedness this night had brought.

His parents—the failures.

This woman—the healer.

"Thanks for all of this," he said brokenly. "I don't know what the hell I did to deserve you."

She let him hold her, listening to him gulp down great knots of emotion until at last he freed her and she raised up to see his face.

"Feeling better now?"

He nodded and dried his eyes with his knuckles.

She kissed his mouth with extreme tenderness and whispered, "See you in the morning. No digging in the socks till everyone's up."

* * *

Janice awoke first, shortly after sunrise. She tiptoed to the kitchen and plugged in the electric coffeemaker, then stuck her head around the archway of the living room. Christopher lay on his side with both hands up near his face, one knee updrawn, protruding from the covers along with one bare foot.

She studied his foot—medium length, bony, with some pale hair on the toes. She studied the palm of his right hand, fingers curled above it in repose. She studied his hair, so thick and manageable it scarcely looked mussed from his night's sleep. She studied his mouth, open a sliver as he slept, and imagined kissing it someday.

Down the hall a bedroom door opened and Christopher's eyelids flinched. The bathroom door closed and he woke up, saw Janice half-hidden around the doorway and went into a stretch with one elbow pointing at a corner of the ceiling.

"Oh . . . hi . . ." His words were distorted by the stretch. "Did I sleep too late?"

"No, everyone's just starting to wake up." She smiled. "Merry Christmas."

"Yeah, thanks, same to you. Is that coffee I smell?"

"Sure is. There'll be a jam-up in the bathroom, so go ahead and have a cup while you wait your turn."

"Thanks, I will."

"I heard you and Mom talking last night after I went to bed."

She waited while he wondered what she expected to hear him say.

"Yeah, I had something I needed to talk to her about."

"How long did you talk?"

"Not long. Ten minutes maybe."

"She's great, isn't she? You can talk to her about anything."

"Yeah, you sure can. But I knew that from Greg. He always told me that about her."

"It's been pretty awful around here without him since the holiday started, but we're all putting on a brave face."

"I know. I miss him, too."

She laid her cheek and one hand against the archway. "Thanks for filling in for him, Chris. Your being here means a lot to all of us. Especially to Mom."

* * *

264

How he and Lee managed to keep their feelings hidden throughout the rest of that day was an act of sheer determination. They sat on the living room floor and pulled the booty out of their stockings, still dressed in bathrobes and sweat suits, laughing at such findings as edible candy worms, bubble-gum "mosquito eggs," false eyelashes as long as spaghetti, socks with bear claws and footpads painted on them and red clown noses, which they all put on while they continued digging. Janice had bought Joey a sex manual for teenagers, which caused some laughter and some blushing, while Lloyd had gotten everyone coupons for McDonald's. In Christopher's stocking he also found tiny bottles of aftershave, a deck of playing cards, a key holder, a rubber stamp with his home address (from Joey, which surprised him because it meant they'd had long-term plans for his presence here this morning). And from Janice, two tickets to a Timberwolves game.

"If you need company, just let me know. I love the Wolves," she said.

"Gosh, thanks, Janice," he answered. "I just might."

When the stockings were emptied, they all got juice and coffee and settled down in the living room to open the gifts beneath the tree. Christopher had put plenty of thought into the gift he gave to each of them. For Joey, the object of every teenager's covetousness: a pair of Oakley sunglasses with dragonfly-blue lenses and Croakies to match. For Janice, a trip to Horst, which the gals at the police station assured him was the beauty shop of note in the Twin Cities. For Lloyd, a membership to a health club with a walking track. And for each of them, the last photograph he'd taken of Greg, blown up to a five-by-seven and framed.

The pictures brought tears, of course, but Lloyd put it best when he held the frame in one hand, wiped his eyes with the sleeve of his bathrobe and said, "We all needed this. We've been missing him a lot and haven't said anything. I don't know about the rest of you, but I've been sneaking off to wipe my eyes whenever he came to mind, which has been often. Now, thanks to Chris, he's here with us in this room again, in all our hearts at once. Thanks, Chris . . . thanks a lot."

When the emotional moment passed, they finished opening gifts. Joey gave him a paperback novel about a police detective, Lloyd a billfold, Janice a compact disc by Wynonna Judd, and Lee a coordinated sweater and shirt. It was only later, when he was taking the shirt out of the plastic sleeve and removing the pins, that he found, in the pocket, a fourteen-karat gold bracelet. Hanging from it by a golden thread was a small, flat red foil heart upon which the manufacturer's name was stamped in gold. Inside, on the space provided, she'd written *Love, Lee.*

He modeled his clothes—they fit—and kept on the wrinkled new shirt with his police trousers while they cleaned up the living room and ate a ham dinner, and tried Joey's new video game, and got a portion of the frame of a jigsaw puzzle put together. Finally, when he was getting ready to go home, he found a moment alone with Lee.

"I found the bracelet," he told her. "But it's too much."

"It's what I feel. Are you wearing it?"

He extended his wrist, proving that he'd had no intention of giving it up, too much or not. "Thank you, Lee. I really love it."

She touched the links with one finger. "So do I."

"And the heart."

She kissed his wrist where the warm gold chain crossed it.

"I wish you could stay."

"So do I. Are you going over to Sylvia's later on?"

"I'm not sure. It's awfully nice, just lolling around here."

"If I drive by, I'll give a honk. Well, I'd better say goodbye to the others."

Lloyd and Joey were in the living room playing the video game. They paused to say goodbye. Janice was in her bedroom trying on clothes. He knocked on her door and she came into the hall wearing a sweater with tags hanging from its wrist.

"Gotta go," he said. "Thanks for the best Christmas of my life."

"Thank you, too." She caught him around the neck with one arm and held him for only a moment. "And don't forget—call me if you want company at the Timberwolves."

He patted her back and they parted.

Lee saw him out. When he stood on the step and she held the door open behind him, he turned back and said, "I change shifts in three days, back to day shift, plus I have the whole New Year's weekend off. I want to take you out on New Year's Eve, so think up some excuse. Better yet, tell them the truth."

He left her with that challenge. She closed the door already beginning to scour her mind for explanations.

Chapter 14

*T*wo days after Christmas, Lee received a beautiful greeting card from Christopher. In it he'd written:

Dear Lee,

Although I tried to tell you on Christmas Eve just how much it meant to me to be with you and your family for the holiday, I don't think I did a very good job. Your family is all that mine isn't, and being with you has been an education as well as a pleasure. If there were more families like yours, guys in my line of work would be put out of business. Being with you personally has come to be the best part of my life right now. You're a great lady, a special person, and a wonderful friend. Thanks a lot for everything you do for me, and especially for the Christmas gifts. The shirt and sweater are just what I like, but the bracelet—wow! I sure wasn't expecting that. I wear it every day and think of you when I put it on and when I see it there on my wrist. I'll never forget this Christmas as long as I live, and I have a feeling the same will be true about New Year's Eve. I just can't wait.

Love,
Christopher

It had been years since she'd received an affectionate greeting card from a man. Reading his words she felt romantic again, vibrant, eager— all the entirely feminine reactions of the wooed woman. It struck her as unusual that a man without a mother's positive influence would write a note such as this. He, too, was special to have done so. She reread the note time and again, sitting at home in the kitchen where they'd first kissed, thinking how unexpected was the advent of this young man into her personal life when she had not been looking for anyone to fill a gap. Indeed, she hadn't known the gap existed, now here he was, putting anticipation in her life, excitement in her days and a flurry in her widow's heart, which had been content to go unflurried for so many years.

How bizarre and unexpected to end up kneeling beside a man— especially one of Christopher's age—on a sofa on Christmas Eve and hearing that he loved her, telling him she loved him. Yet it was absolutely true. She loved him. What was to come of it, she had no idea, but the change it had wrought in her life felt so incredibly glorious she would go on gifting herself with his presence and enjoying each moment they spent together.

He called as she was sitting there reading his card for the fifth time. His voice had the power to turn her radiant within. He could say, simply, "Hi," as he did now, and in her breast happiness flowered, filled her with a wondrous sense of well-being, a benefaction that flowed on long after the conversation ended.

"I was reading your card," she told him, ". . . again."

"I meant every word in it."

"I loved every word in it. It's been years since I got a card like that from a man."

"You say that often—it's been years."

"Well, it has been. Do you mind?"

"No. Actually, it's sort of a thrill when I hear it. I like being the one bringing you back to life."

"You certainly are doing that."

"So how about dancing? Has it been years since you've done that, too?"

"Actually, it has been."

"Want to give it a whirl on New Year's Eve?"

"Yes!" she said, excited. "Oh, yes! I haven't bought a dancing dress in years!" He laughed. She laughed. "I said it again, didn't I?"

"A bunch of the guys from the department have reserved a block of tables at the Bel Ray ballroom. High Noon is playing."

"Who's High Noon?"

"The best country band around."

She gave a moment's thought to his invitation. "The department guys, huh?"

"You ready to face them as my date?"

"What do you think they'll say?"

"They'll tease me, but not when you're around."

"Well, if you can take it, I can take it. Are you a good dancer?"

"Passable. How about you?"

"I've got rhythm, but I'll probably be a little rusty."

"Want to go out to dinner first?"

"Dinner too? Christopher, you'll spoil me."

"I'd love to. How about if I pick you up at seven?"

"Fine." After a pause, she said, "Christopher, I'm so excited. I haven't been out on New Year's Eve since 1983."

"We'll make it a night you'll never forget."

She said to Janice and Joey, "Do either one of you object to Christopher taking me out on New Year's Eve?"

Joey said, "Not as long as you give me money to order a pizza."

Janice's expression drooped. "Oh, shoot! If I'd known, I wouldn't have made plans with Nolan and Jane."

Lee gazed at her daughter feeling somewhat miffed. Was she so old and decrepit that it was inconceivable Christopher might want to take her out *without* her children? Unbelievably, Janice failed to realize this was a real date. If it was a case of hiding in plain sight, so be it. Lee wasn't going to elucidate.

"The police department guys have reserved a bunch of tables at the Bel Ray ballroom and we're going out there."

"*Dancing?*" Janice exclaimed.

"Yes, dancing. Is there anything wrong with that?"

"Well, no, but . . . gosh, Mom, it's been a while, hasn't it?"

"Yes it has, and I'm pretty excited. What are you doing that night?"

"Going to a party at one of the girls' houses I worked with at The Gap last summer. She said I could bring anybody I want so I asked Nolan and Jane if they wanted to come along."

"What about you, Joey?"

"Could I have Denny stay overnight?"

"If it's okay with Denny's mom, and if she knows I won't be here till later. And no girls."

"No girls. Sandy is skiing in Colorado with her family, but will you pay for pizzas?"

"I'll pay for pizzas."

"All *right!*" He socked the air. "We can play video games all night!"

Lee bought a new dress. It was fun-loving, flouncy and had a two-tiered skirt in solid red. She bought red pumps to match, and real silk panty hose, then hung multicolored earrings on her ears and a glob of matching color above her sweetheart neckline.

Christopher came to pick her up dressed in jeans, sport coat, string tie and cowboy boots. He escorted her out after complimenting her looks, holding her coat, opening the door and in general acting as attentive as any normal young swain who comes a-courting.

When they'd left and Janice was still standing in the front hall with her saliva glands pumping, Joey said, "I think he likes Mom."

"Well, of course he likes Mom. *Everybody* likes Mom."

"But, I mean, I think they're going steady or something."

"Going steady! Oh, Joey, for heaven's sake, Mom is forty-five years old and Christopher's only thirty! He's just being nice to her because Greg is dead and he knows she'd be lonesome otherwise."

"Open your eyes, nipple-head! Look at how she was dressed! She didn't look like any old lady to me."

Janice rolled her eyes and headed back to the bathroom to finish combing her hair. Fourteen-year-old brothers could be so *dense!*

Janice was partially right. Christopher *was* being nice to Lee. Four blocks away, he had pulled his Explorer to the side of the street and was kissing her masterfully enough to suck off half the new lipstick she'd just applied. His left hand was inside her coat, caressing her breast, and his tongue was inside her mouth. When the kiss finally ended he said with his forehead against hers, "Are you sure you want to go dancing?"

"Yes," she answered, smiling. "First."

They ate at Finnegan's—lightly, because they talked and laughed and flirted so much that when the waiter came to claim their plates for the third time, they let him take them even though the food wasn't gone yet.

Christopher said, "Good God, you look pretty."

Lee said, "Good God, you look handsome."

"Is the dress new?"

"Everything's new. Me too, I think."

"You're going to be, before this night's over." He was holding her hands across the table, adoring her with his eyes. "I've got something for you." He released one hand, took a paper from his pocket and handed it to her. It was a green sheet, folded like a business letter. She opened it and read across the top "Lufkin Medical Laboratories." Lower down the page a single item jumped out at her: *HIV negative.*

Color leaped to her face. All within her seemed to surge to the sexual parts of her body. She gaped at him over the paper.

"Christopher . . . my God, you did it!"

"It seemed the wisest thing to do in today's world. But I don't want you to feel pressured because I did. The choice is still up to you."

She pressed a palm to her right cheek, then her left. "Mercy, am I blushing?"

"Yes, you are, and it's quite becoming."

"I can't believe you actually *did* it!"

"Why? I told you I would."

"But . . . but that was just . . . just speculation."

"Was it?"

She let her eyes be held by his. Her tone softened. "No, I guess it wasn't." And after a pause, "I didn't do anything like that though. Do you want me to?"

"Not if you and Bill were monogamous, and I think you were."

"Yes, we were."

"And there's been nobody else since, so I was the only one in question. Now that question is answered."

She took both his hands again. "That's quite an act of faith, Mr. Lallek."

He looked down at her knuckles while rubbing them with his thumbs. "That's what good relationships are built on, and I want ours to be the best."

She studied him with a loving expression in her eyes, then asked softly, "Would you mind very much if I got up, right here in the middle of this restaurant, and came over there and kissed you?"

He let a grin spread up one corner of his mouth . . . slowly. "You wouldn't sling your leg over my chair like you did that other time, would you?"

She grinned back, picturing herself in the red dress and high heels sitting astride him in this fancy restaurant with its candlelight and real linen. "I'll try to control myself."

He pulled on her hand and she got up to do as promised, surprising herself and him with her lack of compunction, even though they weren't sitting precisely in the *middle* of the restaurant, and even though the waiter wasn't anywhere in sight, and even though neither of them saw anyone they knew among the clientele.

She held his face in her two rough hands and put her mouth on his for only the briefest second. When their lips parted she kept her face close and whispered, "Do we really have to go dancing?"

And made him smile.

He could do the Texas two-step!

She watched the couples circling the floor counterclockwise, and balked as he tugged on her hand.

"But I can't do that!"

"How do you know?"

"Christopher, I'll embarrass you."

"Never. Come on, give it a try. We'll go out in the middle where we'll be out of traffic and I'll teach you a move or two."

She relented and let herself be taught, noting that there were others out there in the middle of the floor struggling through basic steps, too. Christopher told her, "They give lessons here a couple nights a week before the band starts playing, so there are always beginners."

As she'd told him, she *did* have rhythm, and it turned out to be less difficult than she'd imagined. Soon she was swinging under his arm, he was dipping under hers, and they were performing basic moves—the promenade and the wrap—quite smoothly as they circled the floor.

"I wouldn't have taken you for a dancer," she said while the *shh-shh-shh* of cowboy boots sandpapered the floor all around them.

"The last girl I dated—the one who moved to Texas—wanted me to learn. She and I took lessons together."

"I should thank her. This is fun."

"Ready to try something new?"

"Is it hard?"

"Naw, you can handle it. Now, get ready, I'm going to take you 'Around the World.'"

He lifted his hands and led her around his body in a full circle, spinning her round and round.

She laughed breathlessly as she faced him again and resumed the basic step.

"I did it!"

His smile was uncomplicated, pleased, and filled her with happiness.

At the tables reserved for police department personnel there were a lot of celebrating cops and wives, who were designated drivers. The mood was gay, at times raucous. Much to Lee's surprise, she was accepted as Christopher's date with none of the double-takes she'd expected. Pete Ostrinski asked her to dance and she followed him quite smoothly. Toni Mansetti inquired how her son was doing. The wife of Sergeant Anderson told her a ribald joke about panty hose that created a new round of laughter from all the other women who'd already heard it, and started them all casting dubious glances at their ankles, which played off the punch line and signaled more laughter. Christopher attempted to teach her an advanced move called the whip, but they got tangled up time after time and ended up laughing so much they gave up and decided they'd save it for next time.

The band struck up the Collin Raye song "Love Me," and Christopher took Lee's hand, sauntering onto the dance floor. "Come on," he said, "let's polish some belt buckles."

The mood had shifted. Couples were locked together in full-length embraces. The circling had stopped in favor of swaying in place and making gentle turns. The hall became dim with a bluish cast from the overhead canister lights trained on the band. A mirrored ball strewed reflected jewels of light across the faces and shoulders of the dancers. Christopher wrapped both arms around Lee, joining his hands on the shallows of her spine. She linked her fingers behind his neck, settled her hips against his and lifted her face to his happy one.

"Having fun?" he asked.

"Mmmm . . . you're the most fun this life has had for a long, long time."

He touched the end of his nose to hers, then tilted his head as if to kiss her.

"Your friends are watching," she murmured.

"I don't give a damn."

He kissed her and put pressure on her spine until his body changed the shape of her own and seemed to become an extension of it. Swaying, he dovetailed against her while the chorus of the song called repeatedly, "Love me . . . love me . . . love me . . ."

He put space between their faces and looked into her bedazzled rust-colored eyes. "What would you say if I said, 'Let's go, let's get out of here and get alone.' "

"Right now? Before the first set is even finished?"

He nodded, holding her hips flush to his, swiveling in rhythm with the music.

"I'd say, 'Let's.' "

"Do you mean it?"

"Let's just walk off this dance floor and get our coats at the coat check and not come back."

"They'll miss us and wonder where we went so early."

"I really don't care. Do you?"

"Not at all."

They sealed their pact with a smile, turned and threaded through the dancers, across the light-speckled floor toward the entrance, knowing full well they had made a silent covenant to consummate this relationship before the night was over.

Outside, it was bitter cold. They walked to Christopher's truck with their arms around each other. Inside, while he started the engine, he said, "Sit here by me." So she ignored her seat belt and rode to his apartment sitting on one foot with her arm around Christopher's shoulders and her cheek against the rough tweed of his shoulder. Once she kissed his jaw, once his ear. He found her free hand and pressed it upon his warm thigh beneath his own, where she could feel the muscles shift each time he moved his foot from the gas pedal to the brake and back again. He had the radio on, playing soft country songs that made conversation unnecessary. While they rode, he kept softly rubbing the backs of her fingers with the pads of his own.

At his apartment they parked in the garage and rode the elevator up. She watched with some residual amazement this young, virile man with his attractive close-cut hair as he bent to fit the key in the lock and open his door, knowing what would happen on the other side of it.

He switched on an overhead light, leaned his backside against the door, removed his cowboy boots and disposed of their coats. Then he took her hand and said, "Come this way." She allowed herself to be towed down the hall to his bedroom while he hummed "Love Me" and loosened his string tie. In his bedroom, lit only by the negligent hall light that straggled around the doorway, he turned and kissed her, dipping his knees and circling her waist with both arms, then lifting her free of earthly ties and transporting her to the bed.

Their lives had been leading toward this for so long, and the decision to do it with full accord, thus they approached the next hour with both freedom and delight.

"Oh, Christopher," she whispered, as he came down upon her. "I want you so much."

"Then we're even . . . but say it again. I've waited so long to hear it."

"I want you so m—"

His mouth cut off her words and in the midst of the first wild and rolling kiss their hands dove straight as arrows to the objects of their desire. Through their clothing they petted the first time, telling one another with the curve and thrust of palms how it would be, how they wanted it to be, feeling warmth and arousal and the parting of limbs to give access. They were still for a moment, exploring, riveted by the combination of feelings beneath their own hands and the hands of the other. They lay apart, eyes open, faces tinted by the bisque light of the distant fixture that seemed to fall upward from their chins, highlighting their features as they went on accepting these gifts of feelings.

Her high-heeled pumps hit the floor . . . *thump* . . . *thump*. She closed her eyes and breathed "Ohh . . ." and rolled to her back, one foot flat on the bedspread, dress rucked up to her hips, giving herself over to the pure fleshly pleasure of feeling male hands upon her once again. He leaned over and kissed her breast, through layers of feminine apparel.

She said, "Please . . . could we get our clothes off, Christopher?"

He knelt in the middle of the bed and tugged her to her knees. "There's not much grace in taking clothes off. I didn't know how you felt about it."

"There's not much grace in having clothes on at a time like this. They do best on the floor."

He took off some of hers, she took off some of his, and each of them managed the most difficult pieces of their own. When they were naked, still kneeling in the middle of his bed, she abruptly straddled him, much as she had on that kitchen chair, their bodies close but unlinked.

"Hey, what's this?" he teased, surprised by how unceremoniously she took to his lap and flung both arms around his neck.

"I'm hiding."

"From what?"

"From your eyes. Sometimes, since that day we decorated your Christmas tree, I'd lie in bed and think about this moment and long for it and dread it at once."

"Why?" He leaned back and lifted a hand to touch her hairline with his fingertips.

"Because . . . I imagine the girls you've been with were young and perfect. Their skin was probably tight and tan and they didn't have stretch marks or wrinkles or veins that show, or terrible beat-up hands, or any of the unsightly things that forty-five-year-old women have."

"Lee," he said, tipping her off his lap and arranging his limbs half on top of her. "You're forgetting one thing." He kissed her once, his hand moving up her body, and whispered into her mouth, "I didn't love them."

With such simple words he stole her self-consciousness, which, like their clothing, seemed relegated to a puddle on the floor, leaving her free to enjoy her femininity. He lay on his side, braced up on an elbow, brushing a widespread hand up her leg, stomach and ribs, capturing first one breast, then the other, dipping his head to taste them, naked, for the first time. When he wet her skin, she wet her lips and reached a hand down for him, took him in hand and learned, with much pleasure, his intimate shape. It took little for him to bring her to climax—mere touches after all the years of dormancy. She lay in the wash of weak light from the hall and allowed him the greatest trust of all: to watch her at his mercy while her body quaked and spilled, while she uttered a coarse note in her arched throat and gripped his tangled bedspread in two fists.

Then he was above her on all fours, whispering into her mouth, "Do you want to put it on or should I?"

"What would you like?" she asked, realizing it had been a long time for him, too. There were parts of this ritual he'd undoubtedly spent time imagining.

"You do it," he answered, and laid the tiny packet in her hand.

He rolled to his back, hands thrown above his head, small sounds issuing from his throat as she touched him and ministered to him.

"Two years is too damn long," he said, his voice rumbly and deep while he lay with his eyes closed. "I can't imagine how you went without it for nine."

"Neither can I, now that I'm here."

"Please hurry . . . I'm dying."

"Oh, don't die," she begged, finishing, throwing herself across his chest, kissing his face. "Please don't die just yet. I've got some other things in mind I'd like to do with you." His arms scooped her in and he rolled at the same time, their limbs twining.

"Ah, sweet woman, you've just saved my life," he said.

They were avid and eager, stumbling through these initiate steps with the uncertainties of all first-time lovers, calling on playfulness to get them through the precarious moments of unset precedent.

The playfulness vanished, however, as their roll across the bed ended and two lovers found themselves captured in one another's eyes. A reverence stole their tongues. They could speak, at that moment, only with their eyes. Christopher centered himself above her, then in her, slowly and deeply.

"Lee . . . Lee . . ." he whispered against her lips. "At last."

Then together they became harmony and rhythm. The beat of their bodies became the culmination of the loving friendship they had formed in the past half-year. The sorrows of those months slid away. All those tears, all those talks, all those consolations had been leading to this. This! Christopher and Lee, making something extraordinary out of their ordinary selves.

"You . . . you," she said fiercely, gripping him with her heels and hands. ". . . All the time it was you and I didn't know it."

"I thought you'd say I was too young for you and you'd turn me away."

"I thought I was too old for you and I'd look foolish for even thinking this could happen."

"Never . . . I wanted this long before I first touched or kissed you."

"You feel so good. I've missed this so much."

"Tell me what you want . . . anything."

She wanted nothing, for she had the best life had to offer. Still he touched her, kissed her, caressed her in myriad ways, whispering, "Like this? Like this?"

And she whispered, "Yes . . . like that . . . oh yes."

She felt him stretch, and heard the snap of the bedside lamp. It brought her eyes flying open, staring up at him while his arm was still extended above his head.

"I want to see you. Do you mind?"

Shyness struck Lee. She wanted to say, Turn it off! In the light, their differences would be too boldly displayed, and all the faint cobwebbing of her age would leap out of hiding in the amber radiance from behind his shoulder. She wanted the room to remain dark, but while she was still caught by surprise, he settled astride her.

His crisp brown hair was disheveled by her finger tracks. His eyes loomed blue as oceans. By their insistent gaze he held her as he played with her breasts, reshaping them, stroking them, watching the backsides of his fingers circling round and round their florid tips, then beneath them, scribing half-moons before covering both mounds fully with his two broad hands.

"Say you don't mind," he beseeched in a husky lover's voice.

"I don't mind."

He could see that she did, that she was still self-conscious though he—her lover now—found her body beguiling. He bent forward, running his palm up over her brow as if feeling for fever, pushing the hair back from her face.

"Don't mind," he whispered, "don't mind, Lee. Let me love all of you the way I love the inner you."

She crooked an arm around his neck and drew his open mouth to hers, making a soft, acquiescent sound in her throat, wondering if the other man in her life had ever filled her with this much feeling, for at the moment, it hardly seemed possible. To kiss so, with tenderness tempering lust, yet lust an insistent accomplice, brought a luxuriance to their arousal. They had time and privacy and a healthy physical greed pressing them from within. "Oh, Christopher . . ." she murmured in a shaken voice. "You make me feel all the ways a woman wants to feel."

Again, he began moving within her.

She stroked his legs, spread her hands on his hips, watched the lamplight shift over his firm hide, his brow become beaded and his face sobered by passion. When his breathing grew forced, he fell forward, hands spread, elbows locked, blinking so slowly she thought he did not see her across the inches separating their faces, but watched instead his own inner feelings playing within some gilded screen in his mind.

He made some sounds, unmusical to all but her, the source of his pleasure.

When he came, he shuddered and collapsed like a craft running aground, falling upon her. She collected his thick bulk in both her arms and laced her fingers into his hair, finding his skull damp. The scent of him came from it—cosmetics and warm scalp and a touch of dance hall smoke.

She ran her nails over his head again and again, slowly, and he shivered once with his face out of sight above her shoulder.

When his pulse had slowed and his breathing evened, he caught her behind one knee with his heel and rolled them to their sides. He found a pillow and stuffed it beneath their heads, then for a long, serene time they studied each other's countenances, gauging their repletion in the tempo of their blinks and the laxness of their lips. She touched his lower one with a fingertip, then kissed him with a moth's touch.

He smiled.

"What are you thinking?" she asked.

"I'm not. I'm just being happy."

She rubbed his bottom lip. "It was very good for me."

"It was very good for me, too."

"What do you think are the chances of a woman coming the first time with a man?"

"I don't know."

"Pretty slim, I think."

"I was never sure if any girl did it with me before."

"Are you sure now?"

"Not a question in my mind, but it's probably because it's been so long for you. You were more than ready."

"You really think that?" She was still rubbing his lip.

"I told you once, I'm not really what you'd call a ladies' man."

"Well, you're this lady's man."

He clamped his teeth on her fingertip and sawed sideways, putting a faint white dot beneath her nail. He released it with a kiss and her fingertips settled against his chin. They closed their eyes for a while and rested, neither of them in a hurry to disjoin, enjoying the flaccid warmth of afterlove, the texture of his hirsute legs between her smooth ones, lazily moving a finger or a toe against one another. She thought about how liquid and relaxed her body felt. He thought about her reaching orgasm the first time with him.

In time he spoke quietly, his voice opening her eyes.

"Would it be tacky of me to ask about your sex life with your husband?"

"No, I don't think so. What we just did together removes a lot of barriers, don't you think?"

"So what was it like?"

She put some thought into her answer. "Guilt-ridden before marriage. Much better afterward, though it ran hot and cool. Sometimes we'd do it four times a week, sometimes only a couple of times a month. Just depended on what else was going on in our lives. We had to work a little harder at my orgasms than you and I did, though."

After a spell of silence, he lifted his head off the pillow and kissed her full on the mouth, then lay back as he'd been.

"You want to know something ironic?" he said. "I was scared to death that it wouldn't be as good for you with me as it had been with him. Everything you read says these things take time and patience to get right, so I figured . . ." He shrugged and his glance flickered away, then back at her, leaving the thought unfinished. "Once I said to you that I wasn't going to be scared of what might happen between us, but a lot of that was bravado. I was plenty scared, and most of it had to do with my being only thirty and you being so much older and experienced. That can be pretty intimidating for a man, you know. I thought, What if I make a play for her and she slaps my hand like I'm some naughty child?" After a pause he added, "But you didn't."

"Did you really think I'd do that?"

"I didn't know."

"Couldn't you tell I was falling for you?"

"Yes, but I thought you'd resist because of the unwritten social laws governing ages."

"Since we're making confessions, I have one of my own. When I first suspected that you were getting a crush on me, I thought, Gosh, he's so young. And I have to admit—I'm human—I had this other totally awful, unforgivable thought that did wonders for my ego: Wouldn't I look smart landing a boyfriend so young? It's been a real hang-up for me ever since, because it would make me a very shallow woman if that were my reason for going to bed with you, just to snag a younger man. Now we've done it, and I didn't do it for that reason at all; I did it because I love you and like you and respect you and have so much fun with you, but I have to admit—your age, your youth, your young, perfect body is a thrill I hadn't imagined."

He braced his head on one hand and used the other to push her slightly away so he could stroke her. He centered the butt of his hand between her breasts while fanning his fingers left and right, left and right, almost as if he were dusting her off.

"I'm glad we don't have to go through these firsts again. They're nerve-racking. Next time it'll be so much easier."

She smiled and teased, "Oh, so we're going to do this again?"

He went on watching his hand play across her soft skin. Goose bumps of pleasure had raised on her breasts, lifting the fine hair and puckering her nipples. "We're going to do this many, many times. As often as we can."

"A full-fledged affair, then—that's what we've started?"

He gave up dusting her breast and cupped her jaw instead while crooking an elbow beneath his ear.

"You can call it anything you want. Whatever it is, it's too damned good for a one-timer."

She studied him in the lamplight, which came from above and behind him, taking in the honey-hued nimbus outlining his brown hair, the russet lashes framing his blue eyes, his symmetrical features, which pleased her immeasurably. She studied his mouth, softened and polished by all the kissing they'd done . . . touched it as if unable to help herself. "Everything about you pleases me so much. I just can't believe this has happened, that we actually got beyond all those barriers. I'm liable to be insatiable for a while, making up for lost time."

"I won't mind." He caught her hand and began nipping its edge with his teeth. "Insatiable women are the best kind."

It was a toss-up who was more insatiable when she pushed him to his back and rolled atop him.

Later, she awakened him, lifting her head to read the alarm clock on the nightstand. They were beneath the covers by now, and her face held an irregularly shaped red blotch where it had been stuck to the hollow of his shoulder while she slept.

Coming awake, he looked down at her and smiled sleepily.

"Gotta go home," she whispered.

"Aw, no . . ." He rolled to face her, made a wishbone of his arms and captured her within them. "Noooo."

"I can't stay. Joey's at home with his friend Denny, and Janice will be coming home, too."

He lifted his head and left wrist, read his watch behind her back, then let himself go limp against the bedding again. "It's not even twelve yet."

"So, we jumped the gun a little bit."

He chuckled deep in his throat, eyes closed, arms lying loosely around her. "I wish you could stay here till morning."

"I know, so do I." She turned back the covers and got up. "But I can't."

He rolled to his back, joined his hands beneath his head and watched her begin to get dressed. Watched her step into her underwear, contort her arms to hook her rear-closing bra, then sit on the edge of the bed and skin her panty hose up her legs. Next came her dress, and when she had it on, he said, "Come around here. Let me zip it." She circled the foot of the bed and sat down with her back to him. He sat up and kissed her nape, threaded his arms inside her open dress, doubled them beneath her breasts and rested his mouth on the slope of her shoulder.

"I love watching you dress, watching you move around in my bedroom where I've imagined you doing just that."

She covered his arms with her own, felt them firm and warm inside the red crisp cloth of her bodice, tipped her head to one side and closed her eyes.

"I love this," she whispered, "just the feel of your arms around me. A man's arms are so different than a woman's. When you're without a man like I've been, you miss the sex, of course, but sometimes you miss this even more—just the touching, the rubbing together, letting your weight sag against somebody who's bigger, and smells different, and feels different than you. Promise me we'll do this sometime . . . just enjoy the feel of each other without having to make love."

"I promise. Now you have to promise me something."

"What?"

"To dress for me sometimes, the way you just did, slow and relaxed while I lie and watch you. It struck me a minute ago—anybody can watch a person undress, but watching them dress is even more intimate. You learn the order they do things—pants first, bra second, panty hose after that. Tonight, after I take you home, I'm going to picture that while I fall asleep."

She sighed, and let her head drop back, and they rocked gently with his arms still coiled about her and his lips on her neck. It would have been easy to fall back asleep, they were so contented with each other. But duty intruded, and she was forced to make her limbs move.

"I really do have to go. Zip me."

When he had, and she'd retrieved her jewelry from the nightstand, and slipped into her pumps, she took a page out of his notebook and watched while he rolled up to sit on the edge of the bed and find his discarded clothing, while he stood and pulled them on, buttoned his shirt before zipping his fly, then stuffed his tails in and tugged on the waist of his jeans, closed the waist button and—finally—zipped up.

"You're right," she said, sauntering over to stand before him, resting her elbows on his shoulders and toying with his hair. "There is something more intimate about it. I'd never thought about it before."

"Glad you enjoyed it," he said, smirking, buttoning his cuffs behind her back.

"And I thought of something else," she said.

"What's that?" He held her lightly by the ribs, his thumbs in the hollows just below her breasts.

"That if you'd just had sex with a stranger, you'd have trouble watching him dress. It would seem tawdry, wouldn't it? But watching you"— she kissed him lightly—"seemed like reading the P.S. on a love letter."

They rested their hips against each other and shared a single, splendid, soporific kiss.

When it ended, he said, very seriously, "I love you, Lee."

She imbibed the words, remaining silent while they seeped into her, filling all the empty troves that had been waiting years for this treasure.

Saying it became a reaffirmation, the ideal closing for this night of first intimacy.

"I love you too, Christopher."

And on that very fitting note, he took her home.

Chapter 15

ON New Year's Day everyone in the Reston household slept late. It was 9:50 when Janice awoke. She opened her bedroom door and slogged down the hall toward the bathroom, noting with lazy indifference that her mother's door was still closed. The rarity of Lee Reston sleeping till late morning struck Janice as she returned to her room and opened her mother's door to peek inside.

Lee lay on her stomach with one arm crossed beneath her face and the other flopped up against the headboard. She was sprawled diagonally beneath the covers, breathing evenly. Her red dress lay neatly folded over the back of a chair. One standing red pump accompanied one fallen on the floor beneath her panty hose and bra.

Janice studied her mother and experienced a surge of embarrassment at the thought that Joey's deduction might be true. If it were, she, Janice, would look like a stupid fool. It must be true: Her mother had bought a new dress, a red dress with a tiered skirt and shoes to match! Lee, who seldom bought clothes, hadn't even showed it to Janice in advance, hadn't oohed and aahed over it the way one would expect her to. Had she been hiding it hoping Janice wouldn't be around when Christopher came to the house to pick her up?

She silently closed her mother's bedroom door and opened Joey's. It was stuffy inside, smelled like old sweat socks and some dried-up orange peels that were sitting on his windowsill. He, too, was sound asleep, on his back with his chin in the air at an odd angle and his hands, with their huge knuckles, relaxed on the bedclothes. Denny Whitman was dead to the world in a sleeping bag on the floor.

She went inside, closed the door behind her, picked her way carefully over Denny and tiptoed to her brother's bed.

"Hey, Joey," she whispered, sitting down beside him in her long flannel nightgown. "Hey, Joey, wake up."

Joey pushed her away with one leg and rolled to face the wall, mumbling some syllables that sounded like *gold* and *myrrh.*

She jostled him and whispered, "Joey, wake up. I've got to talk to you." She jostled him harder. "Darn it, Joey, will you turn over here!"

He did, with all the good nature of a pit bull.

"Jeez! Leave me alone, will ya? I'm still sleeping!"

"Joey, I have to ask you something. Be quiet so we don't wake up Denny."

"Ask me later."

"I just want to know what time Mom got home, that's all."

"I don't know."

"Well, were you up?"

"Yeah. It was early."

"Early?" Her heart lifted with hope.

"Yeah, before midnight, I know that much, 'cause Denny and me had the TV on." He was rubbing his eyes, then gave a huge yawn.

"Was Christopher with her?"

"No, he just dropped her off."

"He didn't come in?"

"No. Jeez, why don't you ask *her* all this stuff?"

"I can't ask her, not if what you said is true and she's dating him seriously. Do you really think she is?"

"Heck, I don't know. He's here all the time."

"But he wasn't here at midnight? You're sure?"

"No!" he whined, disgruntled. "I told you, he just dropped her off, and she came in and ate some popcorn with Denny and me, and she made us turn off our video games so she could see some stupid mob scene in Times Square."

"Well then, maybe she's not dating him. I mean, maybe they're just friends after all."

She stared hopefully at Joey. He only shrugged and said, "How should I know?"

"Wouldn't they have stayed together at least till midnight if they were going steady, as you put it? I mean . . . if you were with Sandy on New Year's Eve, what would you do at midnight?"

He blushed and said, "Jeez, why don't you leave a guy alone?"

"Joey, listen . . ." She put her hand over his and went on sincerely. "You're my brother. This is important. If she's dating Chris, and if it's serious, I think we should talk to Aunt Sylvia or somebody about it."

"Why?"

"So Aunt Sylvia can talk some sense into Mom."

"Why?"

"Well, she's fifteen years older than he is, for heaven's sake!"

"So what?"

"So what! How can you lie there and say 'So what'? Do you want her to make a fool of herself?"

Joey stared at her awhile and said, "I don't get it."

Exasperated, Janice doubled forward at the waist and scratched her head until her hair looked wiry. Joey was too young, after all. She was talking in a circle around the subject of sex, but he wasn't old enough to grasp it, and she realized it would be wrong of her to bring it up in the context of her mother and Chris. When Joey had used the term "going steady," Janice had translated it into "having an affair."

Yet she had no more proof than Joey did.

"Just listen," she advised. "You're around her more than I am now that I'm in school. But pay attention, will you, after I go back for third quarter?" She paused, but he kept looking at her blankly. "If she starts staying out late, or . . . or . . . well, you know . . . anything that keeps her away a lot, call me."

Before Joey could answer, Janice sensed herself being observed and looked down at the floor to find Denny Whitman awake and listening.

She jumped up off the bed. "Go back to sleep, you guys. Sorry I woke you."

When Lee got up, Janice studied her with sensors a-quiver, but her mother only came out of the bathroom smelling like toothpaste and put the coffeepot on, as usual. " 'Morning, dear," Lee said. "Did you have a good time last night?"

"It was okay. Did you?"

"I had a grand time, until I tried to do something called the whip. Nearly tore my arms off."

"The whip?"

"It's a country dance move. Christopher tried to teach it to me, but I messed it up so badly I'm afraid we gave up."

Janice studied her mother moving about the kitchen, opening drawers and finding bagels, slicing them and putting them under the broiler, getting out cream cheese and jam, finding a carton of orange juice and shaking it, doing all the ordinary things mothers do in the morning. What was she, Janice, staring at? Did she really think that if her mother was having an affair with Christopher it would show? That she'd look *different* this morning? A glimpse of a thought beamed across Janice's mind's eye, but she kept the beam narrow, so that it flashed too fast for her to picture her mother as the sexual partner of the man Janice herself had been trying to attract ever since she'd met him. But the thought had struck, and it left Janice grossly uncomfortable. Mothers simply were not to be considered sexual beings. Oh, maybe if fathers were still alive—but with anyone else the thought was unpalatable.

"Mom?"

Lee finished pouring a glass of juice and looked up at Janice, holding the carton stationary while its spout dripped. Janice was leaning back against the countertop, gripping her elbows tightly against her ribs, her bare toes curled into a scatter rug in front of the kitchen sink.

What's going on between you and Chris?

The unspoken question was foretold by the scowl on Janice's face, by her tight, self-imposed body hug, by the pinched look on her lips. Lee instinctively guessed what Janice was thinking, but if Janice wanted to know, let her ask. Lee herself was uneager to broach the subject, afraid of hurting Janice and reaping her censure. Furthermore, what was going on between herself and Christopher was too new, too fragile yet to broadcast and hold up to the family's dissatisfaction.

"Yes, honey?" Lee replied.

The question hovered between them, unspoken, while Lee poured a second glass of juice. As she was handing it to Janice the phone rang.

Janice answered, swinging to face the counter, presenting her back to her mother.

"Hello?" After a pause, Janice handed Lee the receiver, knuckles down over her shoulder. "It's for you."

Lee set down the juice glass, took the phone and said, "Happy New Year."

"Happy New Year to you too," Christopher said, sounding happy and smiley.

"Oh, hi, Christopher. How did you survive last night? Did I break any of your arms on that dance floor?"

"Not a one."

"I had a good time but my calves ache from dancing in high heels."

"I think maybe your calves ache from something else."

She laughed and he said, "I love you."

For Janice's sake she put a lilt of deceptive laughter in her voice. "Do you really? Heavens, I never would have guessed it."

"Could I bring over some lo mein later this afternoon and see you?"

"Do you think the Chinese restaurants will be open?"

"If they're not, we'll eat toast and watch football games."

"Fine. Let me get a nose count." She dropped the receiver from her ear and said, "Christopher wants to bring Chinese over later. Should we count you in?"

Without turning to face her mother, Janice said, "Sure," and walked from the room, leaving her orange juice untouched.

Janice watched them like a cat the entire time Christopher was there, but if they were intimate, they gave nothing away. Christopher sat most of the day with his nape caught on the davenport cushions, his ankles crossed, watching bowl games with Joey and Denny, rehashing plays with them. Lee, dressed in a gray sweat suit and terry-cloth footlets, read a book curled up in a living room chair. At five o'clock she got up to warm the car in preparation for taking Denny home. Christopher roused himself and offered, "I'll take him if you want."

"No, you're all comfortable there. I'll go. Back in ten minutes or so."

Janice thought, *If these two are messing around, I'm Mae West!* They both acted as if they needed a shot of testosterone.

Lee returned, warmed up the Chinese food in the microwave, brought everybody a plate in the living room and returned to her comfy chair to eat hers and continue reading.

At eight o'clock, Christopher stretched and said, "Well, I think I'll go."

Lee had difficulty pulling her eyes away from her book. "Just one min . . ." She raised a finger and kept on reading to the end of the paragraph.

"Don't stop reading. I can find my way out."

"Oh, no! No!" Lee returned to reality, leaving her chair with the book plopped facedown on the cushion. "It's just that I haven't read a book for so long. I kind of got lost in it."

"Well, keep on. You don't have to see me out."

She yawned, linked her fingers and inverted her hands straight out in front of herself, stretching everything from her waist up.

"Lazy day."

"Yeah, it was." He got his jacket and put it on in the front hall. "Thanks for letting me hang around underfoot." He kissed her cheek, making no secret of it while the two kids looked on from the front room. "Hey, Joey, Janice . . . see you, huh?"

When the door closed behind him, Janice decided with some relief, I was wrong, Joey was wrong, Christopher is no more to her than Greg's replacement.

It was 2 P.M.—Lee's lunch break—on the first business day following New Year's when she knocked on Christopher's apartment door. He flung it open and the two of them nearly ripped each other's skins off, lunging together. They kissed as if tomorrow it would be outlawed. He pinned her against the apartment door, then changed his mind and dragged her away from it to skin off her coat and drop it to the floor. The kiss was openmouthed, sexual, impatient—the lush, pervasive kind that ends imposed suppression and begins to mark territory. In the midst of it he captured her breasts, flattened them and her hard against the closed door. Their combined weight hit it with a bang that shuddered up their hipbones and echoed outside in the hall.

When it ended she held him none too gently by two fistfuls of hair above his ears. "Don't you ever do that to me again! I've never spent such a miserable day in my life! I wanted to come over to that sofa and flatten you underneath me, but all I could do was sit there across the room reading a silly book!"

He laughed and said, "Are you saying you wanted me?"

She put pressure on his hair and raved, "Wanted? Wanted!" then, growling, used his hair as a handle and wobbled his head around as if to tear it off his neck.

"How are your calf muscles?" he inquired with a crooked smile.

"Kiss me nice and I'll tell you."

He kissed her nice, gently this time, while she smoothed the hair she'd been clutching and left her hands gently cupping the back of his head.

When he once again looked down into her eyes, she said quietly, "My calf muscles could use some physical therapy."

"Ah," he replied, "I've got just the thing in mind."

He picked her up and carried her like a bride into the living room where the Christmas tree was gone and the furniture in its customary place. He dropped down on the sofa, tipping her off his lap and curling forward to hold and kiss her while her legs trailed over his thighs. Exploring her lips and tongue with his own, he freed the buttons up the front of her lavender smock. Beneath it she wore a sweater. His hand was already skimming up underneath it when she halted the kiss and told him, "Christopher, I have some really bad news."

His hand stopped and he sent a look of concern straight into her eyes.

"I got my period last night."

For three beats he only stared disbelievingly. Then he flung himself backward against the sofa as if he'd been shot, his head flopping back, eyes closed, hands dropping free of her while he groaned, "Ohhh . . . nooo . . ."

"Sorry," she said with a shrug and a grimace.

"How many days?"

"Four or five."

He raised his head, opened his eyes and laid a finger across her mouth vertically. "Then you're no good to me, madam, because that's all I want you for, you know."

She kissed his finger and said, "Here I thought you loved me for my popcorn balls."

He squinted at one corner of the ceiling, thought for a moment, then turned a grin down her way. "Now that you've reminded me ... I guess I *can* stick around for four or five days longer." He grabbed her elbows and hauled her up. "C'mere." When he'd righted her, amid some awkward adjusting of her weight and limbs, she ended up straddling his lap, his hands at her armpits between her sweater and smock. He tilted her forward and kissed her with the pressures of pre-intercourse set aside, replaced by a laxness perhaps even more enchanting. His lips were sublimely soft, moist and relaxed beneath hers as they exchanged four winsome, crisscross kisses—noses left ... right ... left ... right. They took time, after the exchange, to study each other's eyes and faces appreciatively, their hands fluttering upon one another as idly as the fins of unswimming fish, his beside her breasts, hers at his back hairline. They were fine, rewarding minutes, those silent ones, while they recognized that sex could wait while their true allure for one another grew each moment they were together ... and, too, each moment they were apart. Their eyes imparted the message, then they exchanged small possessive smiles at very close range.

"I'll tell you something," he said softly, "New Year's Day was hard on me, too. I knew I shouldn't come over, but I just had to."

"I'm glad you did. If you hadn't come to me, I'd have come to you, and I didn't have any idea how I'd explain myself."

He began to rebutton her smock. "It's hell having to explain yourself, isn't it?"

She combed his hair back with four fingers, enjoying the crisp coil of it, the combination of scents—shampoo, laundry, skin—that created the effusion peculiar to him.

"Janice knows," she said, scraping his skull lightly with her nails.

"I suspected as much. She was pretty aloof yesterday."

"I think she almost asked me in the morning."

Her smock was closed. He rested his hands on the crook of her waist. "What would you have said?"

She quit furrowing his hair. "I would have told her the truth."

"Would you really?"

She nodded so infinitesimally he believed her. "I just wanted some time for us first. We deserve that, I think, before I stir up the cauldron that's bound to boil over when everybody finds out."

"You really think so?"

She nodded, her eyes dropping to the V-neck of his sweater. "Everybody but Joey. He's crazy about you, and he's young enough that he doesn't have preconceptions. But Janice is going to be mortified. Sylvia is going to be shocked. And my mother . . ." Lee rolled her eyes, then settled them on something at her left. ". . . My mother will be the worst one of all."

"Does it matter so much, what they think?"

"Well, of course it matters." She needlessly adjusted his shirt collar over the neck of his sweater and left her hands flat on his collarbone. "They're my family."

"Are you saying they'll disown you or something?"

"No, they won't disown me."

"Then they'll disown me." He said it without rancor, looking up into her eyes, stating the likelihood as if it were something they must face and deal with.

She sighed and wound her arms around his head, drawing his face to her chest. "Oh, I hope not. I'd like to think they're less hypocritical than that."

They sat on, in the caramel light of afternoon that slanted through his windows, so happy to be together, accepting this unconventional pose in all its intimacy as their own. His face was turned aside while she plunged one hand into the hair at the crown of his head and worked her fingers as if shampooing, then stroked the hair to the limits of its short length before repeating the motion again and again. She couldn't get her fill of pleasure in touching the myriad textures of him after the many years' dearth of male textures. His hair, his jaw, his brow, the lobes of his ears, his ribs and chest, even the textures of his clothing seemed different from hers, draped over muscle so much firmer and a bone structure so much broader. His hand was up her back again, between the smock and sweater, absently marking time across her shoulder blades like an inverted pendulum.

He closed his eyes and drifted, enjoying, too, the distinct femaleness of her, the pressure of her legs wrapped around his hips, her nails on his skull, her palms on his clothing and her breath on his forehead. The sun warmed his left cheek while her breasts—soft and pliant—warmed his right. She was scented much like her flower shop, herbal and lavender and floral all mixed together. His elbows, at her ribs, outlined a body circumference that seemed fragile compared to his own. Her shoulder blades, when his fingertips brushed them, felt as insubstantial as bird wings.

Man . . . woman . . . different . . .

So incredibly, enjoyably different . . .

"You want something to eat?" he asked when they had both grown lazy and indifferent to all but the sun and the motion of their hands.

"Mm . . ." she said against his hair, her eyes closed. "What have you got?"

"Some salami and cheese. Bagel chips. An apple."

"Mmm . . . do I have to?"

"You should eat something."

"I could live on this."

He smiled, nearly shivering beneath the gentle strokes of her hand on his hair.

"What time do you have to get back?"

"I shouldn't stay long. Sylvia's got a dentist appointment this afternoon."

He sighed and regretfully withdrew from her arms, looking up at her with his hair ruffled.

"Look at you, straddling me again. You're such a tart."

She clambered off, catching his hand, hauling him up behind her. "Come on, let's find that salami."

Holding hands, they walked toward the kitchen, stone in love. But as they went they wondered how much longer to keep their affair secret, and what it would lead to and why whenever they discussed its outcome their tones became somber, as if they were altering forever the future of their lives, though they did not know how.

Shortly after winter vacation ended, the school called Christopher. It was a silver-bright winter day warm enough to raise steam off the melting sidewalks. Inside the police department, where he was filling out an accident report, it smelled of late morning coffee and gun-cleaning oil. He took the call and heard a woman's voice inform him, "This is Cynthia Hubert, the principal at the junior high. We have a seventh-grade student here, Judd Quincy, who's gotten into some trouble. He says if we call you you'll come over here and bail him out."

Christopher sighed and let his shoulders sag, tilting back in his swivel chair.

"What's he done this time?"

"Stole some money out of a teacher's purse."

Christopher closed his eyes and pinched the bridge of his nose. Damn that kid. He thought they'd been making progress.

"You sure he did it?"

"She caught him red-handed."

"Is the liaison officer there?"

"Yes, Judd is with him."

"Listen . . . don't do anything with him till I get there, okay?"

The principal's pause sounded strained with indecision. Finally she sighed and said, "All right, we'll wait."

They had Judd in a counselor's office of Fred Moore Junior High when Christopher entered, in uniform. The room held an impacted, high-tension stillness often accompanying proven guilt. Judd sat in an aqua vinyl chair staring at his Air pump tennies. He looked skinny and unkempt. Christopher nodded to the liaison officer, Randy Woodward, from his own department. Behind Chris the principal entered, a stylish, thin, salt-and-pepper-haired woman wearing a straight gray dress and gold-rimmed glasses. He turned around and shook her hand. "Thanks for calling, Mrs. Hubert." He glanced down at Judd, still staring at his Air pumps, which by now looked as if they'd marched across Prussia on a foot soldier.

"Could I talk to him alone for a minute?" Chris asked.

The others went out and left the two of them alone.

Christopher shuffled over to stand before Judd, looking down on his bent head with its burry hair and birdlike neck, his rumpled, dirty T-shirt under a filthy denim jacket and jeans with tears across both knees. He stood a long time with his hands on his hips, the room quiet while from the outer office came the muted sounds of voices, and someone using a stapler, and a phone ringing persistently.

Finally Christopher asked, "Did you steal some money, Judd?"

The boy said nothing, only hung his head and studied the tongues of his tennies.

"Did you?" Chris repeated softly.

Judd nodded.

Words of rebuke somehow refused to form in Chris's mind. He'd lectured Judd so many times, had taken the tough-guy stance and made the kid realize the world wasn't fair but he'd just have to live with it, muddle his way through to adulthood, when he could finally make his own decisions. It struck Chris today, however: The kid was only twelve years old. To Judd, muddling his way through to seventeen, eighteen, whenever he might graduate from high school, must seem like asking him to become a Rhodes scholar. He was a scared, mixed-up, unloved little boy who probably hadn't been fed breakfast this morning, never mind kissed goodbye on his way out the door.

Suddenly Christopher found himself doing what he'd never done before: He went down on one knee and took Judd in his arms. Judd clung and started crying. Christopher held him firmly, swallowing hard to keep himself from doing the same, his nostrils narrowing at the stale smell coming from Judd's skin and clothing. He and Judd stayed that way, close and silent, while the secretary in the outer office seemingly used up an entire bar of staples, and every absentee in the school population called in sick. When Christopher tried to pull back, Judd clung harder.

"What went wrong?" Christopher asked. "Something at home?"

He felt Judd shrug.

"You want to get out of there? You want to live in a foster home?"

Judd said, "I want to live with you."

He pulled the boy's arms from around his neck and forced him to sit back on his chair. "I'm sorry, Judd, you can't. A person has to be licensed to give emergency foster care, and besides, what would I do with you when I work nights?"

"I'd be okay." Judd dried his eyes with the backs of his wrists. "I'd just watch TV and go to bed anytime you said I should."

It nearly killed Christopher to reply, "I'm sorry, Judd, it wouldn't work."

Judd looked up with more sincerity in his eyes than Christopher had ever seen there. "I could do stuff for you, maybe vacuum your place or warm up your can of soup for you."

That was Judd's idea of a meal, warming up your can of soup. Chris put his man-sized hand around Judd's boy-sized neck, wondering how much dirt was disguised by his dusky pigment. Then he got up and sat on the aqua-blue chair beside Judd's. He bent forward and rested his elbows on his knees.

"Tell me what happened at home."

"They took my free lunch tickets to buy coke with. Then they tried to give me some of it, said they was gonna turn me out—woo-hoo."

"Turn you out?"

"Yeah, you know—introduce me, sort of, to something new."

"The cocaine, you mean?"

Judd nodded while Christopher's adrenaline shot a stream of heat through his chest. It wasn't all that uncommon for parents like Judd's to fence their kids' subsidized lunch program tickets, but trying to get their own kid hooked on drugs was a new one on Chris. His innards seized up and he experienced the unholy desire to find Wendy and Ray Quincy and drive his fist into their faces until they needed plastic surgery.

"Now, let me get this straight." He lifted the kid's chin and forced his direct attention with a straight-line gaze. "Your mother and dad bought cocaine with your lunch money, then tried to get you to use it. You're sure that's how it was?"

Judd jerked his chin free. "I said that's how it was, and that's how it was."

"So you stole the money to eat lunch with?"

Judd had returned to shoe staring.

"Judd, I've got to have it straight this time, no lies, no half-truths. Is that why you stole the lunch money?"

The boy mumbled, "Yeah, I guess so."

"You guess so?"

"And 'cause I knew if I did, they'd call you."

Christopher left his chair and hunkered down facing Judd, sitting on one heel. "Hey, listen to me, okay? 'Cause this time it's really important. I can't put you in foster care without your parents' okay, and I don't think they'll give it. But we've got one other possibility. I've got the power to get you out of there and put you on a police hold for twenty-four hours. As soon as I do that a social worker will start proceedings with the county attorney, and there'll be a detention hearing before a judge. If we go that far, you'll have to tell the judge what you just told me, about your parents trying to get you to use coke. Will you do that?"

When it got that far, children often refused to testify against their parents, fearful at the last minute of losing their parents and home after all.

"Will you do that, Judd?"

Judd stared down at his dirty hands through plump tears that trembled on his lower eyelids.

"Can I live with you then?"

Don't break my heart like this, boy. "No, you can't, Judd. But there's a good chance I can be appointed your guardian during the proceedings."

"My guardian?" Judd looked up.

"It would be my sole purpose to look out for your welfare and make sure the correct decisions were made for you. But you have to understand—if I start this, if I put you on a twenty-four-hour police hold and talk to child protection, once they get in touch with the county attorney we're talking about taking you away from your parents permanently."

Judd thought that over for some time before coming up with one paltry defense of the mother who didn't deserve him. "My ma—sometimes she cooks supper."

Chris felt his throat thicken. When he spoke his voice sounded as if he were trying to swallow and talk simultaneously. "Yeah, I know. Sometimes they're okay. But most of the time they're not. They're sick, Judd, but they refuse to get help. Maybe if you don't live with them anymore they'll get it. We'd find you a good foster home where you'd get baths and meals and lunch money every day. But the choice is up to you—you've got to say."

"Could we still play basketball sometimes, you and me? And go to the workout room together?"

"Yes, Judd, we could. I'd make sure we did."

Judd found it impossible to make the final decision, so Christopher made it for him. He rose to his feet and put a hand on the boy's head. "Tell you what—we're going to get you out of school for today. You wait here, okay?"

In the principal's office he found Randy Woodward, Mrs. Hubert, and the teacher whose money had been stolen, Ms. Prothero. He closed the door and said without preamble, "I want to put him on police hold and get a court hearing."

"You think it'll do any good?" asked Woodward.

"I'm going after a CHIPS petition."

"A CHIPS petition?" said Woodward. "You're sure?" A CHIPS petition—Children in Need of Placement or Supervision—meant trying to remove a child permanently from his home. No responsible police officer or social worker began such a procedure without questioning himself to make sure it was the right thing to do.

"He stole the money because his parents fenced his subsidized lunch tickets and used the money to buy cocaine, then tried to get Judd to sniff some of it."

Ms. Prothero—a clean-cut all-American-girl type perhaps two years out of college—visibly blanched and put a hand to her mouth. Mrs. Hubert sat behind her desk looking sober but thoughtful. Randy Woodward said calmly, "I'd like to tie those sonsabitches on about a thirty-foot cable behind my snowmobile and go for a four-hour ride through the woods."

Christopher replied, "Trouble is, when they came to, they'd only ask for a snort. The boy needs a bath and some food. I don't think he's eaten in a while. He also needs clean clothes, which I don't think you'll find at his home. Will you contact Social Services?" he asked Woodward.

"Right away, if it's all right with Mrs. Hubert."

She nodded and said, "I think that's best."

"Ms. Prothero?"

The young woman came out of her daze, looking ill. "Yes, of course. Dear God, I had no idea it was that bad at his house."

Christopher said to Woodward, "I'll take him to the foster home myself after you make the call. He knows me. He's going to be scared."

"Sure. Glad to have you do it. These are the ones that break your heart."

Break your heart—sweet Jesus, this one damn near shredded Christopher's. He transported the scared little kid to a small, neat house on the southwest side of Anoka and walked him between the snowbanks up the driveway. Judd stared straight ahead, wearing a stoic expression and a denim jacket scarcely warm enough for midwinter. All the while Chris remembered how hard Judd had hugged him in the counselor's office at school.

A buxom fiftyish woman in a moss-green sweater and slacks opened the door and let them inside.

"This is Mrs. Billings," Christopher told Judd.

She said, "Hello, Judd," with such false brightness it made Christopher feel guilty as hell for leaving the boy with her, though the house appeared clean and had holy pictures on the living room walls.

He said to the woman, "He needs food and a bath. He's on a twenty-four-hour hold pending a detention hearing."

Before leaving, he put a hand on Judd's shoulder. The boy was too tall to be knelt before, yet too short to be hugged chest to chest, so Christopher settled for a squeeze of the shoulder before he could no longer help himself and gathered Judd against him in a mismatched farewell hug. This time, before a stranger, Judd gave no hug in return.

"Hey, listen, you're going to be okay now."

"When will I see you again?"

"There'll be a hearing within twenty-four hours. The law won't allow me to be present at it, but I'll come to get you for it myself, in the squad car."

"You promise?"

"I promise."

"Will I go to school tomorrow?"

"No, probably not tomorrow. The hearing will probably be then."

"What's the hearing for?"

"Well, the legal language says it's a hearing for probable cause. That means the judge will decide if there's enough reason to keep you out of your home permanently. The county attorney will be coming to talk to you about it beforehand. Just tell the truth. Tell him what you told me at school."

Judd studied his friend the policeman with a downcast expression.

"Well, now, listen, I've got to go. I'm on duty, you know."

Judd nodded.

He ruffled the boy's hair, thanked Mrs. Billings and left. As he was opening his car door he glanced back at the house to find Judd standing motionlessly in the front window, watching him. Inside the squad, he had to blow his nose and clear his throat before he could pick up the radio and report to the dispatcher.

He realized something as he headed back toward Social Services to find out about when the hearing was scheduled: The kid hadn't lapsed into rap talk once today. Fear had robbed him of all vestiges of bravado.

He called Lee that night and said, "I've got to see you."

"Something's wrong," she said.

"Yeah, it's . . ." What was it? His job, his damned thankless job during the training for which he'd learned never to become emotionally involved with the people he served. "It's Judd."

She gave him permission straightaway, without asking a single further question. "Come anytime. I'll be here all night."

He got there at 8:30 feeling heavy-limbed, heavyhearted, and needing . . . needing something . . . something he couldn't quite put into words. Succor, maybe.

She let him into the shadowed front hall, took one look at his drawn face and said, "Darling, what is it?"

Without even removing his jacket, he took her in his arms and put his face against her hair. She folded her arms up his back and they stood in the dim entry behind a stub wall that left the back of her quite visible through the living room archway. The entry lights had been left off, as had those in the kitchen. One dim lamp cast light onto their ankles from the living room where, for once, no television chattered, no Joey sprawled.

"Just one of those days I could have done without."

"What happened to Judd?"

"I started legal proceedings to try to have him taken away from his parents permanently."

"What started it?"

He told her about the lunch tickets, the cocaine, the scene in the principal's office and taking Judd to the foster home. "The thing is, after all that kid's been through, I'm still not sure I'm doing the right thing."

"But, cocaine . . ."

"I know. I know." He held her loosely, needing the feel of her warmth and closeness, the faint pressure of her arms bolstering his back. "But

I've been there, Lee, and I know how it feels. It's home, but it isn't like other kids' homes. Still it's the only one you've got, and if you lose your mom and dad, how do you know there'll be anybody there at all for you? I saw it in Judd's eyes today. I felt it when he latched onto me so damned hard I thought he'd break my neck. Then he said, 'I want to live with you, Chris,' and I had to say no. Jesus, Lee, you should have seen him. There he sat on that hard office chair, looking like some little refugee, dirty, bedraggled, smelling bad. He didn't even have on a decent winter jacket, and I knew damned well nobody'd fed him breakfast . . . and I've got an empty bedroom, and I make enough money that I could easily take good care of him, but what am I going to do with a boy of twelve when I work nights half the time and there's nobody to watch him?"

She had no answers. She only held him and let him go on whispering gruffly, working out his feelings.

"They warn you not to let this happen, never to get too close to kids like him, but what kind of a heartless human being would I be if I didn't?"

"Judd is warm and fed and being taken care of tonight. You did that much for him."

He sighed and rested his chin on her head, closing his eyes. He tried to draw strength from her, enough to blot out the difficult memories from that day, but they persisted. In time, he said, "The kids are the hardest part of this job. Not the felons, not the crooks, not even the accident victims. It's the kids that get to you."

"I know," she said, rubbing his back. "Greg always said the same thing."

"A couple years ago, the first year Greg joined the force, I got a call from the North Side saying someone had spotted a little girl walking down the street barefooted. It was a beautiful summer day, about two o'clock in the afternoon when I found her. I'd guess she was about three years old or so, and I swear to God, nobody had done one single thing for her that day. You could tell by her clothes that she'd dressed herself, poor little thing. She was wearing some dirty little dress and no panties underneath it at all, and then those bare feet, and her hair all scruffy and snarled. She was just toddling down the street dragging a hairless doll by one arm, blocks away from home. She'd just wandered out and nobody had even missed her. When I pulled the squad up beside her and got out, she was sucking on her fingers and crying, and even before I got to her, she reached up both arms, and once she'd put them around my neck, nobody could pry them loose. I had to call for a backup because she cried when I tried to let her go to drive my squad. I took her to the emergency foster home myself, and when I tried to give her to the woman there she sobbed and refused to let go of my neck." He was quiet awhile, then added, "I'll never forget that day as long as I live."

When he grew quiet, she said, "You mustn't feel guilty for not taking Judd."

"But I do. I started this big-brother relationship with him and I feel like I'm letting him down."

"You're too softhearted."

"How can a person be too softhearted?"

"Dear Christopher, this is one of the reasons why I love you."

"Oh, Lee . . ." He drew back and took her face in both hands, holding it like a chalice from which he would drink. He kissed her in gratitude, in beatitude, then continued holding her face.

"Tonight I wasn't sure if I needed a lover, a mother or a wife. So I came to you for all three."

"A wife?" she repeated.

"Cops have to lay a lot on their wives and I haven't got one." He grazed her cheeks with his thumbs. "Thanks for being here."

"If I was any help at all, I'm glad, but I have my own reasons for opening my door to you, and they're not totally altruistic." She went up on tiptoe and reached up one arm to draw his head down. "I thought about you all day long."

They were kissing when Joey came out of his bedroom and walked down the hall, stockingfooted. He entered the living room from the opposite end and came up short at the sight of his mother standing beyond the far archway of the room in the shadows of the entry hall, wrapped tightly in an embrace with somebody, kissing him.

He got a funny feeling in the pit of his stomach. A lift. A stir. An odd buoyant sensation that made his inner thighs feel liquidy and weak. It was Christopher, Joey was pretty sure, though all he could see was his jacket sleeves and his hands on his mother's back and head. He knew that jacket, though. Chris's left arm slipped down and caught his mother around the hips, pulling her deeper against himself. She whispered something Joey couldn't make out, and the murmur from a masculine voice confirmed that it was Christopher whose open hands came down and grasped his mother by both buttocks while she went up against him the way he'd seen in the movies.

He felt a blush cover his body and backed off into the hallway, standing motionless and undetected. He listened to their quiet murmurs and the long silences in between, then the more novel sound of slurpy kisses and humming sounds like he himself made when eating something he liked. He peeked around the corner again and saw Christopher's hand leave his mother's back and slide up under her sweater. The edge of the archway cut off his view, but he knew perfectly well Christopher was feeling up her breasts. Jeez! His *mother?* She still did stuff like that at her age? Wow, then they probably went all the way, too. Joey got all jacked-up feeling, all strange and tight and hard everyplace, and his breathing got windy. He took one last peek, then slipped silently into his mother's bedroom where the house's second telephone sat on her nightstand. He closed the door noiselessly, picked up the receiver and dialed by feel in the dark, then flopped on his back in the middle of her bed and said, "Hey, Denny, this is Joey. I gotta talk to you about the weirdest thing that just happened . . ."

Chapter 16

THE judge ruled in favor of leaving Judd in foster care until a formal court hearing, which was scheduled for late February, though he denied Christopher the appointment as Judd's guardian, stating that the boy already had a county attorney and a social worker looking out for his welfare. Christopher returned Judd to Mrs. Billings's house and left him there with the promise that the two of them would work out together in the police weight room every Tuesday that Chris's schedule permitted.

Joey Reston decided he wouldn't tell anyone but Denny Whitman what he'd seen in the front hall at home. If he told Janice, she'd break up Christopher and their mother, and that would be the end of the rather sexually stimulating scenarios such as the one that had so fascinated him he'd decided to try a little of that stuff with Sandy Parker. Of course, he'd have to talk it all over with Denny first and make sure that when he finally put the move on his girlfriend, he did it right and didn't scare her off.

Janice had returned to college, and Lee made plans for an unabashed sexual reprise with Christopher on the first night it was possible.

She called him and said, "Joey has signed up for a class to get his driver's permit. He'll be gone for two hours tomorrow night, starting at seven o'clock. What are you doing?"

"I'm off. Can you come over?"

"Yes." She released a pent breath. "Just try to stop me."

"And I've got Friday off, too. What are you doing Friday night?"

"Nothing. And Joey's going to a basketball game."

"Two nights in a row. Shazam."

"Oh, Christopher, I haven't felt like this in years."

"Like what?"

"You know."

"Maybe I do, but tell me anyway."

"Sexy. Turned on. Thinking about it all the time. I suspect I should feel guilty, but I don't."

"Why should you feel guilty?"

"I'm lying to the kids."

"No, you're not. You're just reserving some of your private time for me and not telling them about it."

"A slanted view if I ever heard one."

"I've told you, anytime you want to tell them, straight to their faces, 'I'm dating Christopher,' just let me know. I'll come and tell them with you."

"Not yet," she said, a hoarder savoring her booty, "not just yet. I want you to myself for a while."

A silence fell while they pictured each other, and felt lucky and happy and yearny, as all new lovers feel when they must be apart.

"I wish I was with you now," he said.

"So do I."

"Are you in bed?" he asked.

"Yes." She called him every night at eleven, after lights out. "Are you?"

"Yes, in the dark. What are you wearing?"

"A really ugly old faded flannel nightgown. It must be ten years old."

"Are you lying on your back?"

"No, on my side, curled up with the phone on the pillow."

"Is the nightgown caught between your legs?"

His question did unbelievable things to her libido. "Is this one of those kinky telephone conversations I've heard about?"

"Yes, I suppose it is, but I've never had one like it before either, so don't go thinking I make a habit of this. Only with you. Is the nightgown caught between your legs?"

"Yes," she whispered, then closed her eyes, breathing as if his hands were upon her, picturing his face, his sturdy fingers, his unclothed body, while only silence connected their two telephones.

"Lee?" he whispered after a long while.

"Yes."

"Don't waste a minute getting over here after you drop Joey off."

She didn't. At 7:07 she was walking through his door, and by 7:09 neither of them had a stitch of clothing on. They didn't make it as far as his bedroom but tumbled to the living room floor where the radio was playing and two lamps were lit beside the sofa. This time, she hadn't a single inhibition about being seen in the light, but rolled with him, and spread her limbs at his bidding, and let him kiss her in the most intimate of places, which had been scented for that purpose.

Their coupling was greedy and untamed, a splendid natural compulsion carrying them from one pleasure to another after their forced celibacy. They explored poses balletic and profane, submitting completely to the unutterable joy of this act.

They had been kneeling, face-to-face, when she fell back, her arms upflung, her ribs forming a bridge where he spread one hand.

Her words came as an afterbeat. "I can feel you . . . clear up to . . . my heart . . . my God . . . my God . . . my God . . ."

"I never thought you'd be like this."

"I've never been . . . before . . ."

He hauled her up and she came with the same loose freedom as she'd fallen back, to kiss him and move upon him and mess his hair and wet his mouth with her own.

"Lee . . . Lee . . . I still can't believe I'm with you, and doing this."

She was forty-five, and flying free, and making up for so much lost time.

When she climaxed, he stifled her cry with a sofa pillow, afraid the tenants in the apartment below would hear. When he climaxed, she watched, smiling down their bodies, taking joy in the sight of them joined. In paroxysm he was beautiful, bowed back upon her with his jaw fallen open and his breath strident. She touched his damp brow and ran a finger into his open mouth, which settled closed as his eyes came open.

Afterward, they lay on their sides on the turfy texture of the carpet, holding one another with their legs and their gazes. Near their heads a branch of the ficus tree fluttered in the forced air rising up through the hot-air vent. The low bass beat of the radio reverberated along the floor and up into their ribs. Outside, snow pecked at the windows and wind prowled, but in the saffron light from the lamps Christopher and Lee felt warmed from within.

"You're something," he said, exhausted.

"I don't know where it came from."

"Too long without it."

"Something more, I think. This is a different me."

He touched her lower lip, misshaped it and let it spring back to its natural contour. "When I first started thinking about you in a sexual way, I imagined that you'd be very straight, very proper about it."

"I used to be. You've changed me."

"How did I manage that?"

"I don't know. You just . . ." She rolled to her back, one elbow jutting up, one breast flat and stretched, attracting his idle hand while their bodies remained in a liquid link below. "There you are, thirty and sturdy and making me into this sex-crazed woman where I used to be so . . . well, so functional, so oriented all day long at work. Now I lose track of what I'm doing, and I scheme to get away from the shop to meet you and do this, and a day without you seems like a month."

"It's the same for me. But it's more than sex. You're there for me in more ways than that."

"What ways?" she said, still lazing backward while he ran a fingertip over her ribs and around one nipple, down to her navel, inside it, then back up her center.

"The day after New Year's when you came here at noon and we couldn't make love, I felt contented just sitting with you on my lap in the sun. And when my job gets me down and I can come to you the way I did the other day when I put Judd in that foster home . . . that's all part of it for me. And that part is just as good as this part."

Smiling lazily, she rolled her shoulder toward him slightly, giving shape to her breast once more, so that it fit nicely into his hand.

"Just as good?" she teased.

"Well," he amended, grinning, "just about as good."

Her throat fluttered in a silent chuckle, then she rolled to lie face-to-face with him, lifting the hair at his nape with four fingers, studying his features while her laughter dissolved into something much more profound.

"For me too," she whispered.

She lifted her weight from the floor and bore it on one elbow, rolling slightly onto him to kiss him more affectionately than passionately.

"You've made me so happy," she said, strumming his hair back from his ears as if it were lute strings.

"I'm glad."

"And you know something?"

He waited, sated, for her to go on.

"I truly believe that the quality of a relationship can be measured by the quality of the time *after* making love. What do you think?"

He thought he wanted to spend the rest of his life with this woman, that's what he thought. Catching her neck in the crook of one elbow, he sighed her name, "Oh, Lee . . . ," and settled her in the bays and cays of his body, letting the unsaid speak louder than any words he could have replied.

She dreamed of Greg that night for only the third time since his death. The dream was simple, just a glimpse of him smiling and saying, "I took care of that hose, Mom," as he walked into the kitchen adjusting a red bill cap. She awakened disoriented, believing during those few fragile seconds before total wakefulness that he was still alive. Full awareness brought the hammer blows of her own heartbeat against the bedding, reminding her that he was truly dead and she'd never hear his voice or see his face again.

She touched things to make certain she was awake: the bedspread, her forehead, the nightstand, cool and solid at the tip of her outstretched arm.

What had the dream meant? And why had it come tonight right after she'd spent time with Christopher? Was it a signal that she truly was substituting Christopher for Greg, if not in the physical sense, then in the emotional?

That day, still melancholy from the dream, Lee received a second reminder of Greg—a telephone call from Nolan Steeg. "Hello," he said simply, "just wondering how you're doing." The sound of his voice clutched her with a deeper wistfulness, though she never failed to be touched by the sensitivity of the young people who continued calling this way instead of forgetting she'd ever known them and been part of their lives. Dear, thoughtful Nolan—how heartwarming to realize that he'd cared enough about Greg to continue caring about his family. He and Lee had a ten-minute visit about Nolan's job, Joey's driving, Janice's return to school, the winter weather. Finally, when they'd spoken of everything except the subject that was on both of their minds, Nolan said, "I don't know why, but I've been thinking of Greg so much today."

What a relief it was to speak directly of him at last.

"Oh, Nolan, me too . . . I dreamed of him last night."

"I never dream of him. I wish I would. It'd be nice to see him again."

"I can't believe you called today, just when I needed it. Not everybody realizes that I still need to talk about him sometimes."

"He was my friend my whole life long. It takes longer than a few months to get over losing him. I can't imagine how long it's going to take you. I'm just glad you're the kind I *can* talk to."

After Lee hung up she found her spirits fluctuating between happy recollections of the past and present self-pity. Nolan's call had sparked so many vivid memories of the two young boys through the years—in elementary school together, then in junior high like Joey was now, then in senior high, double-dating, going out for sports, polishing their first cars in the driveway, working barebacked in the sun while their car radios shook the leaves on the trees. At times during that day these images would bring a sting to Lee's eyes; at other times they would bring an unconscious smile, a healing acceptance.

But as if fate was out to undermine all the progress she'd made since last June, it had one more reminder in store. On her way home from work that night, she switched on the car radio, and what should be playing but Vince Gill's "When I Call Your Name." The chance of her hitting that particular song during the five-minute drive home was remote. Yet there it was, crooning out of the cold speakers, the third and most powerful reminder of Greg.

Music. Its nostalgia hit with an insidious impact. It was the most recent of his likes, this song that was still pouring forth from radios all over America, speaking to people's emotions on multiple levels. But not to Greg's. No longer to Greg's. What had he felt when he'd heard these words? Who had he thought of? Had there been a special girl he'd loved and lost and still longed for? A girl he might have eventually married? Had children with? Spent a happy life with?

That song began the thought that Lee had trained herself during the past seven months to shut out:

If only . . .

If only . . .

If only . . .

She didn't quite make it home before beginning to cry. Joey was there in the kitchen dropping some macaroni into boiling water when she walked in.

"Will you make some macaroni and cheese, Mom? But you gotta hurry. I've got to be at . . ." His expression grew fearful when he saw her tears. "Mom, what's wrong?"

He came to her straightaway and they hugged.

"Greg," she said through a stuffy nose. "I'm missing him something awful today."

He hugged her harder, standing very still.

"Me too. I wonder why."

"I don't know. Nolan called, too. He said the same thing."

"Why would we all be thinking of him at the same time?"

"Who knows? Earth rhythms, biorhythms, the pattern of the stars. We think we're healed, then we find out we're a long way from it."

"Yeah," he said in a croaky voice against her hair. "Bummer."

She rubbed his shoulder blades, smiled sadly and repeated, "Yeah . . . a real bummer." Over the last half year Joey had surpassed her in height. The realization only added to her gloominess: Soon he, too, would grow up and be gone from her. She drew back in spite of the thought, perhaps because of it, and forced life to take precedence over death.

"So. You've started some macaroni and cheese." She found several tissues and offered a couple to Joey. They blew their noses and wiped their eyes, and she turned down the stove burner before the macaroni boiled over. "And you've got to be at the high school at seven-thirty."

"Yeah," he said without much spirit. "Anoka's playing Coon Rapids." It was the biggest rivalry of the year.

She took his face in both hands and gave it a little love pat and

311

smooch. "And pretty soon I won't have to give you a ride to these things anymore."

"Denny's mom is giving us a ride tonight."

"Well, good. Now, let's get this cheese sauce made."

When he was gone she cleaned up the kitchen and changed into blue jeans and a sweatshirt. The house was very quiet. The dishwasher made a rhythmic *thump-thump-thump* and sent out the lemony smell of steamy detergent. The houseplants needed watering but she suddenly despised the thought of watering one more plant, of touching one more leaf after a day, days, years of doing so. Suddenly she missed Janice so terribly much the center of her chest hurt—now where had that come from? She, who had adjusted to Janice's going off to college within months of her doing so. She dialed Janice's dorm number but nobody answered: Friday night, and what healthy, well-adjusted, pretty young coed wouldn't be out with friends? Lee hung up, braced both elbows on the kitchen counter and poked the tip of one finger into the leftover macaroni and cheese left cooling in a plastic storage dish.

Poke . . . poke . . . poke . . .

Holding her feelings at bay . . .

Holding . . . holding . . .

Until a sob burst forth with such ferociousness it laid her flat against the countertop, her hand lying limp beside the macaroni.

Christopher arrived when she was mopping up her face. He stepped inside with two rented videos and a red pie box from Bakers Square.

He asked the same question Joey had.

"Lee? What's wrong?"

She sniffled and said, "It's dumb."

He set down the videos and pie.

"What's dumb? Come here . . ." He went to her instead, and gathered her into his arms against the cold nylon of his jacket with the smell of winter captured in its filaments. Gently cupping the back of her neck, resting his lips on her forehead, he asked again, "What's dumb?"

"Greg," she got out before she began crying again.

He was the only one who didn't say anything, and it was precisely what she needed. Simply to be held, loved, rocked, petted, understood in silence by this man. The comfort of others mattered—it certainly had—but all day long she had yearned toward this minute when she could curl into a cocoon in Christopher's arms and feel at last the perfect consolation, for that's what he had become to her. No others, no matter how she loved or cared about them, could fulfill the need he had begun fulfilling in her day-to-day existence. Much as *he* had come to *her* when life got too complicated and sad, *she* now turned to *him.*

He let her cry for as long as she needed, then turned with one arm around her and walked slowly to the living room where they sat on the sofa in darkness softened only by the peachy light from the distant kitchen. She coiled up tightly against him like a snail beneath a leaf while he turned her legs to the side and draped them over his lap, laying his cheek on her hair.

In time she began telling him about her day, the trio of reminders that had rekindled her grief: the dream, Nolan's call and Greg's favorite song. She confessed her disappointment in discovering she wasn't healed of her grief after all.

"I guess I'm still what they call vulnerable, even after all these months."

" 'They'—who is 'they'?"

"The books, the magazines, the people who appear on talk shows. They all say you're vulnerable for a long time after a loss, and you should give yourself time before making changes in your life."

"Vulnerable to me, is that what you mean?"

"Oh, Christopher, I don't know what I mean. I thought I was over the worst of it, that's all; now here I am right back where I was seven months ago."

"Hardly. You've come a long way since then."

His coolheaded common sense reassured her. "I suppose you're right, and deep down inside I realize that I tend to get melodramatic. But this doesn't feel like melodrama. It feels like a great big empty ache that's never going to go away."

He could tell perfectly well what had happened today: She'd experienced a relapse of grief and had stepped back to assess her sexual relationship with him, which had begun to look suspiciously much like overreaction in the wake of loss. Were the two of them greedily grasping at life, proving they were not squandering it by engaging in this coital merry-go-round with each other? Were they fooling themselves about being in love in order to justify what they were doing on couches and floors and in his bed every chance they got? When the true period of mourning was over, would they find out they had merely used each other to get through it?

"You know, Lee, you're not the only one who's vulnerable here. What about me?"

She sat very still, with her legs still across his lap, one hand on his chest, feeling his heart beat along at a normal pace.

"Do you think we're both going to end up hurt when this is over?" she asked.

He gave no reply.

"Each of us will lose our best friend then, won't we?" she asked in a diminished voice.

He remained stone still. "You seem awfully sure this is going to be over someday."

Lee's mind ticked off the paramount reasons it would be: *His age. Her age. Mother. Janice.* What other outcome was possible? Surely someday there would be a painful breakup.

"Is this just a temporary fling for you, Lee?" he asked.

Now it was her turn to sit absolutely still.

"Is it?" he asked. When she made no reply, he pressed his point. "Are you waiting to get over your infatuation with me so you never have to tell your family?"

She pulled back sharply, looking up toward his shadowed face. "I don't know what you mean," she answered.

He rolled his head and looked at her. "You know something, Lee? That's the first lie I've ever heard you tell."

She bristled and lurched up from the couch, but he caught her arm and hauled her back against his side.

"Forget it," he said. "Tonight isn't the time to discuss it, right after you've had such a bad day anyway. I brought some pie. You want some pie? It's cream cheese and apple."

"I'm not in the mood right now." She rose with no resistance from him and walked out of the room. Left behind, he sighed and pulled himself to the edge of the sofa almost wearily, dropping his elbows to his knees and considering the situation for several minutes before pushing to his feet and following her to the kitchen.

She had put away the leftover macaroni and cheese and stood at the kitchen sink staring out the black window.

"Lee," he said with a a note of apology, dropping a hand on her nape. She stood stiffly beneath it. "What do you want me to do?" she asked.

"I don't know."

"Well, neither do I. Once people know about us everything will change, and I don't want that."

"All right." He dropped his hand from her. "All right. I just thought it might be easier if we were honest with them, and we could stop sneaking around."

They stood in the kitchen refusing to look at each other, wondering exactly what they wanted. Starting an affair was the simple part; continuing it was more difficult. If it were to be a temporary fling and nothing more, there was no reason for her children to know. If it was not, this was too soon to talk about it.

"Do you want me to go?" he asked.

"No."

"Then what do you want?"

"I want . . ." She turned and he saw uncertainty on her face. "I want to be bold and fearless, but I'm not. I'm afraid of what people will say."

He stood staring at her, part of him understanding, another part alienated by her reluctance to defy heaven and earth on his behalf. He was willing to defy it; why wasn't she? Yet he did understand. She had lost a husband and a son. She didn't want to lose a daughter, too, and who knew what reaction an outraged, infatuated twenty-three-year-old might have when she found out she'd been upstaged by her forty-five-year-old mother? And what about Lee's mother, father and sister?

He had no answers, so he escaped momentarily into serving up pie. He opened a cabinet door and got out two saucers, cut two pieces and found forks, then carried everything to the table. He sat down with his back to her and defiantly rammed one bite of pie into his mouth. It tasted like sadness.

"Aren't you going to eat your pie?" he asked.

She came, finally, and sat down, picked up her fork and took one bite, then stared at the wedge without eating more.

He studied her downcast face, her eyes that refused to meet his, her stubborn chin and the mouth that was trembling again after all the crying she'd done today. Hell, he hadn't intended to make her cry.

"Lee," he said in a tortured voice, "I'm sorry."

When she looked up he saw tears lining her eyelids, not quite plump enough to fall.

"I love you. You didn't need this tonight of all nights. I'm sorry."

They dropped their forks at the same moment and catapulted from their chairs into each other's arms, their hearts aching with love and fear and the realization that the hurt each of them had foreseen was already beginning.

"Sweet Jesus," he said, quite desperately, with his eyes closed, "I love you."

"Joey will be home in half an hour," she said. "We have to hurry."

He picked her up and carried her to the bedroom where they made love with an unmistakable tenderness, for here now was a new sexual mood: apology. It permeated their touches, murmurs, gazes.

For in Christopher lingered a profound regret for having added to her burden tonight rather than mitigating it, and in Lee the haunting suspicion that he was right, that she was hoping she'd get over him before her kids found out.

In the weeks that followed, however, life atoned. It gave them redemptive times together, rescuing them time and again from themselves, for in the presence of one another *self* tended to matter less. *Self* was somehow seen to, in all its wants, by their giving to each other.

Their primary frustration during that time was having so little time to themselves.

They stole hours.

They hoarded noons.

They grew expert at making love in ten minutes or less. Sometimes, though, friendship supplied the sustenance and sex waited. Friendship—by its thriving, simple force—drove their relationship to a new level of satisfaction.

Sex, they said to themselves, *well, yes, sex. But in all honesty anyone can achieve a certain level of expertise at sex, can't they?* Ah, but to be friends, now there was an accomplishment.

Perhaps they overplayed friendship because they'd been spooked by that exchange the night he'd suggested she might use him and lose him once this period of mourning had ended.

Christopher's deeper feelings caught up with him, however, one morning when everything had been so perfect his entire being was sated: all but that tiny corner of his wishes where a nagging hangnail of desire flapped each time it rubbed against his contentment.

Joey had spent the night before with the Whitman family at a motel with an indoor pool celebrating Denny's fifteenth birthday. For the first time ever, Christopher awakened at dawn with Lee in bed beside him.

He opened his eyes and saw her there, on her stomach with her left arm under the pillow, her right canted against his dark pine headboard. The daylight held too little candlepower to cast shadows, thus she reposed in the dusky prelight that gave her an allover hue of Spanish moss. Only her eyelashes stood out against the delicate gray colorlessness covering her exposed shoulder blades, arms and face. Her lips were open but she appeared unbreathing. Only her left eye showed. Beneath it a tiny furl of skin took on a first morning shadow along with another beside her nose, and yet another leading from it to the corner of her mouth. As he watched, her right thumb flinched, then her left leg, which was updrawn near his hip beneath the covers. That thumb—rough, slightly spatulate—bore the remnants of yesterday's work beneath its stubby nail. He loved, he'd discovered, her self-consciousness about her hands and the hands themselves, workworn, stained, crosshatched on the inner fingers by the abrasiveness of soil and colored by chlorophyll.

He rolled to his stomach, arranging his body in a mirror image of hers: pillow beneath his cheek, knee cocked and touching the tip of hers, his hand at the headboard seeking and finding hers, linking their fingers loosely while she continued slumbering, unaware of his touch. With his thumb he touched hers, rubbed its sandpapery pad and contemplated her face. He wanted the right to wake up beside her like this always. He wanted her coarse hands and her changeless hair and her relaxed mouth in his line of vision when he opened his eyes every morning for the rest of his life.

He waited to tell her so, watching in patience as the dawn gained strength and the light brought out pale hues upon her hair and skin. Her hair became bronze, her lips pink, her freckles rusty across her bare shoulders.

She opened her eye and found him watching her. Lifting her head, she scrubbed hard beneath her nose, squinting her eyes shut, then curled onto the pillow again. With their fingers still loosely linked, her left eye open, half her mouth visible, she smiled against her pillow.

"G'morning," she said, muffled.

"Good morning."

She closed her eye. "You've been watching me."

"Mm-hmm."

"For how long?"

"All night. Didn't want to waste a minute."

"Liar."

"Since dawn."

"Mmmm . . ." She acted as if she wanted to snooze some more, so he let her. His heart began racing, wondering how to pose the question, fearing she'd say no and force an end to their relationship. He thought about all the years he'd lived without really searching for the right one, then finding her in the most unlikely person of all. Thirty years of life funneling down into one crystallized moment that would affect all his days that followed. He'd never even thought of rehearsing this. He figured he'd know when the moment was right, and as for words—well, hell, a man just had to stumble through the best he could in spite of his hammering heart and his fears of rejection.

She might have dozed again, all the while he claimed her lax fingers and kept their thumbs matched, all the while the lump of anxiety rose from his chest to his throat and lay wedged against the pillow.

God in heaven, what if she said no? Where would he ever find another woman to equal her?

Her thumb began circling his slowly; she hadn't been dozing after all.

"Lee?" he said quietly.

Her left eye opened, its rusty iris dotted by deeper markings, like a tiger lily. "Hm?"

He lifted his head, carried her right hand down from the headboard and kissed the base of her thumb. Dread of her answer kept him mute so long that she said, "What, honey?"

He studied their joined hands while saying it. "I love you and I want to marry you."

Her head came up. Her face appeared in full, eyes wide while reactions volleyed across her face: stunned surprise, rejection of the moment for which she wasn't prepared, a weakness for him tempered by a realization of the strength she found with him.

"Oh, Christopher," she said, scuttling up, backing to the headboard, sitting with the blankets held above her bare breasts. "I was afraid you'd bring this up sometime."

"Afraid? I said I love you. You've said you love me. Why are you afraid?"

"There are fifteen years between us."

"We've known that since we first met, but we started this affair anyway." He sat up against the headboard, too, covered to the hip, the pillow at his back, his legs crossed and stretched straight out before him. "You'd have to do some pretty fancy talking to convince me that matters one single bit."

"You're blocking out what matters."

"For instance."

When she stubbornly refused to cite a reason, he did.

"Public opinion—shall we start with that?"

"All right, let's." Her voice had taken on an edge. "Or more to the point, family opinion, and I don't mean my mother's, or my sister's, or my father's, or Joey's. I mean Janice's. Let's start with her opinion."

"Let me reiterate something I've told you on several occasions. I never once—not by word, action or innuendo—made the slightest move on Janice. I hugged her a few times right after Greg died, but everybody was hugging everybody else then, so that doesn't count. Neither have I ever made any bones about the fact that I was taking you out or doing things with you. And if you recollect with any kind of honesty, you'll realize, neither did you."

She slid a thumbnail between her bottom teeth.

"*Did* you?" he insisted.

She locked both arms around her knees and replied meekly, "No."

"In fact, there were times when you asked your kids if they had any objections, weren't there?"

"Yes."

"As recently as New Year's Eve, right?"

"Yes."

He let that sink in before continuing. "Any feelings Janice supposed she had for me were strictly one-sided; and if you raised the kind of children I think you raised, she'll realize that you've got a right to happiness and she'll give us her blessings. If not . . ." He spread his hands and let them drop. "We'll face it when we have to. I don't have all the answers."

"But Janice would be mortified after the way she confided in me that she liked you, and after she bought you those tickets at Christmas and practically spelled it out that she'd like to go to that ball game with you."

"But is that our fault? Should we back away from each other just because Janice has a crush on me? I'll concede . . . she might be shocked when we first tell her, but she'll get used to the idea. So what other objections do you have?"

"They aren't objections, Christopher, they're common sense."

"What other common sense do you have, then?"

"I don't like your tone of voice."

"I don't like your answer!"

"I don't like any of this! We've never fought before."

"Well, damn it, Lee, that's what a man does when a woman turns down his proposal; he starts fighting for her!"

"All right," she said, spreading her hands as if pressing down the air at her hips. "All right." The blanket slipped down her breasts. She tugged it into place and pinned it beneath her arms. "You can disregard everything that's changeable but you can't disregard our ages. That part is never going to change."

"I don't want it to. I love you the way you are, you love me the way I am, and I don't see that changing as we grow older."

"But, Christopher—" She broke off her own objection, wagging her head as if this was all too exasperating.

" 'But, Christopher, what about kids.' That's what you were going to say, isn't it?" Their eyes met and he saw that some of her temper had dissolved. He felt his do the same and realized that this, above all, would be the most difficult to convince her of. When he spoke he put a wealth of earnest sincerity into his voice. "I don't want any, Lee. I've never wanted any. I told you that weeks ago. I've known since I was a kid myself that I didn't want to put any kid through what I've been through myself. And since I've grown up and become a police officer, I've seen so many poor, unloved, hungry little bastards that I just don't want to bring any into the world and risk putting them through that."

"But yours wouldn't *be* poor, unloved, hungry little bastards. You'd be such a good father," she said plaintively.

"I can be that to yours if I marry you. Maybe not to Janice, but to Joey. I love Joey already, and if I'm not mistaken he feels darn close to the same thing for me. I've been playing a father's role with him ever since Greg died, and if I marry you that'll just make it official."

She knew he was right about Joey, who worshiped the very breeze left by his passing.

He was hurrying on. "And you've forgotten about Judd. I've made a promise to myself that I'm going to stick by Judd till he's got a diploma in his hand and a reasonably firm foot into adulthood. He's going to need it. I'll have all the fathering I want, getting him over the hump . . . and you're right, I think I'll be good at it. Good enough to head that kid in the right direction, because whether he goes back to his parents or stays in foster care, he's got a hell of a lot to overcome, and I'm the one who can help him do it . . . me, who overcame it myself.

"As far as Janice is concerned, I don't think I'll ever be a father figure to her because she's too old, but I can round out the family and fill that space that's been vacant since Bill died. I know it'll take time with Janice, but once she falls in love—really falls in love with some nice young man she'll meet someday—she'll forget she ever looked at me twice. And when she sees that you're happy, she'll be happy, too."

Lee let her head fall back against the headboard and her eyes close. What peculiar and bittersweet luck they'd had to find each other and fall in love. How unfair that a chance thing like a number—fifteen—divided them and created a barrier to their happiness. She loved him—oh, her heart didn't question it for a moment—but with that love came a responsibility to look into a future that he was too young to heed, so she, with her greater life experience, must heed for him. She rolled her face toward him.

"You make everything sound so logical."

He took her hand and held it on the sheets between them. His voice was quiet when he replied, "There's nothing logical about love, not the way it happened to me. I just . . ." He shook his head in wonder. "Hell, I just fell. Hard. Sudden. Boom, there it was: *This is the woman I want to spend my life with.* It rattled me when I first realized it, but not for the reasons you think. I never cared that you were older or that people would talk. I got scared because I knew that when this day came and I asked you, you'd say exactly what you're saying."

He was staring at their joined hands, and she could see how devastated he'd be at her refusal. She loved him so incredibly much at that moment that she allowed herself the fantasy of picturing herself as his wife with everyone she knew ideally happy for her. But their situation offered too many obstacles for idealism. She tried to put all she felt into the quiet, loving tone of her voice.

"Please understand, Christopher . . . I have to say this. I'm a family woman, committed to family. To rob you of having children, who can bring so much joy into your life, seems like an act of selfishness, not of love."

"I told you, Lee . . ." He met her eyes and said with unflappable certainty, "I don't want any of my own."

"Everybody wants children of their own."

"You're wrong. You can't judge everybody by your own standards."

She sighed, deep and long, and let her shoulders droop as her gaze drifted beyond the foot of the bed. He rubbed his thumb over hers and said, "Fifty percent of American families aren't traditional anymore, did you know that? Fifty percent. We'd fit right in."

It might be true, but somehow she felt distanced from statistics, and unhumored by his pithy observation. Fifty percent . . . fifty. Lord, what had happened to this country?

They sat silently for a long time, involved in their private thoughts: he with disappointment creating a new knot in his throat, she with the worry that if she said yes he'd come to regret what he gave up years from now, when she aged before he, and when he wished he'd married someone younger and had children of his own, maybe even when her sexual drive died before his did. Within the next decade, possibly half a decade, she'd be facing menopause while he would hit the prime of his life saddled with her. There seemed, upon honest consideration, an actual edge of immorality to the idea of accepting his offer and doing that to him.

"Oh, Christopher," she sighed, "I don't know."

When he spoke, there was a note of appeal in his voice.

"Could we lie down, Lee? Please? Here it is, the first morning we ever wake up together, and you're over there against your pillow, and I'm over here against mine, and I'd rather be holding you while we talk about this."

She gave in to his gentle humoring and let him stack both their pillows. They settled down belly to belly, covered to the shoulder by blankets. They hugged, twining their legs and caressing one another's backs, though the embrace remained reassuring rather than sexual.

"Oh, Christopher," she sighed again, happy to be returned to his long, warm nakedness beneath the covers, but uncertain about their future just the same. "I'm sorry I got angry with you but this is such a hard decision."

"Do you realize," he said, "how fully I've already blended into your life? I do everything a husband would do. I help you buy your Christmas tree. I put it in the stand for you. I fix your hoses and level your washing machine and mow your lawn, and give your kids a talking to when they're sloughing off on their obligations to you. I comfort you when you're sad, and make love to you when you're happy, and sometimes I fill in that man's chair at the end of the table, and you love having me there, don't tell me you don't. I take your son out driving for the first time, and I go to his football games, and I'm the one who comes running when you're scared to death he's dead at midnight. Now, mind you, I didn't do this on purpose. I didn't mean to inveigle myself into your home life, but the fact remains, it happened. For you to tell me a marriage wouldn't work between us is damned unbelievable, Lee."

"I never said it wouldn't work. I said there are obstacles."

"Life is full of obstacles. They're there to be surmounted."

She digested this piece of wisdom, the kind that usually came from her mouth. His warm palms worked at persuading her. Lord, how good it felt to lie like this with him, to feel him growing aroused against her. How easy it would be to say yes and enjoy this luxury every morning for the rest of her life. She had awakened alone for so many, many years. This was how men and women were meant to be, together. She imagined telling her mother she was going to marry him, then pushed the idea away because it interfered with the pleasure brought by his hands, his scent, his warmth and the sexuality he was stirring within them both.

"So, tell me something," he said, drawing back, finding her eyes. "If all the extraneous issues didn't exist—not the age difference, not Janice's crush, not all the public opinion we'll have to stand up to—if it were just you and me, knowing me the way you do now, loving me and knowing I love you . . . would you marry me?"

She looked into his beloved blue eyes and answered the way her heart dictated.

"Yes," she said without pause. "Yes, I would . . . but, Christopher, life isn't that ea—"

He laid a finger across her lips.

"There . . . you've said it. Yes, you'd marry me. You want to. Concentrate on that for a while—will you?—instead of examining the negative side of everything?"

They hugged full-length again, her smooth legs between his coarse-haired ones. "Oh, Christopher," she sighed—how many times had she sighed his name this morning? "I wish I could just say yes and it would be as simple as that."

"There was a spell a while back—we didn't talk about it, but I know what you were thinking. That maybe you had turned to me out of nothing more than desperation, just trying to get over losing Greg. I hope that's gone by now."

"It is . . . and I'm sorry I get those spells."

"Quit reading those books," he said. "They put ideas into your head. We're together because we love each other, not because we're leaning on each other out of desperation, right?"

She drew back to see his face. "Right," she whispered, "because we love each other."

He said it again, straight out, holding her face in both hands. "Marry me, Lee."

She closed her eyes and kissed him to give herself time to reason, but when she was under his naked influence, reason came with much more difficulty. He was fully aroused now, their legs were dovetailed tightly, and every sense within her responded to him.

"No fair," she whispered against his lips, "asking me when we're in a state like this."

"Marry me." They carried on this dialog between plucking kisses.

"May I have some time to think about it?"

"How much?"

"A day, a week, maybe just long enough to get rid of this enormous lump of morning insistence beneath the covers. I don't know how long, Christopher. I wish I did, but I don't."

"But do you love me?"

"Yes."

"Will you keep thinking about that while you're deciding?"

"Yes."

"Are you going to talk to anybody about it?"

"Probably not."

"Good, because I know a few of them who would try to talk you out of it."

"So do I."

Giving up the playfulness, rolling her full length beneath him, he declared with true passion, "Oh, God, I love you. Please say yes."

"I love you, too, and I'll try."

Chapter 17

N<small>EAR</small> eight o'clock that morning they arose and showered. Lee used the bathroom first, got dressed and was looking into his refrigerator when he came out into the kitchen toweling his hair, wearing gray sweatpants that hung low on his belly.

"I want to cook you breakfast to celebrate our first night together, but there's nothing in here to cook."

He stood beside her searching the refrigerator, smelling like fresh shampoo and soap.

"Sorry, babe. I usually go out."

"Want to go to my house and eat? I've got lots of good things to put in an omelette. Joey won't be home yet, so it should be safe for you to take me home."

"Your house it is," he agreed, and went off to get dressed.

They drove separate cars and arrived at her house shortly before 9 A.M. When Lee pulled into the driveway her blood took a leap to her face: Janice's car was parked in front of the garage. Lee sat staring at it, gripping the steering wheel, holding her breath, then letting it gush out in resignation. Christopher parked behind her and walked past her window on his way to the garage. He raised the door and, when she'd driven inside, was waiting to open her car door. They stood in the cold garage gazing first at Janice's car, then at each other.

"Well, this is it, I guess," he said.

"I had no idea she was coming home."

"She didn't call and tell you?"

"No."

"So what are you going to tell her?"

"We could tell her we've been to church."

"In our blue jeans?"

"You're right. Besides, I always go to the ten o'clock service. I wonder when she got here."

"Judging from the frost on her windshield she's been here all night."

"I hope nothing's wrong. I'd better get inside and see."

When she turned away, he grabbed her arm. "Lee, I want to go in with you."

"She's going to be very angry."

"I can handle that."

"Embarrassed, too."

"I want us to face her together. Anything you're guilty of, I'm guilty of. Besides, if she's up she probably saw us both drive in, and I don't want it to look like I'm slinking off and leaving you to explain."

They went in together through the front door. Janice was standing by the kitchen table holding an ice pack on her jaw, glaring at them.

"Janice, what's wrong?" Lee moved straight toward her without stopping to remove her jacket.

"Nothing!" Janice snapped, her mouth cinching tight.

"What's wrong with your jaw?"

"A wisdom tooth. Where have you been, as if it isn't obvious!"

Lee removed her jacket and hung it on a chair. "At Chris's."

"All night? Mother, how could you?" Janice's face was flaming. She refused to look at Christopher.

"I'm sorry you found out this way."

"Where's Joey?"

"He spent the night at the Holiday Inn with the Whitmans."

"Does he know about what's been going on?"

"No."

"Oh my God, I can't believe this." Janice covered her face with one hand and turned away.

Christopher stood behind Lee's shoulder without touching her. "Your mom and I discussed whether or not to tell you but she decided she needed a little longer to sort out her feelings."

"Her feelings! Hers!" She spun on him. "What about mine? What about Joey's? This is disgusting!"

"Why?" he asked calmly.

"I'm not ignorant!" Janice snapped. "A woman doesn't stay out all night at a man's apartment without sex being involved. It is, isn't it?"

Lee snapped, "Janice, you're being rude."

Christopher remained calm. "Your mother and I have been seeing each other a lot since last June."

"Since my brother died! Say it the way it is! That's what started all this, isn't it? The classic mourning woman turns to the younger man for sympathy."

"I turned to her, too."

"Well, you could have told me! You could have . . . have said something before I . . . before I . . ." Mortified, she escaped to the working part of the kitchen, turning her back on them once more. Christopher brushed around Lee's shoulder and took Janice's arm to gently turn her around.

"Things were complicated, Janice," he said quietly. She averted her burning face, refusing to look at him. "You know why." He released her arm.

She said to the floor, "I must have looked like a fool, giving you those tickets for Christmas, saying the stuff I did."

"No. I was the one in the wrong. I should have told you long before that, that I had feelings for your mom."

She glared up at him. "Then why didn't you?"

"Because we were no different than anyone else when we started dating. We didn't know what it would lead to."

Too embarrassed to stand so close to him, Janice shouldered around both him and Lee and stood defiantly at the opening where the hall led toward the bedrooms.

"Mother, he's thirty years old, for heaven's sake! What are people going to say?"

"Exactly what you are, I suppose. That he's too young for me. So should I give him up because I'll upset people?"

"You should give him up because you'll look like a fool!"

Lee felt herself begin to grow angry. "Do you think so, Janice? Why?"

Janice glared from her mother to Christopher and back again, her mouth clamped tightly shut.

"Why will I look like a fool, Janice? Because this *is* a sexual relationship?" Christopher opened his mouth to speak, but she held up a hand. "No, it's all right, Christopher. She's twenty-three years old; she's old enough to hear the truth. You're angry with me right now, Janice; well, I'm angry with you, too, because you're implying that because there's fifteen years difference between Christopher and me, he's using me. Do I have that correct?"

Janice blushed brighter and looked at the floor.

"Is that the kind of person you think Christopher is?"

Janice was too mortified to speak.

"You might as well know that it's been a big issue between us, one that we've talked about. Only it isn't only whether or not Christopher is using me, but whether I'm using him to get over Greg's death. I'm not. I love him. I'm sorry if that doesn't fit into your image of how a mother should act, but I do have feelings, I do have needs and I do get lonely. I even think about my future. I'm not old, Janice, I'm only older than Christopher, but who's to say how old is too old? Must I get permission from my family before I date a man?"

Janice looked up miserably. Tears shimmered on her eyelids. "But, Mother, he's Greg's friend. He's . . . he's more like your son."

"No. That's your viewpoint, not mine. Our relationship has totally changed in the last eight months. You might be interested to know that we became very, very good friends first before our relationship became intimate."

A hint of challenge came into Janice's voice when she asked, "What's Grandma going to say?"

Lee resisted the urge to look to Christopher for help. "Grandma will be very outspoken, and it won't be pleasant, but Grandma doesn't run my life. I do."

"Well, I can see that nothing I say is going to make you change your mind, so I'm going to bed. I've been up half the night waiting for you and my tooth hurts like the devil."

"Why didn't you call? I think you knew I'd be over at Christopher's. I would have come home."

"Because I wanted to know for sure. Now I do."

She spun on the ball of her foot and marched to her bedroom. When her door slammed, Lee and Christopher stood in the vacuum left by her anger, their emotions in chaos. The faucet was dripping. Lee went over and tried to turn it off, but the steady, monotonous sound continued. Finally Christopher moved up behind her and curved his hands over her shoulders. Wordlessly he turned her around and took her in his arms.

"I'm sorry," she said, feeling close to tears now that the first rush of rebuttal was over. "That must have been terrible for you."

"It was about what I expected. How about you?"

"What she said was. How I reacted was a surprise."

"A surprise?" he said.

"I thought I'd be brimming with guilt. Instead, when she started passing judgment I found myself getting angry. What right has she got to dictate my life? The trouble with my kids is, they've never seen me as a sexual person. All I've ever been is *Mom*. Ever since Bill died I've always been there for them and I guess they thought I always would be—exclusively. The idea that I could need a man for *that* stops them cold in their tracks."

"Still, I'm not sure you should have said that."

"Said what?" She drew back and cast him a bristly look.

"That our relationship is sexual."

"Why not? I have a right to that in my life, damn it, with you or any man I choose. I wanted her to know that."

"It was a jolt for her though, the way you said it."

"I wanted it out in the open."

"And now it is, that's for sure."

"Christopher, I don't want to fight with you, too!" She pulled away from him and put away a pot holder that was lying on the countertop, slamming the drawer with her hip. "And anyway, I don't know why we're fighting! First you say you want me to tell my kids, and we fight because I won't. Then I tell them and we fight because I did."

"Lee . . . Lee . . ." he said, taking her by the shoulders again, forcing

330

her to face him. "Come on. I'm feeling my way here, too. I'm just trying to think of the best way to break this news to the rest of your family, because we're going to get more of what we just got from Janice, only I have a feeling it's going to be worse when it gets to your mother and your sister. They're really going to lay the guilt trip on you."

She lunged into his arms and held tight. "Oh, Christopher, I hate it when we argue. I love you. I want us to be together, but look what happens when we test the first person, and I haven't even mentioned marriage yet."

He drew back and gaped at her in surprise. "You mean you're thinking about it?"

"Well, of course I'm thinking about it. How could I not be? I love you. I don't want to spend the rest of my life alone."

"Oh, Lee . . ." The look in his eyes told her how she'd surprised him. Celebrating, however, took second place to the more serious message he had to impart. He held her by the slope of her neck and spoke earnestly into her eyes. "Then promise me you'll try to keep from getting angry when they tell you you're robbing the cradle, and when they accuse you of being a lonely, sad woman who doesn't know what she's doing, and when they say that you're being used and that I'm only after your house and your car and who knows what else, and that I'll grow tired of you as soon as the first young chick walks by in tight shorts and twitches her butt at me. Because unless I miss my guess, you're going to have to listen to that and a lot more. But the best way to fight that kind of attitude is by showing them that we're happy together, not by getting pissed off, okay?"

She rested her forehead against his chin and shut her eyes wearily. "Are they really going to say all that?"

"I think so."

They stood that way for a spell, taking strength from one another. Finally Lee asked, "Will you?"

"Will I what?"

"Grow tired of me as soon as the first young chick twitches her butt at you?"

He put a finger beneath her chin and lifted it. "What do you think?"

"I've thought about it some—I won't lie to you and say I haven't."

"You wouldn't be normal if you hadn't, but that's one I can't combat with words. That's where trust comes in. If I say I love you and I want to commit myself to you for life, you just have to believe that I mean it, and we take it from there. Okay?"

Within a corner of her heart, peace settled. How convincing he was. How wise. Had he vowed never to look at another woman she would have been much less assured. His simple statement of ineluctable fact gave her pause to realize he had just put his finger on the basic element upon which all lasting marriages are built. Theirs—should it happen—would be strengthened by this belief, which she shared.

She reached up and kissed him in reply—not heavily, as if stamping her initial in sealing wax, but with a glancing touch of reassurance.

"I'd better go in and check on Janice's tooth. She'll be too stubborn to come back out here, and I think her jaw was swollen."

"Should I stay or go?"

"Stay. You came for breakfast and I'm going to fix it for you. I'll see to her first though."

Janice was lying on her side facing the wall when Lee sat down behind her.

"Is he gone?"

"No, he's still here. I'm going to make breakfast for him. What's happening with your wisdom tooth? Did it flare up suddenly?"

"It's all infected. I need to have it pulled."

"Which one? Upper or lower?"

"Lower."

"Turn over here."

"You *don't* have to worry about me. I can take care of myself," the girl declared.

"Janice, don't be so stubborn. I'm not going to stop worrying about *you* just because I'm dating *him*."

Janice flung herself onto her back and fixed her eyes on a piece of furniture behind Lee, who felt her brow.

"My heavens, girl, you have a fever. Have you taken any aspirin?"

"Yes."

"How long ago?"

"About three in the morning." The implication was clear: She'd been up waiting for her mother to return.

"I'll get you some more. Are you in bad pain?"

"It doesn't feel too pleasant but what can I do on a weekend? I'll just have to wait till morning to call Dr. Wing."

"Open your mouth. Let me see."

"Mother, it's infected and probably impacted, too. What's there to see?"

"Is there a bulge by the tooth?"

Janice rolled her eyes. "Yes, there's a bulge. But I won't die before morning, so just leave me alone."

Lee had no choice. When she returned with the aspirin and a glass of water, she said, "There *is* such a thing as emergency treatment for teeth, you know, so if it gets to that point I'll drive you to the hospital."

Janice popped the aspirins and chased them with water, handed the glass back to her mother and flung herself down facing the wall again. The message was clear: I'm not thanking you. I'm not forgiving you. I don't want to be mothered by you!

Lee stared at her daughter's back and left the room with a sigh.

On Monday afternoon at one o'clock an oral surgeon extracted both wisdom teeth from the right side of Janice's mouth. One was impacted and infected. The other, he said, would follow suit shortly, judging from its crowded condition and the angle at which it was pushing her other teeth.

She awakened from her sodium-pentathol slumber crying inexplicably—a natural reaction from the drug. One of the nurses on the office staff gave Lee instructions on how to care for her, how woozy Janice would be for a while and what to feed her to avoid a painful dry socket. Lee left the dentist's office carrying a prescription for pain pills and supporting a blubbering daughter, who continued to cry and babble, "I don't know why I'm crying so hard. I just don't know."

"It's from the drug," Lee explained. "It'll go away in an hour or so."

At home, Lee settled Janice into bed with a towel beneath her cheek and a mixing bowl to spit into. She gave her a pain pill and offered to heat up some chicken broth for her, then watched Janice's eyes fall shut as she was drawn down into the residual effects of the anesthetic.

Lee leaned over the bed and rubbed Janice's hair back from her forehead and kissed her.

In that moment, mothering became uncomplicated again as it had been when her children were babies. Smoothing a brow, administering a pill, cooking special foods when they were sick: These were the needs easy to fill. She found herself soothed—even healed—to be touching her daughter and seeing after her physical needs, especially after the rift created the previous day.

Janice, she thought, *please don't withdraw your love from me. Please don't make me choose between you and Christopher. There's no reason, darling, and it will break my heart if you keep turning away from me this way.*

Christopher called shortly before suppertime. "How's Janice?"

"She's asleep now, but she'll be hurting tonight. The dentist prescribed some pain pills though."

"Does she need anything? Can I do anything for you?"

"Just continue to be patient with my children," she replied. "It may take some time to win them over."

"That I can do, as long as I know there's a reason to. Have you thought any more about marrying me?"

"Yes, I've thought about it. It's *all* I've been thinking about."

"And?"

"And it sounds very appealing, but I still don't know."

"You know what?" he said.

"What?"

"I'm doing it again."

"Doing what again?"

"Playing the role of a husband and stepfather right this very minute. Think about it, Lee."

When his shift ended he stopped by on his way home.

"Hi," he said when Lee answered the door. "I can't stay. I've got a date with Judd, but I wanted to bring this for Janice. Tell her I hope she likes it."

He handed her a set of audio tapes of a current best-seller. "I thought it might be more relaxing for her to listen than to read it today."

She kissed his jaw and realized he was making it harder and harder for her to say no to his marriage proposal.

And too . . . he was doing it again.

What any good husband and dad would have done.

"Christopher brought you these."

Janice glanced back over her shoulder, studied the tapes her mother had dropped on the bed and said with asperity, "I already read it." She left them right where they'd fallen, turning her face to the wall.

Being shunned by her daughter hurt worse than Lee had ever imagined it could.

Being hurt by one child quite naturally drew her toward the other. In need of understanding, of an ally perhaps, maybe only a friendly smile, she went to Joey's room later that night. She found him sitting on the floor of his bedroom wrapping silver duct tape around his favorite pair of dilapidated Nikes.

"Hi," she said, leaning against his door frame.

"Oh, hi!" He looked back over his shoulder.

"May I come in?"

"Sure. How's Janice?"

"Sleeping. Grouchy."

"Man, I hope that never happens to me. Denny's dad says he's still got his wisdom teeth and they never gave him any trouble."

"It's more than Janice's wisdom teeth that's bothering her."

"What else?" He stopped taping and watched Lee cross to the bed and settle herself dead center on it, sitting Indian fashion. She was dressed in an oversized purple sweat suit with the sleeves pushed up to her elbows.

"She's upset with me."

"About what?"

"I'm going to be very honest with you, Joey, because this is really important to me."

"She must've figured it out about you and Chris, huh?"

Lee couldn't have hidden her surprise had she put a bag over her head. "Well, *you* don't seem too shocked. How long have you known?"

He shrugged and ran his hand repeatedly over the edge of the silver tape, smoothing it around the sole of the shoe. "I don't know. I saw you guys kissing one night, but I sort of figured, even before that."

"So what do you think about it?"

"Heck, I think it's cool."

Lee grinned. Who said girls were fun to raise? Give her a son anytime. Their temperaments were a lot less volatile.

"It's really serious, isn't it, Mom?"

"Yes, it is."

"That's what I figured. So, do ladies your age marry guys his age, or what?"

"I don't know of any who did, do you?"

He just shrugged and cut off another strip of tape.

"Would it bother you if I did?" she asked.

"Heck no. Why should it bother me?"

"People might tease you, say your mother's a baby snatcher, things like that."

"Jeez, people can be such dorks. If they said something like that, they don't know you. Or Chris either."

"He asked me last night," she admitted.

"To marry him?"

"Yes."

"Does Janice know that?"

"Not yet."

"Does Grandma know?"

"Grandma doesn't know any of this."

"Jeez, she'll shit a ring around herself when she finds out."

Lee laughed before she could stop herself. "You're not supposed to use language like that, young man."

"Yeah, well, I did, so ground me, Ma."

Lord, he was really growing up fast. She was going to enjoy the next three years with him. He was so refreshingly straightforward.

"So what'd you tell Chris?" Joey asked.

"I told him it was tempting."

"You wanna marry him?"

"Yes, I do."

"But you're scared of what Grandma will say, right?"

"Grandma, Janice, Sylvia, you. Well, not you anymore. You seem to be all right with the idea."

"Heck yes. You've been alone since Dad died. Sometimes I don't know how you stand it. I mean, me and Denny, we talk sometimes, you know? Like the night I saw you and Chris kissing the first time. I called him and I said to him that you were awful happy since you've been hangin' out with Chris, and it seems like you would have done stuff like that a long time ago."

"Kissing guys, you mean? I never wanted to until Chris came along."

"Really, Mom?" He studied her with a crooked grin on his mouth. "Then I think you should go for it."

No doubt about it, this son of hers was a gift. Lee sat on his bed with her elbows on her knees, smiling down at him while he slapped one more circuit of tape around his tennis shoe.

"I guess you know by now how much I love you. Are you going to wear those things that way?" she asked.

He held up his handiwork. "Heck yes. They're *hot!*"

"I seem to remember buying you some new ones for Christmas."

"Well, sure, and I love you, too, but not enough to throw these away just because they need a little tape job. These are my best ones."

She shook her head in wonderment, got off the bed, kissed the crown of his head and went into her bedroom to call Christopher and give him the latest *Children's Attitude Report.*

Janice stayed home one more day, then returned to school, still acting aloof toward her mother.

Lee worked that day, as usual, and returned home in the late afternoon to begin fixing supper. First she went down to the basement to throw the morning's load of laundry from the washer into the dryer. She was just coming up the basement stairs when the doorbell rang.

"Why, Mother!" she said, answering it. "What brings you over? And, Sylvia . . ." She had just left Sylvia at the store a half hour before.

Peg Hillier pushed past Lee with an officious air, removing her gloves.

"We've come to talk to you, Lee."

Lee watched her mother's back—stiff as a pikestaff—the swirl of her coat, the erectness of her neck, and knew she was in trouble.

"Oh. I bet I know what about."

"I'll just bet you do." Peg swung on her. "Janice called me."

Lee said, "Would you care to come in, Mother? Take off your coat?

Sit down, maybe, and have a cup of coffee? You, too, Sylvia." She glanced outside. "Is this the whole army, or have you brought more? Where's Dad . . . and Lloyd? They should be here for this, too, shouldn't they?"

"Your attempt to be cute isn't fazing me in the least, Lee. Shut that door and tell me what in the ever-loving world has gotten into you! A woman of your age latching onto a boy your son's age!"

Lee shut the door resignedly and said, "Put your coats on the sofa. I'll make some coffee."

"I don't want any coffee! I want an explanation!"

"First of all, he's not my son's age. He's thirty years old and—"

"And you're forty-five. Good God, Lee, have you gone crazy?"

"Hardly, Mother. I fell in love."

"In love!" Peg's eyes seemed to protrude from her skull. "Is that what you call it? You've been sleeping with that boy! Janice said you admitted it!"

Sylvia added, "Lee, this is so shabby."

"So what did Mother do? Call you immediately and spread the news so you could come over here and bombard me together?"

"I agree with Mother. Your having an affair with Christopher is disgraceful, but we understand all the stresses you've been under since Greg died. It's natural that you'd want to turn to someone, but, Lee, a boy that age."

"He's not a boy! Will you quit saying that!"

"He might as well be, given your age difference."

Peg said, "I must admit, I never would have guessed he'd behave like this either. I thought he was such a fine young man. What in the world is he after?"

"After?"

"Yes, after! A man that age with a woman so old."

"So old. Gee, thanks, Mother."

"You may be willing to delude yourself, but I'm not. He was after exactly what he got! But to think he did it after you were so good to him, after you opened your doors to him, and took him into this family, and acted like a mother to him. To think that you'd let him seduce you!"

"Mother, I am telling you, we fell in love! It wasn't as if Greg died and I rolled into bed with Chris the next day! We began seeing each other and had so much fun together, and only then, after months, did our relationship become intimate."

"I don't want to hear it." Peg's face grew pinched and she looked aside.

Sylvia picked up the gauntlet. "You admitted to your own daughter that you've been sleeping with him. . . . Lee, what were you thinking of?"

"Am I not supposed to have any sex ever again? Is that it?" Lee's two attackers stared in stupefaction while she went on. "Am I supposed to be some dedicated little mama, waiting to darn my children's socks and cook their favorite foods when they come to visit me? Am I never supposed to want a life of my own?"

Sylvia replied, "Of course you can have a life of your own, but for heaven's sake, choose someone your own age to have it with."

"Why? Why is it so wrong that I chose Christopher?"

"Lee, be honest with yourself," Sylvia admonished. "This thing looks mighty quirky. You treated him like a son for how many years? Then when Greg dies the two of you grow thick as thieves, and pretty soon you're in bed together. How do you think it looks? And how long do you expect him to stick with you?"

"You might be interested to know, Sylvia, that Christopher has asked me to marry him."

"Oh, dear God," Peg breathed, putting a hand to her lips and dropping down hard on a kitchen chair.

"Marry him?" Sylvia, too, sat as if poleaxed.

"Yes. And I'm considering it."

"Oh, Lee, you don't know what you're doing. Greg hasn't been dead a year and, granted, you needed someone to get you through this terrible time, but to tie up with someone that young for life. How can it possibly last?"

"How can any marriage possibly last, given the divorce rates in this country today? If you love somebody, you have faith in them, you marry them assuming it will last because you've both said it will."

Peg took over. "You never joined any of those grief groups, but if you had you'd realize that you're doing exactly what they warn you not to do—jump into a relationship out of desperation. You're lonely, you've gone through a terrible ordeal losing Greg and you're facing the time when all your children will be gone. I understand that, dear, but look ahead. When you're sixty, he'll be forty-five. Do you really think he won't want a younger woman then?"

Lee refused to reply.

"And what about children?" Sylvia put in. "Doesn't he want any?"

"No."

"That's not natural."

"It's really none of your business though, is it, Sylvia? He and I have talked about all these things you two have thrown at me today, and if we've worked them out and I want to marry him, I expect you to honor my choice."

Peg and Sylvia exchanged glances that said Lee had truly lost good sense and just how were they going to convince her she was making the mistake of her life. Peg sighed dramatically and fixed an absent stare on the fruit basket in the middle of the table. She tried a new tactic.

"I just wonder what Bill would say."

"Oh, good God." Lee rolled her eyes. "Bill is dead, Mother. I'm alive. I have a lot of good healthy years ahead of me. It's unfair of you to suggest that I should remain faithful to a dead man."

"Oh, don't be so silly. I'm not suggesting that. But Bill was the children's father. What can this man ever be to them? Which brings up another nasty point. Janice told me that she confessed to you some time ago that she had feelings for Christopher herself."

"Yes, she did. But did she tell you if he ever returned the interest in any way whatsoever?" When Peg didn't answer, Lee hurried on. "No, he did not. Her attraction to Christopher complicated things for us, but we talked about it, too, and decided our own happiness counts for something. And we're the happiest when we're together."

"So you're not going to end it?"

"No, I'm not. He makes me happy. I make him happy. Why should I throw that away?"

"The day will come when you'll regret it."

"Maybe. But you could say that about half the choices you make in this life. On the other hand, the day may *never* come when I'll regret it, and how sad it would be if I'd thrown him away for nothing."

"So, are you really going to marry him?" Sylvia asked.

"I think so . . . yes, Sylvia."

Sylvia said, "Honestly, Lee, if it's just because of the . . . well, you know . . ." Sylvia stirred the air with her hand.

"I think the word you're looking for is 'sex,' Sylvia, and if it were just that, don't you think I'd have taken up with some man long before this? Sex is just one part of our relationship, and I'll freely admit that after so many years without it, it's sensational to have it available whenever I want it. But friendship and respect play equally important parts."

Sylvia had turned pink as a rare steak and didn't know where to rest her eyes.

"I'm sorry, Syl. I know it's a subject you never talk about, but you brought it up."

Sylvia's mouth was pinched as she went on superciliously. "I understand you stayed all night at his apartment Saturday night. What will your children think?"

"My son thinks I should marry him."

"He's fourteen years old. What does he know?"

"He knows Christopher. He loves him. He said, 'Hey, Ma, I think you should go for it.' "

Peg angled a disparaging look at her younger daughter. "And if you take Joey's advice, I'm still convinced you'll live to regret it."

"I think you'd better get used to the idea, Mother, because I'm going to say yes to Christopher."

Peg buried her face in both hands and propped her elbows on the table. "God in heaven, what will my friends say?"

"Ahh . . . There, you've hit upon your real problem, haven't you, Mother?"

"Well, it is a problem!" Peg spit, lifting her head suddenly. "People talk, you know!"

"Yes. Starting with my daughter—thank you, Janice."

"Don't you go blaming Janice!" Peg was getting angrier. "She did the right thing by calling me."

"Oh, yes, I can see that. This has been such an enlightening conversation. But it's true, Mother. You've saved your greatest worry for last: What will people think. You've always been so concerned about that. What will they think if I play Vince Gill at my son's funeral? What will they think if I bury him in his favorite cap? What will they think if I marry a handsome thirty-year-old man instead of some nice balding middle-aged bore who'll make me settle down and act my age?

"Well, the truth is, Mom, I don't care what they think. Because if they're looking down their noses at me, they aren't the kind of friends I'd value in the first place."

"You always were good at talking your way around things, Lee, but you won't be able to talk your way around this. People *will* whisper behind your back. Your children will undoubtedly be asked all kinds of pointed questions, and everyone at your father's and my country club will ask if it's true that he's only thirty."

"Then answer them honestly, Mother. Why can't you do that? Why can't you just say, 'Yes, he's thirty, and he's a fine man who's kind and considerate and cares about his fellow human beings, and who's made my daughter so happy, the happiest she's been since her first husband died.' Why can't you say that, Mother?"

"That's right!" Peg said self-righteously. "Turn the blame on me, as if I caused this disgraceful situation. Child, you exasperate me so!"

"Mother, I've always loved you, but you've never been able to admit when you're wrong, and this time you are."

"Lee, for heaven's sake!" Sylvia chided.

"You, too, Sylvia. You're wrong, too. I love this man. I'm going to marry him and make myself happy."

"Well, marry him then!" Peg shot up from her chair and marched toward the living room to get her coat. "But don't bring him to my house for Easter dinner!"

Chapter 18

"THEY said exactly what you said they'd say." Lee was on the telephone with Chris later that night.

"It was bad, I imagine."

"Horrible. But I held my temper like you asked me to."

"I take it that didn't help much."

"No. Except that I was proud of myself."

"You're really down though, I can tell." When she made no reply, he asked, "Aren't you?"

"Ohh . . ." She blew out a breath. "You know . . ." A moment of sadness came to complicate her irritation with this group of people she loved. "They're my only family."

"Yeah . . . I know the feeling. Ironic, isn't it? My family alienates me by caring too little, yours does it by caring too much."

"I suppose that's true, but it's hard to believe they care for me *at all* when they're trying to control my life."

"Honey, I'm really sorry you have to go through this." He sounded very sincere and sad on her behalf.

"Want to hear the funny part? My sister Sylvia, who's the world's biggest prude, couldn't even get herself to say the word when she wanted to chide me about my rampaging sex drive and how it was probably the only reason I wanted to marry you."

"You told them you were going to marry me?" His voice sounded as if he'd suddenly straightened his spine.

"Yes, I did, but, Christopher, I don't think that's the wisest thing to do right now. Everybody's all bent out of shape and giving me lectures, and I think it's best if I give them a chance to get used to the idea first."

"But you'll do it? You're saying yes?"

"I'm saying I want to."

"When, Lee?"

"I don't know when."

Some seconds passed while she sensed him visibly deflating. "All right." She could tell by his voice he was forcing himself not to push too hard. "I understand. But don't wait too long. Honey, I just love you so much. I don't want to waste any more time apart."

At the floral shop things became strained. From the very next day, Sylvia began cornering Lee when the others were beyond earshot, haranguing her with denunciations about her affair, scolding her for upsetting their mother so terribly and for setting a bad example for her children. Couldn't she see how improper it was? Hadn't their parents taught her such behavior was reprehensible? And with a man young enough to be her son! Didn't she realize he was only out to use her and would make a fool of her in the end? It just wasn't natural for a boy that age to fall for someone their age. Didn't she care at all that Mother and Dad's social circle would ask embarrassing questions? Why, even Sylvia's own children were already asking them.

"How did *they* find out?"

"They overheard me talking to Barry."

"Oh, great. Thanks a lot, Sylvia."

Sylvia threw down a stack of envelopes she'd been leafing through. "I'm not the guilty one here, Lee, so just watch it! Someone's got to make you come to your senses, and who else is it going to be? Mother? Janice? They're both so appalled they won't even speak to you!"

* * *

Unfortunately, it was true. Joey celebrated his fifteenth birthday, but Janice—who'd made a point of coming home on his birthday last year— remained at school and only sent him a card. Peg and Orrin sent a gift by mail and called with the excuse that they couldn't come over for birthday cake because Orrin had had some bridgework done on his teeth that day and his mouth was too sore.

Lloyd came, however, and brought Joey a big maroon sweatshirt with a big white *A* on the front, for next year when he'd be attending Anoka Senior High. The three of them went out for supper at Joey's favorite restaurant and Lloyd very discreetly mentioned, "The party's kind of small this year, isn't it?"

The whole story tumbled out, but Lloyd—kind, nonjudgmental Lloyd—merely said, "My, that is a problem, isn't it?"

Orrin came to Absolutely Floral one noon and said, "Lee, I'm taking you out to lunch," during which he told her seven times how upset her mother was, and how this foolishness of hers had to stop and she must tell that *boy* that he should go find someone his own age!

Lee's outrage boiled over. "You're all a bunch of backbiting hypocrites! Christopher was good enough for me when he was comforting me and acting as my support system after Greg died, and when he was picking up Janice at the airport, and sending you and Mom sympathy cards, and taking over a lot of the supportive duties that otherwise might have fallen to you! But now that he's been in my bed you treat him— both of us—like we're some sexual perverts! I don't think I like what that says about you!"

The meal ended on a bitter note with the two of them scarcely able to tolerate each other another minute.

Lee called Janice at college, as she usually did once a week, only to get perfunctory grunts for answers, delivered in a voice that said quite clearly, *I'm only tolerating this conversation, not taking part in it.* Lee asked when Janice would be coming home again and got the blunt reply, "I don't know."

*   *   *

Lee's attack on her father was immediately telegraphed throughout the family, and Lee received another sermon from Sylvia on right and wrong, this one more vitriolic than the last, as Sylvia defended her parents and chastised Lee for her treatment of them. The tension at Absolutely Floral got so pronounced that the other employees began to get grouchy, too. Then one day Pat Galsworthy said to Lee, "Are you *really* going out with a man who's only thirty years old?" Lee blew up at her and said it was none of her damned business, and if she wanted to keep her job she'd better stick to discussing floral trends with the *bookkeeper* when the two of them were holed up together.

Lee later apologized, but the truth was, the business was being affected by the rift between her and Sylvia. Finding it difficult to be civil to each other, the two of them became reluctant to sit down and discuss the ongoing daily matters—orders, billing, scheduling—which were so essential to having the enterprise run smoothly. This lack of communication was reflected in the botched routine, the scheduling snags and the general tension among all the store's employees.

Christopher called one Thursday and said, "Dress up in something classy. It's my night off and I'm taking you to dinner at the Carousel in downtown Saint Paul."

In the revolving restaurant, with the twinkling lights of the city dotting the night all around them, he produced a diamond ring with a rock so large it could not be worn beneath a leather glove.

"Oh, Christopher . . ." Lee said, gaping at the engagement ring in its blue velvet box. "Oh, look at this . . . what did you do?"

"I love you, Lee Reston. I want you to be my wife." He took her hand and put the ring on the proper finger. As usual, her nails were stubby and her skin rough.

"But it's so big. And what will I do with it when I'm handling dirt and flowers all day long?"

"Put it in a dresser drawer and put it on when you get home. Will you marry me?"

She looked up and felt tears beginning to gather.

"Oh, Christopher, I can't believe this is happening. I want to . . . you know I want to. But how can I?" The weight of the family's reaction bore down upon her, bringing a confusion of feelings. She loved this man and thought they could have a happy life together, but her decision was not as simplistic as that. "Everything else in my life is falling apart." She added in the gentlest voice she could muster, "I'm sorry . . . I can't wear this." She removed the ring and put it back in the box. "I just can't. It's much too beautiful for my ugly hands anyway."

He stared at the ring, forlorn, then at her, so disheartened she found it hard to meet his gaze. Finally he took her hands and held them on the tabletop.

"Lee, don't do this," he begged earnestly. "Please."

"You know what I'm going to say, don't you?"

"Don't. Don't say it, please . . ."

"But everybody's turned against me. Everybody."

"Except Joey."

"Yes, except Joey. But it's even affecting him. Janice didn't come for his birthday, and neither did his grandpa and grandma. Sylvia and I hardly speak to each other at work. Our business is becoming affected by all these bad feelings. What should I do?"

He dropped his eyes to their joined hands and rubbed the backs of hers with his thumbs. The expression on his face got even sadder, and his lengthening silence told her he recognized the problems he'd brought into her life, and that if she married him they would probably get worse. He hadn't the wherewithal, however, to cut her free by putting the ring back in his pocket.

The waiter came and presented their plates, steaming, fragrant, each a work of art. They mumbled "Thank you" and picked up their forks, pretending to eat, prodding the food instead.

Lee went on speaking in a hurt voice. "You know how important family has always been to me. I fought so hard to keep mine together after Bill died. My mom and dad have always been there for me, and Sylvia and I were best of friends. When we opened up the shop we got along so well even my mother couldn't believe it. And now . . ." She shrugged. "Now it's all falling apart."

"And so you're cutting me out."

"Don't put it that way."

"But it's true. I thought our relationship stood for something, but you're willing to write me off because your family doesn't approve. How do you think that makes me feel?"

"It hurts me too, Christopher."

He fixed his eyes on the night view outside the windows. As the restaurant revolved, it changed from the distant Minneapolis skyline to the dark strip of river. He had given up all pretense of eating and sat with his fingers on the stem of his water goblet. Finally, he turned back to her.

"Lee, I've never said one word against your family. I think that in spite of what they're doing to you, they're a good bunch of people. But they're condemning me not for myself but for my age. I honestly believe they know I'm a decent, law-abiding, fairly honorable guy who'll treat you the best he can for the rest of his life. But I'm only thirty, and you're forty-five, so they tell you you're crazy and it won't last, and they fill your head with all that garbage! But it's so damned unfair, and you're wrong to knuckle under to their pressure!"

"Maybe I am, but for the time being, that's the way it's got to be."

"For the time being—what does that mean?"

She took a deep breath and said the words that would break her heart. "It means I don't think I should see you anymore for a while."

He held himself still, as if to absorb the impact of her unwanted words. They both knew "for a while" could mean interminably. If her family disapproved now, would they be likely to change their stand in the future?

He set his teeth and studied the distant lights again, his face a mask of dejected stony lines.

"Please, Christopher, don't look that way. It's not what I want either."

He continued brooding while their suppers congealed into cold lumps on their plates. Finally he took his napkin from his lap, folded it, laid it beside his plate and, without looking at her, said, "Well, if it has to end let it end without harsh words. There's no sense in my being one more person to add to your woes. But if it's okay with you, Lee, I'd just as soon leave now. I'm not very hungry anymore."

It took them thirty minutes to drive from downtown St. Paul to Anoka. Through the entire trip he was painfully solicitous, holding her coat while she donned it, taking her elbow on their way to his truck, opening the door for her, seeing her safely inside. He adhered to the speed limit religiously all the way to her house, handling the vehicle perfectly, slowing for red lights with so much lead time her body scarcely swayed when they stopped. He kept the radio turned to a moderate level, adjusted the heat to hit her feet and signaled every turn.

All the while Lee felt as if a balloon were inflating inside her chest, shutting off more and more of her air, pressing against her lungs until there was less than enough left to sustain her.

Her heart ached.

Her eyes burned.

Her throat felt like a garden hose with a kink in it. If only he'd supplicate, rage, drive like a maniac. Instead, he maintained this perfect, stoic control.

At her house he left the engine idling and walked around to open her door, giving her a hand while she managed the long step down in her high heels, taking her elbow as they trod the icy sidewalk to the front step.

There she stopped, torn by what she was doing, aching already with the emptiness that was sure to slam her even harder when he drove away. The outside light had been left off, and the night wind swirled around their ankles. The late winter snow had grown dark with age and lay like a compressed gray blanket in the yard around them. The air held a chill dampness that permeated clothing, skin, going clear to the heart, it seemed.

He took her gloved hands in his and they stood with six inches of space between them, their chins lowered, staring at the dark concrete between their shoes.

She looked up.

He looked up.

And in that second when their eyes met, his life-saving control snapped. He clutched her against himself, hard, kissing her in an agony of forced farewell. It was a kiss that stamped love, possession, hurt and blame upon her, telling her in no uncertain terms how much he, too, would suffer when he walked away.

As suddenly as he'd grabbed her, he set her back by the arms and told her, "I won't be calling you. You know where I am if you want to see me."

Abruptly he spun, descended the two steps in one leap and stalked to his truck.

* * *

She had wept this hard before. Three times in her life she had wept this hard, so surely she would live through it. This was as fierce, consuming and debilitating as it had been when she'd cried for baby Grant . . . and for Bill . . . and for Greg. The difference was, she'd brought this on by choice.

Yet what other choice could she make?

She was a woman unused to hopelessness, so the question felt foreign going through her mind again and again that night. Another question glimmered: *How could people who love you put you through such hell?*

Over and over she relived Christopher's parting kiss, watched him turn and hurry away, heard the angry slam of his truck door and saw him squeal off down the road like a lunatic, accelerating with a roar that sent the rear end of the Explorer fishtailing up the street, hitting a snowbank on the opposite side and rebounding to the center. He had turned the radio up so loud she had heard it booming through his rolled-up windows. At the end of the block he'd blasted through a stop sign without slowing down.

This policeman.

This obeyer of laws.

This man whose heart she'd just broken.

She, with a broken heart of her own, lay on her bed as if she'd jumped from a tenth-story window, sobbing so loudly that her son woke up and opened her bedroom door a crack, whispering with fear in his voice, "Mom? . . . Mom? . . . What's wrong, Mom?"

She could not answer, did not want to answer, went on weeping and leaving Joey to worry and wonder—thoughtless wretch of a mother that she was.

She cried the tears of the lovelorn—the all-consuming spasmodic weeping that racked the entire body for hours on end, so bitterly sorry for herself that she didn't know how she'd survive the lonely days without him. Who would call to ask how her day had been? Who would show up at her door with a pie, or call to ask if she wanted to go walking or shopping for a Christmas tree? Who would hold her when she needed holding, and understand when she needed to cry sometimes, and be there to laugh with her during the happy times?

She lay sprawled on her side, inert, uninspired to act on her own behalf, to get up and find a new box of tissues, to get under the covers, to remove her clothing or her jewelry.

Her temples throbbed. Her eyes ached. Her nose felt raw. She couldn't sigh without shuddering.

I don't want to cry anymore. Please, don't let me cry anymore.

But even that thought brought fresh tears.

The last time she looked at the clock it was 4:34 and it hurt to pick up her head.

She awakened at 10:13 and jerked upright when she saw the time. She was over an hour late for work! She managed to get to her feet, then plopped back down, cradling her aching head. The bedspread was rucked into ridges like a topographic map. Her pillowcase needed washing. A pile of soggy tissues lay around her feet.

Oh God.

Oh God.

Oh God.

Let me get through this one day and then I'll be better.

When she forced herself to rise and began shuffling around, someone knocked on the door. Startled, she swung about just as Joey opened it and said doubtfully, "Mom, you all right?"

"Joey, what are you doing home? Isn't it a school day?"

"I didn't go today."

She was still dressed in the clothes from last night, wrinkled and misshapen—skirt, dress, nylons, sweater and all. It struck her suddenly how she must have scared him.

She closed her eyes and put a hand to her head, trying to stop it from bonging.

"Mom, what's wrong?"

It seemed as if he stood a quarter mile away. She trudged to him and draped her arms around him loosely. "Christopher and I broke up last night."

"Why?" he asked innocently.

His simple inquiry started the flow of tears again. The salt stung when it reached her raw, swollen eyelids.

"Everybody's having a shit-bird, that's why!" she said defiantly. "And it's so unfair, and I . . . I . . ." The damned bawling started again. She hung

351

on Joey's shoulders and showed him how girls act when they lose their boyfriends, wailing like wind in a knothole, abashed but unable to stop herself. Lord almighty, what was she doing blubbering on the poor kid's shoulder? He'd have enough of this when he was seventeen and broke up with some girl of his own.

Awkwardly he put his arms around her. "It's okay, Mom. Don't cry. I'm still here."

"Oh, Joey, I'm sorry . . . I'm sorry. I didn't mean to sc . . . scare you."

"Gosh, I thought it was going to be something awful, like you got cancer or something. If it's just Christopher, why don't you call him up and get back together? He really loves you, Mom, I can tell he does."

She got control of herself and withdrew from his arms. "If only it were that simple," she said, shuffling toward the bathroom. She switched on the light, made it to the mirror and mumbled, "Ye gods afrighty."

Joey had followed her to the doorway and stood looking in. "You do look like something on the floor of the meat-processing plant."

"Gee, thanks." She pushed the hair back from her forehead, what few strands weren't already standing up like dandelion stalks. She'd never known a face could have so much color without having been beaten up.

"Don't you think you'd better call the shop and tell Aunt Sylvia why you're late?"

"I'm not telling her one damn thing," she stated evenly, "except that I'm not coming in today. If she doesn't like it she can go suck a dead gladiola. What about you? I suppose I'd better call school and tell them I'll be bringing you in late."

"Could I not go today, Mom?"

That got her attention. She leaned back from the mirror and focused on him, still standing in the bathroom doorway. "Not go?"

"Let's both play hooky," he suggested. "We can think of something fun to do together."

Last night's engulfing cloud of depression began to show a sunny underbelly.

"You mean you want to spend the day out gallivanting with an old broad with purple sags all over her face and eyes that look like cow guts?"

"Yeah," he said, giving her a cheeky grin. "Sounds kind of fun."

She wandered over to him and leaned against the bathroom wall, propping one hand on her hip. "What are we going to do?"

He shrugged. "I d'know. We could . . ." He thought awhile, then finished brightly, ". . . go play a few games at the video parlor or go out shopping at the Mall of America, or how about having breakfast someplace, then going to a matinee? I could drive."

Out of the pit of her stomach started a gut-chuckle that grew as it rose, bringing an actual smile along with it.

"Oh, so that's your motive, is it?"

"Actually, I just thought of it now, but the whole program sounds better than going to school."

She surprised him by boosting off the wall and kissing his forehead. "Okay, it's a plan. Give me a half hour to repair the locker plant damage and I'll be ready to take off."

They decided they'd take turns choosing what to do next. They started at Circus, dropping thirteen dollars and fifty cents into various machines until Lee finally won a round of Afterburner over her son. Their next stop was the Dairy Queen Brazier, where they ate burgers, fries and banana splits. After that they drove clear over to St. Paul to Joe's Sporting Goods to check out the end-of-the-season ski sale, then to the Minneapolis Institute of Art, where they decided the Dutch artists were their favorites.

The day became one of those memorable pages out of the book of life that they would, in the future, turn to again and again. It was something they'd never done before, playing hooky. She had raised her children under the good old upper-midwest work ethic, but abandoning it for once bonded Lee and Joey as no parental guidance ever could.

Joey talked about his girlfriend, Sandy, and how nice she was, and admitted he was beginning to get "those feelings."

Lee talked about Christopher for much the same reason.

Joey said he really liked his math teacher, Mr. Ingram, and was thinking maybe he'd take geometry and trigonometry in senior high because Mr. Ingram said he was gifted in that area.

They talked about what Joey would like to do when he grew up.

"I don't want to be a cop," he said.

That brought up Greg, and how well they'd done in that regard, but what kinds of things still reminded them of him.

Joey asked if she'd ever done anything like this—playing hooky—with Janice or Greg. She said she hadn't; she'd been too busy after

Daddy died, going to school, then starting the business, then worrying that an hour away from it might cause it to fail.

Joey said he liked her a lot better this way.

"Which way?" she asked.

He shrugged and said, "I don't know. You're just . . . happier, looser. I mean, you just said it yourself. A year ago you wouldn't have let me skip school. You'd have put me in the car and hauled me over there, then we wouldn't have gotten to do all this stuff together. You've changed a lot since Christopher's been around."

"Have I?" she asked sadly.

"Well, don't you think you have?"

Was it Christopher who had changed her? Greg's death? Or just getting older and wiser?

"Well, son," she said, dropping an arm around his shoulder, "it's been a heck of a year. Nobody goes through what we've been through without changing because of it. Anyway, I'm glad you like me better."

They were strolling along beside a marble carving called "Veiled Lady" when Joey stopped and looked his mother square in the face.

"Don't let them rip you off, Mom. Grandma and Aunt Sylvia and Janice, I mean. I know they've been telling you all kinds of stuff, but I think you should marry Chris."

She studied the statue, wondering how a veiled face could possibly be carved in stone. Yet there it was, face and veil both clearly visible in solid white rock.

She turned to Joey and took him in her arms. People nearby glanced curiously at the two of them, but Joey had matured enough to accept his mother's public displays of affection without cringing.

"I want to, Joey, so badly. But it's causing so much divisiveness in our family."

"Well, heck, what do they know?"

His unqualified support buoyed her heart. "Thank you, darling."

She released him and resumed moving down the deep corridor, her footsteps echoing, his squeaking as they ambled along.

"It means a lot to me that you told me," she said. "This whole day means a lot to me. Last night I didn't know how I was going to make it through another day. I thought I'd shrivel up and die without Christopher. But look. Here I am, enjoying this art gallery, proving how resilient the human spirit is. You helped me make it through the first day, and if I can make it through one, I can make it through the rest."

"So you're not going to see him again?"

"No, I'm not."

They kept walking.

He gazed up at a painting on his right.

She gazed at one on her left.

"You know what I think, Mom?"

The question repeated itself and came back to them in the lofty space through which they moved. Her wrist was hooked on his near shoulder. His hands were buried in the pockets of his unzipped winter jacket.

Click . . . squeak . . . click . . . squeak. Her flats and his taped-up tennies moved on together.

"I think you're making a big mistake."

That thought returned often during the slow progression of days while Lee and Christopher remained apart. How sluggishly time moved without the impetus of planned happiness to speed it along. How burdensome the duty of work without the leavening of play at its end. How lonely doing alone what one has done with another for so long.

They had eaten so many meals together, listened to so many songs on the radio, been in each other's houses, used each other's bathrooms, refrigerators, hairbrushes, silverware.

Reminders were everywhere.

He had left an Anoka police department ballpoint pen beside her telephone. On it was printed EMERGENCY? CALL 911. She felt as if every day were an emergency in which she was struggling to make sense out of the backwashes of life. Not an evening passed that didn't require immense resistance to keep from calling him the way the pen advised.

Foods she made reminded her of how he liked them. Popcorn. Chinese. Spaghetti and meatballs. Eating supper across the table from only Joey, Lee contemplated how in only three years he would be graduating from high school. Then what? Would she eat alone forever?

One day she turned over a flowered tablet and found a note he'd written when he'd stopped by on duty. It said *Anoka fairgrounds—alarm system.* He'd been called out to check one of the buildings and had left her with a peck on the mouth and an apology for not being able to stay longer.

She opened her glove compartment one night and found a small, powerful flashlight he'd bought and put there, scolding that she was too trusting and needed to safeguard herself more often than she did.

A magazine in her living room lay open to an article he'd been reading last time he'd been waiting for her to change clothes.

The washing machine spun itself off kilter again and she was nearly in tears before giving up and asking Jim Clements next door to come over and get it leveled for her.

She opened a cupboard door and found the vase in which he'd sent her the roses from another florist.

Countless times a day, the black-and-white Anoka police cars drove past the window of her shop. She never saw one without her heart giving a lurch that left her feeling empty and yearning for the rest of the day.

But nighttimes were the worst, lying alone in her bed, missing him with her body as well as with her mind, wondering how many more good years she had left and decrying the fact that she was squandering them to appease her family. Every night at eleven she would battle the urge to pick up the phone and say, "Hi, what are you doing? How was your day? When will I see you?" One night she actually lifted the receiver and dialed, then hung up on the first ring, rolled over and cried.

She tried to hide her despondency from Joey, but it lived inside her like a parasite, sucking away at her ability to enjoy life as she had before, to find fulfillment in her son's achievements and day-to-day activities, to feel satisfaction at the end of a well-worked day, to search out the good rather than the bad.

No, when she'd sent Christopher away she'd sent him with her optimism, humor, satisfaction, happiness—all the positive forces that had always driven her life. She tried to recover them, but her attempts at displaying her old spirit for Joey's sake looked, she knew, pitifully false.

It was much the same for Christopher.

Days without her took on a pointless mechanism. He worked. He ate. He lifted weights. He practiced at the shooting range. He took his

Explorer in for an oil change. He took Judd to see a Bruce Lee movie. He didn't realize how he'd been avoiding his apartment, with all its memories of her, until the day he ran out of uniforms. How long since he'd done laundry? Eaten in the apartment? Opened the living room blinds?

He did what he had to do.

He washed and ironed his uniforms. Vacuumed the carpeting. Watered the plants. Changed his bedding.

The smell of her was still in it. Cosmetics, sex, woman—memories came billowing up out of the hot water when the sheets hit the washing machine.

She'd left a small bottle of hand lotion in his bathroom. She'd said he never had any when she wanted it, so she'd bought a bottle for her ever-rough, stained hands. After their breakup, he would sometimes uncap the lotion and smell it like a recovering alcoholic uncaps his liquor, sniffs it and makes wishes.

There were other reminders, too.

In his bathroom half a box of condoms.

In his refrigerator some strange-flavored pop she'd bought one time on impulse, saying it sounded so weird she had to try it. Chocolate-cherry soda. He kept it there in the hope that someday she'd come back and drink it as she'd planned.

In his Explorer a pack of tissues from the last time she'd had a cold.

In his living room the sofa where they'd first laid full-length together, the floor where they'd made love, the radio station they'd listened to while doing it, the plants she'd let him keep after Greg died and into whose soil she'd often stuck her finger to check for dryness.

The location of her flower shop, just around the corner from the police station, necessitated his passing it countless times a day. He never did so without glancing up hoping to see her watering plants in the window or coming out the door. But he never did. He saw only potted flowers behind the window glass and customers using the door.

Loneliness took on a new meaning during those late-winter days without her. Once he was in a drugstore buying deodorant and razor blades when he passed the racks of greeting cards. At a revolving one he paused, randomly plucked out several cards and read them.

I love you because . . .

I'm sorry . . .

When you're not here . . .

The sentimentality bludgeoned him as he read card after card and thought about sending one to her. One? Hell, he wanted to send her ten, a dozen, a card a day, their messages were so poignant. He loved her, he was sorry, when she wasn't here the green vitality of his life wilted.

They had been apart nearly six weeks when he went one Monday morning to Fred Moore Junior High to deliver some papers to the liaison officer. He was just approaching the glass-walled office when the door opened and Lee came out.

They saw each other and stopped dead in their tracks. Their hearts leaped. Their cheeks took fire.

"Lee," he said as the door drifted shut behind her.

"Hi, Christopher." She touched her chest as if her breath had grown sketchy. The halls were silent and empty with first hour in session.

"What are you doing here?"

"I washed Joey's gym shorts this weekend and naturally he forgot to take them this morning, so I had to drop them off. What are you doing here?"

"Dropping off some papers for the liaison officer."

They tried to think of more to say, but nothing mattered. All that mattered was looking into each other's eyes again, sending the silent messages that nothing had changed, the hurt lived on, the longing remained. They stood face-to-face, stealing these moments to look greedily at each other and feel their hearts come alive after feeling dead within for so long.

She was dressed in familiar clothes—her denim jacket with a lavender smock peeking out at the neck.

He was resplendent in his navy blue uniform with its silver badges and buttons, crisply knotted tie and visored cap.

The shiny floors of the school hall reflected the two of them standing motionless, loath to go their separate ways. But they could not stand there forever with their lips parted and their emotions turbulent.

He recovered first, shifting his weight to the opposite foot and rolling up the papers in one hand. "So, how's—" He cleared his throat and began again. "How's Joey?"

"He's just fine."

"Everybody else?"

"Oh, everybody's fine. How about Judd?"

"The papers are about him." He flourished the roll. "The court put him in permanent foster care and I think he's much happier already. He's in a house with four other children, and every one of them is from a different ethnic background."

"Oh, good. I'm so glad. I know how much you care about him."

A lull fell, then he asked, "So what have you been doing?"

A rapt expression had come over her face, a look filled with utter mesmerization. She acted as if she hadn't heard his question as a whispered admission fell from her lips.

"My God, I've missed you."

"I miss you too," he said, pained.

"Every night at eleven I think about picking up the phone."

"All you have to do is do it."

"I know. That's what's so hard."

"So nothing's changed with your family?"

"I don't talk to my family much."

"It's that bad?"

She couldn't begin to do justice to how bad it had been.

"I thought it was supposed to get better without me," he said.

"I know," she whispered while the force field of longing built and billowed around them.

"Then why are we going through this, Lee?"

"Because I . . . I . . ." If she said any more she was going to cry, so she swallowed her excuse.

"It's still the age thing with you, isn't it? It's not just them, it's you too."

The office door opened and two students came out, chatting, carrying a tagboard sign and some masking tape. Both Lee and Christopher visibly started and stepped back, putting more space between them.

When the students' voices had trailed away, he said, "Well, listen . . . I have to go. Somebody's waiting for these." He indicated the tube of papers.

"Sure," she said. "Besides, this isn't the time or place."

He took another step backward and said, "It was good to see you. Every time I drive past your shop I hope you'll be in the window, but . . ." He shrugged and let the thought trail off.

"Christopher . . ." She reached out as if to detain him, but her touch fell short.

He reached out blindly behind himself for the handle of the glass door through which they could easily be seen by several office workers. "All you have to do is call, Lee."

With those words he retreated and left her standing in the empty hall.

Any progress she'd made was reversed by those few minutes of seeing his face, hearing his voice, learning that he remained in the same tortured state as she. Yearning . . . merciful Lord, she had never felt yearning as powerful as during those fleet, fraught seconds while she faced him in that hallway, while her heart reached and her blood coursed and she maintained a proper distance.

The following day and even the day after that she had only to recall their meeting to react the same way, with an upsurge of emotion spanning the cerebral to the sexual. How simply he elicited such response from her. He had only to step into her sphere to transform it and her into the realm of the extraordinary.

The letdown came with surefire pointedness, however, in the ordinary quiet of her own home.

She was back to crying again, failing to listen when Joey talked to her, sighing often and caring little about domestic duties. At the shop, the halting reconciliation that had begun between herself and Sylvia suffered a setback when her sister came to her one day as she was counting daffodils in a large white bucket.

"Lee, Barry met a man at his office who's about your age and—"

"No thank you."

"Well, aren't you going to let me finish?"

"Why should I? So you can fix me up with this guy and quit squirming over what you did to Christopher and me?"

"I'm not squirming."

Lee gave Sylvia a point-blank stare. "Well, you should be. If it wasn't for you I'd be married by now."

Sylvia had the grace to blush.

Lee put a rubber band around twelve daffodils, trimmed off their ends and stood them in the water. "I've been thinking, Sylvia. Would you be interested at all in letting me buy out your share of the business?"

Sylvia's mouth dropped open. "Lee, my God, is it that bad?"

"Or I suppose I could sell you my interest, but I still need a steady income, and with Joey only three years away from graduation I need to think about helping him out with college, and having something to keep myself busy after he's gone from home. That's why it would work better if I bought out your half rather than the other way around."

Sylvia rushed forward and touched Lee's hand. It was wet and held a Swiss army knife. This was the first time they'd touched since the breakup.

"Do you really want that, Lee?"

Lee removed her hand and concentrated on her work. "Yes, I think I do."

"Well, I don't."

The daffodils were all trimmed and clustered. Lee carried them away toward the front of the shop. "Think about it."

Her mother called her the next day at home, obviously alerted by Sylvia that Lee was beginning to show signs of disassociating herself from the family.

"Lee, Dad and I were wondering if you and Joey would like to come over for dinner one night this week."

"No, I'm sorry, Mother, we wouldn't."

She stunned Peg just as she had Sylvia.

"But . . ."

"Mother, I'm right in the middle of something here. I can't talk now."

"All right. Well . . . call me sometime."

Lee made no reply. It felt fantastic to pull a reversal of tactics on her mother.

Of course, Janice called too. By now it had become obvious the three of them were burning up the wires between their telephones.

Janice said, "Hi, Mom."

She replied coolly, "Hello, Janice."

"How are you?"

"Lonely," she replied.

Score three for Lee, she thought while Janice struggled for a response.

"Mom, Grandma called and said you're thinking about quitting business with Aunt Sylvia. You can't do that."

"Why?"

"Because . . . because it's so successful, and you love what you're doing."

"You know, Janice, I used to. But somehow it doesn't seem to matter much anymore."

"But you're so *good* at it."

"There's not much satisfaction in that fact either lately."

"If I came home this weekend, could we talk about it?"

"No. It's a decision I want to make on my own. And it's going to be a fairly busy weekend. I work on Saturday and there's a bake sale after church on Sunday. Then in the afternoon I planned to go to a matinee with Donna Clements."

Once again she'd flabbergasted her daughter by failing to issue the quick plea for Janice to come home so they could make peace at last.

Lee found she didn't want peace. Anger had taken over and it made her feel more alive than she had since this debacle began. When Janice hung up, Lee could almost picture her daughter standing motionless with her hand on the phone, staring at the wall, watching their way of life disintegrate.

Anger, manifested in that way, however, eroded Lee's spirit in the week following her emotional divorce from three of the people who mattered most in her life.

She grew churlish at work.

She cried at embarrassing moments.

She became snappish with Joey, who didn't deserve it.

He came into the bathroom one night after supper and found her on her hands and knees, scrubbing around the toilet bowl. With her butt facing the door, he couldn't tell she was crying.

"What you doin', Mom?" he asked innocently.

"What do you mean, what am I doing!" she retorted. "Can't you see what I'm doing? I'm scrubbing the toilet seat that you manage to piss on every time you go! Why boys can't hit a hole that big is beyond me! Then they leave it for the women to scrub up! Move! You're in my way!" She backed into his ankles and he leaped out of the way.

"I'll scrub it if you want me to," he said, hurt by her sudden attack.

"Oh sure, now you'll scrub it. Now that I've already done it! Just get out of my way!"

He slinked off and closed himself in his room. Later that night he heard his mother weeping the way she had the night she broke up with Christopher.

The phone rang at work the next day. Sylvia answered and laid the receiver on the counter. "It's Lloyd," she said.

Lee wiped her hands on her smock and felt hope infuse her spirits. Lloyd could always make her feel that way, and it had been so long since she'd talked to him or seen him. When she picked up the receiver her face held a note of gladness that matched her voice. "Lloyd?"

"Hello, dear."

"Oh, it's so good to hear from you."

"How are things over at that shop of yours today?"

"I'm surrounded by narcissus and pussy willows. Does that mean spring is here?"

"It must be, because I've caught a case of spring fever. I've been feeling a little cooped up here lately and I was wondering if you'd mind cheering up the life of a lonely old bachelor by going out to supper with him."

"Tonight?"

"That's what I was thinking. I've eaten a couple of those meals over at the Senior Citizens Center this week and they're enough to make you puke. What do you say to a nice fat juicy steak up at the Vineyard?"

"Oh, Lloyd, that sounds wonderful."

"I thought I'd come by for you at seven."

"I'll be ready."

When Lee hung up she caught Sylvia watching and wondering, but she divulged nothing.

* * *

At the Vineyard, Lloyd ordered a carafe of red wine. When the waitress had filled their glasses and left, he took a sip and said, "Well, I'll get right to the point, Lee." She felt her blood begin to plummet at his clipped, businessy tone. "The point being Christopher Lallek."

"Oh, Dad, not you too."

"No, no, not me too," he said, leaning forward as if with great enjoyment. "I'm not joining the ranks of those misguided fools who think they have a right to tell you how to run your life."

"You're not?" she said, amazed.

"Not at all. I came here to talk some sense into you, but not the kind of sense they'll agree with. Now, what's this I hear about you telling Christopher you aren't going to see him anymore?"

"Joey must have called you."

"He's been calling me quite regularly, as a matter of fact. And telling me how hard you are to live with lately, and how you cry yourself to sleep at night. A while back he told me all about a long talk the two of you had when you were walking through the art gallery. By the way, you made that boy feel like he had the greatest mom in the world by spending the day with him that way. But back to the issue at hand— you've broken up with Christopher."

"Yes, I have."

"Very noble . . . and very unwise, don't you think?"

She was too stunned to reply.

Lloyd covered her hand on the tabletop between them. "Lee, honey, I've known you for a long time. I've seen you sad and I've seen you happy, but I've never seen you any happier than during these past few months while you were seeing that young man. If I may be so crass, I'm not sure I ever saw you that happy when you were married to my son. I'm sure he'd forgive me for saying so because the two of you had a good marriage, and heaven knows I'm not taking anything away from that. But this . . . this young Lochinvar put a glow on you that hurt the eyes of those who don't wear it themselves. Could be some of them got a little jealous." He released her hand, took a drink of his wine, then studied the glass thoughtfully. "It's not easy to be stuck in a marriage that's twenty, thirty, forty years old and watch someone of your age fall in love and walk around looking like a ripe peach again. I'm not saying your mother and your sister don't have happy marriages. I'm just saying that the best of marriages get a little stale and shopworn after a while. And as for my granddaughter. That's pretty easy to understand. Naturally she'd get into a snit, being upstaged by her own mother.

"But don't you let any one of them talk you out of your happiness. You worked hard for it. You raised those kids and gave them nine good years after Bill died, and during that time you hardly ever thought of yourself. When you started dating Christopher you put yourself before them for once, and if you don't mind my saying so, it was high time. Children can get selfish, you know. You can give them so much of yourself that they expect it all."

"I haven't been giving them much of anything lately," she admitted.

"Well, that's a temporary thing. It's because when you're not happy you don't have as much to give. So what are you going to do about it?"

"I don't know."

"Don't you think the time has come for you to stand up to them—all of them, your mother, your sister and your daughter?"

"I thought that's what I'd been doing."

"No. What you've been doing is cutting off your nose to spite your face. What you need to do is go to that man you love and tell him you'll marry him, and let everybody else suck dead gladiolas—I believe that was the phrase, wasn't it?"

Lee laughed in spite of herself. The waitress brought their salads and Lloyd picked up his fork with scarcely a pause in his monologue.

"There's one other thought I've had, and I believe I've considered it quite thoroughly since the night when you told me about this whole ruckus those silly women have kicked up. I think Bill would give you his blessing if he could. He'd want you to be happy. After all, you're the mother of his children. If you're happy, they're going to be happy in the long run."

"Do you really think so, Dad?"

"Yes, I do."

"Mother suggested that I was being disloyal to Bill by taking up with Christopher."

Lloyd just shook his head. "Honestly, that woman. She means well, but sometimes I'd like to kick her butt. Mothers get . . . well, you know.

They have this image in their heads of what's right for their daughters, and when it doesn't turn out that way they can get pretty forceful. They tell themselves they're doing it for their daughters' good, but they're really doing it to get their way."

"Oh, Lloyd, I can't tell you what a relief it is to hear you say these things."

"I'm only telling the truth. I'm not really one of your family, so I can look at the situation a lot more impartially than they can. Now eat your salad and stop looking as if you're going to leap off that chair and kiss me, because people will think I'm the one who's robbing the cradle."

"Lloyd Reston," she said, smiling at him very warmly, "you are the dearest, most sensible, lovable man in the world."

"Well, I'm close, but not quite the most. I expect that honor goes to this fellow you love. I've been around the two of you enough to see how you respect and admire each other and how doggone much fun you always manage to have when you're together."

"Yes, we do."

"And if I may be so bold . . . I understand that your affair was sexual, too. Well, I say, more power to you, Lee. That was probably the real burr under those women's saddles. You'll pardon me for saying it, but I've seen your sister touch her husband exactly once in all the years I've known them. As I remember he had a wood tick on his neck and she picked it off for him one time when we were picnicking somewhere. As for your mother and father—well, I'm not going to make any remarks about them, but I suspect, given their age, that lust has rather lost its stronghold over at their house.

"So I say, if you've found a virile young man who loves you to pieces and wants to sweep you off your feet, get swept. Now eat, I said."

Lee felt so light she was certain she'd float off her chair and bump the ceiling.

"May I say just one thing more?" she asked.

"Make it quick. My stomach is growling."

"I love you."

Lloyd lifted his gaze to his happy daughter-in-law and said, "Yes, I suppose you do. I've been around so long, what other choice do you have?"

He dug into his Caesar salad.

She dug into hers.

They wiped their mouths and exchanged messages over their linen napkins, smiling like conspirators.

Chapter 19

SHE had decided even before Lloyd dropped her at home. His blessing was all she'd needed to make her see how wrong she'd been to turn Christopher away. Lloyd's word carried more weight than all the others combined, for if he—the father of her first husband—could give her the right to second happiness, so surely should the others be able to do the same.

She kissed his cheek and he patted her arm before she stepped from his car and tripped to the house as if there were no earth beneath her feet.

With her impatient heart racing, she dialed Christopher's apartment.

"Be there, be there," she whispered, but got his answering machine instead.

This message was too momentous to leave on a tape recording: She dialed the police station and the dispatcher said, "He's working mid-shift, Mrs. Reston. He'll get off at eleven o'clock."

She checked her watch. It was after ten.

Suddenly she was racing. Into the bathroom, into the tub, out of the tub, into clean clothes, thinking, *Hang on, Christopher, I'm coming.*

At 10:45 she went into Joey's room and woke him up.

"Hey, Joey? . . . Honey?"

"Hm? Mom? What time is it? Feels like I just went to sleep."

"You did." She sat on the edge of his bed while the hall light slanted in a golden fan on the floor behind her. "It's only quarter to eleven. Sorry to wake you but I'm going over to Christopher's. I just wanted you to know in case you woke up and found me gone."

"To Christopher's?"

"I didn't think you'd mind."

"No. Hey, way to go, Mom."

"I may be gone late because he's just getting off work now."

"Grandpa must have done some fancy talking tonight."

"Yes, he did. And I'm going to do what he and you said I should do. I'm going to marry Chris."

"You are?" Even in the deep shadow she could see his crooked smile. "Gee, Mom, that's great."

"I'm going to tell him tonight."

"Well, in that case . . . maybe I shouldn't expect you till morning."

It struck Lee how society's perception of unmarried sex had changed in a single generation. Her own mother couldn't accept Lee's having an illicit affair, yet she could sit here on her son's bed and joke with him about it.

"I promise I'll be here to fix you breakfast."

"Waffles?" he asked.

"Is this extortion?" She hated making waffles . . . too much work.

"Well, heck, you can't blame a kid for trying."

"Okay, waffles."

"All *riiight.*"

"I owe you more than waffles though, don't I?"

"Aw, Mom . . ."

"Well, I do. I owe you an apology. I'm really sorry for how I acted the other day when you came into the bathroom. I had no right to bark at you and say the things I said. I know I hurt your feelings."

"Yeah, well, I figured out why."

"And you called Grandpa and told him to have a talk with me, right?"

"Well, you wouldn't listen to *me.*"

She arranged the covers across his chest and tipped forward, pinning him in place with the blankets. "You're a very perceptive young man, Joey Reston. You're going to make some woman an exceptional husband someday." She pecked him on the face.

"And it won't be long either. I just asked Sandy to marry me and she said yes. We're thinking maybe we'll go to school one more year and then do it."

Lee's mouth dropped open. Before the adrenaline reached her extremities, he laughed in falsetto and said, "Just kidding, Mom."

"Oh my God . . ." She put a hand to her heart. "You scared the living daylights out of me!"

"Just getting even for that tongue-lashing you gave me in the bathroom. I didn't think the waffles and the apology would quite cover it."

With the edge of a fist she thunked him on the chest. "You inconsiderate brat."

"Yeah, but you love me, right?"

"I do." She was laughing inside. "Yes, I surely do." She sat a moment on her son's bed, feeling happiness come and flood her, feeling things finally falling into place. "Well, I guess I'd better get going so I'm there when Christopher gets home."

"Tell him hi from me. And if he says yes, tell him he better be able to pee into the toilet bowl without getting any on the floor if he knows what's good for him."

"Joseph Reston!"

"G'night, Mom. Have a good time."

"Just you wait till April Fools' Day. I'm gonna get you so good."

"Hey, listen, woman. I gotta get some sleep. Tomorrow's a school day."

"All right, all right, I'm going."

She kissed him once more and headed for the door. As she reached it he said, "Seriously, Mom, I'm glad for you."

With a happy heart, she smiled and turned off the hall light.

It was 11:15 when she reached Christopher's place. Approaching his door she felt a quivering of anticipation within, the kind of anticipation a woman in her mid-forties believes gone with her salad days—that green, burgeoning optimism that she'd had when she'd married Bill, fresher perhaps because this love she felt was so unsought. It had chosen her; she had not chosen it. What a fool she'd been to let her family rob her of this happiness for even so short a time. This was *her* life, hers alone, and life was not a dress rehearsal. Fleet and final as it was, she owed herself the taking of all the happiness she could get from it, and Christopher was the key to so much of that happiness.

She knocked and waited, holding a vision of him inside her head and an eagerness within her heart. In seconds his voice came from the other side of the door.

"Who is it?" Ever the policeman, ever cautious.

"It's Lee."

The dead bolt clacked and the door opened, bumping aside his black work shoes, which sat on the rug. He stood before her in stocking feet, still dressed in his uniform, his hair pressed flat from the rim of his hat, holding a yellow plastic container of microwave Beefaroni from which a spoon protruded. The room smelled like the freshly heated food.

"Well, this is a surprise."

"Not at all. We both knew the other day at school that we couldn't stay apart."

"You might have known but I didn't. I thought it was really over for good."

She offered a fey smile, letting her eyes wander up to his hair, down to his dear blue eyes and full lips. "Would you mind, Officer Lallek, if I came in there and kissed you?"

She stepped over his shoes, unceremoniously took him in her arms and kissed him. He kissed her too, holding her with one arm while the other hand was occupied by his snack. It was a kiss of sentimental sweetness, unrushed rather than unruly. She fit so nicely beneath his downturned head with its neatly trimmed hair and closed eyes. The shape and texture of his lips and tongue were as familiar to Lee as the interior of her own mouth. She took her time enjoying the kiss, washing him with an almost lazy swoop of her tongue that said she had been a very silly woman, indeed. When the kiss ended they stood peacefully, smiling at each other.

"Mmm . . . what are you eating?"

"Beefaroni."

"Tastes good."

"You want one? I can heat one for you."

"Hm-mm . . . wouldn't taste nearly as good firsthand. Would you like to finish yours though?"

"Not particularly, now that you're here."

"Do anyway. I'll watch."

He grinned wryly. "You'll watch?"

She rested her forearms against his bullet-proof vest and traced the outline of his lips with an index finger. "I'll watch these," she murmured, "closing around the spoon and moving while you chew. I've missed watching these."

He chuckled and said, "We police officers meet all kinds."

"Eat your cheap noodles," she said in a rich caviar voice.

He freed his hands and stood before her plying the spoon, keeping his eyes on her over the plastic cup. When his mouth was full she kissed his cheek, which was puffed slightly, its muscles shifting as he chewed. He smiled, swallowed and said, "You miss me or what?"

"Huh-uh. That's not why I'm going to marry you. I'm going to marry you so you can level my washing machine and mow my grass, shovel my snow, stuff like that."

The spoon stopped halfway to his mouth. He leaned back to give himself ample space to see her face. "You're going to marry me?"

"Yes, I am, Officer Lallek. I'm going to elope with you."

"Elope!"

"Quicker than you can say Chef Boyardee Beefaroni."

"You don't say."

"I'm tired of people telling me what I should and shouldn't do. I'm tired of sleeping alone and eating alone and watching you cruise by my house at night when you think I'm sleeping and I won't see you."

"Since when did—"

"I *saw* you. You went past on Sunday night at ten, and the next night just before you got off duty, and plenty of other nights, too."

"How about tonight?"

"I wasn't home. I was out with Lloyd getting preached to. Then when I got home I took a bath and put perfume behind my knees and put on clean underwear and told Joey I was coming over here to propose to you."

"Is that so? Clean underwear? And perfume where?"

"In all the places where two can enjoy it more than one."

"Here, hold this." He handed her the container, then swung her up like a hammock in his arms and ordered, "Flip that dead bolt."

When she had, he carried her to the kitchen where the bright lights were lit over the table and the silverware drawer hung open.

"Set that down on the cabinet," he ordered.

She got rid of the container, then doubled her arms around his neck while he carried her to the bedroom. Above the bed he released her knees, letting her slide down his body until she knelt on the mattress. Holding her face in both hands, he kissed her, a long flowing river of a kiss upon which they drifted together, with the promise of a much longer ride ahead. When it ended they remained close, breathing on each other in the dark, setting their hearts on a straight, mutual course toward permanence. The levity they'd shared at her arrival had been dispelled by the import of this solemn moment.

"Christopher, I'm sorry," she whispered. "I loved you and I listened to them. I'm sorry."

"It's been hell without you."

"For me too."

"I didn't want to come between you and your family though. I still don't."

"Lloyd made me see that it's their problem, not ours. If they love me they'll accept you, and they love me. I know they do, so I'm willing to give them a second chance. Will you marry me, Christopher?"

"I'd marry you here and now if I could."

"I meant it when I said I want to elope. Do you think we could?"

"You're serious!" he said, surprised anew.

"Yes, I am. I'm not giving anyone a chance to influence me again. I just want us to get on a plane and go someplace. The only one I'll tell is Lloyd, because I'll have to ask him if he can stay at the house with Joey while we're gone. I always thought it would be so romantic to be married in a garden. Do you think we could use the tickets to Longwood Garden, or is it still winter in Pennsylvania?"

"I'm afraid it's still winter there. But it's spring down South. Maybe we could find someplace down there."

"Oh, do you mean it, Christopher? You'll really do it?"

"I have vacation time coming. I can talk to my sergeant and see what they'll give me off. For a reason as good as this they might be willing to rearrange the schedule."

"Oh good. Now could we quit making plans and take this metal vest off you? It's such a nuisance."

While he began loosening his tie and unbuttoning his shirt, she walked on her knees to the far side of the bed and fell to all fours to switch on a bedside lamp. By its light she returned to him, taking over her share of the duties she so relished, ridding him of the vesture that symbolized his profession, which had brought the two of them together. While they undressed she wondered as she had so often—did Greg know? Could he smile down from some celestial plane and see how happy the two of them were? Did he grin and say, "Nice work, Grandpa?" Had he found his little brother somewhere up there, and were the two of them pleased at this mortal bliss their mother and Greg's best friend had found?

As the last pieces of clothing dropped, her wondering ceased and she fell with Christopher, already embraced. And in their reach and flow to one another they became splendid beings celebrating not only their bodies but also their love.

It took them two days to find the proper garden and make arrangements. On the third, a Thursday, they flew to Mobile, Alabama, where they rented a car and drove straight to the Mobile Infirmary. There they had the required blood tests and walked out four hours later with the results. These they took to the Mobile County Courthouse at the intersection of Government and Royal streets, where they bought their wedding license and made arrangements with one Richard Tarvern Johnson, the administrative assistant to the judge of probate, to meet them the following morning at eleven o'clock at the near end of the bridge spanning Mirror Lake in Bellingrath Gardens.

Lee Reston had never before seen azaleas blooming in their natural habitat. She saw them on her wedding day, more than 250,000 plants, some of them nearly 100 years old, in every conceivable shade of pink, cascading from bushes higher than her head, lining pathways, surrounding the boles of moss-draped water oaks, reflected in the pools, lakes and in the current of the Isle-aux-Oies River, beside which the Bellingrath estate had been built.

The gardens sprawled over an 800-acre setting, boasting latticed bowers, sparkling fountains, bubbling cascades, verdant lawns and flowers . . . everywhere flowers. Christopher had trouble keeping Lee moving while they walked toward their rendezvous with Johnson. She kept gazing overhead at the immense oaks and sighing, "Ohh, look." And at rainbows of tulips and daffodils lining the walkways. "Oh, look at *those*. I've never seen anything like it in my life." And at the flood of purple hyacinths that turned the air to ambrosia. "Oh, smell them, Christopher! I think I'm getting dizzy, they smell so grand!"

He tugged on her hand. "Come along, sweetheart, we'll tour the gardens later on. We don't want to be late for our own wedding."

The bridge at Mirror Lake was arched, with wooden latticework supporting its railings. It spanned the lake across which could be seen the rockery and the summer house, each surrounded by colorful blooms. At the near end of the bridge, Johnson, the marriage official of Mobile County, was waiting. He was a dyed-in-the-wool southerner with the accent to prove it, a man in his mid-forties, with thinning blond hair, glasses and a smile that said he much preferred the jewelled setting of Bellingrath to the libraryish rooms of the courthouse where he usually performed his nuptial duties.

He had sold them their wedding license the previous day and recognized them as they approached.

"Good mornin', Mister Lallek, Mizz Reston. And a fine one it is for a weddin'."

"Good morning, Mister Johnson," they returned in unison.

"Aren't these azaleas something? I swear."

Christopher said, "Mrs. Reston owns a florist shop. I've had trouble getting her here without dawdling."

Johnson chuckled and said, "A place like this would make anyone dawdle. Well . . . shall we get started?"

There were only the three of them: Johnson in his business suit; Lee in a taupe organdy dress and high heels, holding a single calla lily; Christopher in a navy blue suit with a fragrant gardenia in his lapel. Only the three of them and a pair of swans on the lake behind them, and off to one side a wading flock of sunset-colored flamingos going about

their business of eating their lunch and standing on one leg while
digesting it. Some finches chittered to one another in the low flowers
beside the lake, and an occasional sparrow or warbler tattled from the
water oak above their head.

No guests to seat.

No caterers bustling in the wings.

No pomp or circumstance.

Only two people in love, relaxed on their wedding day.

"We can do this however you prefer," Johnson said. "I'm here to make
it official. I can read some words from a book or you can say whatever
you like."

Christopher and Lee looked at each other. He was holding her In-
stamatic camera. She was holding her lily. Neither of them had given a
thought to ceremony. Truly, it had been celebrated on the night they'd
agreed to do this, with only the two of them present.

Christopher decided. "I'd like to say something myself."

"So would I."

"Very well," Johnson agreed. "Whenever you're ready."

Christopher set the camera on the grass at their feet and held both of
Lee's hands.

"Well . . ." he said, then halted to do some thinking. He looked into
her eyes, then blew out a breath containing a trace of a laugh, because
he had no idea what to say. At last he made a good start.

"I love you, Lee. I've loved you for long enough to know that you
make a better person of me, and I think that's important. I want to be
with you for the rest of my life. I promise to be faithful, and to help you
raise Joey, and to take care of both of you the best I can. I promise to
be good to you and to take you to as many gardens as we can possibly
see in the rest of our life, and to respect you and love you till my dying
day, which won't be hard at all." He smiled and she did, too. "Oh, and
one more thing. I promise to respect your family, too, and to show them
in every way I know how that this marriage was the right thing for both
of us." He paused for thought. "Oh, the ring . . ." He fished it from his
pocket, not the immense rock he'd tried to give her earlier, but a plain
gold band they'd chosen together, one with no jewels that would have
to be left in the dresser drawer, just a sturdy circle that could stand up
to the daily beating to which it would be subjected.

"I love you," he said, slipping it on her finger. "And you were right. This ring is much better because you'll never have to take it off." He smiled directly into her eyes, then said to Johnson, "I guess that's all."

Johnson nodded and said, "Mizz Reston?"

She looked down at Christopher's hands within her own, then up at his face, wholly happy and at peace.

"You've been such a gift to me, Christopher. You came into my life when I least expected it, at a time when I needed someone so badly. Little did I know that I'd fall in love with you. How lucky I am that I did. And I'll keep loving you till the end of our days. I'll be there for you when your job gets you down. I know it's not always easy to be a policeman's wife, but who knows better than I what I'm getting into? I promise that I'll support you in all the causes you espouse, especially with kids, because I'm sure that Judd won't be the last one you'll be a stand-in father to. I'll do whatever I can for them, and I'll give you the freedom to do what you must for them. I'll make a home for us, and it will always be open to your friends . . . and your family, if you choose. I'll go to every garden on the face of this earth that you're willing to take me to." She smiled broadly, winning a smile from him. Soon her expression softened. "Somehow the old words are best . . . in sickness and in health, for richer, for poorer, till death do us part. That's how I'll love you." Gently, she said, "Give me the other ring."

He took it from his pocket and she put it on his finger, then kissed it. Raising her eyes again to his, she whispered, "I love you, Christopher."

"I love you, Lee."

They kissed. Behind them on the water a pair of swans floated toward each other, and for an instant as they passed, their heads and necks formed a heart, as if a blessing were being extended upon the vows just spoken.

Mr. Johnson said, "Let it be known that the state of Alabama recognizes this marriage as true and legal and that a record of it will be kept on file in the Mobile County Courthouse."

The ceremony was over but had been so brief it left a lull of uncertainty, as if the bride and groom were thinking, *Shouldn't it have taken longer?* Johnson made it official. "Congratulations, Mr. and Mrs. Lallek."

He shook both their hands and said, "Now if you'll sign the wedding certificate, that'll about do it."

When they'd both signed, he snapped a picture of them with Lee's camera. Then a passing tourist snapped one of all three of them.

"Well, good luck to you both," Johnson bid.

He left them there beside the lake, chuckling into each other's eyes because in some respects the few official words spoken by him seemed like a farce. Vows were, after all, a thing of the heart, not of recorded signatures and dates.

When he'd departed, Christopher captured Lee's hand and swung her against his chest. "Come here, Mrs. Lallek. Let's try that again."

This kiss was overseen only by the swans and the buttermilk clouds that washed the blue sky with an overlay of white. It went on as long as Lee could permit without getting impatient for their tour of the gardens to begin. She pulled away first. Being a creature devoid of coyness, she put it to him honestly, "Kiss me later, Christopher. I'm just too anxious to see all those flowers."

They spent their first three hours as Mr. and Mrs. Lallek strolling the gardens and snapping pictures of each other.

They spent their wedding night at a place called Kerry Cottage, a restored carriage house on the grounds of an antebellum mansion named Sharrow. The owner, one Mrs. Ramsay, a thin, horsey-faced matron with gray hair that waved naturally, tightly against her skull, said she would do some telephoning and put off some relatives who were driving down for the night from Monroeville. "They never pay me a red cent and expect breakfast on the table at the stroke of eight. Cousin Grace can just come another time. Tonight you two newlyweds will have the best room I've got."

She fed them glazed cornish game hens filled with pine-nut stuffing at a table in the garden beneath a hawthorn tree, which she said was planted by her great-great-granddaddy before the Civil War. When dusk fell she lit a hurricane candle and brought them amaretto cream cake poised upon a lake of vanilla cream. On the cream she'd scribed two interlocked hearts of chocolate syrup. She touched each of her guests on the shoulder and said wistfully, "May your lives together be as happy as mine was with the Colonel." Choosing not to elaborate on who the Colonel was, she filled their glasses with something she called iced mint malmsey and disappeared into the shadows.

They toasted.

They drank.

They gazed.

They took time to adore each other while the night beckoned them toward the privacy of their garden cottage. Still, they sat on, savoring the anticipation and the resonance of the feelings stirring between them. The iced mint malmsey was slightly bitter but refreshing. Above their heads the leaves of the hawthorn tree rustled like dry paper in a faint night breeze. Beneath their elbows the pierced metal of the garden tabletop grew cool upon their skin. The light from the candle illuminated their faces to a Rubenesque glow.

Christopher emptied his glass, set it on the tabletop with a soft *tink* and said, "Mrs. Lallek . . . ," testing it on his tongue before going on. "Would you care to retire now?"

"Mr. Lallek," she replied, smiling into his eyes, "I would like very much to retire now."

He pushed back his chair. It resounded like a muffled bell as it bumped over the cobbles. He pulled hers out and she rose, taking his arm.

"Shall we find Mrs. Ramsay and thank her?"

"By all means."

They ambled toward the house on the uneven bricks with the smell of wisteria in their nostrils.

"I find myself speaking differently here," he said. "Listen to me, at home I'd say *talking*, here I say speaking. There I say *should*, here I say *shall*. What is it?"

"The South definitely casts a spell."

It continued casting its spell as they thanked and bid goodnight to their hostess, sauntered arm in arm 'neath a spreading live oak, past their own hawthorn, and made their way to the carriage house with its testered, draped bed. There, the coverlet was already turned down and a pair of good-night candies waited on their pillows.

She was naked when he laid her down and stretched out beside her.

"Lee . . . oh Lee," he murmured. "My wife at last."

She spoke his name and drew him in, close to her body, closer still to her soul.

"Christopher . . . my husband."

Wife.

Husband.

Lovers.

In the rich, rife southern night, they wanted no more.

Lloyd got the idea all on his own. He took only Joey into his confidence before sending out the invitations.

To his granddaughter, Janice.

To Sylvia and Barry Eid.

To Orrin and Peg Hillier.

And to Judson Quincy.

You're invited to a wedding supper honoring the marriage of Lee Reston and Christopher Lallek, who were married at Bellingrath Gardens last Friday. Supper will be served at the bridal couple's future home at 1225 Benton Street, on Wednesday evening at 5:00 p.m. Please don't disappoint them or me.

Sincerely,
Lloyd Reston

They all called immediately upon receipt of their letters, everyone outspoken and miffed, haranguing Lloyd as if he were to blame for Lee's lack of good sense. To each one he'd say, "Just a minute, Joey wants to talk to you."

And Joey would spill out his honest enthusiasm. "Hey, Grandma, isn't it great? You're coming, aren't you? Mom called and she's so dang happy! So am I! So is Grandpa Lloyd! He and I are making the wedding supper and neither one of us knows what we're doing exactly, but we're looking through recipe books for something that sounds good and easy. Are you coming?"

Each one hung up, frowning, hoist by her own petard. Lee's own son was ecstatic. Lee's former father-in-law had given his blessing to the union. The two of them, inept stumblebums in the kitchen, were going to prepare a meal of celebration and asked only that the rest of the family be in attendance.

How in heaven's name could they say no without looking like total jerks?

* * *

Lloyd solicited Judd's help. He picked up both him and Joey immediately after school and the three of them set Lee's kitchen table with her best china. They hung three paper wedding bells on the light fixture. They cut up about five pounds of beef sirloin, seared it in a big soup pot, whacked up some onions and mushrooms, poured in some burgundy and bouillon, put in the proper spices and hoped a woman would show up to thicken it into beef burgundy when the time was right.

They cut up a salad, opened up three cans of whole-kernel corn, prepared instant rice in the microwave, got a bread basket lined with a napkin like Lee always did, tore apart the dinner buns, put two sticks of butter on a plate and hid the bakery-decorated cake on the top shelf of Joey's closet.

Shortly before 4 P.M., Lloyd put on his jacket and said to the boys, "Now, don't forget. If nobody's here by five, take all the extra plates off the table, okay? I should have your mother and Chris back here by five-thirty at the latest. That's if their plane gets in on time."

Christopher drove on the way home from the airport. Lee delivered a monologue on Bellingrath Gardens. Her spiel never slowed until they reached her house only to find there was no room for the Explorer in the driveway.

"... could go back again to ..." Lee interrupted herself in the middle of the thought. She gaped at the collection of vehicles. "That looks like Mother's car. And Janice's ... and Sylvia and Barry's." Her head snapped around and her eyes lit on the man in the backseat. "Lloyd, what have you done?"

"Let's go inside and see."

She looked terrified as she got out of the truck and stood beside it, staring at the house. Christopher took her arm. Above her head, he exchanged glances with Lloyd.

"What *did* you do, Lloyd?"

"Invited them, that's all."

"But, Dad ..." she said. "None of them knows."

"They do now."

"Oh hell," she groaned, and looked for help to Christopher, who had none to offer.

"We might as well go face them," he said.

The boys had loud music playing. Lee's mother was stirring something on the stove. Her father was opening a bottle of wine. Sylvia was fussing over a bouquet of white roses on the center of the table. They all appeared intentionally busy except the boys, who came to the door babbling excitedly.

Lee got a hug from Joey. Christopher said, "Well, for heaven's sake, Judd is here, too!" and got a high five and congratulations from him. The others gave up their preoccupation and hovered on the perimeter while Joey and Judd went on bragging loudly about the preparations they'd made with Lloyd, and the music kept playing, and Lee stood barely inside her own front door afraid to take the seven or eight steps that would carry her to the others. She felt as awkward as a singer who's begun on the wrong key. At her shoulder she felt Christopher waiting for her to move, while behind them Lloyd hung up coats in the closet.

Finally she said, "Well . . . this is a nice surprise," and made her feet move.

She reached Sylvia first, and felt her heart clubbing as they remained that one step apart, their emotions strained and wavering. Who moved first? Lee, perhaps, taking that initial difficult step toward amity.

Their hug was stilted, their elbows in the air above each other's shoulders, their backsides jutting while Sylvia whispered in Lee's ear, "I think you're crazy. It'll never work."

Lee whispered back, "Just watch and see."

Her mother came next. This hug was harder, but bore much the same message. "Have you lost your mind, eloping? When Lloyd told me I nearly died."

"Thanks for coming, Mother."

Orrin's hug was the first genuine one. "Your mother says you're crazy, but I've never seen you look happier, honey."

"Thanks, Daddy. I am." She turned to the last person. "Janice . . . honey, it's so good to see you." Janice was blushing and hanging back. Lee's embrace broke the ice. The two hugged longer and harder than they had in many months, feeling relief sluice in and mend the rift that had held them aloof for weeks. "Oh, Mom . . ." Janice's whisper was unsteady. Lee heard her gulp in a futile effort to control her emotions. She rubbed the center of Janice's back, hard, a connection that said, *Don't cry, dear, everything's going to be just fine now.*

In the hubbub of greetings, those between Lee's family and Christopher were perfunctory at best, but Janice—bless her heart—exhibited grace under pressure and gave her mother the kindest wedding gift she could give by approaching Christopher straightaway and, blushing though she was, offering a genuine hug.

"It's easy to see how happy you both are. Congratulations."

"Thank you, Janice, from both your mother and me."

"I just want you to know, I've met a guy I really like a lot. We're going out on our second date tomorrow night."

Christopher smiled and said, "Good for you. Bring him home soon so we can meet him."

Looking on, Lee felt a welling of emotion that pushed at her throat and seemed to billow within her heart. She turned away and went around the corner of the kitchen to dry her eyes in private. Christopher saw and followed. Coming up behind her he locked an arm across her chest. She gripped it with both hands and tipped her head back against him, closing her eyes, swallowing hard.

"Oh, Christopher . . ." she whispered.

"I know," he replied, and kissed her hair.

Judd came barging around the corner and came up short. "Could I change the CD? Oh! Something wrong?"

Joey came right behind him and said, "No you can't. Come on, dummy, leave 'em alone."

And somehow, eyes got dried, the kitchen got invaded, the beef burgundy got thickened, food got dished up and everyone got seated. Vince Gill was singing from the living room. Some glasses were filled with wine. Some were filled with Sprite. Food and chatter were being passed around the table. The noise and confusion of family mealtime worked its magic at replacing the faltering relationships that would still need some work in the future.

Lloyd arose with his glass in his hand. "If I may—"

"No, Grandpa," Joey interrupted. "This time I think it's my job."

After a hesitation of surprise, Lloyd resumed his chair with a pleased smile and turned the floor over to his grandson.

Joey stood and lifted his glass of Sprite to each person in turn as he toasted.

"To Grandpa Lloyd, for getting us together. To Aunt Sylvia for bringing the flowers. To Uncle Barry for bringing Aunt Sylvia . . ." Everyone laughed. "To Judd, who's just going to have to learn to like country music instead of rap. To my sister, Janice, who I'm glad to have back home. To Grandma and Grandpa Hillier for giving us the best mom in the world. But most of all to Mom and Christopher, the new bride and groom. I hope you guys always stay as happy as you are today, and I hope you go away often and leave me with Grandpa Lloyd, because I get by with all kinds of stuff when he's here. Man, I ate pizza every night and stayed up till eleven-thirty and he let me drive the car over to Sandy's house!"

When the laughter died down, Joey continued. "Seriously . . . I learned some things this year about what really matters. We all did. So I'll just end by saying, Mom, Christopher, we all wish you a long and happy life together. That goes from all of us here"—his eyes circled the table, then lifted toward heaven—"and from those up there. Dad? Greg? Grant? Nice to know you're all together. Put in a good word for these two, will you?"

While around the wedding table glasses touched, hearts softened, and a bride had difficulty keeping her eyes dry, three souls looked down from their ethereal dwelling above, exchanged smiles of satisfaction and, with their arms around each other, ambled off to wait.